Jeffrey Robinson is the international bestselling American author of sixteen books, including *The Risk Takers*; its sequel *The Minus Millionaires*; the acclaimed biography of Saudi Arabia's former oil minister, *Yamani – The Inside Story*; and *The End of the American Century*, a particularly chilling account of the hidden agendas of the cold war. His latest for Simon & Schuster is *The Manipulators – A Conspiracy To Make Us Buy*.

A native New Yorker who has lived in Europe for the past twenty-seven years, including fifteen in the United Kingdom, ~~TV and rad~~ demand th~~United Sta~~ is the 1990 ~~Benedictine After-Dinner Speaker of the Year Award.

The Laundrymen

JEFFREY ROBINSON

POCKET
BOOKS

LONDON · SYDNEY · NEW YORK · TOKYO · SINGAPORE · TORONTO

First published in Great Britain by Simon & Schuster Ltd, 1994
This edition first published in 1995 by Pocket Books
This revised edition published in 1998 by Pocket Books
An imprint of Simon & Schuster Ltd
A Viacom Company

Simon & Schuster Ltd
West Garden Place
Kendal Street
London W2 2AQ

Simon & Schuster of Australia
Sydney

A CIP catalogue record for this book is
available from the British Library
ISBN 0-671-01804-3

1 3 5 7 9 10 8 6 4 2

Typeset by Hewer Text Ltd, Edinburgh
Printed and bound in Great Britain by
Caledonian International Book Manufacturing Ltd, Glasgow

This Book is for Uncle Tonton Robby
With Love from Joshua Seth and Celine Chelsea

Contents

Acknowledgements

This all began with John Hurley, who was, until the end of 1992, Customs Attaché at the US Embassy in London. First he fired my enthusiasm, then he proceeded to open countless doors for me – doors that quite clearly would never have opened without him. I shamelessly admit to dropping his name at every turn because, whenever I did, the immediate response was, if you're a friend of John's, that's all right with me. I hope he knows the extent of the esteem in which he is held by people who have worked with him. I hope, too, that he and his wife Eileen know the extent of the admiration in which they are regarded – especially by my wife and me.

I am also grateful to the many men and women who so kindly assisted me on this project: in the United States, at the Department of Justice, US Customs, the Federal Bureau of Investigation, the Drug Enforcement Administration (DEA), the Criminal Investigation Division of the Internal Revenue Service (IRS) and the office of the District Attorney for New York County; in Great Britain, at HM Customs, the National Criminal Intelligence Service (NCIS) and the Metropolitan Police; in Canada, at the Office of the Solicitor General, the Royal Canadian Mounted Police and the Canadian High Commission in London; in Australia, at the Office of the Attorney General and the National Crimes Authority; and throughout the rest of Europe, in various law enforcement and financial regulation authorities.

For their time, encouragement and support during the writing of this book in 1994, I would particularly like to thank Peter Nunez, former Assistant Secretary of the Treasury - Enforcement; Roger Urbanski, Armando Ramirez and Bob Gerber of US Customs; Fran Dyer of the IRS; US Attorneys Mark Bartlett and Joe Whitley; Charles Hill, Graham Saltmarsh, Terry Burke and Tim Wren at NCIS; Billy Miller and Tony Curtis of the Metropolitan Police; Tony Brightwell of Bishops International; Dr Barry A. K. Rider, Executive Director, Centre for International Documentation on Organized and Economic Crime, Jesus College, Cambridge; Rowan Bosworth-Davies of Richards Butler; Brian Bruh and Anna Fotias of the Financial Crimes Enforcement Network (FINCEN); David Westrate, Bill Simpkins and Bill Alden of the DEA; Jan Van Doorn of the Dutch Centrale Recherche Informatiedienst (CRI); Bob Denmark, Graham White and Trevor Taylor of the Royal Lancashire Constabulary; Lucy Lloyd and Henry Stewart Conference Studies for the superb documentation on their money laundering conferences; Michael Hyland, head of Midland Group Security; John Drage of the Bank of England; Eric and Lynn Ellen of the International Maritime Bureau; Michael Ashe, attorney at law; Ticino State Prosecutor Dick Marty and journalist Pascal Auschlain in Switzerland; and Mark Solly on the Isle of Man. I also wish to thank the nearly 50 bankers around the world who gave me their time, many of them speaking frankly enough about specific banking practices and case studies to jeopardize their own positions.

Those bankers are a perfect example of how research for a book like this is often done on the understanding that certain sources never be identified. It means that there are some I cannot thank openly. As a matter of fact, there are 19 people, not including the aforementioned bankers, to whom I owe a very special debt. Spread out around the world, doing whatever it is they do, they were an invaluable reservoir of information. Needless to say, a few weren't necessarily pleased that I'd managed to locate them and, in the end, spoke with me only on the clear understanding that I would not help anyone else find them. Others, who might have been easier to come across, spoke with me only after I agreed that no one would ever know who they were or what they'd said. Without wishing to make this sound especially dramatic, it's an easy condition to accept when you understand that my divulging any information about these sources could quite easily turn out to be hazardous to their health. I wholly respect their wishes. But I do have a touch of regret that I cannot thank them individually by name. After all, I am not just indebted to them for their confidences, I genuinely respect their trust.

To those names, I would wish to say thank you as well to the many people who helped contribute to this revised edition. Among them are: SSgt Yvon Gagnon, RCMP; Special Agent Bill Malarney, DEA; former Assistant US Attorney Wilmer 'Buddy' Parker; former US Attorney Kendall Coffey; former DEA bureau chief in Miami, now of the Kroll Agency, Tom Cash; Special Agent Hardrick Crawford, FBI; Special Agent John Costanzo, DEA; US Attorney Gaynelle Griffin Jones; Assistant US Attorney Charles Lewis; Assistant US Attorney Charles Dause; the Honorable Filemon B. Vela, Federal District Court for the Southern District of Texas; Assistant District Attorney for the County of Manhattan, City of New York, John Moscow; Assistant US Attorney Bridget Rohde; Assistant US Attorney Bonnie Klapper; Special Agent John Forbes, US Customs; Lieutenant Ron Rose, NYPD; US Asst Commissioner of Customs Bonni Tischler; Special Agent Richard Weart, US Customs; Special Agent Allan Doody, US Customs; Stan Morris, Director FINCEN; Carolyn Savage and Joyce McDonald, FINCEN; Rogene Waite and Jim McGivney, DEA; Jack Blum, Attorney at Law, Washington DC; Jean Spreutels, President, Financial

Action Task Force; Jurgen Storbeck, Coordinator of the Drug's Unit, Europol; Assistant Commissioner Perry Nove, City of London Police; Vittorio Rizzi, Italian National Police; and Bernard Bertossa, Procureur General, Canton of Geneva, Switzerland.

Finally, many thanks to my old pal Gerald Chappell, attorney at law, for his constant support and consistently sound advice; Nick Webb at Simon & Schuster for his friendship, wisdom and elan; and Ingrid Connell at Simon & Schuster for putting up with me.

JR/London 1998

Prologue

When this book was first written in the early 1990s, money laundering was thought of by the general public as one of those strange phenomenon vaguely associated with crooked bankers in foreign tax havens. In spite of the clamour coming from those men and women in international law enforcement who, having seen its effects first hand, were starting to describe money laundering as the crime of the nineties, it wasn't yet considered of any real concern to most people, because most people didn't think they had or ever would come into contract with money launderers.

That is no longer the case.

Today, money laundering is very much the crime of the decade, and one that directly touches each of us. Money laundering is the lifeblood of international drug trafficking, and drugs have become the social cancer of our era.

Because international drug trafficking is a business, it stands to reason that the war on drugs can never be won until it becomes the war on 'the business of drugs'. And because, as in any colossal, multinational industry, drug trafficking thrives on cashflow and reinvestment, the business of drugs becomes the business of money laundering.

The two are absolutely inseparable.

One estimate has it that as much as £200–£300 *billion* is right now spinning around the globe looking to get clean as part of the dirty money washing cycle.

By denying the traffickers the ability to launder this money, we can deny them the ability to properly run their business.

In other words, we can beat them by bankrupting them.

But while this could happen, it hasn't happened yet because dirty money now underpins so much of the world's economy and is starting to talk in such a way that some politicians have felt compelled to listen.

What follows are stories about how money launderers manage their business and how that business affects us all.

What follows are stories about how dirty money becomes the white powder which is killing our children and the underground economy that is shaping our world.

What follows are three promises:

If you walk one mile in any direction from the main central railway station in any major city in Europe or North America – London, Paris, Rome, Frankfurt, Athens, Copenhagen, Amsterdam, New York, Miami, Los Angeles, Chicago, Toronto, Montreal – you will pass within an elbow's distance of a property that is owned by, managed by or has been constructed by dirty money.

At some point in the past 30 days, you did business, knowingly or unknowingly, with a money launderer or otherwise came in contact with dirty money.

After *The Laundrymen*, bankers, lawyers, accountants, money managers and more than a few governments will never look quite the same.

CHAPTER ONE

The Magic Trick

'When the President does it, that means it is not illegal.'
Richard Nixon

Money laundering is all about sleight of hand.

It is a magic trick for wealth creation.

It is, perhaps, the closest anyone has ever come to alchemy.

The lifeblood of drug dealers, fraudsters, smugglers, kidnappers, arms dealers, terrorists, extortionists and tax evaders, myth has it that the term was coined by Al Capone, who, like his arch rival George 'Bugs' Moran, used a string of coin-operated laundromats scattered around Chicago to disguise his revenue from gambling, prostitution, racketeering and violation of the Prohibition laws.

It's a neat story – but not true.

Money laundering is called what it is because that perfectly describes what takes place – illegal, or dirty, money is put through a cycle of transactions, or washed, so that it comes out the other end as legal, or clean, money. In other words, the source of illegally obtained funds is obscured through a succession of transfers and deals in order that those same funds can eventually be made to reappear as legitimate income.

Romance has since been added to myth with the name of Meyer Lansky.

Whereas cronies like Capone, Luciano and, later, Frank Costello made their way through the world using muscle, Lansky – a 5 foot 3 inch, Polish born, New York raised, 9th grade drop-out – used his brain to become the highest-ranking non-Italian in what used to be called 'The Syndicate.' He was affectionately known, in those days, as the mob's accountant. He is often affectionately remembered, these days, as the patron saint of money launderers. It's an epitaph that would have amused him.

Lansky had been particularly distressed in October 1931 by Capone's carelessness in allowing the Feds to arrest him, convict him and send him to Alcatraz for something as obvious as tax evasion. Determined to avoid a similar fate, he theorized that any money the Internal Revenue Service didn't know about was, by default, not taxable. With that as his premise, he embarked on a search for ways to hide money. Before the year was out, he'd discovered the benefits of numbered Swiss bank accounts. Some 20 years later, after helping his long-standing partner in crime, Benjamin 'Bugsy' Siegel, to finance The Flamingo – the first major hotel and casino complex in the desert that would become Las Vegas – Lansky convinced his pals that their non-taxable future lay in offshore expansion. He felt that, even if the IRS suspected there was money outside their jurisdiction, the fact that they couldn't get their hands on it to count it was the next best thing to hiding it. So he took the mob to Havana and, with the blessings of strongman Fulgencio Batista, Lansky almost single-handedly turned the Cuban capital into boom-town. But his dreams of a world beyond the reach of the IRS had a rude awakening when Fidel Castro – who'd battled his way down from the mountains in 1959 with the help of guns provided by American gangsters – threw out all the Americans.

While some of his cohorts brooded over such bad luck, Lansky was typically philosophical. He admitted he'd backed the wrong horse – he'd sided with Batista early on because very few people believed that Castro, his mate Che Guevara and their ragtag band of merry-men could pull off an entire revolution – took his losses and accepted the lesson that the best guarantee for any offshore investment is a politically stable environment.

In pursuit of somewhere safe and sound, he turned to the Bahamas. Thirty minutes by air from Miami and in the same time zone as the eastern United States, the 700 islands and cays that made up the then British colony were ideal. Communications were good, real estate was cheap, access was easy, the market was ripe and, best of all, the local politicians were bent enough that he could successfully fortify their hold on power to insure stability.

The fly in the ointment, where Meyer Lansky's beatification is concerned, is that he was hardly a saint and definitely not a money launderer. His fundamental concern was evading taxes. There doesn't appear to be any evidence that he did anything more than come up with some basic procedures for capital flight. There's nothing to suggest he ever intended to repatriate any money in order to declare it and legally spend it.

Far from being a full-fledged patron saint, he is more to money laundering what the Wright Brothers are to the Concorde. Lansky unquestionably managed to get the business off the ground, but it was left to other people to break the sound barrier.

Interestingly enough, it seems that it wasn't until 1973 that the term money laundering actually appeared in print for the first time. And when it did it had nothing to do with Meyer Lansky. According to the definitive source on such matters – the *Oxford English Dictionary* – the original sighting was in newspapers reporting the Watergate scandal.

At the end of February 1972, Richard Nixon took the first formal steps towards renewing his tenure at the White House. He announced the creation of the Committee to Re-elect the President – abbreviated to CRP and, bizarrely, pronounced 'creep' – and named his former law partner, Attorney General John Mitchell, to run it. But that was strictly for public consumption. The real campaign drive had begun at least a year before with Mitchell and Secretary of Commerce Maurice Stans – who took the chair of CRP's Finance Committee – secretly building a presidential war chest. Among the many contributors was the American dairy industry, willing to reward Nixon for having raised federal milk subsidies. Also on the list was the recluse billionaire Howard Hughes, who reportedly handed $100,000 directly to Nixon's closest friend, Florida banker Charles 'Bebe' Rebozo.

Then there was the disgraced international financier, Robert Vesco. Under investigation, at the time, by Mitchell's Justice Department, he thought enough of Nixon and, evidently, the prospect of some Oval Office sympathy, to arrange a cash donation of $200,000.

When Mitchell and Stans squeezed American Airlines for $100,000, George Spater – then chairman and chief executive of the airline – was faced with the predicament of how to divert corporate funds that were otherwise accountable. He arranged to have a Lebanese company called Amarco submit a fraudulent invoice as their commission on parts sold to Middle East Airlines. American Airlines paid the invoice, Amarco deposited the money in Switzerland, and then wired it to their account in New York. There, Amarco's agent withdrew $100,000 in cash and handed it to Spater, who turned it over to Mitchell and Stans.

Braniff Airlines, also hit by the duo, laundered their benevolence through Panama. The airline's regional vice president for Latin America instructed the company's man in Panama City to raise $40,000 in cash on a false invoice from a local company for 'goods and services.' Headquarters in Dallas then supplied the Panama office with a batch of unaccountable blank tickets which were to be issued only when a client paid for a flight with cash. The money raised on those tickets was funneled through a Dallas construction company before showing up on Braniff's books to cover up for the original shortfall.

Next, Stans turned to the oil industry. Ashland Oil's chairman, Orin Atkins, obliged with money from a subsidiary in Gabon, washed through Switzerland, then withdrawn in cash and returned to America in an executive's attaché case. Gulf Oil laundered their $100,000 gift to Mr Nixon's future through a subsidiary in the Bahamas.

It goes without saying that these contributions went unreported. Although Vesco's donation was eventually returned, technically – under the statutes then in force – it was arguable whether or not CRP was in fact under any obligation to report such contributions. The answer was, however, about to be clarified. Congress had just passed a law, to come into effect on April 7, that specifically prohibited these sorts of anonymous donations. As that would severely cramp their style, Mitchell and Stans decided to pull in as much as they could before the deadline.

So they dusted off an old Mexican connection that would guarantee that anonymous donations could not be traced, and went back to work, now targeting private citizens who would appreciate discretion in these matters. They also went in search of corporations that might otherwise be banned by the new law from making substantial and undeclared political contributions.

Never known for the subtle approach, Stans bulldozed potential donors with stern lectures on the debt of gratitude that all patriotic Americans owed to Richard Nixon while, in the same breath, reminding them that his Mexican connection was not subject to American audits.

With hindsight, the whole thing turns out to have been a fairly adolescent scheme. Among the offerings raked in by Stans, in clear-cut breach of the new law, were four cashier's checks totaling $89,000. Each was drawn on a different bank in the United States and each was made payable to a Mexico City lawyer named Manuel Ogarrio Daguerre. In mid-April those four drafts – in sums of $15,000, $18,000, $24,000 and $32,000 – were forwarded by Daguerre to Miami where, on April 20, they were deposited into the bank account of a local real estate salesman named Bernard L. Barker. Should anyone ever question the money, Barker was under instructions to say that it was his share of a land deal with an anonymous Chilean businessman. Should anyone ever ask why he subsequently withdrew the $89,000 in cash, his answer was to be that the deal had fallen through and he needed to repay the commission.

Had Mitchell and Stans then gone on a binge, blowing the money on wine, women and song, it's likely no one ever would have found out about it. Instead, they decided to finance a crime.

On the evening of 17 June 1972, five burglars broke into the Democratic National Committee headquarters at the Watergate office building, west of Juarez Circle. They were: Virgilio Gonzalez, a Cuban-born locksmith; Eugenio Martinez, a Cuban-born anti-Castro activist and CIA informant; Frank Sturgis, a Miami soldier of fortune with CIA connections; James W. McCord, Jr, a former employee of both the FBI and the CIA; and one Bernard L. Barker of Miami, Florida. As it turned out, he'd also worked for the CIA and in 1962 had been involved in the Bay of Pigs invasion.

As far as burglaries go, it wasn't even worthy of the 'second rate' status Nixon gave it in the days when he was still insisting he knew nothing about it. Bluntly put, it was a stupid and clumsy stunt that wound up being an abject failure. The five men were arrested immediately.

At first, the most interesting member of the group appeared to be McCord because, at the time of the break-in, he was the security coordinator at CRP. Then came the arrest of two more men, G. Gordon Liddy and E. Howard Hunt. They were the brains behind the break-in. And it soon came to light that both of them had direct links to the CIA, the Committee to Re-elect the President and, shockingly, the White House.

Yet the thread that would unravel the conspiracy turned out to be Barker.

Too clever by half, Mitchell and Stans never reckoned that anything could go wrong. Nor had it ever dawned on them that, if anything did go wrong, someone might somehow find those four cheques and trace them back through the Mexican lawyer to CRP. Once Bob Woodward and Carl Bernstein of the *Washington Post* broke the story, however, and it gained enough momentum that they could really run with it, every other investigative reporter in America tried to get in on the act. Competition for front-page scoops became super-intense. In the end, it was the *New York Times* that headlined the Mexican money connection.

Subpoenas flew and investigators got inside Barker's bank account. Now a fifth suspicious cheque was uncovered, this one for $25,000 dated 10 April. Drawn on the First Bank and Trust Company of Boca Raton, Florida, it was made payable to Kenneth H. Dahlberg, a Nixon fundraiser in the mid-west. When a reporter contacted him about the check, he admitted he'd long since turned it over to Maurice Stans.

The $89,000, bathed in Mexico, was just the tip of the iceberg. The figure soon jumped to $750,000. That's when it was revealed that Stans maintained a huge and unquestionably illegal cash slush fund in his office at CRP.

The sheer amateurishness of their money laundering scheme invariably tied CRP to the Watergate break-in. By 21 March 1973 – now so tangled in his own lies that his fate was undoubtedly already sealed – Nixon tried to convince his legal adviser John Dean that by laundering even more money he might be able to buy his way out of the crisis.

Prophetically, in a private Oval Office conversation, Dean warned Nixon, 'People around here are not pros at this sort of thing.'

That was an understatement!

He went on, 'This is the sort of thing Mafia people can do – washing money, getting clean money and things like that. We just don't know about those things, because we are not criminals and not used to dealing in that business.'

It was only a matter of time before Nixon's meagre lines of defence were split so wide open that no one – least of all Richard Nixon playing the laundryman – could have halted the process that brought down a dishonest president.

Like any great thriller, the story is filled with ironies.

One is that Nixon had been so far ahead in the polls, and his opponent, George McGovern, politically so far out in space, that CRP didn't need to solicit illegal funds. Nixon, quite literally, could have stayed in the Oval Office, never once made a speech, never once kissed a baby, never once hit the campaign trail, and still have won in a landslide.

A second is that, in the wake of Watergate, Congress took direct action to prohibit government intrusion into the lives of ordinary citizens. One of the laws that was passed virtually enjoined financial investigators not to compare notes, which has turned out to be a boon for the laundrymen.

A third irony is that, in those days, money laundering was not yet a crime anywhere in the world.

CHAPTER TWO

Doing the Wash

'Money possesses a strange kind of purity.'

Bernie Cornfeld

In textbook terms, there are four factors common to all money laundering operations.

To begin with, the true ownership and the real source of the money must be concealed. There's no sense in laundering money if everyone knows who owns it when it comes out the other end.

Next, the form it takes must be changed. No one wants to wash £3 million in £20 notes only to wind up with £3 million worth of £20 notes. Among other things, when there is a great deal of cash involved, changing the form also means reducing the bulk. Contrary to popular belief, you cannot, for instance, stuff £1 million into an attaché case. A million pound stack of £50 notes is nearly 10 feet high!

Thirdly, the trail left by the process must be obscured. The purpose of the exercise is defeated if someone can follow the money from beginning to end.

Finally, constant control must be maintained over the money. After all, many of the people who come into the picture while the money is being laundered understand that it is dirty money and if they can steal it there's little the original owner can legally do about it.

That said, there are three distinct stages to the washing cycle.

The first is immersion, which means consolidation and placement. A drug dealer who amasses £5 million in cash is faced with the herculean task of putting perhaps as many as a million pieces of paper into the banking system. Unlike the counterfeiter, who needs to get his forged notes into circulation, the laundryman is forced to rely on bank accounts, postal orders, traveller's cheques and other negotiable instruments to funnel the cash into the banking system.

Continuing the metaphor, the second step – known as layering – might also be called heavy soaping. This is where the laundryman disassociates his gains from their illicit source. By moving his money between as many accounts as he can – in and out of dummy companies that he's set up around the world for just this purpose – and relying on bank secrecy and attorney–client privilege to hide his own identity, he deliberately creates a complex web of financial transactions, keeping in mind at every step that his main task here is to obliterate any sort of audit trail.

The final stage is the spin dry – sometimes described as repatriation and integration. This is the point where the washed funds are brought back into circulation, now in the form of clean, and often taxable, income.

With minor amounts of money, the three-step process can be quick.

If all you want to do is wash £20,000, you merely have to walk into ten banks and, at each one, buy £2,000 worth of traveller's cheques. Or, stop by the same number of post offices and purchase a handful of international money orders. Negotiable anywhere in the world, you can deposit traveller's cheques and money orders in any foreign bank account, or hold on to them until you want to spend them. As long as you keep the acquisitions down to realistic sizes – and £2,000 in cash isn't going to raise alarm bells the way a single £20,000 cash transaction might – you've managed it with little or no inconvenience.

If, say, you're sitting on £110,000 in cash, you might swagger into a Rolls-Royce showroom and turn the money into a brand-new Silver Spirit. As cash is not the usual form of payment in places like that, it's fair to assume that the dealer might display some anxiety when you produce a green plastic Harrods bag stuffed with banknotes. He might even go so far as to wonder, is this bloke laundering money? If that thought did cross his mind, he'd be legally bound to report his suspicions. Except, it's a good bet that he isn't aware of his legal obligations or, on the odd chance that he is, that for the sake of a sale he'd be willing to claim he never had any suspicions.

When the Rolls dealer then deposits your cash at his bank, there's no reason to believe that anyone at the bank would question it. After all, he's their customer. They know him. Later, should anyone ever ask the bank staff about it, they could always shrug, logically, if there was anything suspect about the cash, it was up to the Rolls dealer to report it.

And even if the fellow who sold the car knew of his duty to notify the police and even if he actually bothered to do so, by the time the British National Criminal Intelligence Service (NCIS) saw a copy of that report, you'd have had plenty of time to flog the Rolls and deposit your cashier's cheque, made out to a false name, in your offshore bank account.

The principal hurdle here is that car registrations and cashier's cheques can leave a distinct paper trail. Less conspicuous are businesses where cash is the traditional form of payment.

One of them is the antiques trade.

You begin by purchasing a £100 shell company. Formation

agents selling ready-made companies advertise every day in the financial section of most newspapers. Using the company's name and a registered office address, you drive around the country, paying cash for Chinese vases, or Louis XV chairs, or George II candelabras, or fine Persian carpets. Gems, stamps and collectors' coins are also easily converted into and out of cash.

Once you've got your stock – say, ten Ming vases at £5,000 each – you put everything up for sale, splitting the cache between five auction houses, preferably in five different towns. When any item comes up, either you allow it to be sold to the highest bidder or you secretly send your favourite uncle into the saleroom to buy it back.

You are paid for every item sold, regardless of who bought it, by cheque. So when your uncle hands the auction house £5,500 cash for one of the vases – that's the £5,000 hammer price plus the 10% buyer's commission – they return the money to you in a draft for £4,500, which is the hammer price minus the 10% seller's commission. The fees are simply written off as the cost of washing the funds. And, in this case, you also have the vase to sell again.

Auction houses in Britain, like Rolls-Royce dealers, are required to report suspicious cash transactions. But the key word remains 'suspicious'. On any given day, throughout the United Kingdom, you can find loads of people paying for major purchases in cash. And hardly any of it ever gets reported.

Retail stores, bars and restaurants are another cash-intensive area. Take the example of a restaurant that doesn't accept credit cards or cheques. South Florida is filled with them. Pizza goes out the front door, dirty money comes in the back door.

The same thing happens in the video rental business. Like any high-volume cash trade, no one could spot an extra $300 a day coming through the tills of a storefront stocked with 5,000 or 10,000 videos. As long as the money is fed into the system gradually, there's no doubt that it would go unnoticed. Nor would anyone question the accountant whose audit showed that the two owners took a legally declared $60,000 bonus every year. Nor would anyone's suspicions necessarily be raised by those same two owners if they ran a chain of 20 video rental stores and – backed up with the appropriate paperwork – were awarding themselves annual bonuses of $1.2 million.

Here's where the laundrymen have understood that, contrary to Gordon Gekko's philosophy in the film *Wall Street*, greed is not good; that, with a little long-term planning, it's possible to build a network of sinks into a money laundering conglomerate.

Take the case of the Italian gentleman who sets his son up in a grocery store. Papa lends Figlio the money he needs to open the business, and much of that money is cash. Figlio pays his carpenters, painters and delivery people with cash, and they are happy to accept it because they see it as non-taxable.

Figlio stocks his grocery through a wholesaler who just happens to be Papa's brother. And when Figlio orders 50 cases of tagliatelle from Uncle Zio, he receives only 40. Papa then hands Figlio cash to make up for the shortfall. It's the same when he orders milk and cheese and frozen brownies. Zio shorts the delivery and the missing 20% helps gets Papa's cash into the system. At the end of the month, Papa tops up Figlio's accounts with more cash. Figlio's bookkeepers are happy, the taxman is happy and Figlio soon branches out to open a second grocery. Two becomes four and four becomes eight.

As Figlio's empire expands, he decides to get into the business of importing olive oil from the old country. Luckily, Papa's got a cousin in Palermo. But Figlio doesn't buy it direct from Cugino. Papa sets up a business in the Bahamas called Olio di Mio Cugino Inc. His cousin sells 100 bottles to the Bahamian company for $100. The Bahamian company bills Figlio for 120 bottles at $3 each. And at the end of every month, there's Papa at the ready with more cash.

How much money circles the globe, looking to get scrubbed clean each year, no one knows for certain. Reasonably authoritative guesses range anywhere from $100 billion to three times as much. It's called the alternate economy. And, after foreign exchange and petroleum, it is the world's third-largest business.

In order for it to function, two things are necessary: like coffee being poured from a pot into a cup, there must be enough room in the cup to hold the coffee and enough coffee in the pot to fill the cup. In other words, there has to be enough money available to create an infrastructure and, at the same time, an infrastructure capable of handling so much money.

The world's parallel, or underground, banking system takes many forms. Whether it's called *chop* or *hundi* or *hawalah*, it was born out of political turmoil and a hearty distrust of banks. It is based principally on family or tribal connections, which are, increasingly, reinforced with retributive violence.

Best described by the Chinese, who apparently invented it, with their term *fei ch'ien* – literally, flying money – in its simplest form chits or tokens are substituted for cash. Money deposited at a Hong Kong gold shop is exchanged for a small card bearing a picture of a dragon, or a $10 bill stamped with a special seal, or a small, innocuous piece of paper – like a laundry ticket or a torn playing card – that has been secretly coded. When the chit is presented to a money changer in San Francisco's Chinatown, the bearer is given his cash.

During the days when certain European countries had

exchange controls – the UK, France and Italy, for instance – a variation on the *fei ch'ien* system was facilitated by the tourist trade. A Parisian businessman would stake his American friends to whatever money they needed while visiting France. When the Americans got home, they added up what they owed their host and deposited that into the Parisian's undeclared US bank account.

Throughout much of the Vietnam War, a thriving black market throughout Southeast Asia drove the underground economy, which turned out to be the only economy. At least until the Tet Offensive in January 1968, Saigon was alive with all sorts of scams and swindles. The official exchange rate in those days was 118 Vietnamese piastres to the dollar, but the black market rate was closer to 200. A lucrative corner of that trade was controlled by a small group of Indian nationals who'd emigrated to South Vietnam from Madras. They bought dollars at black market rates, and smuggled them out of the country to be deposited in Hong Kong and Singapore. From there, the money was wired either to Europe or, more often, to the Middle East, where it was used to purchase gold. The gold was smuggled back into Vietnam and sold for piastres at a rate far exceeding 200 to the dollar. Those piastres were then sold to the Americans for more dollars, completing the circle.

By the time the South Vietnamese authorities were wise to the Indian laundrymen – and began confiscating dollars leaving the country in contravention of the currency restriction laws – the Indians were already working an improvised version of the *hawalah* system. They traded GIs' cheques drawn on American banks for chits. The cheques were sent for deposit to accounts held by the Indians in New York. When the cheques cleared, the chits were exchanged for piastres. At that point, the New York banks wired the dollars on to pay for the gold.

These days, a staggering and more traditional *hawalah*

business exists between India, where currency controls are in force, and the UK, where a large Indian population has a substantial interest in getting funds from the subcontinent into Europe. Facilities abound for Indians to deposit money with *hawalah* bankers throughout the country and to collect their money within hours, minus a commission of 5–15%, from someone in London. The system works because the market is a two-way street. There are enough people with large cash surpluses in both countries – drug dealers, organized criminals, terrorists and even legitimate businessmen – who are willing to pay handsomely for the privilege of using a paperless banking system.

The British are particularly concerned about *hawalah* networks operating between London and two Indian regions – the Punjab and Kashmir – because money travelling that route has been known to finance terrorist violence, specifically Sikh and Kashmiri secessionists. Additionally, the British claim, this particular *hawalah* network is one of the main channels of finance for drug traffickers working out of Pakistan.

A few years ago Scotland Yard busted a *hawalah* banker whom they'd had under surveillance for several months. When officers finally raided his house – after watching him work 12 hour shifts through the night, seven nights a week – they found sacks of cash in his sitting-room containing nearly £1 million. In the end the man was never charged because the money laundering laws in effect at that time in Britain required the police to link the money directly to drug- or terrorist-related activities and they couldn't make that case. But the man was moving £8 million a week. And he is only one of a long list of *hawalah* bankers working in the UK.

In 1989, British police arrested a consortium of six *hawalah* bankers who admitted to having laundered, annually, £80 million.

*   *   *

Crooks wash money because they need to avoid the kind of attention that sudden wealth brings, to place the proceeds of crime beyond the reach of asset forfeiture laws, and to reinvest in both lawful and unlawful enterprises that will then generate more funds.

In 1986, Dennis Levine, a 33-year-old New York investment banker – at the time of his arrest he was managing director of Drexel, Burnham Lambert's mergers and acquisition department – stood accused of insider trading on a scale never before seen. From June 1978 to February 1985, he used non-public information to deal in the stocks and bonds of 54 different companies. In just under seven years, he amassed profits of $13 million.

Knowing from the outset that in order to have use of this money he had to wash it first, he bought a pair of Panamanian-registered companies – Diamond Holdings SA and International Gold Inc. – both of which came complete with nominee directors. His name never appeared in any company documents. When he opened accounts for the two companies at Bank Leu International in Nassau, New Providence Island, he made equally certain that his name was not used on any of the bank's records. His main contact was the portfolio manager – a Swiss national named Bernhard Meier – who was under strict instructions never to contact him, under any circumstances. Ever cautious, Levine would always phone Meier, and then only from a pay phone so that no one could trace calls back to him. When he wanted to see his money, Levine flew down to the Bahamas, using an assumed name, and only for the day. He never stayed overnight for fear that someone working in a hotel might later be able to identify him.

Unfortunately for Levine, he was very much a victim of his own success. He got his trades right so often that some people – including Bernhard Meier – decided to follow his lead. They piggy-backed, buying and selling whenever he bought or sold. That, coupled with his abnormally high batting average, eventually attracted too much attention. The Securities and Exchange Commission (SEC), which unashamedly monitors big hitters, moved in for a closer look. Its agents were quick to uncover the fact that Levine had accomplices in other brokerage houses. When they put pressure on him, he elected to save himself and sold them down the river. When the SEC managed to intimidate a few Bank Leu officials in Nassau – trading information for immunity – Levine's friends returned the compliment and sacrificed him.

Beno Ghitis-Miller suffered a similar fate. A 32-year-old travel agent from Cali, Colombia, he moved to Florida in 1980 to set up a currency business called Sonal. He opened a corporate account at the Capital Bank, in downtown Miami, and, during the first seven months of his business, got into the habit of depositing fairly large sums of cash. Occasionally they reached $1 million.

Late that spring, a man named Victor Eisenstein waltzed into the bank, introduced himself as Beno's agent – his card noted that he ran a company called American Overseas Enterprises – and said that he would be making deposits for Sonal. And he too began putting large sums through the account.

Within a month, the bank notified Eisenstein that they could no longer accept his cash. On the surface it looked as though the bank was beginning to have some doubts about these particular clients. Eisenstein objected but the branch manager said the decision was irreversible. And it was, at least until Beno went over the manager's head and met with the bank's president. Up to that point, Sonal was paying Capital 0.125% for sorting and counting each deposit. Now, to stay friends, Capital offered to maintain the account as long as Sonal upped the commission to 0.5%. And Beno agreed.

Over the next several months, as the cash deposits fast approached $2 million each, the local manager again expressed his concern. But it had nothing to do with the quality of his clients. He was just wondering, would Beno and Eisenstein mind using a better-equipped branch. They happily switched their account to Capital's North Bay Village office. Next, when Beno was told that the bank had commercial space for rent upstairs, he moved Sonal to North Bay Village, too.

It didn't take long before Beno and Eisenstein were depositing several million dollars, three and four times a week.

Claiming that he didn't know the true nature of Beno's business – after all, he later said, he was acting only as Sonal's agent – Eisenstein decided it might be prudent to ask where all this cash was coming from. Beno explained, in a friendly and straightforward letter to Eisenstein, that the money was received by Sonal in connection with exchange transactions from the importing and exporting of agricultural products and raw materials and sales commissions received abroad by Colombian businessmen. He insisted everything was perfectly kosher, and added that, even though they were handling a lot of cash, none of it should be mistaken for cash derived from illegal operations, 'which are so fashionable these days in Florida.'

Apparently no one spotted the mockery in Beno's reference to 'agricultural products, raw materials and sales commissions'.

More to the point, apparently no one at the bank bothered to walk upstairs to look at Sonal's new offices. If they had, they might have asked why a company dealing in cash – especially handling the sums that Sonal did – had no security. There was no armored door. There were no video cameras. There was hardly had any furniture. There wasn't even a safe.

But then, the folks at Capital liked Beno's business. He and Eisenstein were reasonably friendly. They dealt in big numbers. And they substantially increased the branch's 'cash in' figure, which made the manager look like an aggressive young banker on the way up.

Before long, the folks at Capital liked Beno's business enough to negotiate a flat fee for sorting and counting Sonal's cash – $300,000 per month.

In the eight months from 1 January to 20 August 1981, Beno and Eisenstein and Sonal's 'staff' – 37 different Hispanic-speaking guys who had only nicknames – deposited $240 million at Capital. That included the $7 million they dropped off in the final two days of their operation. Sonal had averaged deposits of $1.5 million per day, until the US authorities said enough was enough and shut them down.

The greedier they are the cockier they become and, given enough time, it is their greed and cockiness that eventually help to undo them. The converse is also true. The French father and son team – Henri and Charles Borodiansky – were slightly less greedy and slightly less cocky than Beno and Eisenstein and subsequently fared slightly better.

But only just.

Their act was maritime fraud in general and phantom cargoes in particular. In early 1990, the Borodianskys claimed to have 14 shipping containers of Hennessy VSOP Scotch whisky for sale. The price was right so a department store in Tokyo took the bait. They forwarded a letter of credit for $3.3 million to a shell company called Mozambico Inc. Ltd, whose registered office was a convenience address in central London.

When the cargo never arrived, the Japanese asked the police to find out why. A full inquiry conducted by the International Maritime Bureau (IMB) in London – the Interpol of the shipping business – revealed that son Charles, using the alias Manuel Martins Casimiro, had negotiated the letter of credit in June through the Banque Bruxelles Lambert in Brussels. He'd then moved the funds to Liechtenstein's V&P Bank, straight into an account opened by papa Henri, who'd sported the alias Jose Costa Da Santos. Over the next few weeks, half a million dollars was wired from Liechtenstein to a bank in Luxembourg. The rest of it, the IMB learned, had been sent to an account at the Commerzbank in Cologne, Germany.

It turns out that the Borodianskys had been at this for several years. Using names such as Deck, Borod and Da Silva – in addition to the ones they chose for the Hennessy scam – they'd set up shell companies across Europe. There were at least four in Belgium, one in the Netherlands, one in Spain, five in Britain, two in Luxembourg, one in Hong Kong and four in Germany. They are known to have sold 2,000 tons of non-existent maize bound for Dakar, $2.6 million worth of non- existent urea – a commercial fertilizer – bound for China, 6000 metric tons of non-existent steel bound for Vietnam, and 2,000 metric tons of non-existent cement bound for Aqaba.

When the IMB discovered that the Borodianskys had paid cash for at least one vessel, they were able to locate the ship and impound it. But they needed to prove that the men calling themselves Casimiro and Da Santos and Da Silva were in fact the Borodianskys. So they published a photo in a Norwegian shipping trade magazine asking if anyone knew the whereabouts of these two men. A ship broker in London identified them immediately and was able to provide enough information for the German police to find them.

For whatever reason, it took the Germans six days to act. When they did, they arrested Charles Borodiansky. But his father was gone. And when Charles led the police to the three safe deposit boxes where, it was believed, they'd hidden nearly $3 million in freshly washed cash, all three safe deposit boxes were empty.

Crooks aren't the only ones who launder money.

Corporations do it to avoid or evade taxes, to defraud their shareholders, to get around currency control regulations and/or to bribe prospective clients.

Some years ago, Gulf Oil moved $4 million through the Bahamas to bribe Korean and Bolivian politicians, while the Lockheed Corporation laundered $25.5 million through a Liechtenstein trust, using cash and bearer drafts to pay off Italian politicians. Lockheed also subscribed to the laundry facilities of Deak-Perera – then an important American foreign exchange dealer – to bribe Japanese politicians. At Lockheed's behest, Deak put $8.3 million into the washing cycle to help secure a large sale. It came out the other end in the form of 15 untraceable payments to, of all people, a Spanish priest in Hong Kong who hand-carried the cash in flight bags and orange crates to Lockheed's customers in Tokyo.

Individuals also launder funds.

They may need to hide money, say from a divorcing spouse, or perhaps simply feel that an erosion of their assets can be neutralized by inventing a business deal that moves those assets through a shell company and into a less taxed jurisdiction. Italian designer Aldo Gucci washed more than $11 million through shell companies, stashing it in Hong Kong to keep it out of the hands of the American taxman.

Governments have been known to do it as well, whether it be to subvert terrorists or to arm freedom fighters. That's what Iran–Contra was all about.

In November 1986, Ronald Reagan confirmed the much-circulated rumour that the United States had surreptitiously sold arms to Iran. His initial version of the events was that it had been intended to improve relations with Iran, not to obtain the release of American citizens held in the Middle East by terrorists. But that soon got changed to an embarrassed admission that, indeed, this had been an arms-for-hostages swap.

Although some of the scandal remains clouded in mystery, the deal appears to have been one in which the United States – with the help of Saudi Arabia's King Fahd – furnished the Iranians with weapons in exchange for payments that then diverted to the Nicaraguan anti-Sandinista 'Contra' rebels for their fight against the Marxist regime in Nicaragua – all of this in direct violation of a Congressional prohibition on any such aid.

CIA Director William Casey wanted to find a way to open a dialogue with the Iranians, the direct route having been shut by the arms embargo that followed the 1979 seizure of US hostages in Teheran. He turned to his old pal King Fahd, who had no trouble securing the services of Saudi arms dealer Adnan Khashoggi. Once wrongly touted as the richest man in the world – he never was, but for obvious reasons didn't mind holding the title – Khashoggi was a professional middleman, a globe-trotting broker who knew how to get a deal going and then cut himself in on the action.

Before long, two other players came into the picture on either side of Khashoggi: Manucher Ghorbanifar, an Iranian middleman who, while having gone into exile at the same time as the Shah, still maintained high-level contacts with the Revolutionary Government; and Yaaccov Nimrodi, an Israeli with intelligence experience and considerable contacts in Teheran.

Enter here Lieutenant Colonel Oliver North, US Marine Corps, deputy director of political affairs at the National Security Council. Beginning in late August or early September 1984 – initially working under the President's National

Security Advisor, Robert McFarlane, and later in partnership with McFarlane's successor, Vice Admiral John Poindexter – North formulated and then executed the plan.

By the autumn of 1985, he'd convinced the Israelis to sell 500 US-made TOW anti-tank missiles to Iran, with the deal being guaranteed by Khashoggi. When the Iranians paid Khashoggi, he took his share, then passed the rest along to the Israelis. They paid North, who diverted the funds through Swiss banks, and eventually sent them on to the Contras. To help, North recruited Richard Secord, a retired US Air Force general, and Secord's business partner, Albert Hakim, an Iranian-American. The three were so successful that, by early 1986, they'd managed to buy some 2,000 TOW missiles from the CIA for $12 million and – again with the intervention of Khashoggi and Ghorbanifar – to sell them to the Iranians for $30 million.

In Switzerland, that money was washed through a dummy Panamanian company North had established under the name of Lake Resources. The chairman of Lake Resources was a Swiss accountant named Suzanne Hefti, who worked for Auditing and Fiduciary Services in Fribourg. Her firm was directly tied in to the Stanford Technology Trading Group International in California, which was controlled by Albert Hakim. In turn, Stanford Technology's Swiss affiliate was headed by a man named Jean de Senarclens, who also happened to run an accounting firm in Geneva called CSF.

And it was CSF that played the paramount role in the Iran–Contra washing cycle.

First, North moved money from Lake Resources' Swiss account to a CSF account in the Cayman Islands. Next, a CSF subsidiary in Bermuda wired the money to Alban Values, a Panamanian corporation in which CSF had an interest. Alban Values then sent it to Amalgamated Commercial Enterprises, a shell company registered in Panama but owned by a Miami freight carrier called Southern Air Transport. And they were the ones who actually supplied the Contras.

It's believed that in just the two years from 1984 to 1986 as much as $50 million might have gone this route. Except that the Contras claim they never got anywhere near that amount. After 250 hours of testimony heard by the Senate Select Committee on the Iran–Contra scandal – including sworn statements from 29 witnesses and some 250,000 pages of documents – it is unlikely that anyone will ever know the full extent to which the government joined the laundrymen in making a fortune evaporate.

One prominent variation on the government-as-laundryman theme is political insurance.

Despots of all shapes and sizes insure against their unexpected retirement by shifting money from their own national banking system into less hostile environments. Most of the more visible political heads of state across the Middle East and Africa have financial arrangements in Switzerland. It apparently goes with the turf. The Shah of Iran laundered a king's ransom into secret bank accounts as an emergency pension fund.

So did Ferdinand and Imelda Marcos of the Philippines. Never able to manage on a presidential salary of $4,700, the couple reputedly stashed $5–10 billion in various parts of the world, much of it laundered through Hong Kong. According to the Philippine government commission originally assigned to track down the Marcos money, Ferdinand and Imelda used at least ten dummy corporations registered in the Philippines, Hong Kong, Panama and the Netherlands Antilles to get half the assets into the United States, a third into Switzerland and the rest into France, England, Italy, Panama and Australia.

Obsessed with secrecy, Ferdinand Marcos was totally committed to building an impenetrable web of deceit around his looted fortune. For instance, to purchase three buildings in Manhattan, he used three different bearer share companies registered in the Netherlands Antilles, each of which was owned by a separate Panamanian bearer share company. In other words, whoever physically held the stock certificates owned the dummy company that owned the other dummy company – as long as the first company had the share certificates for the second company – and in turn owned the property.

By making each and every transaction so complicated that no one could ever have traced anything back to him, Marcos quickly lost track of which name went on which account and which company controlled which property.

He's since been accused of using much the same dummy corporation formula to help friends finance their own property deals – among them, actor George Hamilton's purchase of Charlie Chaplin's former home in Beverly Hills. Hamilton, who has denied those allegations as they were lodged in a lawsuit against him, has since sold the house to a company registered in the Cayman Islands, rumoured to be controlled by the Khashoggi family.

The Marcos' finances became such an international embarrassment that even the otherwise unblushable Swiss decided to give up on him. They froze nearly $1.5 billion in bank accounts he'd used – many of them ascribed to aliases – including 14 he'd set up in the names of various foundations.

Needless to say, Ferdinand and Imelda were not the only ones to have got carried away with providing for their old age. The Ceausescus of Romania harboured their stolen assets in Switzerland, as have most of Latin America's tin-pot dictators. The same goes for literally hundreds of former Communist officials, many of whom raked in fortunes through drug trafficking.

One of the most flagrant offenders was East Germany's Erich Honecker. It's no coincidence that an East

Berlin-registered company, Novum Handelsgesellschaft – controlled by an Austrian Communist named Rudolfine Steindling – moved the equivalent of $260 million out of East Germany within hours of the fall of the Berlin Wall in 1989. The money was washed through the Z-Laenderbank – known as Bank Austria – and its subsidiary in Zurich, which was then called Bankfinanz. While $150 million was eventually transferred back to Communist party accounts in Vienna, at least $3 million was later withdrawn in cash.

It turns out to have been standard procedure for Communist leaders to salt something away – hedging their bets, as it were – on the remote possibility that Marx and Lenin were wrong.

CHAPTER THREE

Taking Care of Business

'You don't refuse a customer just because his money
isn't clean.'

Nicholas Deak

It's like a stone being thrown into a pond.

You see the stone hit the water because it splashes. As it
begins to sink, the water ripples and, for a few moments,
you can still find the spot where the stone hit. But, as the
stone sinks deeper, the ripples fade. By the time the stone
reaches the bottom, any traces of it are long gone and the
stone itself may be impossible to find.

That's exactly what happens to laundered money.

The immersion stage is the moment when the laundryman
is most vulnerable. If he can't get his dirty money into
a washing cycle, he can't clean it. But once his cash is
converted into numbers on a computer screen, and those
numbers are transmitted back and forth across the globe,
it's as if the ripples have long since disappeared and the
stone is now buried in silt.

Realizing that the optimum time to strike is when the
laundryman is exposed, the United States' Bank Secrecy
Act of 1970 attempted to force banks, savings and loans,

and other financial institutions to report all cash transactions over $1,000 to the Internal Revenue Service.

But the ceiling was too low. Even though there was a provision exempting certain retail businesses – higher limits were to be determined by each bank, based on a client's specific requirements – the government was inundated with forms. Because there weren't enough people to process them, most of those forms wound up decomposing in a warehouse. Anyway, far too many legitimate non-retail businesses deal in large amounts of cash. Compliance became so time consuming and awkward that, within weeks, banks either exempted all their biggest and best customers, or simply gave up.

Over the years, the law was widened to include non-bank financial institutions, such as travel agencies, money wire services, credit unions, car dealers, insurance agencies, money changers, brokerage houses and cheque-cashing businesses. Even a local convenience store selling money orders was expected to comply. Two years later, 'all trades and businesses' dealing in cash fell under the scope of the act. More realistically, the $1,000 limit was increased to $10,000.

Although 43 otherwise upstanding banks – including Chase Manhattan and Bank of America – had been penalized a total of $20 million, the currency reporting requirement was still being widely disregarded in 1985. That's when the United States decided to play hardball and squashed the Bank of Boston. The government accused it of gross and flagrant violations of the Bank Secrecy Act, alleging that it had failed to report some 1,163 cash transactions, which totaled $1.22 billion. Among the companies exempted by the Bank of Boston from cash reporting, the government pointed to a pair of real estate agencies controlled by a local organized crime boss.

In the face of overwhelming evidence, the Bank of Boston

pleaded guilty – admitting to an additional $110 million worth of violations – and was fined a then record $500,000.

The government reinforced its point by going after another 60 banks. Chemical Bank admitted 857 unreported cash transactions worth $26 million. Irving Trust Company acknowledged 1,659, worth $292 million. Manufacturers Hanover Trust agreed to 1,400, worth $140 million. When the Bank of New England was found guilty of 31 offences, it was fined $1.2 million. When Crocker National Bank was found to have committed 7,877 infractions, worth $3.98 billion, it was fined $2.25 million.

Instantly, banks across the nation sat up and took notice.

The following year, Congress passed the Money Laundering Control Act, making money laundering a criminal offence when it is associated with other criminal activity. If you simply want to move your own money through a whole series of jurisdictions, in and out of shell companies, to see what comes out the other end, that's your business. But if you're doing it in conjunction with a crime – insider trading, fraud, drug trafficking, income tax evasion, theft, whatever – then money laundering gets tagged onto the charge sheet. And here the federal government has left little doubt that this statute would be used as a catch-all offence, along with such old favourites as income tax evasion and conspiracy to defraud.

When the founder and former president of Phar-Mor Inc. – a well-known discount drugstore chain – was indicted by a federal grand jury for defrauding investors of $1.1 billion and embezzling a further $1.1 million from the company, the charges included four counts of wire fraud, two counts of bank fraud, two counts of mail fraud, two counts of filing false tax returns, one count of conspiracy and 118 counts of money laundering.

When Alex Daoud, the former three-term mayor of Miami Beach, was accused of taking bribes, a grand jury indicted him for racketeering, extortion and money laundering. When four officials of the United Mine Workers Union in Indiana were indicted for stealing $720,000 in union dues, they were charged with theft, embezzlement, conspiracy, mail fraud, tax evasion, racketeering, falsifying union records and money laundering. When the president of the Arochem Corporation in Connecticut was convicted for his part in a local bank fraud, the 22 counts lodged against him included wire fraud, bank fraud, falsely reporting information to a bank, participating in a continuing criminal enterprise and money laundering.

Today, American law not only requires a Cash Transaction Report (CTR) to be filed with the IRS for any and all cash transactions in excess of $10,000, but banks and other financial institutions are also obliged to maintain records for five years of every cash transaction in excess of $3,000.

To get around that, laundrymen have been known deliberately to structure their dealings by never going above the $10,000 ceiling. But whereas a series of $9,500 deposits would raise suspicions – CTRs must be filled out on aggregate deposits, assuming that a bank can spot them – a series of cash deposits kept to around $600 each is small enough to become nearly invisible. In one case, $29 million in cash was put through the US banking system, and eventually moved to accounts in Ecuador. However, to place and layer those funds successfully, the laundryman was forced to lumber through 40,000 separate transactions.

Phoney bank accounts are another obvious method of trying to get around CTRs and, believe it or not, the US government has investigated cases in recent years where accounts were audaciously opened in the names of Marilyn Monroe, Abraham Lincoln, James Bond, Mae West and Roger Rabbit.

Needless to say, there's nothing in any law to prevent someone from handing their bank $1 million in used $5 bills. But when it happens, the authorities want to know who's done it and where the money has come from.

Strengthening the government's hand is the 1990 Depository Institution Money Laundering Amendment Act which put the burden to report transactions squarely on the shoulders of banks' directors. It warned that by turning a blind eye they were risking everything, as the government can now claim the right to take over the running of any financial institution in the United States convicted of money laundering offences.

Once that was in place, law-makers in Washington dusted off the old RICO statutes. The Racketeer Influenced and Corrupt Organizations Act permits them to seize monies being laundered – whether they're generated through drug trafficking or any number of other offences – and to confiscate all assets derived from the use of those funds, in addition to levying fines of up to three times that amount.

Standard operating procedure for prosecutions under federal law empowers the local US Attorney to indict, subpoena and plea bargain. The only exceptions – when he's required to get approval from the Attorney General – are cases where the death penalty might be imposed, or when dealing with racketeering, espionage and money laundering.

Nowhere else in the world is money laundering given the same prestige.

In the United Kingdom, several pieces of legislation have been given Royal Assent with the express intention of penalizing the laundrymen. Yet all of them stop far short of the tough-talking line found in America.

The 1986 Drug Trafficking Offences Act provides the police with the authority to investigate suspected drug-derived assets, to freeze them and, upon conviction, to confiscate them. The law also makes it an offence to assist a drug trafficker in retaining or making use of his drug-related assets. It is, therefore, a crime in Britain to hold or control the proceeds of drug trafficking, to have funds put at your disposal or to help to invest such funds.

Parliament followed that with the 1987 Prevention of Terrorism Act, tagging the same criminal status on anyone who deals in terrorist-related funds. In 1990, the Criminal Justice (International Cooperation) Act made it possible to prosecute anyone who conceals, disguises, converts, transfers or removes property from the jurisdiction of the courts, or helps someone to do just that, when he knows or suspects that the property represents the proceeds of drug trafficking. Additional laws – specifically, the Criminal Justice Act of 1993 – now expand the courts' powers to prosecute money laundering as a crime in itself. But, in all these cases, the accepted defence is to prove that you did not know or did not suspect that you were dealing with laundered money – or, having suspected as much, that you disclosed the facts to the proper authorities.

As banks and other financial institutions in the UK are required to report suspicious currency transactions of any amount – not just those above a certain cash ceiling – the frontline battle against the laundrymen gets bogged down in the definition of the word suspicious.

If a client deposits £50 in cash and someone at the bank thinks there's something odd about it, they are obliged by law to file a CTR. If another client deposits £500,000 in cash and no one finds anything odd about it, the deposit goes unreported. Any bank can, therefore, always defend itself simply by insisting that no one ever suspected anything.

When you ask the British authorities why they didn't impose a quantifiable amount above which reporting is mandatory – say, £10,000 – the first answer you get is, we didn't want to create a haystack to find a needle. Behind that, you discover that the American example has led the British authorities to believe that the manpower necessary to police mandatory reporting would cost too much.

Nevertheless, keeping tabs on who deposits what has become a clear-cut international trend.

The Japanese have copied the British, obliging banks to report suspicious cash transactions. Yet, they've gone one step further in forcing banks to report all domestic cash transactions in excess of 30 million yen (*c.* £160,000) and all foreign cash transactions in excess of 5 million yen (*c.* £27,000). Furthermore, where drugs are concerned, prosecutors can put banks and financial institutions in the dock on money laundering charges.

Australia operates a $10,000 cash transaction reporting system similar to the US version – the only other country to do so – except that, instead of distributing CTRs to individual agencies for processing, it has electronically linked banks and financial institutions to an all-encompassing Cash Transactions Reports Agency.

Canadian banks report suspicious transactions, but it's a strictly voluntary system instituted by the banks themselves – the government does not demand reporting.

The EC took steps a few years ago when it drafted its Banking Regulations and Supervisory Practices. Setting the tone right from the beginning, it lets banks off the hook by acknowledging that it is not their responsibility to detect money laundering. Instead, it politely asks bankers: to know their customers so that money launderers will find it harder to operate; to comply actively with existing legislation and law enforcement agencies in the fight against money laundering; to improve record-keeping systems so that suspicious activities can be detected early; and to train staff so that they can recognize and will report money laundering activities.

The United Nations has also climbed on the bandwagon. The Vienna Convention of 1988 proposed that money laundering become an internationally extraditable offence. Some 80 nations agreed, in principle, to ratify the pact. But 80 nations is much less than half the UN membership.

Five years later, only four of the 80 had actually signed.

Notable among the hold-outs are Luxembourg, Liechtenstein, the Netherlands Antilles, the Cayman Islands, Panama, Uruguay, Hungary, Russia, Pakistan and Bulgaria.

European Union law requires financial institutions to keep identity files on every client who deposits or transacts more than 15,000 European Currency Units (£12,000) in cash, and to inform the competent authorities of any and all suspect cash transactions.

Because they want to be seen as being active in the fight against the laundrymen, seven countries have imposed lower thresholds, including Belgium and Germany where reporting duties apply for transactions just over £6,000 while France has a £4500 threshold. Some member states – notably Denmark, Spain, Germany, France and the Netherlands – have also widened the scope of the laws to cover non-financial industries such as gambling. Precious metal dealers and auction houses fall into that category in Germany, as do real estate agents in Spain.

That such laws are on the statute books is one thing. That the businesses subject to them comply, is another. There is widespread confusion among casino operators, precious metals brokers, auctioneers and real estate brokers as to exactly what their responsibilities are. The fact that ordinances are shrouded in legalese, and are, at the same time, difficult to enforce, has not helped when it comes to adherence to them. In France, for instance, where it is traditional to use cash to buy real estate, it's been found that some notaries openly flaunt the statutes, having no intention at all of changing the way they have always done business. Their claim is that they don't do business with drug traffickers – as if they had some way of telling the good guys from the bad guys – and that, as long as high taxes tagged onto such transactions encourage cash payments, they'd merely be biting their own nose to spite their face by reporting those cash payments.

So even when the authorities make the effort to remind casino owners, precious metals brokers, auctioneers and real estate brokers, bankers and notaries that they now have specific responsibilities to report cash transactions, getting them to abide by rules, when those rules are clearly not in their own personal interests, is a big mountain to climb.

Adding to the confusion, the Council of Europe has also come up with the Convention on Laundering, Search, Seizure and Confiscation of the Proceeds From Crime. Intending to set basic standards that will encourage international cooperation among law enforcement agencies, the convention lays out a set of disciplines that, mirroring those of the United Nations and the European Union, might clearly help to combat the problem.

But, like the others, it requires compliance.

Forty member states, plus three non-members – Australia, Canada and the United States – were presented with the convention for signature in November 1990. A dozen countries, including Great Britain, signed up on the very first day. The next step, ratification, required each of the signatories then to gain parliamentary acceptance. Britain was the first of the group to manage that, putting the convention into law in September 1993.

However . . . all that is signed, sealed and ratified does not glitter. As of the end of 1997, only 29 of the 40 member states have signed the convention and only 17 of the 29 signatories have ratified it. Among the 12 who have signed but are yet to put it into law are Belgium, Germany, Greece, Liechenstein, Luxembourg, Portugal and Spain. Among the non-members, only Australia has even signed the convention. And among those members who have both signed and ratified it, Great Britain has only agreed with reservations, claiming exemptions from the convention for the offshore banking industry in Jersey, Guernsey and the Isle of Man. In fact, of those 17 members who have put the convention into law, not one has done so without reservations and specific exemptions.

While none of the transaction reporting systems is perfect – they all have loopholes large enough to accommodate a cash-laden armoured car – laundering huge sums of dirty money used to be a fairly easy stunt.

In the good old days – that is, before cash transaction reporting – all any laundryman needed to do was send a bunch of runners around the country to feed a lot of bank accounts. Each runner, known in the trade as a 'smurf' (the nickname was first used by investigators in Florida, after a clan of popular television cartoon characters) would be given a daily route, exactly like a postman or a milkman. Once the runners had collected the day's cash from their contacts, they'd work an assigned territory: the north on Mondays, the south on Tuesdays, the east on Wednesdays, and so forth. If each runner deposited £200 in 20 accounts per area – hardly enough in any one bank to raise suspicions – and there were ten runners working each area, £40,000 worth of cash per day would find its way into the banking system. That's £200,000 a week or £10.4 million a year. One California drug trafficker actually bragged when he was arrested that his smurfs had gotten so good at it, they could buy up to 2,000 cashier's cheques a day and deposit them, within a few hours, in 513 different banks.

For the academically curious, the secret of good smurfing is speed. To deposit the most in the shortest amount of time, areas are targeted where banks are close to each other and business isn't too hectic. Small towns are no good because tellers remember clients. Empty banks are no good because tellers have too much time to think about a deposit or a familiar face. The best smurfing is done in affluent suburbs where there are enough banks with just enough customers. Big cities, it turns out, are as bad as small towns. New York, central London and the heart of Paris tend to see very little smurfing. There may be loads of banks, but the queues are much too long.

Anyway, that's the way it used to work, before banks became aware of such capers.

These days, laundrymen have turned to non-bank financial operators such as money changers – or *casas de cambio* as they're known along the US/Mexican border, which is crawling with them – money transmitters like Western Union and American Express, neighbourhood cheque-cashing businesses and Giro houses, which are wire-transfer businesses. The most traditional non-bank financial institution that the laundrymen continue to use is casinos.

A cash-intensive industry – much like main street banking, in that currency is its main product – casinos routinely perform many bank-like services. They cash cheques, exchange foreign currency, offer the use of safe deposit boxes and pay out large sums in cashier's cheques. They also frequently extend credit – which can mean leaving your money on deposit in one casino and getting it back in another casino in another jurisdiction.

Not only is a well-established, organized gambling den an obvious place to reduce the bulk of a stash – to change $10 and $20 bills into $50s and $100s – it is a believable source of revenue. At least in principle, all you have to do is stroll into a casino, buy $1,000 worth of chips, play for a few hours, cash out and tell your bank manager that you won the $500,000 you now want to deposit. Of course you might have to substantiate such a boast. But that's no problem for anyone with a compliant and believable friend high up in the casino's management.

Better still, if you owned a casino, you wouldn't have to bother pretending to play the roulette wheel. You'd simply shove your cash into the till and make sure your accountant lists it in the profit column when he files your tax returns.

Acknowledging this natural alliance for what it is, many governments have attempted to make it more difficult for money to be washed through casinos. In accordance with American law, casinos are subject to the same cash transaction reporting proviso as banks. Additionally, they are required to file suspicious cash transaction reports any time a questionable cash transaction takes place.

Putting such obligations into practice, however, is easier said than done. At the beginning of 1993, the US Treasury Department fined ten casinos in Atlantic City a total of $2.5 million for alleged violations encompassing the years 1985–88. The casinos stood accused of 'wilfully failing' to make reports of cash transactions. In response, the casinos now insist that they have cleaned up their act and fully comply with the law. Needless to say, Treasury officials remain sceptical.

Race tracks provide much the same kind of opportunity.

The strategy here hangs on the reluctance of some winners to let the taxman know just how much they're putting in their pocket. A winning ticket being a negotiable instrument, some people are only too happy to help the lucky punter avoid taxes by purchasing his ticket from him for cash. Race courses across America are filled with these 'flies' who stalk the tracks looking for folk with tickets to sell.

Using a similar stunt to purchase lottery tickets is slightly more complicated because the winners aren't in a single place at any given moment. But here again, it's a no-lose situation for all parties involved, even the taxman. The big prizes in the US lotteries are usually paid out over a 20-year period. So a $10 million win is worth $50,000 a year for the next two decades. From the laundryman's point of view, a

20-year annuity is well worth a suitcase filled with cash. The original winner has his money up front – although the burden of getting rid of so much cash is now on his shoulders – while the laundryman has turned millions of dollars in cash into a totally legal, tax-declarable entity.

This is another aspect of Meyer Lansky's legacy to the money laundering industry. He instinctively understood, and helped to nurture, the natural coalition between organized crime and licensed gambling. Lansky was, after all, the man who once said, 'There is no such thing as a lucky gambler. There are just winners and losers. And the winners are those who control the game.'

One man who controlled the game for a very long time is Nicholas Deak, the uncrowned laundry-king of the non-bank financial operators.

In 1953, the 48-year-old refugee from Hungary helped his pal Kermit Roosevelt launder money for the CIA when America wanted to finance the overthrow of Iran's Mossadegh regime and reinstate the Shah. The empire he subsequently built consisted of Deak and Co. – America's largest retail foreign exchange and precious metals brokers – and the holding company's subsidiary, Deak-Perera, America's foremost retail currency and gold trader.

One service Deak didn't advertise was America's most substantial sink.

President Reagan's Commission on Organized Crime issued a report in 1984 called *The Cash Connection*, which detailed, for the first time, the extent of Deak's laundry services. For instance, on 5 October 1981, Humberto Orozco – who, with his brother Eduardo, was a professional drug money launderer – walked into Deak-Perera's office at 29 Broadway in downtown Manhattan with cardboard boxes weighing 233 pounds. Stuffed to the brim with cash – no bills larger than $50 – it took most of the day to verify the total of $3,405,230, which was put in the Dual International (Interdual) corporate account, #3552.

Over the next two weeks, Orozco deposited $999,980, then $537,480, then $879,000 and finally $1,476,429 with Deak. Before the month was out, he'd topped it up with another $3.3 million. All of it came in as cash and all of it was deposited in the #3552 account.

When the brothers were finally busted, investigators established they'd systematically used 11 banks throughout New York to launder $151 million. But, in the 16 months between November 1980 and March 1982, they'd washed nearly two-thirds of their stake – close to $100 million – through 232 unreported deposits at Deak-Perera.

To coordinate intelligence efforts against the laundrymen, the British formed the National Criminal Intelligence Service (NCIS) and the French formed the Office for the Repression of Large-scale Financial Crime (TRACFIN). Best intentions aside, neither has produced dramatically wonderful results. To date, there has only been one major money laundering case prosecuted in France, and that only came about as a result of a tip-off given to the French by the Americans.

Generally speaking, NCIS has been receiving in excess of 20,000 suspicious cash transaction reports a year for the past few years. But their resources are so limited that they reportedly have never investigated more than a dozen or two in any given year. When pressed in an interview, the former director of NCIS, now retired, refused to say how many money laundering cases the service had uncovered and seen brought to justice. The reason was, there were none.

The American equivalent is the Financial Crimes Enforcement Network (FINCEN). Like the other two, data of all sorts, concerning every aspect of currency, banking and drug trafficking, is fed into a computer that seeks out telltale trends and attempts to identify new targets. But technology cannot keep up. In some cases, by the time programmers sort through the paperwork input and the analysis section sorts through the resulting print-outs, trails have gone cold. But in others, leads literally jump off the computer screen.

Since its inception nearly 10 years ago, FINCEN has compiled a gigantic database of cash transactions – every CTR filed in the United States winds up in FINCEN's computers – so that they can mix and match names, addresses, banks and businesses, hoping to find a pattern that fits into the money laundering cycle and, eventually, pinpoint the culprits.

The information compiled by FINCEN is then made available to law enforcement agencies around the country. This mass diffusion of intelligence on money laundering and the laundrymen has been at the heart of almost every major money laundering prosecution in the United States. It proves – because it helps send bad guys to jail – that a cash transaction reporting system which relies on set limits, instead of suspicions, and is then linked into a properly funded database analysis strategy, has a real effect.

Still, it is not a cure-all. And as the laundrymen have got better at what they do, all sorts of new initiatives spring up to try to stop them.

In the United States, concerned that well organized groups of traffickers have been getting under the $10,000 reporting limits, Congress passed the Geographical Targeting Order, requiring money transmitter agencies to report all transfers to certain countries over $750. The act also allows various law enforcement agencies to monitor the money remittance industry much more closely.

Using the GTO as their main weapon, the Treasury Department, in cooperation with nearly 40 federal, state and local law enforcement agencies, formed a joint operation in the New York area called Eldorado.

They first targeted the Colombians and headed straight

for Roosevelt Avenue in Queens, known by the 200 men and women who work the task force as 'Ground Zero'. The heart of New York's ethnic Colombian neighbourhood, just south of La Guardia Airport, running west from Shea Stadium, the 1990 census showed that the average family there was earning around £20,000 a year. And yet, FINCEN was reporting that the equivalent of nearly $40,000 a year per family, was being wired back to Colombia.

The Eldorado task force quickly determined that, while the 300 wire transmitters who line the mile-and-a-half-long boulevard were not necessarily owned by Colombian traffickers, neither drugs nor money moved in or out of the New York area without someone in Colombia being in touch with someone on Roosevelt Avenue.

It was designed to be a one-step shopping centre for drug dealers.

Traffickers could wire money to Colombia and make local and international phone calls. Businesses up and down the block offer so many phone services, with so many different phone booths in each, that a dealer could use a different one every day of the year to prevent the task force from collecting electronic surveillance. These business also deal in bleepers and cellphones, often without requiring any sort of deposit. The same with mail services. Some locals use the storefront's address for their driver's permits and car registration, so that, even if the police can identify someone with those documents, they wind up chasing ghosts right back to a rented postbox.

So little by little, the task force began taking apart the wire remitters. And over the course of the past few years, three things have happened. The first was that the cost of doing business on Roosevelt Avenue went up. The second was, that the traffickers were forced to look for less expensive remitters, which drove some of the business to Miami. And third, the Dominicans realized that they could pick up some of the slack, so they duplicated Roosevelt Avenue in Washington Heights, along Manhattan's upper West Side.

No sooner had the money remitters moved in there, than a new GTO was issued, this time targeting the Dominicans.

In Europe, realizing that only a common approach in the fight against organized crime can be successful, the European Union formed Europol, an EU-wide police agency designed specifically to share information between member states on drugs and money laundering. Eventually, the intention is that Europol should become a clearing house to coordinate investigations of related crimes in different countries. If it is properly funded and free from the meddling of bureaucrats in Brussels – in other words, if they let policemen be policemen and don't turn them into paper-whipping functionaries – it stands a chance of working. If not, it will simply turn into a typical Community quango where ageing cops can bide their time, until retirement, on yet another EU gravy train. What's really needed is a Europe-wide version of the FBI. But there are serious flaws pre-fabricated in the very concept. Europol was formed by 15 nations with 15 different legal systems and almost as many different languages. Finding a common approach to law enforcement is a near-impossibility.

Worldwide, the phenomenal growth in money laundering has given rise to a growing private sector where investigators follow the money trail for their clients, and advise financial institutions on how not to get caught.

After retiring from his years at the DEA, where he headed up their Miami office and found his name on the hit lists of the Medellin and Cali cartel bosses, Tom Cash now works out of the Miami office of Kroll International, one of the largest and most important private sector investigating agencies.

'This is the world of globalization, where customers move

from Paris to Bangkok to Los Angeles the way people used to travel from Marseilles to Paris. Along with that globalization comes the need for gathering information on the people with whom you're doing business. That's what we do. We help banks manage the risk of doing business with the wrong people.'

While some banks clearly don't care, Cash contends all reputable banks care a great deal.

'They have a very large stake in their brand name. Banks stand for integrity and security and safety for investment and for protecting your most important asset which is your money. So legitimate banks are terribly concerned about having legitimate customers, because when something goes wrong, when a drug trafficker is identified as having dealt with bank X, and that's your bank, you don't know what might happen. You don't know how serious this is so guess what? You're going to take your money out. Worse than that, if you don't take your money out, you don't put in additional money until this is settled. And all the time that bank is losing tremendous amounts of interest and tremendous amounts of spread, because you took your money out. Or you didn't put it in, which is even more important.'

But then, he is also willing to admit, 'Many banks have great money laundering policies. They're beautifully printed, beautifully bound and they're on a shelf somewhere. Nobody has ever tested them. Most of the employees have come into the bank since they were written. Half the employees didn't even know they existed. The bank will tell you at the front door, oh, yes, we have this wonderful money laundering policy. But if the policy has never been tested, how do you know?'

Immoral bankers, he feels, like immoral laywers, are not unusual. But when bankers say, 'the morality of my client is not my business,' he believes they are diffusing their responsibility by accepting the fact that their profit is more important than the legality of their business.

'I would answer someone who says, "I'm not a policeman and it's not my responsibility to look into who my depositors are," with, "if your bank doesn't have trouble now, it will soon."'

The City of London depends on self-regulation to oversee the financial community. There is no equivalent of the American Securities and Exchange Commission – which has the powers of a police force – because the British believe that gentlemen are fully capable of keeping their own house clean. So, in Britain, the poachers are also the gamekeepers. And largely because of that, the London market has, for years, been the Wild West.

During the Wilson and Callaghan governments – when Labour ruled the country from 1974 to 1979 – money laundering was turned into an art form by commodity dealers in the City. Exchange controls, levied in a naive attempt to keep capital in the country, were coupled with restrictive taxes, making for a tyrannical fiscal· regime. Wilson's declared aim was to 'soak the spots off the rich'. His chief accomplishment was to midwife a wave of schemes aimed at helping wealthy Britons move their funds beyond the reach of the tax inspectors.

One of the more audacious ploys was the brainchild of a small-time operator named Michael Doxford. Working out of an office in the fashionable St James's area of Mayfair, Doxford gave the impression that he dealt in what used to be called soft commodities – sugar, coffee, soybeans, cocoa. This was at a time when commodity speculation was little more than an upper-class roulette wheel. Not yet tagged with the slightly more serious cachet of 'futures trading,' a flutter on softs meant you could tell people you were 'in the City'. It offered the same rush you might find by putting a grand on the nose of a horse, without ever having to suffer the down-market storefront ambience of a bookie's shop.

A public school type, then in his late 40s, Doxford moved easily through the cigar mist of the gentlemen's clubs. He had access to people with money and sympathized with their angst. He also had the instinct to know that there was a fortune to be made by helping people with money to escape the clutches of Mr Wilson. The unregulated commodity market was tailor-made for what he intended to do.

Oil prices were shooting up almost daily and the world's front pages were focused on the Gulf. Everyone was heading down there. It was a modern-day gold rush. The oil sheikhs were the hottest clients in town, so it was perfectly natural to open a branch of M. L. Doxford in Bahrain. But unlike those brokers who sent their most aggressive sales people to the Gulf, Doxford staffed his office with one docile Englishman. And then, instead of going after petro-dollars, he went looking for sterling.

Doxford discreetly invited his wealthier acquaintances to let him move their assets out of the UK and help hide them in Switzerland. To launder their funds, he asked for a flat 10% commission. According to one of the fraud squad detectives who worked on the case, Doxford's client list soon looked like a mini-Debretts.

Knowing that the British penchant for self-regulated markets could be turned into a licence to steal – gentlemen, after all, do not question the motives of other gentlemen – Doxford simply matched each client in London with an 'invisible' one in Bahrain.

Commodities are a zero-sum affair, which means you can buy only if someone is willing to sell, and vice versa. Because commodity dealers trade as principals and not in their clients' names, only Doxford knew the true identity of the beneficial owner of any particular trade.

As soon as a friend opened a trading account with M. L.

Doxford London, a series of telexes and letters would arrive from M. L. Doxford Bahrain to announce that a local sheikh – a fictitious one who, therefore, could never be traced by the British police – had also deposited funds with the company to open a trading account.

Clients were automatically put into 'discretionary syndicates' – allowing Doxford to trade on their behalf – at which time he took dual positions. He bought from the sheikh and sold to his pal, then bought from his pal and sold to the sheikh. Doxford's friend always lost and the ersatz sheikh always won. In reality, he didn't even have to trade on the market, as long as he created a paper trail so that it looked like the real thing.

Eventually a telex would arrive from Bahrain saying that the sheikh wanted to close his account. With a pile of paperwork in the sheikh's name, Doxford would trot along to the Bank of England to get the proper exchange control documents so that he could wire the sheikh's profits to a Swiss bank. At the same time, the British client would close his account and receive a statement showing massive losses. There was no way the authorities could ever discover that the sheikh's Swiss account was actually owned by Doxford's wealthy friend.

The scheme was foolproof, so much so that the police managed to find out about it only after the company collapsed. Had the Labour Party stayed in power, Doxford would have stayed in business. But one of the first things Margaret Thatcher did when she moved into Downing Street was to abolish exchange controls. Doxford's high-society clients disappeared and he went bust with £5.5 million in debts. Even then, he might have gotten away with his money laundering, except that one of his employees was involved in a messy divorce and the man's wife – with inside knowledge of how the operation functioned – grassed on her husband for revenge.

At the Bank of England, the official line today is much what it was in Mr Doxford's day – that self-regulation works just fine. They completely disregard the fact that in the years 1987–92, there were only a dozen convictions in the City for insider dealing – compared with nearly 175 in the US.

North American money managers view the United Kingdom as one of the world's great offshore banking systems. And when the House of Commons Home Affairs Committee asked the Bank of England how the nation's money laundering laws could be strengthened, the Governors answered, unflinchingly, that the laws didn't need to be changed.

Haplessly, neither the Bank of England, nor any of the self-regulatory bodies that came into being in the mid-1980s, have ever been able to shift the opinions of the fraud squad officers who work on the ground. They take the view that the City of London is a sieve for dirty money. Noting that many of the big names from Britain's criminal community – men and women who cut their teeth on fraud and extortion in the 1970s and 1980s – have since graduated to drug trafficking, they contend that an entire subculture of professional money launderers has been created to cater to them.

Stories abound.

After spending weeks traipsing around the City, getting nowhere with established sources of finance, a certain British entrepreneur, who'd been planning a hefty real estate deal outside the UK, found the money he needed. An intermediary offered him competitive rates from a pension fund registered in Panama with an office in Liechtenstein. He doesn't know the true identity of his patron. What's more, he doesn't care. It's even possible that the agent acting for the pension fund doesn't know, or much care, either. The entrepreneur got his money and was able to go ahead with his project. The intermediary – whose business is to match clients who want money with clients who have money – says he pays for the food on his family's table with commissions, not curiosity.

In 1988, when James Edward Rose was arrested in connection with the importation into Britain of 13 tons of cannabis – estimated at £40 million – the money trail led to a life assurance salesman who, since 1986, had been helping Rose launder profits through single-premium investment bonds.

Acting first for a small company, then for one of the UK's major insurance firms, the salesman racked up a series of achievement awards for his skill in marketing investment packages worth £50,000–250,000. When the company underwriting the bonds started noticing that so much of this man's business was done in cash – and questioned him about it – the cash payments stopped. Yet the money kept rolling in, now in the form of cheques drawn on companies, all of which later turned out to be non-existent. Overall, the salesman washed more than £1.5 million through premium investment bonds.

It must be said that these are not isolated examples.

Case in point: a City commodities dealer, interviewed by Scotland Yard on information supplied from a foreign source, recently admitted to receiving $1 million a month from a source he claimed he did not know. The deal was that every 30 days he supplied the appropriate paperwork to show how this client lost $100,000. The phoney contract notes, together with a check for $900,000, were then returned to the client. The broker kept the hundred grand for his trouble.

Case in point: a pair of London hoodlums are known by the police to have been manipulating shares on the Stock Exchange over the past several years, trading through a dozen different accounts located at some 15 brokerage firms in the UK, Europe and North America. Typically, those accounts are registered in the names of bearer share, limited companies with offices in the UK, the Channel Islands and Ireland. One of those companies purports to be a mutual fund, whose sole purpose is to put in large buy orders for targeted securities. As the share price rises, an option on it is called in, with the immediate profits being invested – again through offshore accounts – into metals, commodities and government paper. These are then used as security for loans that go towards further manipulating share prices. The profits are laundered back through the maze of companies, put into a commodities trade and brought out the other end as a legitimate, taxable income.

In both instances, by creating complex paper trails, taking advantage of the fact that brokers still deal as principals, using wire transfers and being able to bask in the relative anonymity afforded by the enormous volume of business that speeds around the world every day, these people have been able to turn a small portion of an otherwise legitimate business into a profitable laundromat without any serious risk of ever being brought to trial.

Even when the police can trace funds along a straight line – with money originating someplace like Boston, coming through London and winding up in someplace like Belfast – the odds are against them ever identifying the source of those funds.

Case in point: NORAID, the Northern Irish Republican sympathizers' group in the States, is known to subsidize the IRA with the compliance of certain London-based commodities brokers. But pinpointing the trades, stopping them and prosecuting the brokers is another matter.

CHAPTER FOUR

The Professionals

*'There's no such thing as good money or bad money.
There's just money.'*

Charlie 'Lucky' Luciano

When a group of Canadians with lots of money to wash stumbled across the ever-affable Aldo Tucci at the City and District Savings Bank in Dollard des Ormeaux, Quebec, they couldn't believe their luck.

A friendly bank manager is every laundryman's dream.

So they invited him to administer six of their companies and he was so flattered to be asked that he cheerfully opened several accounts to handle their cash deposits. Their total that year came to US$13 million.

To keep his new clients happy and encourage more of their business – on a single day in June 1981 the gang delivered $1.2 million in small bills – Tucci took it upon himself to make special arrangements for the group to deliver their cash-laden tote bags at the bank's back door. The gang and Tucci got along so well that, when their bank manager was transferred to another branch in Montreal, the gang followed him, moving their accounts to his new office.

But then this bunch made it a habit to charm bank

managers all over Montreal. One became so concerned with the amounts of cash they were bringing into his downtown branch of the National Bank – between November 1981 and October 1982, $14 million stuffed in suitcases and paper bags was washed there – he asked them please to be kind enough to tie the money into $5,000 bundles. Naturally, they obliged.

A few years ago in London, a 20 year old opened a student's account at a high street bank with the minimum deposit of £1. Over the next several months, $500,000 was wired into that account from Geneva and then – almost immediately – wired out to Indonesia. There was no other movement on the account. To welcome his new client, the bank manager sent the student a Porky Pig money box and a kid's paint book.

Admittedly, someone in the bank's chain of command had doubts about a student with £1 in his pocket and half a million dollars in his account, and duly filed a suspicious transaction report. But when the British police turned to the three banks involved – one British, one Swiss and one Indonesian – they were told in no uncertain terms that banks have a serious obligation of confidentiality to their customers and that, unless the police could make a satisfactory case that drugs were somehow involved, they could not expect any assistance to be forthcoming.

Just like that, the banks' doors were shut.

And just like that, the student disappeared.

Banking confidentiality is often compared with the privilege extended to a priest in a confessional. Except, under English law, there is no such right. If a priest is called to testify in court, he cannot legally refuse to do so by claiming clerical privilege.

It's the same with a journalist who refuses to name a source. Chances are, neither the priest nor the journalist would testify – and it's difficult to imagine that a priest would even be called to testify – but neither has the legal right to refuse to bear witness if they are put on the stand.

Nor, for instance, does the law grant blanket confidentiality to doctors. If you go to a doctor to be treated for a bullet wound, most jurisdictions oblige the physician to report your visit to the police. It's the same if you admit to a psychiatrist that you've been involved in child molestation and are likely to commit the crime again. There is usually an obligation on the psychiatrist to notify the proper authorities.

Because the law doesn't acknowledge secrecy in a confessional, in a newsroom or even on a psychiatrist's couch – one argument goes – why should it extend secrecy to banks?

The answer is, it doesn't, in spite of the fact that many bankers think it does. At least it doesn't in the United States, Canada, the UK, Australia, New Zealand or any of the countries in the EC. More and more – as a direct result of the growing industry in money laundering – courts are forcing banks to reveal information about their clients that was once considered inviolable. As a result, drug traffickers have turned to other businesses, seeking out professionals who can sidestep whatever regulations the authorities gradually manage to put in place. In some cases, the traffickers have managed it without those professionals ever knowing that they're dealing in dirty money. The latest gimmick, coming out of Colombia and centring on the well established black market peso exchange, takes a page out of the *hawalah* banking manual.

Agents in Colombia seek out legitimate businessmen needing to buy western currencies for the purchase of goods in, say, the States, Britain or Germany, and then match them with legitimate businessmen in the States, Britain or Germany selling goods for export.

Take the case of the importer in Bogotá whose business

is small appliances and who is looking to order £1 million worth of kettles from a firm in the UK. He can either go through the usual, commercial channels – which means paperwork, bureaucratic red tape, bank transfer fees and various taxes – or he can save himself perhaps as much as 20 per cent of his costs by bringing the traffickers into the middle of his deal and purchasing foreign funds on the black market. Having pulled £1 million off the streets of Liverpool from cocaine sales, the cartel's British-based agents then use that money to buy kettles. The businessman in Bogotá pays the traffickers in Colombia with one hand, the traffickers in Liverpool pay the supplier in the UK with the other, the importer gets his appliances, the kettle company gets their export, and the drug traffickers have successfully washed £1 million through two legitimate businesses, at least one of which – in this case, the kettle company – never realized that they've become money launderers.

Because it is such an efficient scheme, and because drug traffickers are always in search of ever more creative ways to wash money, they've since come up with a scam that works off the back of this one, in a sense reversing the process.

A Colombian coffee exporter has orders to fill for a major UK-based supermarket chain. But before shipping the coffee, both he and the supermarket chain file a series of export documents through their respective banks, guaranteeing that in exchange for the coffee leaving Colombia, payment will be forthcoming from a correspondent bank in Britain.

Valid for up to one year, these export papers not only offer preferential exchange rates, but, more importantly, justify funds coming into Colombia. So after the coffee exporter uses them – and without the British supermarket chain having anything at all to do with the scam – the traffickers buy the export papers to justify opening several new accounts at several different banks. Drug funds are then wired in from overseas, now appearing as legitimate receipts for coffee sold to a British importer.

It was only in October 1997 that the size and breadth of these combined schemes – which make up a near-foolproof system that has, in recent years, included, unwittingly, some of the world's largest companies – came to light. A young woman, who for her own safety was kept behind a security curtain and known only as Ms Doe, was escorted under armed guard into a US House of Representatives' subcommittee hearing room to testify before the members who had convened to investigate the black market peso exchange. She'd been a lawyer by profession in her native Colombia, but worked there as a money broker for the cartels before they sent her to New York as one of their black market currency agents.

'In Colombia,' she explained, 'I established accounts in banks where drug money was deposited. From these accounts, I arranged payments to exporters on behalf of Colombian businesses. To facilitate my brokering activities, I utilized accounts in many prominent international banks, including Citibank, Chase Manhattan Bank, Chemical Bank, Bank of America, Wachovia Bank, Bank of New York, Nationsbank, BarnettBank, Texas Commerce Bank, Republic Bank, Sun Bank, Mega Bank, BancoAtlantico, Atlantic Bank, Philadelphia International Bank, National Westminster Bank, Marine Midland Bank, International Bank of Miami, City National Bank of Florida, First Union Bank, North Carolina National Bank, National Bank of Miami, Korean Exchange Bank, Swiss Bank Corporation and Bank Leumi.'

While also naming several banks in Colombia – among them Banco Occidente, Banco Cafetero, Banco Ganadero, Banco del Estado and Banco Industrial Colombiano – she was fast to point out that she could not say if any of the banks knew that she was using them to launder money.

Although she did add, 'Without their services, we could not have brokered drug profits.'

As a cartel agent, she also arranged payments to a number of large multinational corporations. Among the companies she named were Sony, Procter & Gamble, John Deere, Whirlpool, Ford, Kenworth, Johnny Walker, Swatch, Chorrera, Orleander Group, Orotex, Italian Telas, Jacobsen's, J&B Importers Inc., US Gear Corp, Merrill Lynch, Taiwan Hodaka Industrial Company, Seattle Bike Supply and Reebok.

'These companies were paid with currency generated by narcotics trafficking,' she said, here too stressing, 'They might not have been aware of the source of this money. However, they accepted payments from me without ever questioning who I was or the source of the money.'

Over the course of the two years she worked as a money broker in Colombia, she operated out of a tiny shopping mall in Medellin, one of several dozen brokers with offices there – she said it was like a flea market – where importers could shop around, going from broker to broker, to look for the best rate they could get on foreign currency. Meanwhile, her contacts in other countries – known as 'Duros', the hard ones – regularly reported back to the mall with the amounts they needed to dump onto the black market. All the brokers in Colombia had to do was match the needs of the businessmen looking to buy with what the Duros had to sell.

When a deal is made, she said, the Duro is said to have 'crowned', the term coming from the game of checkers where a single piece gets to the other side of the board and becomes a king. Because this is cartel money, the newly crowned king holds the broker entirely responsible for full payment, unimpressed by the usual excuses of confiscation and theft. The penalty for misappropriation is death.

With so much money at stake, the black market peso brokers quickly took a lesson from the Lloyds of London insurance market. They learned how to 'reinsure' their interests, protecting themselves by splitting transactions with other brokers, lessening their own liabilities on each transaction.

Every time she successfully put a deal together, Ms Doe said, she took a commission from both sides. 'I purchased $60,000 from the Duro for 800 pesos per dollar. The money was located in a New York stash house. The Duro instructed me to pay him the pesos in Colombia by four cheques. One cheque was made payable to his company and the remaining three to other individuals. All cheques were deposited into their respective bank accounts in Colombia. By receiving four cheques, the Duro avoided the Colombian law of "unlawful enrichment". The Duro's US courier deposited the $60,000 to three United States bank accounts under my control.'

In this instance, she said, she'd sold the $60,000 to a Colombian importer at 890 per dollar. 'Accordingly, my profit was 90 pesos per dollar. This importer owned Colombian book stores and instructed me to wire transfer the $60,000 to his United States book supplier. I instructed the importer to issue five cheques in payment for the $60,000. Four were made payable as instructed by the Duro, and the fifth cheque was my commission. The importer deposited the Duro's cheques in the designated accounts. In turn, I instructed my US bank to wire transfer $60,000 to the account of the US book supplier. At the exchange rate of 890 pesos per US dollar, I made a profit from this transaction of over $6,000.'

Complicating matters slightly, brokers' fees are determined by a number of factors, namely the amount of narcotics on the streets, plus the amount, form and location of the money. The more dollars on the streets the higher the risk to the trafficker which means the broker can charge a higher commission to launder the funds. If the dollars are already in the bank, then there is less risk and fiercer competition in the flea market will drive commissions down.

'A single transaction could typically involve several brokers,' Ms Doe continued, 'and also allow the multiple use of various types of funds. An example of this was when I purchased thirteen cheques, totalling $64,105 drawn on several US bank accounts from another money broker. I purchased these signed cheques with the payee portion left blank for 790 pesos per dollar. I sold these cheques to a third broker who owns a jewellery company in the US at a rate of 802 pesos per dollar. He then deposited these cheques into his US account. He then sold wire transfers from these accounts at a rate of 820 pesos per dollar.'

The system works fluidly and well, she felt, because Colombian bankers were protecting the money brokers. On at least three separate occasions, she claimed, she'd been warned in advance by three different banks that the Government was looking into her own 'unlawful enrichment'.

To keep the supply of banks plentiful, through which they can launder money, brokers constantly hire people to go to New York or to Miami or come to Europe, equipped with sufficient identification, to open as many accounts as they can, using as many variations of their Spanish surnames as they can. In some cases, these same smurfs are also employed to deposit drug money back into those accounts, always in sums small enough to duck under the radar of local currency reporting requirements.

'After opening the accounts,' she said, 'the smurfs receive the chequebooks from the bank, utilizing mail drop locations as their addresses. The smurfs sign the cheques and deliver them to the money brokers in Colombia via the United States Postal Service. Colombian money brokers believe that other delivery services, namely DHL and Fedex are searched by government agents but feel safe with the US Mail. The date, amount, and payee are left blank, pending the sale of the cheque by the money broker. The balances in the accounts are allowed to accumulate to only a few thousand dollars and then routinely cleared by cheques drawn on the accounts. Many of the blank cheques are sold to Colombian importers, and used to pay for exports. Many of the cheques are also negotiated in the Republic of Panama, where US currency is legal tender.'

After two years in the Medellin flea market, she moved to the States where she witnessed first hand the skill with which the cartels' agents had built a laundromat.

'Through my contacts with Colombian money brokers, I began receiving bulk currency from money brokers acting on behalf of narcotic traffickers. At the instruction of these brokers, large amounts of currency ranging in amounts up to $300,000 were delivered to me on a constant basis. A mule would deliver the cash in bags to me. I opened up a second business account under the same name in the same bank. This account was utilized to deposit the narco-dollars. I used an armoured car service to pick up and deliver the narco-dollars to the bank for deposit. At the instruction of the money broker, I transmitted the narco-dollars less my commission of about 5 per cent from my account to various American exporters. The dollars would be either wire transferred or paid as blank cheques.'

She said Colombian money brokers provided her with the amounts and the beneficiary's accounts for the wire transfers. Those accounts included individuals, manufacturing and exporting companies, credit card companies, securities brokers and both real and fictitious charitable organizations. They were located in Panama, Colombia, Spain, Germany, Italy, Britain and throughout the United States.

'The total amount of narco-dollars I laundered while I was in the United States, in a one year period, was approximately $14 million.'

*   *   *

As certain nations have begun to crack down on illicit cash transactions, laundrymen have been forced to seek out 'user-friendly' places where there are no currency controls, where banking secrecy is assured, where no one cares who deposits what.

Putting a border between the crime and the booty frequently entails smuggling. It's true that there are international agreements which are supposed to enhance collaboration among law enforcement agencies and thwart this kind of cross-border ablution. But, compared with the extent of smuggling that goes on, the amount of cooperation is negligible. It seems that where crime is concerned – especially money laundering – jurisdiction all too often ends at the airport.

Stuffing cash inside condoms, just like drugs, that are then ingested is a common technique to get money into a country. But 'swallowing' to get money out of a country – especially out of the United States where there are no laws preventing anyone from exporting as much money as they want – is a relatively odd phenomenon. Yet US customs reported someone tried it in 1991.

Agents at Kennedy Airport in New York detained a departing suspect from Ghana and asked her how much money she was carrying. She told them $9,000. A search of her luggage revealed $24,000 stuffed between clothes and in bottles of shampoo containing wads of $100 bills. They then discovered she had also swallowed a dozen condoms with money rolled inside and was hiding six more vaginally. The total haul was nearly $55,000.

A more brazen approach was used by a South African businessman who faked a badly sprained ankle and convinced his doctor to put a cast on his leg. He was booked on a flight from Johannesburg to London and asked the airline to supply a wheelchair to help him get from check-in to the gate. But, on the day of his flight, an anonymous call came into South

African customs that a businessman with a cast on his leg was smuggling a large sum of money out of the country.

When he wheeled up to the immigration desk on his way to the gate, he was stopped. Officers said they wanted to search him. He refused. They insisted. He demanded that he be permitted to ring his solicitor. Senior officials were called in and the argument continued long past the point where the plane was scheduled to leave. He categorically refused a body search and, by the time his solicitor arrived, the flight had left without him. Now he threatened to sue everyone in sight. His solicitor somehow managed to calm him down and explain that the officers were well within their right. Protesting to the very end, he had no choice but to sit there while his cast was sawn off. And once it came off the officers found – absolutely nothing.

Now the man raised hell. He started ringing everyone he knew in government. Red-faced apologies, though plentiful, were no good. The businessman ordered his solicitor to get everyone's name and file law suits. He intended to sue the government and sue the airlines for allowing this to happen. He not only wanted retribution, he wanted blood. He caused such a huge rumpus that the following day, with a new cast plastered over his ankle – and cash stuffed inside – Customs and Immigration officials personally helped him on to the plane.

A less nerve-racking, more popular method is the identical suitcases trick – one packed with clothes, the other packed with money. As soon as the laundryman gets off the plane, he retrieves the one with the money from the luggage racks and takes it through customs. If he's stopped and the suitcase is opened, he says – with appropriate shock and horror – it looks exactly like mine but it isn't. Insisting that he took it by mistake, he returns to the luggage racks to show the officers the same one with his clothes and identification inside. The money is then abandoned, written off by the traffickers as the cost of doing business.

Professional money smugglers – who exclusively service the laundry trade – are still a rare breed. But the few who do work this market full time are said to be very good at what they do and earn a handsome cut for their skills.

At least so far, Pancho turns out to be one of the more successful players in this game.

His biggest single coup to date was making $18 million in small bills disappear for a New York drug dealer. Working on a fee of 10% plus expenses, Pancho first arranged to have the cash smuggled out of the US and into Canada. That proved no more difficult than driving it to Montreal himself, with his wife and two kids in the car, making the border crossing look like a mundane family outing.

Next, Pancho sent runners to airports, railroad stations, post offices and crowded banks where they posed as tourists to switch $20, $50 and $100 bills into larger denominations. Because of the sum involved, reducing the bulk of the cash took nearly one month.

From Montreal, professional couriers were dispatched to London. They carried cash in attaché cases and stuffed the overflow into their pockets. Well-dressed men travelling alone, or well-dressed couples arriving in Britain together, the couriers walked innocuously through the green channel at Heathrow – 'Nothing to Declare' – just like ordinary businessmen and tourists.

Again, because of the sum involved, Pancho had to hire a lot of couriers. To avoid anyone recognizing them, this part of the operation spanned several months. But Pancho knew – as all professional smugglers must believe – that the system can be beaten.

Much of what Customs do relies on 'profiling' – the officer's ability to spot certain characteristics common to most smugglers. It was a method perfected many years ago by US Customs, when someone high up in the bureaucratic maze at US Customs wondered what might happen if he fed into a computer all sorts of seemingly unrelated facts about people who'd been apprehended bringing illicit goods into the country. The result was a list of several dozen shared traits – the profile of a smuggler – which is these days deeply embedded into the psyche of all customs inspectors.

Hardly mysterious, it's mostly about common sense.

For example, an extremely well-dressed elderly woman, travelling alone, with nothing to declare will almost always get stopped and searched because profiling says she's the sort of person who's probably bought something expensive. An equally well-dressed couple in their mid-30s who hand the inspector a written declaration will almost always get waved through because profiling says they're probably too scared to cheat. A man who is obviously travelling on business, using a Business Class ticket paid for by his company, wearing a rumpled suit with only carry-on luggage and an especially jet-lagged expression will have less trouble getting past customs than a neatly dressed, First Class flying, one-eyed, 22 stone Pakistani man carrying a blonde-haired, blue-eyed, 2-year-old baby girl.

Pancho knows that, unless he makes a serious error of judgement in the couriers he uses, or unless customs is tipped off, or unless an officer somehow recognizes the same courier coming in from North America every third day, the odds are weighted in his favour.

He knows that, unless he hands them a reason to suspect something, it's very unlikely customs will ever get its hands on this money.

With the $18 million now in Britain, Pancho had no trouble shipping the cash to the Channel Islands, where it was deposited – by prearrangement with a friendly banker – into 14 different Jersey company accounts. As soon as the money was bedded down there, it was transferred yet again, this time by wire, out of those accounts and into at least 20 others scattered around the world. To anyone working in any of the banks involved, wire transfers simply gave the impression that the companies were successfully trading. At the same time, wire transfers eliminated any possibility of following the funds. Some of the money is known to have vanished into Luxembourg. The rest evaporated into thin air.

Needless to say, professional smuggling is a high-risk business. But the rewards are compensatory. In order to hugely increase their gain, some laundrymen are willing to increase the risk by combining money laundering with drug smuggling.

According to one – call him John – the ideal place to run this double-barrelled hazard is Gibraltar.

Because 'The Rock' is over-populated with company formation agents – many of whom are known for not asking too many questions – he insists he had no trouble establishing himself there with a £100 import/export company. Now, using the cash he collected from a drug deal in Spain, he bought electronics goods – hi-fis, televisions, VCRs, CD players, telephones, answering machines, camcorders and fax machines. He then went through the exercise of obtaining the necessary export licences, in the company's name, before shipping his inventory across the Straits of Gibraltar to Tangiers. There, after paying import duties, again in the company's name, he sold the lot. With that money he bought more drugs – it's easy in Morocco – which he smuggled into Spain. After selling the drugs there, he deposited the money he made on them in his Gibraltar company bank account, where the income was supported by his export license and Moroccan sales receipts.

The main hazard is, of course, dealing drugs. But because of its historical, cultural and linguistic ties with Central and South America, Spain is Europe's premier port of entry for the Latin drug trade. Furthermore, the Straits are one of the major smuggling routes into Europe. In early 1993, for example, two rings – operating under the names Mufa and Everest and working out of the Spanish North African enclave of Ceuta – were broken up by Spanish customs officials who calculate that over the previous three years they'd brought at least 100 tons of hashish from Morocco, most of it hidden in trucks carrying fresh flowers. They washed their profits – an estimated $220 million – through seven different banks in Ceuta, Morocco and Spain.

Sadly, there is so much smuggling going on in Spain that the police just can't cope. And the possibility of turning $5 million into three or four times as much – with the added benefit of being able to launder your original stake at the same time – makes people like John feel that calculated risks are well worth taking.

But Pancho and John are the exceptions. The difference between them and the amateur smuggler is that they understand risk and have worked out ways of minimizing it. They say that the first lesson in smuggling is, pay attention to details. But it is a rule some amateurs find expensive to learn.

One businessman with a pilot's licence from Ft Lauderdale, Florida, fancied himself a great smuggler when he started moonlighting as a flying laundryman. He made so much money so quickly that he even up-graded his plane. The way he saw it, this was not just an investment in his second career – it would help him carry bigger loads, faster – but a unique opportunity to own a terrific new toy.

He went all the way and bought himself a Learjet.

Obviously, there are plenty of people in the States who fly their own plane, but when you regularly file a flight plan in Ft Lauderdale that says you're going to the Bahamas and air traffic control regularly tracks you to Panama, it shouldn't come as a surprise when the authorities start asking questions.

The usual ruse is to file point-to-point. You go Ft Lauderdale to Nassau. In Nassau you file to Caracas. When you land in Venezuela, you file to Costa Rica. From there, if you want to go to Panama, it's a good bet that the American authorities will have long since lost track of you. But the fellow from Ft Lauderdale insisted on going directly to Panama City.

After several trips in a very short period of time, both customs and the DEA set their sights on him. One morning, just before he left on a run, they stopped him. His plane was searched and they found $5.5 million in cash. When they went to his home, they discovered nearly $20 million worth of drugs and a small cache of weapons, including a submachine gun. They not only arrested him, they confiscated his new toy.

It's well known that the airlines frequently cooperate with law enforcement agencies. Air crews arriving in Miami on flights from drug-related destinations – Colombia, Peru, Ecuador, Venezuela – are offered cash rewards by US Customs for pointing out passengers who did not eat or drink anything during the flight. The idea is that most people would have something on a four hour flight, unless there was a particular reason not to, such as a stomach laden with drug-filled condoms.

Less publicized is the fact that the airlines themselves have been asked to look out for frequent travellers who make unusual journeys. Someone departing from Chicago, going to the Bahamas, on to the Caymans, then to Cali, back to the Bahamas and into Miami every week is certain to draw attention, and information about him will be forwarded to the authorities.

One way to get around that is to own a travel agency.

The laundryman buys his own tickets for cash and writes them to suit his circumstances. There's no need to arrive in Miami on a flight from Cali. He can issue himself tickets in one name from Bogotá to Rio, in another name from Rio to Paris, in a third name from Paris to London and in his own name from London to New York. That way, he not only becomes impossible to track, he also avoids entry into the United States from someplace suspect.

Travel agencies come with the added benefit of being an ideal sink. The Orozco brothers – of Deak-Perera laundromat fame – proved the point by purchasing an agency in New York called Calypso Travel. A perfectly reputable cover, they opened an account for the company at Chase Manhattan, which agreed to place Calypso Travel on its exemption list for cash transaction reporting. On at least three occasions, the Orozcos made cash deposits for Calypso Travel, totalling $150,000. When the bank finally withdrew their exemption, it turns out that it had absolutely nothing to do with the fact that they were money launderers. It was down to administrative procedures within the bank.

A Corsican group, operating out of Marseilles, found they could wash funds through plastic surgery clinics, where wealthy French and Italians paid to have their bodies adjusted. It was no problem for the Corsicans to find physicians willing to cook the books and up their turnover with cash from drug sales.

Another French gang, this one working in Paris, laundered their money through the European thoroughbred market. They registered race horses with the various Jockey Clubs, and hired professionals to help them put their horses up for sale. Other gang members bought the horses back. The nags' names were changed after each transaction and fed through the system again. When suspicious authorities asked to see these phantom thoroughbreds, they were told the poor things had tragically died.

Throughout the world, more and more criminals are turning to white collar professionals to handle their financial interests. It's especially attractive because, with all their trappings of respectability, white-collar professionals – enticed with commissions ranging from 4 per cent to 10 per cent – are generally well equipped to manipulate highly sophisticated laundering schemes.

Particularly where drugs are involved, the guys moving the narcotics no longer have to worry about moving the money and the guys moving the money never have to touch the drugs.

For many, it turns out to be a highly lucrative sideline. A politician from Georgia became a laundryman because it seemed such an easy way to finance an $850,000 mortgage; a California businessman got involved because washing $1.1 million through his company's account required very little effort and the $77,000 he was paid for the use of the account was too much to pass up; while Richard Silberman, a fundraiser for Jerry Brown's 1980 US presidential bid, recently admitted to an undercover FBI agent that he'd been making fast money as a laundryman for 20 years.

In New York, Eddie Antar – owner of the famous, now bankrupt, Crazy Eddie discount electronics chain – got into money laundering because it was a quick and easy way of boosting his share price. Over a period of several years, he siphoned cash from his business. The money was carted away in shopping bags, stored for a time in a bank vault, then deposited in a secret account in Israel. From there, the money was washed through a Panamanian bank before coming back to the Crazy Eddie stores in the form of cheques payable to the company. Increased sales artificially inflated the company's profits, which kept the share price high. He then sold the shares and pocketed $74 million.

Fast money was undoubtedly the motivation for three brothers who turned their auto dealership in the Washington DC area into a sink for drug dealers. Large sums of cash were broken into smaller chunks – careful never to go over the $10,000 reporting ceiling – then deposited in the company's accounts, backed up with false sales invoices.

A few months after busting them, federal agents arrested 19 people at 11 Washington area auto dealerships where drug dealers had bought or ordered some 85 cars for cash. Salesmen had promised to deliver those cars with false registrations and doctored insurance papers so that the vehicles could not be traced back to the drug dealers.

Those arrests came as a result of a two-year investigation, which included a sting operation where a pair of undercover agents arranged to purchase half a million dollars worth of cars for cash, including a $48,000 Jaguar Sovereign. Not only were the salesmen shown bags filled with cash – and allegedly accepted $1,500 tips for falsifying paperwork – they were informed by the undercover agents that the cars were needed to transport drugs and to reward faithful employees of their drug organization.

The amount of money involved there, however, pales by comparison with a recent case in Cranston, Rhode Island. There, 34-year-old Stephen Anthony Saccoccia, his wife Donna, plus seven of their employees at the Trend Precious Metals Company and the Saccoccia Coin Co., were arrested as part of a five-state swoop by federal authorities and charged with almost 100 counts of money laundering and false accounting.

Saccoccia had opened a coin shop after leaving high school in 1973, building up his business by fencing gold and coins for his teenaged friends, who were stealing it from their parents. In 1985, he pleaded guilty to a federal charge of tax evasion. Following his release from prison in 1988, he began laundering money for a local Mafia family. But it wasn't until a few years later that he moved into the big time, opening a sink to service both of the rival Medellin and Cali cartels – supposedly the first and only laundryman ever to do business with them at the same time.

Drug money would be collected at dummy jewellery shops in New York and Los Angeles, bundled in gold shipment crates and sent to Saccoccia's offices in Rhode Island, New York and California. He'd convert the cash to cashier's cheques, which he then deposited in various company accounts. Using falsified invoices and sales receipts to explain the sudden increase in turnover, the funds were quickly wired out of the country, through phantom companies, to Colombia.

Saccoccia worked on a flat 10 per cent commission. And whereas one report noted that, in under 15 months, he and his employees washed $200 million for the cartels, federal authorities now believe that he had laundered at least $750 million. In May 1993 he was convicted on 54 counts of money laundering and conspiracy. He was fined $15.8 million, subjected to a confiscation order for $136.3 million and sentenced to serve 660 years in prison.

Undoubtedly, Saccoccia's was an audacious scam. But the prize for conclusive moxie goes to the money laundering Rabbi.

Abraham Low, an ultra-orthodox Los Angeles clergyman, was arrested by the FBI in early 1993 when they uncovered a $2 million laundry operation that was soon dubbed 'the holy network'. Together with Hollywood physician Alan Weston and Bernadette Chandler – a woman known to the FBI simply as Charlie – Low was taken into custody after he'd agreed to help launder supposed drug money for an undercover agent. It seems Low's synagogue was having serious financial difficulties and the congregation stood to lose $18 million in bad investments overseen by Low.

The FBI first stumbled onto him during an investigation

into a stolen cheque racket. In September 1991, Low's wife went into a bank and turned a single $500,000 cashier's cheque into four smaller cheques. When the bank discovered that the original cheque had been stolen and forged, they called the police. Agents learned that Low had been combining cashier's cheques pilfered from a bank in West Los Angeles with phony loan papers to show a legitimate source for the funds he was laundering. Low had access to bank accounts held by various charitable organizations – hence the 'holy network' tag – through which large cash deposits could be laundered.

Chandler came into the picture when Low purchased a stolen $500,000 cheque from her for $30,000 and two diamond rings. After Chandler set up a $1.5 million money laundering deal with an undercover agent, Low and Weston bragged that they could provide the same service. A special agent – pretending to be a loan-sharking drug dealer named Ronnie – was introduced to them by an FBI informant. Low and Weston offered Ronnie use of their sink, and assured him that they were prepared to handle substantial amounts on a weekly basis. Low even outlined the system, explaining that money delivered to trusted members of his congregation – in this case, diamond dealers – would be washed through the charitable accounts and could then be wired anywhere in the world. Ronnie agreed to a test transaction and provided $10,000 in cash. The moment the deal was done, the FBI moved in.

If nothing else, a money laundering Rabbi must be proof positive that laundrymen these days don't fit any of the usual hoodlum stereotypes.

They are not machine-gun toting men in black shirts with white ties. Nor are they to be confused with street-level drug dealers, who are predominantly black. For the most part, they don't have previous criminal records. For the most, part they are people who might, otherwise, never consider crime but who are keenly attracted to a quick-buck, clean-hands hustle. On behalf of their drug-dealing, fraudster, smuggling, kidnapping, arms-dealing, terrorist, extortionist and tax-evading friends, these people have turned money laundering into the most sophisticated element of organized criminal activity.

White, affluent members of the professional classes have turned money laundering into the world's leading financial growth industry.

CHAPTER FIVE

Lawyers

'I'm gonna get rich patenting a better mousetrap.'
'Not me, I'm gonna get rich finding a bigger loophole.'
  Conversation overheard between two law school students

That privilege does not exist for bankers, doctors, clergymen or journalists might come as a surprise to some people. That it does exist for law makers and lawyers should come as a surprise to no one. Legislators protect themselves with parliamentary and congressional privilege. And lawyers are protected by attorney-client privilege. But then, it's no coincidence that an overwhelming percentage of legislators also happen to be lawyers.

In the United States, attorney-client privilege is generally thought to derive from the Sixth Amendment of the Constitution. In fact attorney-client privilege is not specifically spelled out there. All that the amendment says about attorneys is that anyone accused of a crime has the right to 'the assistance of Counsel for his defense.'

Privilege actually evolves from early ideals expressed in British case law where courts decided that a just defence is only possible when an accused is free to speak to counsel without fear of counsel being an agent for the prosecution.

It is a fundamental concept in an independent legal system. It is also the fundamental reason why lawyers are the perfect laundrymen.

When an attorney holds money in trust for someone else, it is customary for it to be put in his client account – a segregated trust – which is a direct reflection of the business done by him on behalf of his client. Because of that, the particulars of any lawyer's client account are considered to be protected by the same privilege that safeguards almost every aspect of the lawyer's relationship with his client.

It's secret banking, where banking secrecy doesn't exist.

But it is not without pitfalls.

It happens to be against the law for anyone, including attorneys, knowingly to accept dirty money in payment of a fee. If it can be proven that a lawyer has knowingly accepted drug money in payment of a fee, he can be subjected to various penalties, including fee forfeiture. But because the key word is 'knowingly', many lawyers who defend cash-rich criminals either don't ask where their fees are coming from and make certain that their cash-rich criminals don't offer explanations, or they allow their clients to supply just enough information to allow them reasonably to believe the fee was being paid out of legally obtained funds. That way, everyone's virtue remains smugly intact.

At least, it does in public.

In private, there is plenty of drug cash running around, and it's not only on offer to lawyers who defend dope dealers.

A well-known and highly respected international law firm in the UK was approached by a client, for whom they'd acted in the past, to purchase an ocean-going yacht. For the senior partners of the firm, it sounded like a terrific way to make some easy money. The gentleman instructed them to find something that would meet his requirements in the $6–$10 million range.

With a handsome fee in the offing, the attorneys contacted ships' agents in several pleasure ports along the Mediterranean. It was only a matter of days before an agent in France faxed back to them the particulars of a $9 million yacht that sounded perfect. The lawyers forwarded the details to their client and he decided, almost on the spot, that it was exactly what he was looking for. He told them, buy it.

Negotiations were quickly concluded, the conveyancing went smoothly and the appropriate agreements were drawn up. Just before the time came to sign the final papers, the attorneys asked their client how he'd be paying for the purchase.

Under normal circumstances, money would be transferred from the gentleman's bank, somewhere in the world, to the law firm's client account. Once all the documents were exchanged, completing the sale, the law firm would wire the money from their client account to the client account of the attorneys acting for the seller. But evidently, this wasn't normal circumstances. The gentleman buying the yacht told his attorneys that he intended to pay for it with cash.

The lawyers were admittedly bewildered, as it's not every day they do $9 million cash deals. Obviously, there are people in the world who traditionally pay cash for everything. It's common practice, for instance, in many Gulf states. But that wasn't the case here. And although the lawyers knew enough to worry, they were apprehensive for the wrong reason.

Their concern with $9 million in cash was that they might somehow be risking unforeseen tax liabilities. So they called for their in-house tax specialist who inspected every inch of the deal. As the deadline for closing drew near, he reported that while this might be highly out of the ordinary, he could see no material tax risks to the firm. His only recommendation was that arrangements should be made for guards to protect the money en route to the bank.

The idea that money launderers often attempt to put cash into extravagant objects which can then be legitimately resold all over the world, presumably never dawned on any of the lawyers. So, once they were reassured about their tax position, they set a date for the signing. Only one minor detail remained – how the cash would be transferred. The client explained that his money was in a bank's safe deposit box and that he wanted the attorneys to rent their own safe deposit box next to his. They would go into the bank vault together, he would open his safe deposit box, count out $9 million and hand it to them. They would put it in their safe deposit box and give him a receipt for it. At that point he'd walk away with the title and keys to his boat. Once he was gone, he said, the lawyers were free to do anything they wanted with the money.

The senior partners were instinctively nervous about exchanging so much money in such a bizarre manner, but they were looking at a handsome fee and that tended to quiet their anxieties. Then one of the partners, who was highly amused by such a cloak and dagger payoff, casually mentioned it to someone else in the firm. That person suddenly screamed, 'Have you ever heard of money laundering?' And the deal was immediately killed.

Not surprisingly, the three trades reporting the largest amounts of cash income are car dealers, real estate agents and lawyers.

Between 1983 and 1987, a retired British solicitor with entrepreneurial ambitions bought 11 companies in the Channel Islands for a drug trafficking organization. Using those as fronts, he invested $3 million in a St Kitts-registered trust company. As soon as he and one of his drug trafficking clients were installed on the company's board, they were able to wire money from the Channel Islands through the trust company and then, disguised as loans, on to a network of 60 companies they'd established as legitimate businesses in North America and Britain.

In August 1988, James O'Hagan of St Paul, Minnesota, was a partner in the local law firm of Dorsey and Whitney, where he learned – through privileged information – that the British conglomerate Grand Metropolitan was going to take over the American food giant Pillsbury. Over the next three weeks, O'Hagan allegedly purchased so many shares in Pillsbury that, when the Grand Met takeover happened, he made $4.3 million. Having apparently already embezzled $1 million from his client account, he washed his insider dealing profits through the account, which more than covered the missing funds. He has since been charged on 56 counts of securities fraud, mail fraud and money laundering.

And then there was Gary Henden, a Canadian lawyer who became a legend in his laundryman's lifetime by having a 15-year-old boy on a bicycle deliver parcels of cash to banks around Ontario. For some bizarre reason, a child carrying $250,000 in small bills eluded the bank managers' suspicions. The Royal Canadian Mounted Police later claimed the banks should have questioned the teenager's deposits. The banks maintained it was none of their business.

Employed by Canadian drug traffickers, Henden set up a company called Antillean Management and opened foreign bank accounts in that name. He then created one called Rosegarden Construction. When he found property to buy, money would be wired from the Netherlands Antilles company to the M&M Currency Exchange in Canada, yet another Henden shell. From there it would go into Cencan Investments Ltd – also a Henden invention – which would loan it to Rosegarden. Cencan would issue a cheque, which would be deposited by Henden – the attorney acting for Rosegarden – into his client account. Henden then paid for the purchase, but registered the mortgage in favour of 'Gary Henden, Attorney at Law, In Trust'. Needless to say, those mortgages were never repaid.

Henden eventually admitted to having washed $12 million over a three-year period for a drug trafficking syndicate. The police feel a more accurate figure might be five times as much. Still, had they not been able to establish a direct link between Henden's assets and drug trafficking, they could never have broken through the screen he'd erected around attorney-client privilege.

It was much the same for the Vancouver attorney working on a flat percentage when he deposited $7.4 million in cash between March 1985 and July 1987 into his client account at a local branch of the now infamous BCCI. In a single 18-month period, he also turned C$3.1 million into US dollars, walking into the bank with anywhere from $56,000 to $396,000 in his briefcase, pre-sorted into piles of $20 and $50 notes. When the bank manager asked about the money, the man explained that he was a lawyer acting for a client and refused to say anything more about it. The bank manager reassured the lawyer that he understood attorney-client privilege and that his business was welcome.

Harold Ackerman was a 51-year-old south Florida vegetable importer who was arrested in 1992 for smuggling cocaine. At first he staunchly maintained his innocence, a position that was highly questionable, especially when Gilberto Rodriguez Orejuela, then titular head of the Cali cartel, and his brother Miguel went public with a passionate plea for Ackerman's release.

It was a very curious thing for the brothers to do. And a bunch of people at the Justice Department started asking questions.

Described at the time by the DEA as the highest-ranking Cali trafficker to be arrested in the US, Ackerman first came to their attention in late 1991, after a raid on a Miami warehouse uncovered 15 tons of cocaine in hollowed-out concrete fence posts. In the spring of 1992, agents found six more tons of coke in a shipment of broccoli and okra in Ft Lauderdale. The investigation led to the arrest of several Colombians operating in south Florida, plus Jaime Garcia-Garcia, a 43-year-old Cali laundryman in Bogotá. The good guys picked up $600,000 in cash, four planes, a cache of weapons, a network of computers, 94 bank accounts in Latin America and seven more in the States.

Ackerman now changed his tune, contending that he'd been forced to sell drugs by left-wing paramilitary groups in Colombia who'd threatened to kidnap his family if he didn't cooperate. The jury didn't buy his explanation and convicted him. In a show of support, the Orejuela brothers published an open letter to the DEA, pleading Ackerman's innocence and accusing the agency of 'unfounded, permanent aggression'. The DEA responded by inviting the brothers to come to Florida to make their case in person.

Understandably, they refused.

However, as a result of their intervention, prosecutors began looking beyond Ackerman and towards some of the seemingly legitimate acquaintances he had in common with Gilberto and especially Miguel. Financial documents and Ackerman's computer files had been seized at the time of his arrest, and a closer appraisal of those turned up what appeared to be a group of lawyer criminals.

One of the men who caught their attention was Michael Abbell, a partner in a Washington DC law firm with an office in Florida. In 1981, his fourteenth year as an attorney at the Justice Department, he'd worked on a case that the government was making against one of the Cali cartel leaders, José Santacruz Londono. Part of his job was to try to secure information from the Swiss about bank accounts held by Santacruz.

When he left the Justice Department in 1984, he joined the law firm of Kaplan, Russin & Vecchi where within six months he was hired to help Gilberto fight an extradition charge. He'd been arrested in Spain and the US wanted him to face charges in New York. After obtaining a conflict-of-interest clearance from the Justice Department, Abbell testified as an expert witness against the very people he'd worked with at Justice, who'd prepared the extradition request. Instead of being extradited to New York, the Spanish returned him to Colombia. Orejuela was tried there and Abbell was in the courtroom. Apparently he'd been hired to brief Gilberto's lawyers because of his extensive knowledge of the evidence. In 1987, he was again working for Orejuela, this time writing a legal opinion about Colombia's ban on extraditing its citizens to the US. The next year, he submitted statements to the Senate Foreign Relations Committee during a review of evidence-gathering provisions in legal assistance treaties with various countries. Abbell's position was consistent with an often heard plea from lawyers defending Colombian drug traffickers, that defendants should have greater use of foreign-obtained evidence. In 1989, he showed up in Miami for the drug trafficking trial of Luis Echeverri Santacruz, José's half-brother. Supposedly retained by Orejuela and Santacruz to assist on legal and factual issues, he was not otherwise participating at the trial. Sitting next to him throughout the case in the back of the courtroom was Joel Rosenthal, a defence attorney in Miami who'd been similarly retained to help the defence.

It was around this time when Abbell and the firm of Kaplan, Russin & Vecchi parted company, citing incompatible interests. He went into practice with his friend Bruno Ristau, who'd directed the Justice Department's Office of Foreign Litigation for 18 years. They opened an office in Washington and another in Florida which they eventually stocked with Francisco Laguna, a Bogotá-born attorney.

Next, Abbell found himself representing Santacruz's wife.

The DEA had uncovered a significant laundry cycle with a money trail leading to Luxembourg and $60 million that they said belonged to Santacruz. They also located $12 million in New York. Abbell, now accompanied by Laguna, attended court hearings in both places, then filed a claim for the money in New York on behalf of Ampara Castro de Santacruz. He asserted her right to it as her inheritance from her father, but the jury said no.

Ironically, after the US District Court judge who'd heard the case labelled Santacruz a well-organized, multinational drug trafficking fugitive, Abbell wrote a letter, criticizing him for misrepresenting his client's husband. This, just nine years after Abbell had pursued her husband's money because it had belonged to a well-organized multinational drug dealer.

Five years later, in part through evidence uncovered in Ackerman's files, Abbell stood accused of knowingly securing false sworn statements from arrested members of the Orejuela faction of the Cali cartel; submitting fraudulent documents to courts in New York and Luxembourg on behalf of the cartel; arranging, receiving and transmitting cartel drug money; racketeering; conspiracy; drug trafficking; and money laundering.

By this time, Laguna was also attracting attention. During a 1992 DEA sting operation, undercover agents picked up cash for Santacruz in various cities around the country. When $1.2 million was seized in Chicago, the undercover agents were contacted by a cartel representative who'd come to the States to investigate the bust. He ordered them to speak with Laguna. Questioning the undercover agents whom he believed to be laundrymen, Laguna allegedly demanded, 'Why don't you tell me what you know? We're trying to find out what is happening here.' Some months later, a federal indictment charged 21 people with money laundering, and Laguna as an unindicted co-conspirator.

Also under investigation was Joel Rosenthal, along with three other Florida attorneys linked to Ackerman and the Orejuelas.

William Moran, a former federal prosecutor in Miami, was a partner in Moran and Gold, and first dealt with Gilberto Orejuela in 1985. He was hired to represent members of the gang who'd been arrested in Florida. Ackerman was introduced to him in 1990 by a mutual friend, who supposedly identified Ackerman as the person to call if and when any gang member got arrested. Donald Ferguson had also been an assistant US Attorney in Miami and now worked for himself. He was recruited by Abbell in 1990 to help with the civil forfeiture suit in New York and since then represented arrested members of the Orejuela gang. Robert Moore was the attorney hired by the cartel to defend Ackerman.

Moran was indicted on a multiple of charges, including arranging bail for gang members whom he knew would jump bail; aiding and abetting the flight of gang members whom he knew to be criminals; preparing, presenting and arranging knowingly false affidavits; and arranging for and forwarding monthly subsistence payments from Orejuela to the families of arrested gang members to ensure that they would not cooperate with the government. Ferguson was similarly indicted on multiple charges that included the delivering of drug money to be used for legal fees, bail and subsistence expenses.

The 163-page indictment that named Abbell, Ferguson and Moran also charged 56 other people at all levels of the cartel, among them the Orejuela brothers and Santacruz. Laguna, Rosenthal and Moore were not named as they'd already pleaded guilty to reduced charges. In fact, Ferguson cut a deal with the government, pleading guilty to conspiracy to obstruct justice and money laundering and, in exchange for a minimum sentence, an agreement to testify against the remaining two.

That left Abbell and Moran to tough it out, facing possible life imprisonment for their part in a massive drug trafficking and money laundering scheme.

'Lawyers represent a very special dynamic in the context of money laundering,' notes Kendall Coffey, a former US Attorney in Miami and now in private practice, 'because, on the one hand, all of us know that we don't have any rights that mean anything unless there are lawyers who are going to zealously and aggressively safeguard those rights. On the other hand, traffickers in the 1990s and money launderers in the 1990s are real sophisticated. They know that lawyers have a special kind of hall pass, that attorney-client privilege allows certain kinds of protections that don't apply to other people. If you send a courier to deliver a message, that person can be subjected to examination and questioning. If you use your lawyer to deliver a message, lots of issues arise. Important shields surround the use of that lawyer. Of course, lawyers are not above the law, and yet their role is so essential in a society like ours that it becomes a very difficult job balancing the needs of law enforcement and our rights that have to be vindicated by lawyers.'

Coffey, who initially prosecuted the Miami-based lawyers, says that someone in the Cali cartel clearly got it wrong by concluding that if they used lawyers to deliver threats or, as intermediaries to gain false evidence, their actions passed through some sort of protected zone. He says they almost certainly believed that just because a client's communications with his lawyer are privileged, lawyers could therefore get away with anything.

In other words, they assumed attorney-client privilege was a substitute for accountability.

'There's an extremely difficult balance between what lawyers have to do to represent their clients and the use of lawyers as accomplices in trafficking and laundering. When the government indicted these six, its position was that they were part of the narcotics trafficking efforts of the Cali cartel. One of the most difficult questions we had to ask ourselves was, when were these lawyers acting as lawyers and when were they acting as criminals? That presents a challenge to law enforcement to determine where the limit is. This prosecution spelled out the fact that there are no protected zones for criminal conduct.'

The essence of the charges against them was that they were not acting as lawyers, that they were not practising law, while they were acting as criminals. The government claimed that they were delivering threats to intimidate witnesses, that they were creating false evidence, that they were betraying their responsibilities as officers of the court.

'If a lawyer zealously represents his client,' Coffey continues, 'you know, represents him aggressively and does everything he can to win a trial, then that's what the system is all about. But when a lawyer acts as a participant in narcotics trafficking and money laundering, that person ought to be put away, to be put in jail. He must be held fully accountable for the consequences of his act.'

The charges against those six attorneys indicted in Miami outline some 59 transactions totaling $6,911,497. Many of the transactions involved cash. Most of the transactions passed through one client account or another.

It goes without saying that given enough time and determination, the courts can get inside an attorney's client account. And in this case they did. But it's a long, involved process and one which legislators are naturally disinclined to make any easier.

If exiled dictator Jean-Claude 'Baby Doc' Duvalier can still afford champagne and caviar, he has British solicitors to thank for it.

In September 1986, eight months after Haiti's President for Life was forced into exile on the French Riviera, attorneys acting for him put $41.8 million worth of Canadian Treasury Bills into their client account at a Toronto branch of the Royal Bank of Montreal. Within a matter of days, the T-bills were moved to a Jersey account held at the Hongkong and Shanghai Bank in Montreal.

Duvalier's representatives then separated the ownership records from the money – a common ruse to complicate the paper trail – sending the records for safe keeping to a bank in London, while taking the T-bills to yet another bank in Montreal. Two months later, those T-Bills were moved to an account of the Royal Trust Bank of Jersey, which is a subsidiary of Canada's Royal Trust Company. To complicate the audit trail as much as possible, that particular account was part of a larger one held by Manufacturers Hanover Bank of Canada at an office in Toronto used by the Royal Bank of Montreal. Shortly thereafter, the money was wired into a pair of accounts at the Royal Trust Bank in Jersey owned by a locally registered shell company called Boncardo Ltd.

As the virtually invisible owner of Boncardo Ltd, Duvalier was issued with bearer cheques on Boncardo's accounts. The scheme worked for more than a year, until February 1988 when French police – acting on embezzlement charges lodged by the Haitian government – raided Duvalier's villa and confiscated private papers that led to the discovery of the two Jersey company accounts.

Duvalier's lawyers promptly hustled the money out of Jersey, nesting it in the Swiss accounts of two Panamanian shell companies, Minoka Investments and Modinest Investments. A week or so later, $30.8 million was wired from Credit Suisse in Geneva to the Royal Bank of Montreal.

Canadian Treasury bills were purchased and a Duvalier agent took possession of them. For anyone hoping to trace the funds, the scent ended right there. The T-bills were left at two nearby banks, but not for long. As the case in France intensified against Duvalier, it was felt his money would be safer elsewhere and it was subsequently wired to Luxembourg.

That's when fate stepped in to save Duvalier's bacon. The government that succeeded him had located assets and frozen them, but that government was overthrown in a September 1988 coup by General Prosper Avril, a Duvalier compatriot. Avril allowed the case against Baby Doc to disintegrate, along with all traces of what remains of that original $41.8 million.

No suspicious cash transaction reports were required, nor would they be required today, because no cash came into Britain. Anyway, even if it had, Duvalier's attorneys could have readily claimed, we know the beneficial owner of the money and do not consider it to be suspicious. What's more, those attorneys remained snug in the knowledge that, as long as they were not breaking the law – and they are fast to point out that they were not in violation of any statute at the time on the books in the UK – whatever instructions they received from their client, remains privileged information.

Many lawyers in the States argue that by grouping attorneys with all other businessmen and requiring them to put the name of a cash-paying client on the IRS Form 8300, the government has found a way around attorney-client privilege.

The staunchest test of this 'lawyer as secret banker' prescript began in 1989 when the US Internal Revenue Service took aim at lawyers, their clients' accounts and cash-paying clients – notably drug traffickers, who pay for most things, including legal services, with cash – stipulating that they must fill out Cash Transaction Reports for any cash received in excess of $10,000. It was, the IRS said, exactly the same condition that had been imposed on banks and other trades. And as it is with banks and other trades, an attorney's failure to file reports is a felony offence.

Significantly, the first and loudest protest to the IRS came from criminal defence attorneys who objected on the grounds that the ruling unquestionably violated attorney-client privilege.

John Zwerling, a partner in the Richmond, Virginia firm of Moffitt, Zwerling and Kemler recently found himself in the middle of just such a controversy. 'Our system is founded on an individual's right to seek counsel. So putting a client's name on the IRS Form 8300 is perhaps not a problem for a person who's willing to have the Government know that he's gone to see a lawyer. But, for someone who decides that he doesn't want every IRS agent, every Assistant US Attorney, every bureaucratic cop in the federal system to know his business, in the end, he may choose not to seek counsel. By threatening attorney-client privilege you strike at the heart of the right to seek counsel.'

An obvious contention is that in a criminal defence practice, people who come bearing cash to seek counsel are probably criminals who have obtained that money through criminal procedures. And they should not be permitted to use their ill-gotten gains to further their own defence. Despite the arguments of lawyers who claim that the Constitution guarantees representation by the counsel of your choice, it says no such thing. And under our system, anyone who cannot afford counsel, whether it be of his choice or not, is guaranteed counsel by having one appointed to serve him.

Zwerling however does not quite see it that way. 'There are a lot of people who have cash. Retailers have cash. Restaurateurs have cash. There are a lot of people in this country who don't use banks. Or, if they do, they only use banks minimally, so they can write cheques to pay the rent. They keep the rest of their money under the mattress. It may be not very bright but they do it because they're afraid of losing their savings in a bank. Why shouldn't they be able to pay in cash without inferring that they're criminals?'

A criminal defence lawyer's first responsibility is, quite plainly, to provide competent, legal counsel: to stand up on his client's behalf; to make sure that any evidence presented against his client has been lawfully obtained; to make certain that the Government's proof is adequate; to assure that his client's side of the story is presented in a meaningful way; and if his client is convicted, to see that the sentence is no greater than is required under the law. Zwerling argues that the government's use of the IRS Form 8300 where it pertains to lawyers is putting the entire system in jeopardy because it becomes a weapon with which the government can turn a lawyer against his client.

In May 1990, the FBI busted a 35-year-old, northern Virginia auto mechanic named William Paul Covington for drug trafficking. In the course of the investigation, they obtained seizure warrants for a safe deposit box, several vehicles and Covington's residence. To defend himself, Covington hired a local law firm. But in July 1991, the FBI hit Covington with another series of search and seizure warrants, which got them into several of his bank accounts. At that point, Covington decided to seek new counsel. Claiming that the government had scared his lawyers out of the case, he approached Moffitt, Zwerling and Kemler.

When William Moffitt and John Zwerling met with Covington, he explained that as the target of a federal cocaine investigation, many of his assets had already been seized by the government based on probable cause. He admitted to them he'd dealt cocaine since 1985 but insisted it was always small quantities. He claimed that the government's allegations against him were drastically overstated.

During that initial interview, which took place on Wednesday 21 August 1991 and lasted nearly five hours, Moffitt and Zwerling asked extensive questions about Covington's background. He told them that since 1970 he had been steadily employed as a mechanic and had earned substantial sums of legitimate money. He said his father had always advised him to keep a nest egg of cash, something for a rainy day, so he'd hoarded cash all his life. He referred often to times pre-dating any drug trafficking when he had as much as $100,000 in his safe deposit box, all of it legitimately earned. That's about when Covington asked if he could pay Moffitt and Zwerling in cash.

The lawyers responded that cash would only be acceptable under three conditions: first, the cash would be deposited in a bank so there would be a record of it. Second, they would comply with the law and file an IRS Form 8300 reporting the transaction. While they would not name Covington as the source of the cash, claiming attorney-client privilege, his identity might have to be disclosed if the government petitioned the court to know it. Third, they would not accept drug money.

The next day, Thursday, Moffitt and Zwerling informed Covington that their fee to defend him would be $100,000. He handed them a down payment of $17,000 in cash and returned Friday with a further $86,800 in cash. Myth has it that Covington delivered the cash stuffed in a Ritz cracker box. Zwerling recalls it was, instead, a shoe box. In any case, the lawyers deposited it in their bank on Monday, the 26th, and filed the required Form 8300 a week or so later. Keeping their word, they did not name the source of the cash.

Meeting with the prosecutors, Moffitt and Zwerling were able to establish several critical points: that Covington did indeed have access to large amounts of legitimate cash through his business; that he had always hoarded cash; that he'd been a nickel-dime dealer; and that the assets already seized from him more than covered the amount he most probably earned from drug dealing. They then set about trying to get their client a deal. But the government insisted that Covington admit to distributing 15–50 kilos of cocaine, which he refused to do, maintaining his position that the actual quantity was significantly lower. When the negotiations failed, a Grand Jury indicted him.

Two weeks into October, the government monitored a conversation with Covington's girlfriend where he discussed the cash payment to Moffitt and Zwerling. Immediately, the prosecutors dipped into an IRS database and found the law firm's CTR. With just six weeks to go before the trial was scheduled to begin, the government served a subpoena on Moffitt and Zwerling, demanding to see the firm's fee records relating to its representation of Covington. They threatened felony tax prosecution against the lawyers for having withheld client-identifying information from the IRS Form 8300 and, unbeknownst to the lawyers, executed a search warrant for the firm's bank records.

Immediately, Moffitt and Zwerling retained separate counsel for Covington, for the law firm and for all three principals of the firm. They then filed motions to quash the subpoena and moved to order withdrawal of the threatening letter. In response, the prosecutors sought approval from the Department of Justice Asset Forfeiture Office to claim back the $103,800 fee Covington had paid Moffitt and Zwerling, claiming it was drug money. Approval was granted by that office, which is merely a formality, so they filed against the firm. Moffitt and Zwerling quickly filed a defence.

In the meantime, the subpoena was quashed and the threatening letter was withdrawn. But the damage had been done. The government had successfully set up a series of smoke screens, which not only prevented Moffitt and

Zwerling from properly defending their client, it created a situation where Moffitt and Zwerling could be called as witnesses to testify about cash against the very person who'd come to them for help. The government had used the IRS Form 8300 and the attorney-client privilege issue to drive the defence attorneys out of the case.

On 16 July 1992 the government asked the court to disqualify the law firm. Four weeks later, Moffitt and Zwerling were officially removed from the matter. Shortly thereafter, Covington pleaded guilty and was sentenced to 21 years.

Moffitt and Zwerling were now in an even more dangerous situation.

Once a person is convicted under the sentencing guidelines, there's only one avenue for him to take to get the sentence reduced. It's called, 'substantial assistance to the Government'. In other words, that person is invited to sit down with the prosecutors and say, 'I will help you make a case against another human being, and in turn you will reduce my sentence'. So they go after their friends, their family, and sometimes, their attorney. And if cash has been involved in a criminal defence – which the government can determine through the IRS Form 8300 – especially drug related crimes, the convicted man's lawyer has to worry that he's going to be the next defendant because his former client is trying to get his sentence reduced.

Which is exactly what the government did in this case.

They offered Covington a chance to reduce his sentence by convincing him to help them in their fee forfeiture case against Moffitt and Zwerling. The courts have proven reluctant to order the entire fee forfeited, the government has scored points in every round. Moffitt and Zwerling continue to appeal and promise to do so up to the US Supreme Court.

Several questions lie at the heart of the matter. Can a drug dealer use illicitly obtained funds to pay for the counsel of his choice? Apparently not. Is it a breach of attorney-client privilege if the attorney is forced to divulge the nature and/or source of his fees? There are those who argue it is. Would the government have been able to split Covington away from his lawyers had he paid for their legal services with a cheque? Clearly not. Has the government violated any of Covington's rights by using the IRS Form 8300 to get around attorney-client privilege? The American Civil Liberties Union seems to think even if they didn't, at the very least, they've taken a very dangerous step in that direction.

In a brief submitted as a friend of the court, the ACLU held, 'If the government can unilaterally inject fee forfeiture into a criminal case in a manner that leads to defence attorney disqualification, the government can improperly deny an accused the constitutional right to counsel of choice in cases the government selects.'

Adds Zwerling, 'We don't believe that the Department of Justice has the ability, in and of itself, to void the language that's on every dollar bill in the United States where it says, this is legal tender for all debts, public and private.'

The case against Moffitt and Zwerling is not an isolated one. New York attorney Gerald Lefcourt has been placed in a similar situation.

The DEA, FBI and New York City Police Department knew they'd scored points against the Cali drug cartel in November 1994 when they arrested two lawyers, a Bulgarian diplomat, an assistant manager at Citibank, a cop, a stockbroker, a firemen and a pair of rabbis for washing more than $100 million of drug proceeds. After a 10-month investigation, 23 people were charged with participating in a ring whose business stretched from New York, Los Angeles, Houston, Chicago and Miami to Canada, Germany, Switzerland, Italy, Puerto Rico and Colombia.

Believed to have been in operation for at least two years, one of the leaders of the group – fireman turned businessman Richard Spence or law partners Harvey Weinig and Robert Hirsch – would be contacted by traffickers and told that money needed to be picked up. A courier would be dispatched to a designated hotel room or a meeting point on a street to get the money and deliver it back to one of the three leaders. After being counted, it would be taken to the Bronx, where a low level employee at a Citibank branch would accept it. From the Bronx, it would be wired to Europe. There, under the watchful eye of the Cali cartel's representative, Juan Guillermo Ocampo, the money would wind up in Zurich, where the husband and wife team of Leon and Rachel Weinmann would move it through their Swiss bank before sending it on its way to a senior cartel trafficker, Miguel Omar Garrabito Botero in Cali.

The group managed to wash $70–100 million before it was taken down. The major players were all arrested and some of them quickly pleaded guilty as part of a deal with the prosecution.

One of the people charged with a money laundering offence in the Federal Court in New York – but not one of the principal gang members – came to Lefcourt seeking counsel. He paid part of Lefcourt's fee by cheque and the rest with cash. The amount of cash exceeded $10,000 so Lefcourt duly filed an IRS Form 8300.

Just as Moffitt and Zwerling had done, he too refused to name his client, having made the determination that disclosure of his client's identity in connection with the cash payment could and almost certainly would be used against him by the government.

'Being an officer of the court is not the same as being an undercover agent for the prosecution,' Lefcourt insists. 'It's obvious that the prosecutor would view the fact that my client had cash, whether he was guilty or not, as something that he would like to put before the jury. And how would the prosecutor do that? He would call me as a witness to say that I received this money from this person. So instead of providing effective counsel, which is what the Constitution says my client is entitled do, I've become a witness for the government. This is unacceptable. That's not the way the right to counsel should work.'

Unlike Moffitt and Zwerling, the prosecution didn't go after Lefcourt, but the IRS did. They promptly slapped him with a $25,000 fine for failure to comply. Being a pay now, appeal later situation, Lefcourt had no choice but to pay the fine and then begin the lengthy appeal process. His suit against the IRS claims that he was wrongfully assessed in that he did not intentionally disregard the filing requirement. Instead, he claims to have acted in the good faith belief that he had ethical obligations towards his client and that he was obliged, at a minimum, to let a court decide whether or not there were special circumstances which might have exempted him from naming his cash-carrying client.

In fact, it turns out that the law does permit exemptions for lawyers under 'special circumstances' from naming a cash-paying client on the IRS Form 8300. But the law does not spell out what those special circumstances should be.

Lefcourt maintains, 'There are all sorts of people who prefer to do business with cash and none of them should be suspected of being drug dealers, simply because they use cash. The Latino community doesn't necessarily use banks, for cultural reasons, which began with language barriers. That's also true of the Hassidic Jewish community. I've represented members of both groups and they often come in with cash. In addition there are all kinds of people who hoard cash, for any variety of reasons. Some of them may be tax cheats. But then some of them may not want his or her spouse to know that they have this extra money. All kinds of people pay cash, including those who are guilty of crimes that generate cash. Simply because they have cash, it doesn't mean they're guilty.'

He agrees that if someone goes to a Cadillac dealer and buys a car for cash the car dealer must fully comply and report that cash transaction. But he claims that the IRS doesn't see the difference between a Constitutional right to counsel and a Cadillac dealer.

'To them, they're exactly the same. You have no constitutionally protected right to buy a Cadillac. But the right to come to an attorney to discuss your needs in private is based on a Constitutional right. A free society should not in any way interfere with a citizen's opportunity to defend himself by consulting an attorney. That is of paramount importance in a free society. The Sixth Amendment allows and requires counsel in criminal cases, and the effective assistance of counsel is interfered with if the first thing the attorney does is to violate the ethics of confidentiality by becoming an investigator against the person who walked in for help. Citizens accused of crime mustn't have their Government interfering with attorney-client privilege.'

Although there have been some dissenting opinions among attorneys, the profession as a whole continues to voice concern over the matter. The American Bar Association, along with the National Association of Criminal Defense Lawyers, has met on several occasions with the Department of Justice and the IRS, asking them to stop this. But so far, the government has refused to budge. Some lawyers hope that, eventually, the law requiring a cash-paying client's name will be struck down as unconstitutional. But so far, the Supreme Court has declined to take an IRS Form 8300 case. Although the Justices often watch how an issue is treated in the lower courts before they look at it.

At the end of 1995, the government brought out a revised IRS Form 8300, making it shorter and slightly easier for banks to use. But it did not make any sort of gesture towards attorneys.

And therein lies another contradiction.

Generally speaking, it is the honest lawyer who fills out the form – or in the case of British attorneys, would willingly report a suspicious cash transaction – and then refuses to disclose the identity of his client. He's the one reporting the information, telling the IRS about it, ethically trying to live up to the responsibility of keeping a client's confidence. By contrast, it is the unethical lawyer who tells the Government what he knows about the client in direct conflict with attorney-client confidentiality, or the lawyer-criminal who doesn't fill out the form or bother making any type of report.

Case in point: Not one single instance could be found anywhere in Great Britain of a solicitor filing a suspicious cash transaction report on business transacted by one of his own clients!

Case in point: The number of IRS 8300 Forms filed for the cash transactions that the six indicted Miami lawyers made on behalf of the Cali cartel is none!

CHAPTER SIX

The Marlboro Murder

'The crooks keep so far ahead of us, we'll never completely close the net.'

The US Department of Justice

David Wilson was a fool.

At times a bit too gullible, at other times a bit too susceptible to a touch of greed, he was the sort of man who was always just within arm's reach of the next get-rich-quick scheme.

Born in England in 1944, Wilson had studied accountancy, but he left school without qualifying and, after working locally at various jobs in East Lancashire, he set himself up as a financial adviser. He couldn't certify accounts – he wasn't chartered – so he did tax returns for small firms and dabbled in whatever business ventures came his way.

Basically, he was an honest man. The people who knew him in Lancashire liked him. And the people who hired him to handle their bookkeeping also spoke well of him. More importantly, the police have never found any evidence that Wilson was personally involved in any criminal activities. But because he wasn't above the odd accounting fiddle – he was fond of dubious offshore shelters and prone to showing his clients how to pay their personal taxes out of company funds – it wasn't long before he found himself operating on the fringe of some intelligent, well-connected, company-owning criminals.

If he was guilty of anything – if he committed any sins – it must be that he had long ago convinced himself that he was sharper, more intelligent, more talented than he really was. Or perhaps, even worse, that, when he did go for the pie in the sky, he gambled with his family's future by staking his own money.

It's no surprise, then, that the moment he heard about the untold wealth on offer in black market Marlboro cigarettes, he could taste the millions pouring in.

David Wilson was a fool.

But that doesn't mean he deserved to be executed.

Colonel Hector Moretta Portillo held a privileged place in the Mexican army. As a relative of Mexico's ex-President, he was an accredited member of his country's delegation to the United Nations and came complete with a fancy Mexican army uniform.

Stocky, 5 feet 6 inches, with black hair and a black moustache, at one point in his career he'd been murdered – fatally shot in the head – while on holiday at the home of the Mexican Minister of Interior on the island of Cozumel. Press reports noted that his body was found in the swimming pool and that his killer was still at large.

At another point in his career – a few years after his murder – he turned up in Santo Domingo as Colonel Gomez, an officer in the army of the Dominican Republic and a relative of that nation's former president.

When, towards the end of 1990, he and Wilson crossed paths, he was Hector Portillo again, alive and well and living in New York.

A man known to use up to 30 aliases, he'd been arrested

in the Dominican Republican in 1988 when the authorities uncovered a scheme of his to sell non-existent sugar. Under questioning, he admitted his real name was Michael Austin Smith. That might be the closest he's ever come to telling the truth because that is his name, except it wasn't the name he was born with. When he came into this world, in Brooklyn, New York, in 1955, he was Michael Sporn. He changed his name to Austin somewhere along the way, much the way he changed his accent from New Yorkese to broken English. A keen linguist, he's fluent in Spanish and more than capable of mimicking the speech pattern you'd expect from your average Mexican Colonel.

Now in New York, Portillo – who in the past had been known to run hustles in gold, bonds and whiskey – was onto a new game. This time it was Marlboro cigarettes.

An ideal commodity for a con, Marlboros have a well-recognized, globally traded brand name and are easily and frequently bought and sold outside the manufacturer's normal distribution routes. Besides the fact that their popularity makes them a prime target for the counterfeit market, Philip Morris produces the cigarettes for worldwide consumption and enormous parcels of legitimate Marlboros are forever spinning around the world through all species of wholesale channels – a state tobacco monopoly buys too many and sells the surplus, a cargo gets stolen that needs to be fenced, a middle man buys a very large shipment at an advantageous price and wants to unload them quickly, someone defaults on a payment and his cargo must be sold to recoup costs. Whatever the reason – from oil, pork bellies and timber to grain, steel, cardboard boxes, recording tape and cigarettes – the world is awash with commodities of all shapes and sizes in the parallel markets.

In many Third World countries – notably the former Communist bloc – Marlboro plays a particularly eminent role, in that it has become a kind of currency. Cartons of

Marlboros are often the icing on the cake. They can cap a deal. In Russia, for example, where no one wants roubles, you barter first with dollars, then with Marlboros. In fact, the best way to get a taxi on the streets of Moscow is to wave the familiar red and white box – a signal that you've got something to offer which even non-smoking taxi drivers can use.

It's the old joke about the soldier with his single pack of Marlboros, which he sells to another soldier for a dollar. The second soldiers sells it to a third for two bucks. The third sells it to the fourth for $3, and so on until the price reaches $15. The soldier who paid that for the pack rips it open and starts smoking. The other soldiers are aghast. What's wrong, puffs the soldier with the cigarettes? The first soldier points to the Marlboros. Those, he says, are not for smoking, they're for buying and selling.

So Portillo knew what he was doing when he chose to go into the Marlboro business, intending to put 100 containers-full into the parallel market where he knew that literally thousands of middlemen would be interested. By the way, 100 containers is one helluva lot of cigarettes. There are 20 per pack, 10 packs per carton and 50 cartons per case. Each 40 foot container can take 960 cases or 9.6 million cigarettes. Multiply that by 100 containers and you're talking about 960 million cigarettes or 48 million packs – enough to supply the entire Russian market for four months.

In order to move a shipment like this, he did everything that is regularly done in genuine parallel market commodity trading, except for the minor fact that Portillo's containers of cigarettes didn't exist.

To make this racket work – or, for that matter, to make any scam work – there must be what criminologists call 'evidence of reality'. In other words, you can't sell someone the Mona Lisa when they know full well that it's sitting securely on a wall in the Louvre. So the first requirement is that product must be believable. That's why he chose Marlboros.

At the same time, everyone must believe that the seller has access to the product. To convince any doubters, Portillo cooked up a few variations of the same story. One went: factories in Mexico that Philip Morris had closed were back in operation producing fraudulent Marlboros in cartons and boxes made for the American market. Another version claimed: factories that never had anything to do with Philip Morris were banging out counterfeit Marlboros. A third story was: through his connections with the Mexican government, he'd acquired the cigarettes nefariously and now wanted to move them as quickly and as surreptitiously as he could. And he supported all three contentions with official-looking documents proving that the cigarettes were in fact waiting for him in Mexico.

Finally, the punters must believe that they're getting a bargain. A good con man understands how, when a punter thinks there's a big, fat profit to be had simply for the price of admission, half his brain shuts off. It's the half that should warn all punters, when something is too good to be true, it generally is.

Playing to their greed, providing plenty of room for everybody to make a killing off his back, Portillo said he was looking to wholesale each container for the bargain price of $160,000.

Now, commodities of any kind – whether they're on offer in these twilight parallel markets or moved openly in the main market – are bought and sold on letters of credit. It's the accepted way, as one bank guarantees payment to another without money changing hands before the cargo does. The buyer pays his bank and they hold the money until the seller delivers the cargo, which he does once the buyer's bank promises to pay the seller's bank. The whole system is predicated on mutual trust between banks

– guaranteeing that payment has been arranged – because, when high-priced cargoes are at stake, there seems to be little reason for either the buyer or the seller to trust each other.

From his own experience – notably the failed non-existent sugar scam – Portillo knew that very specific documents were required, not only to make people believe in the 100 container cargo but to get them to pay money for it. In this instance he would need to provide: bills of lading that adequately defined the cargo; a certificate of inspection, to guarantee that the cargo, as described by the bills of lading, was on board a ship going to the buyer; a certificate of freshness, which is peculiar to the cigarette business so that the buyer knows his assets have not passed their sell-by date; and a certificate of insurance to protect the cargo.

For Portillo, forged certificates were not a problem. He had access to people who could forge anything – and did on his behalf – including passports. But maritime transport documents always list the name of the ship carrying the containers. And the whereabouts of any ship, plus the cargo on board, are something that a punter can readily verify. So, to get the scam going, Portillo decided he needed to own a ship.

This was where David Wilson came into the deal.

It's a fact of life that in most businesses the players who have to know each other do know each other, or at least they know how to find each other. Portillo was looking for an accountant in Europe – preferably in England because of the language – to set up a company and help him buy a ship. Some of the less-than-scrupulous people he knew happened to know some of Wilson's less-than-scrupulous clients and they were the ones who put the two men together.

It was a perfect match. Right from the start, Portillo could tell that Wilson was the kind of guy who is always available for a deal. The type of man who let logic take a back seat to avarice. In essence, he was the perfect patsy. And Portillo had no trouble convincing him that, this time, the pie was so huge there'd be plenty of thick slices available for him.

With the biggest get-rich-quick scheme of his life in the offing, Wilson bought a company called Alamosa Ltd in the Isle of Man, housed it at his office in Lancashire and went in search of someone to finance a ship. He found the backing he needed in Norway, where a man with some shipping interests agreed to put up £1.6 million to purchase a 3400 ton bulk carrier built in 1970 called the *Gregory*.

On paper, the deal was sweet for everybody. The vessel would be purchased by Alamosa, then transferred to Wilson Overseas Ltd, a holding company he registered in the Bahamas. For his money, the Norwegian would be the main shareholder of Wilson Overseas, which meant that he would retain title to the ship. As a bonus for the Norwegian's participation, Portillo was willing to agree that for every ten containers of cigarettes he purchased, he would be given one free. It worked out that, if the Norwegian took the entire cargo, he'd be paid back in full for the ship, and therefore wind up owning it for nothing.

Once the papers were signed, Wilson changed the name of the ship to the *Lisa Marie*, after his youngest daughter.

The way Portillo designed his scheme, there was an impenetrable shield protecting him from the punters. None of them could deal directly. They all had to go through agents. When any of those agents – to whom he'd offered big commissions on each container – wanted to know why he wasn't selling them himself, he explained that, because of his position with the government of Mexico, he couldn't be seen to be taking part. It was plausible enough. The truth however, was that, because the world is filled with these middlemen who earn their living on the back of the parallel markets, there was no reason for Portillo to take any unnecessary risks that might expose his true identity.

Not even the agents acting on his behalf could contact him directly. They had a New York phone number for him, but when any of them rang the best they ever got was someone on the other end saying Colonel Portillo wasn't in and asking if the caller wanted to leave a message. Portillo always rang back promptly, but the New York number turned out to be nothing more than a legitimate answering service.

Realizing that the big money was to be made in acting as an agent, Wilson convinced Portillo to let him sell some containers and quickly landed a client named James McMillan. A Scotsman living in Houston, Texas, McMillan put up nearly $350,000 in cash – no letter of credit this time, it was money on the table – in advance for two containers. Alamosa used that cash to refit the *Lisa Marie* so that she could carry containers. Except that, after the refit, there was still no way the ship could handle 100 containers. It might have taken, at best, 90.

But that didn't seem to concern Portillo's agents, who sold several times the ship's maximum cargo. Whether or not any of those agents knew that the cigarettes didn't exist is a matter of conjecture. Some of them must have realized what was going on – after all, they had their ears to the ground – because suddenly there were too many containers of Marlboro cigarettes available in the parallel market.

Then again, if any of those agents did know, they didn't appear to be especially worried about it. They were acting only as agents and most of them would have figured that a minor detail, such as how many containers actually existed, was Hector's problem.

Now that he had a ship, Portillo's next step was insurance. Again through the mutual friend network, he was introduced to an ex-public school boy – one of those frightfully British 'Hooray Henry' types – who'd worked at Lloyds, been thrown out of Lloyds and was otherwise available for dubious projects. He was the one who supplied Portillo with the necessary insurance papers.

Bills of lading were no problem – they were easily forged – but to get the certificates of freshness Portillo needed the services of a maritime survey company. The most convenient way to arrange that was to invent a company called Sealand Maritime Surveyors. Because the *Lisa Marie* was getting overhauled in a Miami dockyard, Portillo put Sealand Maritime there too. At least, the company's address was in Miami and its phone number appeared to be a Miami number. But, thanks to the advanced communications services available through American telephone companies, Portillo could subscribe to Call Forwarding, which meant that, every time someone dialed Sealand Maritime's Miami number, the call was automatically diverted to an Englishman who answered the phone in Spain. Except for those odd occasions when someone asked what the weather was like and the Englishman said it was sunny when Miami was deluged with rain, no one ever suspected that they weren't speaking to Sealand Maritime Surveyors in Florida.

In his opening gambit to the story of the cigarettes, Portillo had claimed that the 100 containers were waiting for the *Lisa Marie* in Vera Cruz, Mexico. But on 12 November 1991, the necessary paperwork was completed to show that 50 containers had already been loaded in Miami. So when she sailed 11 days later, instead of going to Mexico to pick up the cigarettes, the *Lisa Marie* was reported already on her way with cigarettes bound for Hamburg.

Then came a second batch of paperwork. This one showed the *Lisa Marie* loading three containers of Marlboros on 3 December 1991, destined for Naples, Italy – but still in Miami.

David Wilson's confusion quickly turned into suspicion.

To protect his own clients, he'd built into the contract of conditions the clause that letters of credit could not be exchanged until a full inspection of the cargo was carried out at the port of delivery. He must have felt his clients were safeguarded by that. Yet something about all of this wasn't ringing true.

Sadly, his suspicions were about to become his greatest nightmare.

After paying cash for the two containers he purchased from Wilson, James McMillan had also signed on as a Portillo agent. Hoping to interest a group of punters in some or all of the 50 containers supposedly en route to Hamburg, he set up a 2 December sales meeting for prospective clients at the Rotterdam Hilton.

His idea was to get everyone into a single room and give them a great sales pitch. To entice people to the meeting, he furnished them with copies of the 12 November documents showing that the shipment had already left Miami. But one of his clients had a gut feeling – something kept gnawing at him – that this was indeed one of those too-good-to-be-true stories.

With enough common sense to seek professional advice, he forwarded the paperwork to the International Maritime Bureau. And much to his chagrin, the IMB's director confirmed the man's doubts.

A former Chief Constable for the Port of London Police, Eric Ellen has been trying to stop maritime fraud all his life. An acknowledged, world-class expert in the field, he spotted the fly in the ointment immediately. The 12 November bill of lading showed the containers on board the *Lisa Marie* to be numbered 440001–440050. Although every container bears its own serial number, because they are constantly on the move around the world – each one carrying different cargoes to different ports – finding 50 consecutive numbers like that on one ship is as unlikely as finding 50 cars in a traffic jam with consecutively numbered license plates.

In fact, unlikely is an understatement. Fifty consecutively numbered containers on one ship is a virtual impossibility.

Ellen knew that and reported as much. The Dutch police were informed. And they raided McMillan's meeting.

The Scotsman's excuse was that he was acting only as an agent. He swore that he firmly believed the cargo existed and reminded the police that he'd even put his own cash where his mouth was, having paid for two containers. He said, if you don't believe me, ask David Wilson.

McMillan was held until a Dutch magistrate could question Wilson in the UK – the date of that meeting was 3 March 1992 – and, after listening to what Wilson had to say, McMillan was released the following day.

When Wilson heard of McMillan's arrest, he demanded to know where the ship was. So did Wilson's Norwegian backer. Portillo tried to reassure them, explaining how, at the last minute, he'd decided that the ship was not coming to Europe first, but had been diverted to Hong Kong to deliver cigarettes there. Bizarrely, Portillo tried to make Wilson and the Norwegian believe that, instead of going through the Panama Canal and into the Pacific, the *Lisa Marie* was taking the long way, via South Africa and the Cape of Good Hope.

Because he wanted to believe, Wilson might well have believed. But then he received a distraught phone call from the *Lisa Marie*'s captain. When he couldn't reach Portillo through the answering service in New York, the captain phoned Wilson to say something about the ship taking salt water into the engine's cooling system and having had to limp into Puerto Cabello, Venezuela, for repairs.

In a total panic, Wilson and the Norwegian jumped on a plane and flew to South America. They found the *Lisa Marie* there, sure enough, with 50 containers securely strapped down onto her decks. But when the two men ordered the crew to open the containers, all 50 were empty.

Immediately, Wilson took steps to stop the ship from leaving Puerto Cabello and also – significantly – to notify his clients that the whole thing was a scam. By mid-February 1992, certain people were getting the distinct impression that David Wilson had deliberately set out to ruin Hector Portillo's deal.

Three weeks later, on the night of 5 March, two men – their faces shielded with ski masks – forced their way into David Wilson's house, tied his hands behind his back, marched him into his garage and, at point-blank range, shot him twice in the head.

There were a lot of things that David Wilson didn't know when he arrived in Venezuela looking for the *Lisa Marie*.

He didn't know that Puerto Cabello is one of the main drug transit ports for Colombian cocaine.

He didn't know that numerous police authorities around the world had begun to collect some evidence which suggests that Portillo had Colombian drug contacts.

He didn't know that Portillo had already written him off.

To hedge his bets, Portillo had bought a second ship – the *Wei River* – planning to work the same swindle without Wilson. Among his new clients was a buyer in Greece who'd agreed to purchase five containers for just under $1 million. Portillo forwarded the necessary paperwork to assure him that the shipment had been loaded on board the *Wei River* in Houston and that she was expected to sail to Holland on 24 February. In fact the *Wei River* was still in a Houston dry dock.

Then Portillo began thinking that if all this worked so brilliantly with two ships, he could make it work half again as brilliantly with a third ship. So he got hold of one called the *Infanta* and now supplied his agents – who in turn supplied their punters – with identical paperwork for identical cargoes on both ships.

Before long, he was also using the names of six other ships – six ships he knew nothing about, almost as if he'd picked them out of a hat – forging documents to prove that the promised cargoes were loaded and on the way.

With tens of millions of dollars at stake, Portillo had no intention of allowing anyone to get in his way. Wilson would be dealt with. As for the police, Portillo was boldly confident that there was no real international cooperation among the various law enforcement agencies, which might otherwise put him out of business. And in that assumption, he was fundamentally correct. It would take months before the numerous authorities in Europe and the United States – all of which had been alerted at some point to Portillo's scam – started comparing notes. And, even then, some of those authorities were not willing to share everything with the others.

But in the long run, Portillo obviously knew, this hustle – like real Marlboros – also had a sell-by date. He could fend off the growing league of disappointed customers – and much-hassled agents – only for so long. His excuses – and invariably his luck – would eventually run out.

One agent in California moved $1.6 million worth of Portillo's phantom cargo to a businessman in Hong Kong. A month later, when the cigarettes hadn't arrived, the man in Hong Kong refused to be placated any further and changed the tone of his complaints from mild to very angry. Luckily for Portillo, the California middleman was skilful enough to switch gears, turn the anger around and sell the man another $800,000 worth.

Around the same time, a second punter took all the documents given him by an agent to his bank to secure a letter of credit. The bank studied the papers and pointed out a whopping 40 errors, leading them to conclude, beyond any doubt, that this was a hoax. The client didn't want to know. The bank's officers spoke to him until they were blue in the face. But he insisted they pay out. And they did.

To avoid his day of reckoning, Portillo resolved to cover himself with the perfect excuse – a sinking ship. And there is every reason to believe he planned to sacrifice the *Lisa Marie*.

One theory is that the 50 empty containers he'd taken to Puerto Cabello were to be filled there with drugs – or arms – which he intended to off-load on the high seas somewhere off the coast of South Africa. As soon as the containers were empty again, he'd scuttle the ship.

With his profits from the cigarette fraud, the money he could raise on the drugs and/or the arms, plus the ship's insurance, it's reasonable to expect that he could live in the lap of luxury for the rest of his life. At that point, because Hector Portillo didn't really exist, the Mexican Colonel could disappear into thin air. Either that or a resurrection in another guise – another cousin of some *presidente* – could rise from the ashes for the next hustle.

Whatever his plans, he might have gotten away with everything had David Wilson not been murdered.

In an earlier guise, Hector Portillo – this time as Michael Smith Austin – is said to have had dealings with the Pentagon. Word has it – according to those sources who are usually referred to as 'well informed' – that he'd once tried to arrange a defence contract as a supplier in the aerospace industry.

Later, as Portillo-unmasked, Austin made claims to the FBI that he had – and still has – connections with the CIA.

Not surprisingly, neither the Pentagon nor the CIA publicly admit to knowing him.

However, as he tells the story, the markers he holds with the CIA are as a result of the minor role he played – this time under the banner of Colonel Rodriguez, a Nicaraguan army officer – in the Iran–Contra affair.

In fact, there was a Colonel Rodriguez listed under the Nicaraguan column of Iran–Contra, as revealed by the US Senate Hearings. And sure enough, during a television programme in the States about Iran–Contra, a man claiming to be the aforementioned Colonel Rodriguez was dredged up for the cameras. He didn't look anything like Portillo, but that doesn't necessarily mean anything. The man on camera may or may not have been the real Colonel Rodriguez. It is known, though, that when Portillo – as Colonel Gomez – got arrested in the Dominican Republic in 1988, he confessed to fraud and to dealing in forged passports, among other things. It is, therefore, reasonable to expect that he would have been charged and brought to trial. It is equally reasonable to expect that, after pleading guilty, he would have been sentenced to prison in the Dominican Republic.

Except, at the very last minute, the Dominican authorities set him free.

The official reason was that he'd been released 'by instructions of the judiciary.' But no one is quite sure what that means. And the judiciary never offered any explanations. Portillo says he bribed someone $1 million to get him out of Santo Domingo. At other times, though, he says that his friends in high places – unnamed American authorities – arranged his release as a thank you for his help in Iran–Contra.

If, in fact, he does have some connection with the CIA – and the more you know about them the more you realize that anything is possible, especially the most unlikely affiliations – it didn't help him this time. The Lancashire police opened an incident room into David Wilson's murder on the morning of 6 March and, as the investigation became more complex, more officers were called in to help. At one point – and for a period of nearly six months – there were over 100 officers working full time on the case.

On 15 July, some 17 weeks after David Wilson was assassinated, Hector Portillo was arrested in New York on his way to pay $3.2 million in cash for an apartment in Trump Towers. He was charged with murder and ultimately extradited to Britain. His trial took seven weeks, but the jury only needed two hours. In February 1995, they convicted Portillo of first degree murder and sent him to gaol, without the possibility of parole, for the rest of his life. He appealed the conviction and was granted a new hearing. In February 1997, an appeals' court upheld that decision. Two months later, in Liverpool Crown Court, Stephen Playle and Michael Crossley – the contract killers who'd assassinated Wilson – were convicted of his murder and, like Portillo, caged for life.

Unfortunately, the tragedy of this story did not end there.

On the day before Portillo's appeal was rejected, Barbara Wilson fell ill and passed away. She'd suffered the extreme stress of the case but, sadly, did not live to see that justice was, in fact, done.

The Marlboro cigarette scam could have been worth hundreds of millions of dollars.

There are some suggestions that each of the 100 containers Portillo claimed to have on offer might have been sold as many as five times. His agents had, after all, lined up customers in Bulgaria, Poland, Italy, Denmark, the United States, Hong Kong, Austria, Sweden, Greece, Russia – including a customer claiming to represent the Russian Army – the United Arab Emirates, China, Holland, the UK, Germany, Belgium, France, Australia, Singapore, Jamaica and Bermuda.

To handle all the money pouring in, Wilson – in the

name of Alamosa Ltd – had opened bank accounts in several countries. He'd moved money through Switzerland, Belgium, Holland, Luxembourg, Germany and Britain. The largest account was at the Bank of Greece in Rotterdam. But the most active account was in the name of a holding company registered in St Kitts, which was placed with Credit Suisse in Zurich. That's where the bulk of the money eventually went.

Three weeks before the murder – at precisely the same time that David Wilson set out to queer Portillo's racket – Portillo set into motion steps to get the money out of Switzerland. In particular, he contacted, negotiated with and then engaged a professional money laundering service operating out of the UK.

For a fee, this bunch will reliably move any amount of money in any direction for anyone who employs them. They run a full-service underground banking facility, dealing in all aspects of money laundering, in addition to providing a host of affiliated functions, such as false passports, forged documentation, smuggling, drug trafficking and arms dealing.

And their track record is impressive. It is known, for example, that some years ago members of this group sold $6 million worth of arms to Sierra Leone, the government of which subsequently fell to a coup. The shipment was, therefore, never delivered. The money for the guns, minus expenses, was returned to an official whose death was subsequently reported in the papers. That same official has since turned up in Europe, living on the arms money.

There is good reason to believe that Portillo had secured this group's help in whatever his proposed drugs/arms deal was in Puerto Cabello and engaged their help with whatever plans he might have had to sink his ships.

It is known that within a day or two of David Wilson's

flight to Venezuela, Portillo asked someone to arrange overnight accommodation in Zurich for seven to nine people.

It is also known that those same seven to nine people travelled from Zurich to New York and that at least three of them arrived on the same flight. When they walked into the cavernous International Arrivals Hall at JFK, they deliberately got onto three different lines at US Customs. As they are legally required to do by American law, all three affirmed that they were bringing cash into the country. The proper forms were filled out and, because the only restriction on anyone bringing more than $10,000 into the US is that the money be declared, once they did that, all three were permitted to go about their business.

Together the three declared a total of $700,000. But at no point did anyone at US Customs at Kennedy Airport notice that three large cash declarations had been made off the same flight. In fact, it was only when the British authorities asked US Customs for certain records that the Americans were made aware of this delivery.

However, bringing cash from Zurich to New York is not what makes this a money laundering story.

There is a neat twist in the tail.

No one knows for certain how much money Portillo ever got his hands on. Only a relatively small amount of money has turned up. If he did make tens of millions of dollars, no one has yet been able to find it. At least, according to the US authorities, Portillo – or, Austin né Sporn – didn't live like a man with tens of millions of dollars. Yet four unrelated sources have confirmed that, at one point, the main Credit Suisse account contained $80–90 million.

Some people close to the case doubt the account ever held that much. The total amount officially claimed as lost – by those people who have come forward and filed statements with the police – amounts to only $20 million. Several people close to the case are convinced there was more.

So the question is, how much was there and what happened to it?

Consider the fact that the discrepancy between the amount of money four people say there was and the amount of money that is admitted to have been lost stems entirely from one simple premise – that many of the people involved with this matter can't come forward because they have no way of legally accounting for what they put into the deal.

That is a common phenomenon in con games.

It is also a constant in money laundering.

And the suggestion here is that Portillo was working both. He was conning some people while offering others – certain, very specific people – a way to wash substantial amounts of dirty money.

This wasn't merely a sting that turned sour because of a murder; it was a gigantic and adroitly managed money laundering operation – a major sink purpose-built to accommodate major players.

Portillo stole what he could from the punters and washed what he could for his heavyweight clients, bringing their money out the other end of the cycle in some, as yet, undefined form – perhaps as genuine cigarettes that he purchased in the parallel market, perhaps as a phony insurance payment on the non-existent cargo or perhaps simply by having moved it from one numbered account to another.

If it was just a scam, then where is the money?

But if you also see it as a phenomenally well thought out money laundering operation, then that explains why no one has ever found the missing $20–90 million.

Nor is anyone ever likely to.

CHAPTER SEVEN

Sorting out the Sinks

'It's not our business to inquire into our clients' morals.'
Banker in Hong Kong

Ready-made companies, registered in places that many people have never heard of, can be bought from formation agents, who sell them the same way that Safeway sells baked beans.

A stock is always available for purchase 'off the shelf'. Ownership is shifted in the time it takes to fill out a form. And for the convenience of their customers – again, just like Safeway – most company formation agents these days happily accept credit cards.

Legally speaking, a company is a separate entity, recognized by statute, for the purpose of carrying out certain objectives, which are often, but not exclusively, the running of a business. Other objectives might include owning assets, entering into contracts and incurring liabilities. A limited company is one where those liabilities are assumed by the company and not passed along to the management, shareholders or beneficial owners.

Although every company must have a registered office, that is not necessarily the place where the company trades.

Instead, it is the required address for the service of writs, notices and other legal communications.

Every company must also list the names of its directors. But directors do not have to be shareholders. In many cases, they are merely residents of the offshore jurisdiction, who are paid a fee for putting a brass plaque with the company name on their door and for filing the company's annual report. Directors do not necessarily know who beneficially owns the company. As shares in companies can, at times, be issued in 'bearer' form, it's the person who holds the share certificates who therefore owns the company.

When forming a company, authorized capital is declared. That's the nominal value of the shares, multiplied by the number of the shares the company is permitted to issue, in keeping with its own Memorandum of Association. In other words, a company can authorize itself to issue one million shares at a nominal value of $10 each, and thereby claim that the authorized share capital of the company is $10 million. It looks impressive on the bottom of the company letterhead but is otherwise meaningless. A company boasting $10 million of authorized capital might have issued only a couple of shares for a total amount of $2.

Off-the-shelf companies can come with names that are totally innocuous, like Acme Trading and Ajax Holdings, or have an ever-so-slightly familiar ring: Kingfisher International, a non-resident Irish company, is not necessarily associated in any way with the UK-based Kingfisher PLC, which owns the British Woolworth stores; Casenove de Vries Financial Brokers of Panama are not necessarily associated in any way with the international stockbrokers Cazenove; nor is Hilton Construction Inc. of Delaware necessarily associated in any way with the hotel chain of the same name. Of course, no one who understands the word libel would dare to suggest that such similarity was anything but coincidental on the part of the ready-made companies.

Then too, a 'trading company' need not trade, a 'finance company' need not have anything to do with finance, a 'holding company' need not be holding anything. The London–New York Financial Exchange SA, registered in the British Virgin Islands, does not necessarily have anything to do with a financial market operating between London and New York; Piccadilly Properties Ltd (Delaware) does not necessarily have anything to do with real estate in central London; nor does Palm Beach Management Inc. (Panama) necessarily have anything to do with anyone in Florida. The letters 'RE' on the end of an offshore company name do not automatically mean it is in the reinsurance business; the words 'fund management' do not automatically mean the company is a fund manager; nor do the words 'trust company' automatically mean the company is a bank.

Ready-made companies are often synonymous with the term 'tax haven.' Scattered around the world, there are about 50 established and operating tax havens – onshore and offshore – from Liechtenstein, Luxembourg and Monaco in Europe, half way around the globe to Nauru and Vanuatu, lost in the middle of the Pacific Ocean.

For many Europeans – especially the British – offshore tax haven usually translates to mean the nearby Channel Islands of Jersey and Guernsey, and the Isle of Man in the Irish Sea. Dependencies of the Crown, the territories are locally governed according to their own constitutions. Banks are domestically regulated, off-the-shelf companies are cheap, and nominee directors readily available.

The islands' authorities are proud to say that money laundering laws have been tightened over the past few years and that, even if they were once famous for providing laundrymen with sinks, no washing is done there anymore. What they really mean is, anyone arriving with a suitcase filled with cash will have to satisfy his banker that the money isn't of suspicious origins.

It's true that on the Isle of Man banks are now required to report all cash deposits of more than £25,000. And while the Financial Supervision Commission may not take any direct action, it does note the transaction in its files. Bank communication with the FSC is supposed to be confidential, but as the Manx authorities are so jumpy about money laundering – especially with all of the drug trade implications – they have been known to compare notes with the UK authorities.

Of course, they still sell bearer share companies and formation agents there provide nominee directors, and it's fair to say that any nominee director who wires money in and out of offshore banks on the instructions of someone he has never met might be aiding and abetting a laundryman. It matters only to a judge whether or not someone does it wittingly. There is sufficient evidence in recent cases to say that plenty of money comes through these jurisdictions at some point in the washing cycle. The Isle of Man and the Channel Islands have long been used by people wanting to wash funds. After it had been revealed that 'Baby Doc' Duvalier's money had been hidden there, Jersey authorities shrugged and wondered, had anyone actually broken any laws? In the UK, money laundering statutes then in effect applied only to drug or terrorist money. Besides that, they insisted, there were no laws that they're aware of which prohibit the movement of money from one jurisdiction to another, even if the sole motive for moving that money is to keep it out of the hands of a third party. They're keen to emphasize that they don't want laundrymen as clients. But, in the end, they're forced to admit that there's no sure way of telling who's laundering what for whom.

You get much the same response in next door Guernsey. We don't want that sort of business, they reiterate, and go so far as to wince at the term 'offshore.' It seems they're trying to clean up their image with the shinier designation, 'finance centre.'

Whatever, over 14,000 limited companies are registered there – more than ten times the per capita equivalent of the UK. But, unlike the UK, the only information Guernsey authorities supply about a company is the names of directors and shareholders. They do not furnish annual accounts. Nor do they release the names of the beneficial owners.

Clearly they must be doing something right, as banks on an island once famous for nothing more than a breed of cows currently sit on assets of £27 billion.

With stakes running into those kinds of sums, no one has to remind local legislators that, if they even so much as hinted at tightening up the regulations, every tuppence on the island would fast wind its way to Jersey.

Of course, they think the same way in Jersey. And they think the same way on the Isle of Man. All three vehemently deny any assertion that their local economy is that much better for the presence of a laundromat. But then, one man's sink is another man's full-service financial institution.

The Principality of Monaco came under a great deal of criticism for allowing money launderers to use the local banking system. A French parliamentary report concluded that the Mafia's presence in France was steadily growing and singled out Monaco as a major European sink. They said that its proximity to Italy – only 20 minutes from the border which since January 1993 is wide open – together with its secret banking system and the presence of casino gambling had combined to give the Mafia a unique opportunity to launder funds through real estate, golf courses and gambling.

A French newspaper then accused the casino at Monte Carlo of being a prime launderette for Italian crime gangs. The Societé des Bains de Mer, the company who runs the casino, instantly denied the charges. But Prince Rainier III openly admitted that an inquiry into the SBM was already under way.

Having very little patience for such charges the Prince, who has always taken a strict no nonsense approach to crime in his country, insisted that measures be taken to crack down on money laundering. He moved to tighten legislation which obliged banks, insurance companies and stockbrokers to report suspicious transactions, and to disclose the identity of those involved. In line with French law, he required the casino's management to report payments for chips that were suspected to come from drug trafficking or organized crime and set stiff prison sentences for anyone using illegal gains to buy property. He agreed that the Principality would work with the French police where drug money laundering was involved, but drew the line on how much information could be passed along by explicitly forbidding any financial information being handed on to French tax authorities. It gets back to not killing the goose. There are, reportedly, in excess of $13 billion on deposit in 40 banks in Monaco, a country with a population of just 30,000.

As Monaco tightened its rules, real estate began to boom in the tiny Republic of San Marino, hidden inside Italy, where banking is completely secret, almost exactly the way Switzerland was years ago.

Towards the end of February 1993, police in Colombia announced that they'd seized $5.9 million and arrested 250 people during a 15-month crackdown on drug trafficking and money laundering. The money is a mere drop in the bucket and the arrests, while perhaps significant in number, didn't touch any of the major players in either of the cartels. However, by getting inside 900 accounts at the nation's five largest banks, the authorities were able to trace cartel money through fictitious import/export companies and exchange houses in 16 countries. Significant among them were the former Yugoslavia, Pakistan, Russia, Czechoslovakia, Hungary and Bulgaria.

Private banking still operates in what used to be Yugoslavia, offering incredibly high interest rates – 10–15 per cent per month – way out of line with the rest of Europe. One of those banks, Jugoskandic, is estimated to have four million savings accounts, with a total of $2 billion in hard currency. Paying that kind of interest on that kind of money is an expensive proposition. While this is not to suggest that Jugoskandic is in any way involved with anything illegal, there are private banks in the region that are known to be using hard currency deposits – at the behest of the Socialist regime – to do drug deals which in turn pay for weapons to finance the civil war. The money is washed through Austrian shell companies. The game is called 'triangular trade.' The shell company buys a product – in this case arms – from Hungary or Bulgaria, for delivery in Montenegro or Serbia. Disguised as a legal business deal and protected by strict banking secrecy, the Austrian authorities have no way of knowing that someone is breaking UN sanctions.

Recently, the Panamanian government admitted that arms traffickers operating out of the Czech Republic had attempted to furnish the Bosnians with $21 million worth of weapons – 26,800 machine guns, 128,000 magazines, 5,000 pistols and 17 million bullets -- using Panama as the third side of their triangle. In this case the weapons never got shipped. The traffickers were unlucky. But the route through which the money was being washed carbon copies a whole series of deals that are known to have been successfully concluded.

As long as there are third party countries willing to wash funds, the unsuccessful deal will remain the exception.

In Pakistan, for example, banks happily accept large cash deposits. When foreign exchange controls were removed in 1991 – permitting banks to offer accounts in foreign currencies – a presidential decree guaranteed banking secrecy on an unprecedented scale. The central bank even instructed Pakistan's bankers not to ask any questions about the origin of foreign cash deposits. Since then, literally billions of dollars have flooded into the country.

The situation is further exacerbated by the fact that Pakistan is the most fecund part of the 'Golden Crescent' – the opium poppy region that stretches from Pakistan, through Afghanistan and into Iran. Nearly 70 per cent of the world's highest-grade heroin moves into Europe from Pakistan.

It turns out that opium poppy has been the main crop for the people of the Mahaban Mountains along Pakistan's North-West Frontier Province since the nineteenth century, when British colonials planted it there because they could legally export the drug. It is an ideally suited location – with thin soil, steep slopes and optimum rainfall – and the people of Pushton have a long placed high value on land ownership. Furthermore, there are very few opportunities for non-agricultural incomes.

Drug traffickers in the nearby village of Gandaf – Pakistan's version of Medellin – have little trouble encouraging the peasants to devote their tiny plots to opium poppy as it nets those farmers more than ten times per acre what they could otherwise expect with tobacco or fruit.

By growing the raw materials, providing the laboratories to refine them and offering banking facilities for the traffickers, Pakistan is on the verge of becoming the most dangerous power in an already unstable part of the world.

But it has been the breakdown of draconian control, coupled with food shortages, hyper-inflation and the resulting general despair, that has led to a massive increase in all kinds of law breaking in the former Communist bloc.

Hard currency is seen by the people as the only antidote for their understandably pessimistic view of the future. It's not simply the passport to the black markets, it's the key to the world's free markets. And here is one instance when Gresham's Law proves wrong. In this case, good money has driven out bad. Throughout the former Communist world, local currencies are worthless. No one wants roubles, korunas, forints, lev or zlotys. So, to get dollars, Eastern Europe has turned itself into one giant sink.

The Czech government in Prague, for instance, chartered a record 150 new banks in 1990. Most, if not all, were nothing more than brass plaques on an office wall. And there is no fraud squad.

Poland is an even better example. Publicly, the Poles are trying to turn themselves into the Spain of Eastern Europe – offering western manufacturers a large, inexpensive workforce with an economic infrastructure relying on manufacturing and farming. Privately, the Poles are desperate for hard currency and have gone into money laundering in a big way.

Poland today is a country where businessmen walk around carrying suitcases filled with cash. It's a country where credit cards and cheques are still extremely rare. It's a country that enjoys a relatively stable political environment, where the national currency is convertible, and where an infrastructure exists for transferring money abroad. It is, at the same time, a nation hindered by an obsolete financial system – it is estimated that as much as one-third of all business is conducted through the alternate economy – where banks haven't yet learned how to cooperate, where bankers are inexperienced and naive, and where financial law enforcement is impotent.

In short, Poland today is a laundryman's wish come true.

According to the weekly newspaper *Polityka*, many of Poland's most important financial institutions happily open their doors to laundrymen because they lack capital, are unable to collect on bad debts and find this the surest route to solvency. The banks have welcomed the Colombian drug cartels. They've welcomed the Turkish drug barons. And they've welcomed the Palestine Liberation Organization. A few years ago, £50 million of PLO funds were deposited in the Bank of Warsaw and have not been seen since.

Under Lech Walesa, the government tried to put a stop to it, and in 1992 passed a law requiring banks to register the identity of all customers depositing more than $12,500. Chides one Warsaw banker, 'They might as well have asked the entire population to whistle Paderewski.'

Hungary is just as bad, if not worse, because it has been at it longer. Bank secrecy is iron-clad, without any way for anyone to obtain any information, under any condition whatsoever.

And then there is Bulgaria.

When the government in Sofia announced that it would sell off 1,600 previously state owned industries, it explained that, unlike similar sales in other former Communist countries, they would not be accepting scrip or vouchers, they would be selling everything for cash. Informed by European and American advisers that such a sell-off would be a field day for money launderers, the Bulgarians said they would prevent anyone from doing that by asking all investors to declare the origin of their funds – as if a Colombian drug dealer would admit that he was buying Balkan Airlines with $50 million worth of crack receipts!

For the record, the Bulgarians were one of the first Eastern bloc countries to comprehend the advantages of money laundering. Under the regime of Todor Zhivkov – he ruled for 35 years, from 1954 to 1989 – the government dealt drugs, washed the profits through shell companies that had access to Swiss banks, and then used that money to finance a major international illicit arms business.

Zhivkov's trading outlet was the state-owned import–export company, Kintex. Set up in 1968, it was operated exclusively by the KDS, the Bulgarian Security Service. It sold heroin and morphine base to Turkish drug traffickers – important suppliers to the lucrative Western European market – and with that money was able to build up its gun running. Kintex became so adept at converting drugs into weapons that it furnished the Nigerians with guns to put down the Biafra civil war in the 1960s; it furnished various Christian militias with guns to escalate the civil war in Lebanon in 1975; it furnished South Africa with guns in direct violation of various embargoes; and, for more than 20 years, it was the primary outfitter of guns to the PLO. For their efforts, the Bulgarians reputedly earned up to $2 billion a year in much-needed hard currency.

The extent of Kintex's connections with organized crime in the west came to light only in the early 1980s. Italian police raided a Mafia drug refinery in Trapani Province, on the western tip of Sicily, and uncovered a laboratory that, to their surprise, was stocked with Bulgarian machinery and Bulgarian-supplied morphine base. This one lab alone was capable of producing a staggering 4.5 tons of refined heroin per year. At wholesale prices, in those days, that represented $1.125 billion. Over the next few years, no fewer than 15 refineries were uncovered in Sicily and on the Italian mainland, most of them with Bulgarian supplies.

By this time, the CIA had also compiled evidence to prove Kintex's role in international drug trafficking. When the Reagan administration formally protested, Zhivkov – largely to placate the Americans – cracked down on every amateur drug dealer in the country. Tons of marijuana were seized and assurances were given that the business had been ended. But Kintex continued to trade.

Five years later, as a result of continued American protests, Kintex finally became too much of an embarrassment. So, for all intents and purposes, Zhivkov put Kintex out of business. In its place he installed son-of-Kintex, a state-owned import–export company called Globus. So the KDS was still in charge. And its primary mission was still drug trafficking, arms dealing and money laundering. In effect, the only change was the company stationery.

Enter here, the Shakarchi Trading Company.

The founding father, Mamoud Shakarchi, was a highly successful Lebanese banker who, to save himself, his family and his business interests from the civil war in his homeland, moved to Switzerland and established Shakarco, an import–export company. Both his sons, Mohamed and Marwan, soon joined him in business. In 1980, Mamoud split the company in two. Marwan kept the name Shakarco, while Mohamed called his half the Shakarchi Trading Company.

According to several sources, until his death in 1985 Shakarchi Sr was known in some circles as 'Le Blanchisseur' – the laundryman. He had in fact, been under investigation by various authorities – US and European – who'd suspected him of washing Kintex/Globus funds from Turkey, including Sicilian drug money, through Switzerland and into Bulgaria. But Mamoud Shakarchi always denied any involvement. Later, when American and Swiss investigators followed the offshoots of a huge Los Angeles money laundering operation to Europe, and the trail led to the Shakarchi Trading Company, the suspicions that had haunted Mamoud Shakarchi were levelled at Mohamed. The question was, had he simply taken over the family laundromat? Like father like son, he too denied the allegations. But his was a difficult case to maintain.

In February 1987, Swiss police seized 100 kilos of Turkish heroin that had direct links with the Sicilian Mafia. The police were able to establish that the money for this heroin was coming into Switzerland from Bulgaria and being washed through the Shakarchi Trading Company. At least 1.3 billion Swiss francs – just under $1 billion – had been washed through 31 separate deposits into the Shakarchi Trading Company's account with Union Banque Suisse in Lugano.

Mohamed Shakarchi continued to renounce any knowledge of the affair. As the pressure on him mounted, he finally got to the point where he acknowledged that the family had indeed at times laundered money, but only for the CIA.

According to him, over a seven-year period – from 1981 to 1988 – a CIA front company called Argin Corporation had washed $25 million through the Shakarchi offices, to buttress the Mujaheddin rebels in Afghanistan in their fight against the Soviets.

Mohamed's boast was met with continued denials by the CIA.

That is, until 1989 when the American Ambassador in Switzerland issued a terse press release substantiating Shakarchi's relationship with the agency.

That same year, the US State Department went public with its wrath, damning three of the world's banking centres for having sold out.

Under the heading of the *International Narcotics Control Strategy Report*, the Bush administration named the Bahamas as the major transit country for cocaine and marijuana entering the United States, and condemned it for having allowed itself to become such an important money laundering centre. It named Hong Kong as the money laundering heart of the Pacific Rim, and condemned it for having become the major transit centre of Southeast Asian heroin. And it named Panama for continuing to be the principal money laundering haven for the South American cocaine trade.

That report made the papers.

A more revealing document, which didn't, was circulated around the US Drug Enforcement Agency. Specifically not for public release, this greatly widened the picture, singling out 18 'major conduits and repositories' for illicit drug funds. The list of the world's greatest sinks consisted of Hong Kong, Liechtenstein, Luxembourg, the Channel Islands, Andorra, Switzerland, Singapore, the United Arab Emirates, the Cayman Islands, Mexico and Panama. Four American cities were also named: New York, Los Angeles, Miami and Houston. And then the DEA pointed an accusing finger north – at Montreal, Toronto and Vancouver.

Hong Kong is an obvious nominee.

Ever since the mainland territory and offshore islands that are Hong Kong were ceded to Britain as retribution after the Opium War of 1842, the former Crown Colony has been one of the world's major trading and smuggling ports.

Today, it is a designer money centre, born out of jet travel, electronic communications and the mystique of the East. It's a gold market and a diamond market and a stock market that looks more like Las Vegas than Wall Street. It's a Portobello Road for shell companies – a formation agents' paradise where nominee directors forsake wallpaper for brass plaques. Arms smugglers, black marketeers and organized gangs have always used Hong Kong to wash their funds. So have the Chinese, since Mao's Great March.

But Hong Kong had never seen anything like the kind of action the heroin traffickers brought to town. When Law Kin-man, one of the world's most successful laundrymen, pleaded guilty in the US in 1994 to a host of federal charges, he confessed to using 362 bogus bank accounts in Hong Kong to wash an estimated $93 million of Golden Triangle drugs through the territory. A further eight in the States were private brokerage accounts so that he could wash funds through the Hong Kong stock market. Just as banking secrecy laws tightened and Hong Kong's regulatory infrastructure loosened, the drug trade exploded, creating an unprecedented level of prosperity. Banks were awash in liquidity.

The place was Disneyland with dim sum!

The bubble might easily have burst the day the British agreed to return Hong Kong to the Chinese. And some people contend that it did. The money men in Hong Kong took fright. No one knew what the world would look like 15 years down the line; 1997 seemed uncomfortably close. Capital headed west, in haste, most of it finding its way into the US and Canadian real estate markets. Over the next few years the situation worsened. People with money bought their way out. People without money tried selling what they had to raise a ransom. Prices hit rock bottom.

And that's when the law of supply and demand changed gears.

Having moved into the Colony to cater to people wishing to get their money out, western banks had inadvertently established the infrastructure that would now give birth to a second coming. With prices way down and black money still readily available, business opportunities appeared. Beijing made enough of the right noises to encourage western bankers that business under the Communists would be as glorious as it was under the capitalists. So those western bankers revised their view of 1997. They suddenly decided they were in the right place at the right time, and that it was indeed time to gamble on a prosperous future. Now, as native money poured out, foreign money – encouraged by those banks – poured in. The Hong Kong that rose from the ashes of the 1982 crash is today the world's third financial centre, after New York and London. Shell companies generally cost less than they do in Europe or the Caribbean. Bankers are supposed to ask questions, but tend not to bother. Why should they? The territory is crammed with more than 400 banks. It's clear that this is a buyer's market, so much so that the volume of small-denomination American bank notes circulating around Hong Kong today far exceeds the total volume of all currency transactions within any single European country.

It's true that the 'crash' of 1998 sent tidalwaves of doubt through all the Asian markets, hitting Hong Kong with particular ferocity. It is equally true that in the years leading up to the shift from British control to Chinese control, offshore money in Hong Kong slowly began to drift to Singapore and to the Caymans. But neither the crash nor Chinese control necessarily mean that those monies aren't being managed from Hong Kong. It simply means that the corporations and the bank accounts are somewhere else.

And that's a typical scenario in the offshore world.

You can be anywhere, use accounts from any jurisdiction, do anything you want, mix them, match them, and never have to worry too much about any authority catching up with you because the entire process is merely a figment of someone's imagination, translated into computer code on a hard drive somewhere else.

Just across the Pearl River delta is Hong Kong's little bad brother, the Portuguese colony of Macao. And this is what Las Vegas would have looked like had Genghis Khan beaten Columbus to the New World.

Nearly 80 per cent of Macao's annual revenue comes from the $1 billion a year, Hong Kong controlled, gambling monopoly – through which hundreds of millions of dollars are washed every year. Not only do the Chinese gangs have a marked presence in Macao, but the government of North Korea maintains a consular office there, brazenly taking advantage of the colony's easy – and highly secretive – westernized banking system.

With Chinese rule set to return to Macao in 1999, little seems to be cooling down. The Portuguese have stipulated that banks in Macao must identify people involved with 'significant transactions,' and that 'involuntary involvement with money laundering or with any criminal activity must be carefully avoided.' But that's as far as they go. They don't want to upset the Chinese.

In fact, no one appears overly anxious to rock the Hong Kong/Macao boat – least of all the Chinese. They draw nearly half of their foreign currency earnings through Hong Kong. So the wheeling and dealing continue. Perhaps the idea is to hand the Chinese a pair of diamonds as big as the Ritz so that there won't be any question in their minds about what to do with them. As most of the money laundered through Hong Kong and Macao is foreign, it's clearly in everyone's interest to keep the coffers full because that reinforces the case for maintaining the status quo. With so much money riding on the future, it's easy to see why the laundrymen are concerned with political stability – why they want to insure that the Chinese won't do to them what Fidel Castro did to Meyer Lansky and his comrades in 1959.

CHAPTER EIGHT

Islands in the Sun

'We have no natural resources and we have to survive.'
Aruba's prime minister, Nelson Oduber

The fact that there is no Meyer Lansky Street running through the middle of downtown Nassau – or for that matter, through the heart of any capital on any other island in the Caribbean – has got to be one of the most arrogant oversights in history.

Lansky not only built the financial skeleton for postwar organized crime, he opened Caribbean eyes – wallets, safe deposit boxes and secret bank accounts – to the delights of tax havens. He helped show the island nations how to become the world's biggest collection of sinks.

Whether or not they'd ever openly admit to it, a huge debt of gratitude is outstanding.

The Caribbean is home to 31 million people, nearly two-thirds of whom natively speak Spanish. Another 20 per cent are French or Creole speaking. Separated by water, culture, history and politics, the region is anything but homogeneous. It is easier to reach Barbados from New York than it is from Curaçao. The most convenient schedule from Kingston, Jamaica, to Santo Domingo in the Dominican Republic is through Miami. One of the few characteristics most of the islands share is that they are generally considered to be in America's backyard. At the end of World War II, sugar was the region's main crop and the United States was the region's primary market. Since then, sugar exports to the US have steadily declined and so have earnings for oil and bauxite. But the islands are still America's backyard. The US remains the primary market. Except now the main product is narcotics.

It's no coincidence that a powerful Sicilian family – the Caruana–Cuntrera clan, who control organized crime in Venezuela – has been buying sizable tracts of real estate in the Caribbean. When Pasquale, Paolo and Gaspare Cuntrera were arrested at home in Caracas in September 1992 – on heroin trafficking charges that dated back ten years – they were deported to Italy. Known to have commanded a major international money laundering ring and believed to have been behind the 1992 assassinations of a Sicilian judge and prosecutor, they left behind an organization that is said to own two-thirds of all the land and two-thirds of all the businesses on Aruba – a resort island 45 miles west of Curaçao, just off the coast of Venezuela.

Aruba is also home to the La Costa cartel – said to be the world's third-largest cocaine smuggling group after the Cali and Medellin operations – who came to prominence when 16 of their ilk were charged in Miami with racketeering, drug conspiracy and money laundering. They had reputedly brought 80 tons of cocaine and 250,000 pounds of marijuana into the United States since 1980, generating an estimated $800 million in profits until the indictment against their chieftain, Randolph Habibe, in 1993. Habibe has also been charged with a failed attempt to free a fellow cartel member – José Rafael 'El Mono' Abello – currently serving a 30-year sentence for drug smuggling in Oklahoma. To emphasize the amount of money available to these groups, the escape plot as engineered by Habibe was budgeted at $20 million.

One reason places like Aruba are vulnerable to outfits like the Caruana–Cuntreras and La Costa is because small governments – local citizens going up against international crime syndicates – are ill equipped for the fight. Their tourist-based economies are largely cash intensive, almost as if they were consciously designed for people wanting to hide money. Families like the Caruana–Cuntreras had no trouble taking over a large chunk of the island through their control of casinos and hotels. And what the Caruana–Cuntreras and La Costa have done in Aruba, others have managed in Bonaire, Curaçao and Sint Maarten.

The larger, more important islands, which include Haiti, the Dominican Republic and Jamaica, have been turned into 'aircraft carriers' – that's the term they use at the DEA in Washington – because the gangs use them as staging points for their US-bound cocaine.

Although coca doesn't grow in the Caribbean, the ships and planes that bring it from Central America pass through there. So does the money generated by those drugs. Haiti, in particular, has been singled out by a confidential 1993 US Senate report, which named Port-au-Prince Police Chief, Lt. Col. Michel François – the second most powerful military man in the country – as personally handling in excess of $100 million in annual drug trafficking bribes. The three-page document, which was compiled from CIA files and witness accounts, notes that more than 1,000 Colombians are 'stationed' in Haiti, many of them under the direct authority of Fernando Burgos Martinez, a Colombian drug trafficker who's lived there openly since 1984. He's described as the resident manager and bag man who oversees transshipment of a ton or more of Colombian cartel cocaine each month. One estimate puts his annual turnover at $200 million. Another has it as high as $500 million.

His payments to government officials are to guarantee access to the Port-au-Prince airport. And the report quotes a man who once worked for Burgos Martinez as testifying, 'Haiti was our parking lot.'

In more touristed nations, like Jamaica, the authorities strongly object to being tarred by the same brush. Fearing the effect that could have on tourism, they insist that anyone saying the Caribbean is awash with drug money is wrong. Ironically, Jamaica is the only island with a substantial marijuana crop.

Until Castro came along, the Cubans were the entrepreneurs of the Caribbean. In many ways, they still are, although now they run business in the Dominican Republic, Puerto Rico and Miami – a city that is 40 per cent Cuban. Having lost a huge chunk of his foreign income to ideology, Castro has tried to make up for it by operating a freeport for drug shipments coming through the Gulf of Mexico on the way to the United States.

Reports of Cuban involvement in drug trafficking first came to American attention in 1960. But those reports were largely unsubstantiated. Ten years later, as tales of conspiracies grew, there was still no solid evidence to authenticate the claims. But in 1982, a US district court indicted four Cuban officials on charges of conspiring to smuggle drugs into the US, firmly documenting the fact that Castro has sold safe haven to the Colombian cartels for hard currency. The *Wall Street Journal* reported in 1984 that the Colombians were paying Castro as much as half a million dollars per shipment for the privilege of using Cuban territorial waters to avoid interdiction by the US Coast Guard and US Customs.

To contend with Cuban transshipment, the United States has increasingly put the burden on the shipping companies, which are, it must be said, often the innocent victims of the drug traffickers. When the Americans found marijuana on board an Evergreen Line freighter, they fined the German company $29 million. As a result, Evergreen stopped bringing goods from Jamaica to the States.

The possibility that Castro might be linked to cocaine trafficking hit the headlines again over the summer of 1989 when Cuban General Arnaldo Ochoa Sanchez – the third-ranking military man in the country after Fidel and his brother Raoul – was convicted on drugs charges.

Ochoa was put into the dock in a televised show trial, together with 13 senior officers and civil servants, publicly accused of drug dealing. They'd all made money in Angola – illegally bringing home gold, diamonds and ivory while serving with Cuba's African Expeditionary Force – which, the prosecution claimed, had then been invested in narcotics. Never stated was the fact that six of them – led by Ochoa – had invested some of their money in a failed plot to overthrow the Castro brothers. Those six were sentenced to death and summarily executed by a firing squad at the end of the trial.

Now American agents renewed their undercover contacts in Cuba.

And it took the better part of two years before they hit pay dirt.

The man they eventually coerced into providing them with proof positive was Cuban Army Major Luis Galeana. In October 1991, while his plane bound for Moscow was making a refueling stop in Madrid, Galeana defected into the arms of American DEA agents who were waiting for him just outside the Barajas Airport transit lounge. Within two days he was being heavily guarded in a Washington DC area safe house.

Assigned to Cuba's Interior Ministry, Galeana brought with him information – supported by half a dozen reels of microfilm – that documented two years' worth of Castro-sponsored cocaine shipments from Cuba to Texas and Louisiana.

Those were the same cargoes that Castro had tried to pin on Ochoa.

The Americans understood that, with the ending of Russian subsidies, Castro needed foreign trade to keep the Cuban economy from totally disintegrating. But his options were severely limited. So he turned to drugs – an obvious commodity for him – with its high markup, his Central and South American contacts and Cuba's proximity to the United States.

At the same time, he had been bartering what few nuclear secrets his Russian allies allowed him to know. Castro not only backed Saddam Hussein in the Gulf War but offered to aid Iran in its development of nuclear technology. Apparently he's also approached the Chinese and the North Koreans, proposing to help them develop their nuclear capacity in exchange for oil.

Advising Castro is the international financier, money launderer and fugitive, Robert Vesco.

Indicted for fraud, Vesco had absconded from the United States in 1972 with whatever remained of the $224 million he'd stolen from investors in Bernie Cornfeld's International Overseas Services. He went first to Costa Rica, then to the Bahamas, where he followed Meyer Lansky's lead and supported Lynden Pindling. When that contact turned sour, Vesco returned to Costa Rica. He wore out his welcome there and headed for Nicaragua.

In 1983 he turned up in Cuba, where he lives today in a beach house outside Havana, officially protected by the Interior Ministry. Myth has it that he paid Castro $1 billion to avoid extradition to the US. But people who know say the figure is hugely exaggerated as Vesco never had that kind of money.

Vesco sings for his supper as a consultant, helping the Cubans get around the American embargo on their goods, counselling Castro on how to run an international drug trafficking conglomerate and doing whatever miscellaneous drug trafficking and gun running he can, on the side, without being too obvious and therefore upsetting his hosts.

According to Galeana's debriefings in the United States – which clarified a number of matters, including Vesco's status – Castro is petrified by the indictment that the US authorities levied against General Noriega. Furthermore, he is furious that Carlos Lehder Rivas – the Colombian drug baron with whom he personally negotiated transshipment deals in 1987 – had been willing to testify against his former chums.

Until Galeana's defection, Castro could fall back on General Ochoa's confession that he and the others masterminded drug runs into the US, 'for our own personal gain and without the knowledge or approval of our superiors in the Cuban government.'

If anyone believed Ochoa's confessions at the time – and there couldn't have been many who did – Galeana's evidence has since changed their minds. He detailed the extensive use of Cuban territorial limits – of both water and air space – military refuelling and repair facilities, military radar cover and a prevalent reliance on military communications networks. He also outlined how the Cuban navy and air force played substantial roles.

Such a ploy would be categorically unthinkable in a dictatorship like Cuba without the express knowledge of either Fidel or brother Raoul – who is Cuba's Minister of Defence – or both of them.

Based on what Galeana revealed to his American handlers, a plan was drawn up to hasten Fidel's overthrow. It was suggested at high enough levels of the Bush administration that, by indicting Castro on drug trafficking and money laundering charges – exactly as they'd done against Noriega – then broadcasting those charges to Cuba, any high-ranking officers in Castro's army who lived in fear of their own lives after the Ochoa gang firing squads might suddenly spark a coup that could force Castro into exile.

In the end, the plan was rejected by the White House for reasons never stated.

It is the rule, rather than the exception, throughout the Caribbean, to hear politicians say that the drug problem is not one of supply as much as it is one of demand. And the biggest demand comes from the United States. Their concern is, therefore, that Caribbean economies are being destabilized by a situation – drug dependency in America – over which they have no control. In other words, their largest, most important neighbour, which has always been seen as the patron of Caribbean security, has now become the greatest threat to it.

But their argument falls flat when those same politicians have shown they are not willing to risk total isolation by dropping back to a safer position. They've replaced sugar with off-the-shelf bearer share companies, granting permission to operate in banking or insurance. They try to sweeten the pot by providing an abundant supply of nominee directors; banking and commercial secrecy; a free flow of currency; a modicum of political stability; and easy access – physically and electronically – with modern telephone systems, plenty of fax machines and airports offering regular services to North America and Europe.

From their point of view, survival is at stake.

A few years ago in the Bahamas, the Ministry of Finance set up the Financial Services Secretariat 'to identify and to encourage all types of investment and financial service opportunities.'

Put another way, the Bahamians are willing – for a fee – to provide the kinds of financial services required by people who want to hide money. Supporting those objectives in 1990, the legislature passed the International Business

Companies Act, which soon became known as 'the instant registration package.' In less than 24 hours, and for only $100, you can own a Bahamian company – including one with a legitimate-sounding European name, such as British Mercantile Financial Asset Management Holdings – whose assets can be nothing more than the bearer shares of some other off-the-shelf company, which in turn can control bank accounts anywhere in the world, through which money can pass like water down a funnel.

To prove the point, a phone call to a company agent in the Bahamas went – word for word – like this:

'I need to buy a company and would be grateful if this could be arranged as quickly and as discreetly as possible.'

'That is no problem, sir.'

'I've seen your list of names, you know, of available companies, but none of them suit my purposes.'

'These things are easily arranged. Once you buy a company, we can file to change the name of it to anything you want, as long as there is nothing currently registered with that name.'

'I was thinking of something along the lines of a commercial banking corporation.'

'That is not a problem.'

'Perhaps something like Manhattan County First Fiduciary Trust?'

'We will be delighted to look into that name, or any other you choose, and secure one for you that will suit your purposes.'

'Will you also be able to provide an introduction to a friendly banker who will accommodate whatever needs I have, including cash transactions?'

'Yes, of course.'

The response is hardly surprising, considering how the Caribbean is famously overpopulated with bankers who do not ask questions when large sums of cash are deposited.

They're supposed to. But what people are supposed to do and what some are willing to do in order to make a living are often two very different things.

That has never been more evident than a few years ago, when a branch office of an international bank opened its doors at the end of a runway on the Island of Anguilla. It has since been closed – this time it was a little too obvious, even for the Caribbean – but the shack, with the bank's name painted boldly on the front, did unabated business for several years, servicing private pilots who arrived on the island to make cash deposits before flying off again. This was drive-in banking Caribbean style, where no one even had to shut down his engines.

The ironic thing is that when you go to some of these offshore centres, you find that the island's government isn't solving the social problems of their people. There is some added employment – clerical staff and hotel clerks who might not otherwise have jobs – but you don't necessarily find real prosperity. The average citizen is dirt poor, the roads are a mess and communication is primitive. Offshore banking has not necessarily solved any of the island's real problems, although the people at the top – the government leaders who permit and protect it, and the wealthy expatriates who run it – are doing very well.

The bad guys no longer have to rob banks. They can buy them.

St Kitts and Nevis are a pair of tiny English-speaking islands in the Leewards, about 1,200 miles southeast of Miami. A popular stop on the cruise line circuit, the local economy has always thrived on tourism, sugar cane, cotton and pineapple. But the 44,000 residents of the two islands have, in recent years, come to understand that there is big money to be made by selling banks.

One of these ready-made financial institutions – as advertised by a Canadian firm in British Columbia – is an entity called the Keystone Bank Ltd. According to the prospectus, it is chartered in the 'tax free ecclesiastical sovereignty of the Dominion of Melchizedek.' Precisely where that is, the brochure doesn't say. Frankly, you'd think someone could have come up with a less suspect-sounding place. However, along with ownership of Keystone Bank Ltd. comes the Keystone Trust Company, which seems to be the main asset.

For just $15,000 – paid to the Canadian company – you can become the proud owner of a stack of official documents, suitable for framing, plus one brass plaque on the wall of a company formation agent somewhere in St Kitts.

As the bank is chartered in Nevis, no annual financial returns are required of the trust company. Directors, shareholders and principals may be of any nationality and may live anywhere. The value of the stock may be quoted in any company and bearer shares are permitted. A corporation may serve as a director and no shareholder meetings are necessarily required. The trust company can be merged with other corporations and administer the Keystone Bank Ltd.

In short, for $15,000, plus annual fees of £450 payable to the local government, you can run your own bank and put as much cash through the tills as you want to.

This is not simply a laundryman's fantasy, it's a recurring vision.

There are loads of formation agents hawking banks throughout the Caribbean. One of them, Jerome Schneider of the WFI Corporation in California, touts banks at seminars across the United States. His sales pitch hangs on the undeniable fact that investors 'wield power and influence' with their own private offshore bank. For under $10,000, he provides his clients with 'a fully chartered private international bank in the Caribbean, plus a management subsidiary corporation in the Bahamas, plus connection with a professional Bahamas Management service.'

Once Schneider has sold a bank to a client, that's the end of his involvement. WFI does not manage assets or perform any administrative services for the companies it sells. So when it turned out that a woman in Houston, Texas, named Daisy Johnson Butler had bought a company called European Overseas Bank Ltd from Schneider – this one was chartered in Grenada – and used it to defraud 60 investors of $1 million, Schneider could quite innocently raise his arms and say, this has nothing to do with me. In fact, he even claimed that when he heard about Butler's misuse of the bank he acted promptly to get the authorities on Grenada to revoke the bank's registration.

What Schneider does is roam the Caribbean, looking for island authorities who will sell him, in bulk, banking charters. In 17 years, it's estimated that he's bought and sold nearly 1,000 of them.

A favourite spot – a short hop from St Kitts – is the tiny British dependency of Montserrat. When the locals discovered there was a booming market for banking licences, they went into business and were soon invaded by an army of laundrymen with money to wash. Allowing corporations to call themselves banks even though they were not was an uncontrollable exercise in greed. At one point, the island – which has a population of 10,000 – could boast 350 chartered banks.

Some of them had slightly familiar names: Chase Overseas Bank Ltd, Deutsche Bank (Suisse) Ltd, Fidelity Development Bank Ltd, Manufacturers Overseas Bank Ltd, Prudential Bank and Trust Ltd. There was even one called World Bank Ltd. Of course they were never anything more than a brass plaque in a registered office. Although it must be said that was not necessarily the case with the Zurich Overseas Bank. According to an indictment by the US Justice Department against several Detroit loan brokers, who bought Zurich Overseas from WFI, this one actually had an office – a table at the Chez Nous bar in Plymouth.

Montserrat banking was nevertheless good enough for the Panamanian laundrymen who bought banks there to wash funds for the drug cartels and their former President, Manuel Noriega. It was good enough for Israeli Mossad agents who used their Montserrat bank to launder money in a weapons deal with Colombian drug barons in the mid-1980s.

It was also, presumably, good enough for Robert Graven, alias Brother Eduardo, of the Circles of Light Church. Working out of Montserrat, with the stated mission of feeding starving children around the world, he convinced 30,000 Americans to send a total of $3 million to the island's First American Bank. The FBI, working alongside British police officers, ultimately established that Brother Eduardo's mission on Montserrat was Graven's own bank and he has since been convicted of fraud in Philadelphia.

Such is the demand for these banks that it created a cottage industry of Montserrat bank wholesalers. Recently, the situation got so out of control, Britain was forced into the unprecedented step of amending Montserrat's constitution. Responsibility for the financial industry was taken away from local politicians and placed under the authority of Her Majesty's appointed governor. And the first thing he did was to revoke 311 banking licences.

The laundrymen were forced to move on. But they never have to go very far. It has become a simple fact of life that any offshore haven which dares to frighten away depositors who are looking to hide dollars is committing economic suicide.

The British Virgin Island (BVI) bragged that you could get a corporation there instantly for very little money, that no one would ever be able to trace the ownership of the corporation, that you'd be assured of complete anonymity and that you'd pay no taxes. There was only one condition, that you didn't do business there. So today there are somewhere around 190,000 corporations chartered there but not doing business there. Many are being used by every manner of tax cheat, fraud artist, laundryman and drug dealer. Thirty-six dots of land – with names like Tortola, Virgin Gorda, Anegada and Jost Van Dyke – poking out of blue waters northeast of Puerto Rico and west of the Leewards. The year-round population of just 12,000 is culturally linked to Great Britain but constitutionally independent. More importantly, it is very interdependent on its neighbour to the south, the US Virgin Islands. So much so, that US dollars are the official currency.

The weather is perfect and English is spoken. And when a young Irish accountant named Shaun Murphy heard about BVI – and saw the possibilities there for a struggling laundryman – he figured that was for him.

A gentle man with a soft accent, he opened a small practice there, forming off-the-shelf companies and helping people hide money. Initially, when a client came to Murphy with money to wash, he'd put it through a fairly straightforward cycle. He'd form a company for his client in the BVI, use that company to open an account at a UK bank on the Isle of Man and deposit the cash there. He'd then form a second company, open an account for it at a Swiss bank in Panama and wire transfer the money there. Next stop would be a third company, with an account at a UK bank back in BVI. From there, the money would be wired on to his client, anywhere in the world.

It was as good a method as any. Except, after a while, Murphy started thinking it wasn't complicated enough. He reckoned he could provide his clients with a better service – with as many cut-off points as possible – to make their money virtually untraceable.

So he hung a huge map of the world on the wall behind his desk, and he'd sit in his swivel chair for hours, staring at it, picking out all sorts of strange places to open accounts. For one client, he formed 40 different companies and opened 90 different bank accounts in 40 different places around the world. That was the same client who once dropped a Samsonite suitcase to him from a passing airplane, with $2.3 million stuffed inside. It took a local bank two days just to count it.

The more complicated Murphy could make these transactions, the better it suited him. Even his own company, Offshore Formation, wasn't too obviously his. It was owned by two other companies: Romulus, which he secretly owned, and Remus, which was secretly owned by his friend Cyril Romney, who happened to be the prime minister of the BVI.

As sophisticated and connected a laundryman as he soon became, it didn't take long before Murphy had clients like Ben Kramer, who, together with his father Jack, was a high-profile powerboat builder in North Miami.

Ben Kramer was also a heavy-duty drug dealer.

An habitué of the Miami to Bimini powerboat race, Kramer had worked out a near-foolproof gimmick to bring drugs into the US. He'd enter three boats in the race, one of which would invariably break down. Kramer's boat would sit dead in the water while the rest of the race disappeared over the horizon. At which time a mother ship would come alongside and load the stricken boat with drugs. When that was done, Ben's rescue boat would show up and tow the racer back to Miami.

Finely tuned powerboats were breaking down all the time. So no one thought twice when one of Kramer's was winched out of the water, loaded onto a trailer and driven away. Over a five-year period, Ben Kramer smuggled $200 million worth of cocaine into the US with his boats.

Being the professional that he was – this was about accountancy, not about drug dealing – Shaun Murphy set up two shell companies for the Kramers. One was supposed to be a clothing firm – it even had a Saville Row address – but otherwise didn't exist. The second, chartered in the Netherlands Antilles, was called Lamborghini. It was not, however, a motor car company, although Murphy and Kramer never said that, especially if someone thought it was.

Murphy purposely chose two companies that had an air of legitimacy about them so that Kramer could use them as official sponsors for his powerboat racing team. Drug money went into the companies, which financed the boats, which financed the drug running, which financed the companies. Somewhere along the line, Murphy also bought Kramer a car hire franchise in Florida and some real estate in Los Angeles.

At the same time, Murphy established a company for Kramer in Liechtenstein called Cortrust. Kramer quickly filled Cortrust's accounts with drug money, which just as quickly came back to Kramer, filtered through several other shell companies, in the form of loans to build a brand-new marina and to finance bigger boats.

Quite apart from any dealings Murphy had with them, the Kramers got mixed up in the investigation of the murder of Don Aranow. He was the man who built the famous Cigarette and Blue Thunder power boats. And that was the beginning of the end of the story for the Kramers.

Murphy's walls came tumbling down in a totally unrelated incident. He was named as part of the major money laundering investigation that became the Brinks-Mat gold bullion robbery case and, when the British police found him, he sang. They immediately realized he had serious clients in the United States and, after hearing what he had to say about Brinks-Mat, they passed him on to the Americans.

He not only told the DEA everything he knew about the Kramers, but helped them get 70 separate indictments against other drug dealers and money launderers. In fact, the DEA came to like him so much, they spent three years debriefing him. For his help, they paid him $200,000, gave him a brand-new identity and sent him off to live somewhere almost as beautiful as BVI – the Mediterranean.

The Caymans are a small string of islands northwest of Jamaica, a relaxed 90 minute luncheon flight from Miami.

Once the hideout for Edward Teach – Blackbeard the Pirate – they have come to be known over the past 20 years as one of the world's preferred financial hideouts. Sometimes called 'The Geneva of the Caribbean,' the islands – Grand Cayman, Cayman Brac and Little Cayman – are big on sand, sun and confidentiality. At the same time they're particularly short on regulation and taxes.

Georgetown, the capital on Grand Cayman, boasts 580 banks – one for every 38 residents – with assets in excess of $519 billion. Most of the banks are, admittedly, brass plaques on someone's office wall – booking centres, where loans and deposits are recorded, but where nothing more than paperwork changes hands. There are no tellers, no vaults, no free bathroom scales for opening a holiday saving's account. Fewer than 15 per cent of the banks registered and operating in the Caymans ever see any cash.

Originally a dependency of Jamaica, the Caymans elected to take on British Crown Colony status in 1962 when Jamaica declared independence from Britain. Like Hong Kong, the Caymans run their own affairs. There is a British governor in residence, but in reality he does little more than cut ribbons at supermarket openings. The Bank of England has no say, nor any control, over banks in the Caymans.

In 1976, the legislature passed the Confidential Relationships Preservation Law, which – similar to codes in

Switzerland – made it a criminal act for anyone to reveal information about someone's banking or financial associations. Not surprisingly, most of the major American banks have offices there. It turns out that a large percentage of the 25,000 Cayman companies and trusts registered on the island are beneficially owned by Americans. Whether or not these companies and the accounts they control ever get reported to the IRS – as required by US law – is another matter. Almost certainly, most of them do not. After all, if a wealthy man wanted to pay taxes on his income, he wouldn't have to buy a shell company and hide his money in the Caymans. That's why Oliver North set up a dummy company there. That's also why Agha Hasan Abedi opened an office of BCCI there, channeling money through the Caymans to buy his way illegally into First American, the largest bank in Washington DC.

Bilateral agreements exist between the United States and some island governments – the Caymans and the Bahamas included – that are supposed to allow American investigators a glimpse behind the curtains of financial stealth. The Mutual Legal Assistance Treaty, ratified in 1988, says that, if the US authorities request information on specific drug cases and fraud, the Royal Cayman Islands Police will cooperate.

Two years later, under constant pressure from the Americans, bankers in the Caymans drafted a code of conduct, agreeing to refuse any suspicious cash deposits in excess of $10,000. The idea was to put an end to the stream of men in shiny suits with gold chains and attaché cases filled with cash. But 'suspicious cash deposits in excess of $10,000' doesn't necessarily exclude suspicious cash deposits under $10,000 or non-suspicious cash deposits of any amount. So the men with the shiny suits and gold chains changed clothes.

On paper, all of this is fine. In practice, it falls pitifully short of the mark. One obvious reason is that it's left to the Cayman police to decide whether or not the Americans should be granted cooperation. And, in cases of tax fraud, the answer is always no because tax fraud is not a crime in the Caymans.

Equally obvious, the good guys are up against a simple, undeniable fact: allowing the bad guys to hide their assets is big business. Any offshore government that decided to put an end to it would not only be cutting off its financial nose to save face with the Yanks, it would serve no real purpose other than to drive the laundrymen to other offshore jurisdictions where the politicians are less holy.

It is no accident that so many islands – Montserrat, BVI, the Bahamas, the Caymans, Aruba, Antigua, Bermuda – have one thing in common, the British Commonwealth flag. And therein lies a great irony – while Britain has done much to thwart drug money from being washed on the mainland, there is little or no embarrassment, or apology either – when it comes to having sold its sovereignty to the laundrymen.

For that matter, the Dutch are hardly blameless either. As significant participants in the colonization of the Caribbean, they've left behind some considerable problem areas, namely Aruba, Sint Maartens and Curaçao.

In the case of Sint Maartens, banks on that island have been known to receive cash by the mailbag-full, largely the proceeds of drug trafficking and gambling. The ability of the Dutch government to control it or, in fact, to do anything about it has always been extremely limited. At the same time, Curaçao has become a major money laundering centre. Not surprisingly, like most of the other islands in that part of the world, the local government doesn't appear to have much interest in stopping it, because dirty money is a major source of revenue for many influential people.

There, the importation of large amounts of cash is easy,

customs controls are for all intents and purposes non-existent and bankers can't be bothered to ask questions. One estimate has it that shell companies in the Netherlands Antilles control nearly 40 per cent of all foreign-owned farmland in the United States.

Because of the direct link to Holland, it's a smooth wire transfer from Sint Maartens to the Rotterdam account of a Panamanian-registered shipping company in Malta. They send the funds to Singapore, for deposit into the account of a Liechtenstein-registered insurance company on the Isle of Man, which transfers the money on to a Hong Kong-registered real estate company working out of Monaco, with an account in Los Angeles. Timed right, the whole thing can be managed in under an hour.

To get use of the money, the laundryman simply borrows it from himself. It's known in the trade as 'the Dutch sandwich' or a loan back. He walks into a legitimately licensed financial institution and negotiates a loan, using the Hong Kong company as guarantor, which secures the transaction with the laundered funds in LA.

A practical variation on that theme involves a pair of property development companies operating with total impunity today in the United States – one in the Washington DC area, the other in south Florida. The offices are staffed by Americans who act as agents for a group of foreign companies in apparently legitimate business centres such as Liechtenstein or Luxembourg. These companies specialize in property loans to developers who might be having trouble getting large loans through more obvious sources. And in certain cases the American staff at these offices don't have any idea that the primary source of the funds they're lending are being laundered.

Their clients come to them with a speculative idea, such as the development of a shopping mall. They're looking for, say, a seven-year, $7 million loan. But, for one reason or another, these clients are not able to get the project financed through normal banking channels. Either their idea is a bit too speculative for the average banker, or they haven't established a solid working relationship with a major financial institution.

What these outfits do is arrange a $10 million loan, to be repaid in seven years. With the extra $3 million, the developers are required to buy a zero-coupon US Treasury bond, which they immediately sign over to the property company. They are then directed to a bank where they secure a letter of credit for a sum equivalent to the total interest payment on the $7 million, using the shopping mall as collateral. That letter of credit is also signed over to the property company.

The developers get the money they need to build their shopping centre, while the property company gets a $3 million bond, guaranteed payments of interest and the deeds to the mall if the developers somehow default.

In other words, there is absolutely no risk on the part of the laundrymen.

At the end of seven years, the developers pay off the principal and own a mall, while the laundrymen have $10 million – plus interest – in sparkling clean money.

Because there is so much money to be had by setting up an island haven properly, all sorts of new places have got into the game. Many of them are in the Pacific. Some of them are real islands, some aren't even visible at high tide. Their gimmick is to offer guaranteed asset protection from foreign lawsuits, some of them actually advertising that they will not honour an American court judgement.

One atoll in particular, not only charters banks but has managed to find a few corrupt countries in Africa to recognize them as a nation. Based on that, they've applied for membership of the United Nations. At best it's a bad joke. Unfortunately, it follows a model that Robert Vesco tried to construct in the mid-1970s.

A fugitive then hiding out in Costa Rica, he flew to Libya to ask Colonel Khadafi to cede to him 2 square miles of desert so that he could set up a free trade zone for banking. It didn't work, but possibly only because Vesco might have been ahead of his time.

Today, those two square miles of desert look hauntingly like the island of Antigua which has become a free-trade zone on the Internet. They have banking, virtual gambling and kiddy porn, all of it substantially unregulated and unsupervised.

In 1997, one of those Internet operations was a virtual bank called the European Union Bank of Antigua Limited. Although the company was chartered on the island, the computer that was the bank happened to have been located in Washington DC. It means that, these days, where the bank is has nothing to do with where the server is, has nothing to do where the money is.

In this case, the money was nowhere.

A scam set up to take advantage of people wishing to hide money, deposits came in the virtual front door and, just as quickly, left by the virtual back door. The owners of the bank had a single asset which was a loan to an affiliated corporation in another country. Once that second account was sufficiently full, the affiliated corporation balked on repayment and that was the end of the European Union Bank of Antigua Limited.

One thing is certain, it won't be the last of the Internet banks.

Of course, the government of Antigua has come under tremendous pressure from the United States and Britain to do something about the businesses they charter there. The response has been, sure, we'll get around to it.

So far nothing's happened.

CHAPTER NINE

Down and out in Switzerland

'The Swiss wash whiter.'

Souvenir T-shirt in Zurich

Lugano is an Italian town permanently trapped inside the Swiss canton of Ticino, much like a two-headed mouse fixed in a jar of formaldehyde.

Sheltering on the banks of the large, quiet lake that bears its name, Lugano is – at least at first glance – little more than an overgrown depot on the main line of the St Gotthard railway. There are a few decent hotels. There are some good restaurants. But this is not Lausanne – a sophisticated watering hole. This is not Geneva or Zurich – a crossroads for international business. Nor does anyone ever mistake this place for Gstaad or St Moritz – the beautiful people don't come here to play. The locals like to think of Lugano as the Rio de Janeiro of Switzerland and lumber on about how a nearby mountain peak looks exactly like – well, okay, sort of like – Corcovado. But the beach below is hardly Copacabana. And anyway, the Swiss do not samba.

In the past, the main reason for stopping here was because

Lugano was a terrific place to hide money. All that suppos-edly changed a few years ago when the Swiss introduced new banking regulations to combat fraud, tax evasion and, specifically, money laundering. Since then, Lugano is still a terrific place to hide money.

There's a thriving casino across the lake, on the Italian side, with frequent ferry services back and forth. Especially during the summer months, it's not uncommon to find well-dressed men and women stepping off the morning's first boat at the Debarcadero Centrale, to take their croissant and espresso breakfast at one of the cafés on the Piazza Manzoni, or further along the Riva Giocondo Albertolli, near the lush Parco Civico on the lake's shore. It's hardly a coincidence that many of the café tables empty at about the same time the banks open.

According to London's *Financial Times*, 40 per cent of all private assets worldwide are managed in Switzerland – a staggering amount of money. But then there are over 100 banks in Lugano, and three times that many throughout Ticino. As it happens, there are more banks here than in the more populated, more accessible canton of Geneva. In fact, this city has one of the highest banks-per-capita ratios in the world – more than twice that of Switzerland's acknowledged banking capital, Zurich.

While every bank in Lugano is regulated by Swiss banking laws – governed every bit as fastidiously as all banks in the country – the easy approach from Italy and the proximity of a well-established casino make banks here especially attrac-tive for anyone seeking an especially 'discreet' relationship. And because discretion is such a salient commodity, one learns quickly that you can't just walk into any bank and announce that hiding money is what you intend to do.

'I'd like to open a secret bank account,' comes the request in a forthright tone. '*Un compte secret.*'

A woman at the first bank doesn't disguise her annoyance

with such obvious clumsiness. 'We're not interested in any new business of that kind,' she says.

The aspiration is repeated – in a slightly less hearty voice – at the second bank. 'I'd like to open a secret bank account. *Un compte secret.*'

A woman there is hardly more congenial. 'Do you mean, *un compte anonyme*? May I suggest another bank which might be more receptive.'

She does.

It isn't.

'We are not taking on any new private banking business,' a man at the third place explains to an increasingly unobtrusive inquirer. 'Perhaps you might try somewhere else.'

An official at the fourth stop, directly across the street, is even less affable, despite the ever-diminishing decibels. 'There is no such thing here as a secret bank account. I'm terribly sorry to disappoint you. Secret Swiss bank accounts are only for the movies.'

However, at the fifth bank, when a properly hushed desire is expressed to discuss 'various benefits of private banking,' the Special Affairs teller responds with a businesslike nod and directs her prospective client to a carpeted suite of offices behind a locked door. There, an impeccably tailored Gentleman introduces himself, wondering graciously if Signor would care to speak French, Italian, English or German. Signor suggests English. The Gentleman nods and, with a perfectly practiced British accent, offers Signor, 'A coffee? Perhaps some tea?' After two pitch-black espressos arrive, the Gentleman closes his office door and asks how he may be of assistance.

Signor says he's interested in establishing 'a discreet private banking relationship. Perhaps something along the lines of *un compte anonyme.*'

'I must caution you', the Gentleman begins, 'that this kind of facility has been much romanticized over the years. The so-called secret Swiss bank account, the sort you might have read about in James Bond, is strictly for pulp fiction and the cinema.'

'Now where', Signor probes, 'do you suppose they got such a notion?'

He speculates, 'Perhaps they've misinterpreted the banking rules in this country as they actually exist. What we do have to offer is a code that protects all bank accounts. Everything from your conventional current account to your child's savings account. By law, it's a crime in Switzerland for anyone working in a bank, or anyone who has ever worked in a bank, to reveal any information whatsoever about an account. It is against the law even to say that a specific account exists.'

'You mean you'd be breaking the law if you told me your wife kept her cheque account in this branch?'

'That's correct.'

But that's only half the story.

Swiss silence is – by design, and in all but the rarest circumstances – not merely 24 carat gold, it's inlaid with diamonds, rubies and sapphires. Every account is protected, at times to the extreme. Take the case where someone dies and his heirs attempt to discover if he's been stashing money in an account they know nothing about. The only reply they will ever get out of any Swiss banker is a hollow stare and a slightly chilly reminder that banking codes prohibit disclosure of any information concerning any accounts. Although, in this case, there's more to it than a mere requirement to comply with the law. Banks zealously cloister their business behind the strict banking codes because they're permitted to reap the bounty of accounts that have lain dormant for 20 years. If you die and no one knows about your *compte anonyme*, the bank can claim your money. One estimate has it that, at any given time, there are tens of billions of dollars sitting unclaimed in Swiss banks.

So, technically, the Gentleman is right.

What he hasn't endeavoured to say is that, in Switzerland, not all accounts are protected equally – that some are considerably more equal than others.

Banks all over the world offer preferential facilities for customers willing to pay for the privilege. Private banking is standard product in today's financial services industry. Marketed as being extra-exclusive, and therefore appropriately priced, it's readily available in New York, London, Paris and Rome, where banking secrecy is scarcely iron clad. However, when you speak about private banking in Switzerland, the accent really must be on the word private.

'In certain very particular cases, an account might be handled in a particularly special way,' the Gentleman concedes.

'Like in the movies!'

'I wouldn't go quite that far. I'm afraid that the use of encoded midnight phone calls to unlock *un compte anonyme* is nothing but romantic legend. Also, please keep in mind that bank accounts throughout the world are identified with numbers. The notion that someone might be given information by ringing up to ask in a hoarse whisper about account number 12345, is ludicrous. I dare say that information is never given out by any bank anywhere in the world just because someone knows a number.'

'Fair enough,' Signor says. 'But how about "particular cases"? And in a "particularly special way"?'

'By that I mean, certain clients have certain banking needs which we will provide.'

'Such as, hiding money.'

'If that's what you're looking to do, you're probably in the wrong country. In Switzerland today there is a very precise code of conduct which requires us to exercise due diligence in knowing with whom we do business. These days we will only open accounts for people who are willing to disclose to us their identity and explain to our satisfaction the source of the funds they wish to deposit with us.'

What he is trying to say, in essence, is that Swiss banking is not what it used to be.

Once upon a time there were two distinctly different types of account – referred to by the printed form used to open the account. Form A, the standard product, included the name of the beneficial owner. Form B – the really good one – did not involve names. It could be opened by an attorney or an accountant acting as an agent. And although the agent was required to state on the form that he knew the name of his client, he was not obligated to disclose that information to the bank. The beauty of Form B was that, by using an attorney as your agent, you could create a two-storey wall of privacy. Superimposing Switzerland's banking codes over the secrecy afforded client–attorney privilege meant that no one could ever attach your name to the money in the bank. For really good measure, a Form B account opened in the name of an offshore holding company, which was then run by nominee directors, guaranteed that not even the Swiss attorney acting for you knew your name. And if that company was owned by other offshore companies run by nominee directors, beneficial ownership was virtually untraceable. The only danger lay in the fact that, in those circumstances, you couldn't directly manage the account and would have to trust your holdings to various agents. That said, the sort of person who bothered to construct such a complicated maze in order to hide his identity usually had the means – specifically, muscle – to ensure that anyone having signature authority over the account was well aware of the risks involved with mismanagement.

But Form B accounts were abolished by law in July 1992.

'Come on,' Signor urges, 'I'm sure the laws of physics also apply to banking. Voids get filled. How do you open an account today without names attached?'

The Gentleman is naturally cautious. 'Look, even if we used a system based on numbers, you must understand that someone in the bank will always know the name attached to those numbers. It gets down to how many, or how few, will ever be able to link your name with your account.'

'How few is a few?'

'Perhaps three? Perhaps four? Only the bank's top executives. But it's reasonable to expect that someone must know whose money it is. How else could you get it when you need it? How else could we make certain it doesn't go to a person not authorized to use those funds? We need to protect our clients and ourselves from all eventualities.'

Protecting themselves from all eventualities is the unwritten first rule of the banking business everywhere. Protecting their clients from all eventualities is what the Swiss have been doing for centuries.

Bankers there began offering secrecy to aristocrats for a fee during the French revolution. *Les comptes anonymes*, as we know them today, were invented by the gnomes at the end of the nineteenth century – a marketing tool to attract fresh business from around the world. The idea was that if people wanted to hide money, regardless of the reason – tax evasion, fraud, politically unstable environments, whatever – the Swiss were willing to sell them that service. In 1934, secret banking was enshrined into Swiss law, basically because a large number of wealthy Germans were willing to pay to protect their assets against a background of increasing Nazi influence. Yet it was only when these cast-iron accounts were immortalized by a legion of thriller writers – Ian Fleming among them – that legend outgrew reality.

A serious crack in the mask first appeared in 1977. The manager of the Credit Suisse branch in Chiasso, along the border with Italy, had invested in excess of $500 million on behalf of a group of Italian clients. When the money disappeared with the investors, it was discovered that the local manager had been less than diligent. To repair the damage done to the national reputation, Swiss authorities called in the banks and together they wrote a code of conduct. The basis of the code is that responsibility must rest with the bank and its managers to know with whom they're dealing.

Then came the Kopp affair.

In November 1986, US federal authorities, acting on a tip, seized three suitcases at Los Angeles International Airport, bound for Switzerland in the company of a Turkish drug dealer named Dikran Altun. Inside was $2 million of what would come to be known as the La Mina money. Altun was to deliver the suitcases to Jean and Barkev Magharian, Syrian-born brothers who'd been laundering profits for the Medellin cartel for a number of years. A Swiss investigation revealed that the Magharians had washed perhaps as much as $2 billion for their patrons, using 20 different bank accounts in Zurich. One of the banks involved – again, Credit Suisse – eventually admitted that, on those occasions when counterfeit notes had been found in the stacks of cash being deposited by the Magharians, they'd returned the bad notes but had never bothered to advise the police. It also emerged that directors at Credit Suisse had been warned by an internal audit committee that the Magharian brothers were conducting questionable business through their account. Again, the bank did nothing about it.

Banking secrecy laws exist today – in one form or another – in about 50 nations. That's around one-quarter of all the sovereign states on earth. But nowhere does it have the same cachet – the same claim to fame – as it does in Switzerland. Perhaps that's why it's no accident that money laundering is something Swiss bankers and their clients know a great deal about.

The Economist reported that, in January 1992, four Hungarians, wishing to wash some $1.3 million worth of German marks, had arranged an appointment at the main offices of Credit Suisse, on the Paradeplatz in Zurich. They were greeted in the huge, marbled lobby by two men who introduced themselves as officers of the bank. One of the two took the suitcase to another room to count the money while the other invited the Hungarians to have coffee. When the first man did not come right back, the second excused himself, saying that he wanted to see what the delay was. The four Hungarians are still staring into their coffee cups. A week later, a Canadian businessman handed over the $2.5 million worth of Swiss francs that he was trying to wash for another cup of Credit Suisse hospitality. How the fraudsters got into the bank and were able to use the banking hall greatly concerned Credit Suisse. It must be pointed out that the bank was not involved in any way. Still, their coffee is overpriced.

As the investigation into the Magharians' affairs progressed, evidence arose that linked them to the Shakarchi Trading Company. In 1985, Mohamed Shakarchi had invited a prominent Swiss businessman, Dr Hans Kopp, to join him in a venture dealing in metals and precious stones. Four years later, when it was learned that the Magharians had washed funds through Shakarchi's gold bullion operation, Hans Kopp received a very private – and very panicky – phone call from the Swiss Minister of Justice, tipping him off to the investigation. He instantly severed his relationship with Shakarchi. The problem was that the Swiss Minister of Justice happened to have been his wife, Elisabeth.

Scandal ensued – amplified in the press by the arrest and conviction of the Magharians on money laundering charges – leaving Mrs Kopp in an untenable position. Although no evidence ever came to light suggesting that her husband was involved in any illegal activities that might have taken place at the Shakarchi Trading Company, Elisabeth Kopp was forced to resign as the first female member of the country's ruling Federal Council.

Ironically, at the time of her resignation, Mrs Kopp's Justice Ministry was at work framing two new laws that were aimed at putting an end to the influx of criminal funds into Swiss banks.

The first one made money laundering a crime and pre-scribed harsh penalties for related offenses such as insider dealing, market manipulation and tax fraud. Although it did not include tax evasion in a foreign country, the legislation did recognize as an offence the use of fraudulent documents to deny a foreign state its rightfully due taxes.

The second one eliminated all of the existing 32,000 Form B accounts. Under pressure from various foreign governments – including the United States – the Swiss decreed that agents and representatives must now disclose to the banks the beneficial owners of those accounts. An attorney must now sign a sworn statement to the effect that his client is not abusing the Swiss banking laws and that the monies involved have not been derived from criminal activities. The new laws also stripped away a powerful buffer by specifying that any lawyer acting for a client in the capacity of an asset manager could not refuse to divulge information on this aspect of their relationship. In other words, that part of their business is no longer automatically protected by attorney–client privilege.

Under the new statutes, any client wishing to open an account, enter into a fiduciary transaction, rent a safe deposit box or make any type of cash transaction in excess of SFr 10,000 – around £4,500 – must be properly identified.

Furthermore, the Federal Banking Commission has pro-vided banks with a set of ground rules. They want bankers to be suspicious of any sudden activity taking place in a long-dormant account; of cash being withdrawn immedi-ately after it's deposited; of transactions that appear out of the ordinary for the specific client; and of customers who refuse to supply information. Bankers are also asked to be especially wary of any accounts opened with more than SFr 25,000 (£11,500) in cash, while counter staff are supposed to interrogate anyone converting large amounts of cash into other currencies.

Unquestionably, some banks are more vigilent than others. A few even carry it to wonderfully Swiss extremes – a trait peculiar to a people whose reputation, justifiably, derives from their chocolate, not their sense of humour. When the Compagnie de Banque et d'Investissement – now the Union Bancaire Privée – built new offices in Geneva, it petitioned the city council to change the name of its street because, in its opinion, the old name created the wrong image. The city council agreed. It's now the Place Camoletti. It used to be Rue de la Buanderie – Wash House Street.

In Switzerland, today, unless you've got a false passport, you can no longer use an obviously false name. Even with a counterfeit passport, it's easier, and less dangerous, to hop on the next train to Austria, where banks don't much care who you are because they'll open bearer accounts in any name. They call it a password, which means you can call yourself anything from Bill Clinton to Popeye the Sailor Man. While these accounts are limited to a maximum of 10 million Austrian schillings – roughly the equivalent of $900,000 – you're welcome to one each in the name of Snow White and the Seven Dwarfs. Add in all your other favourite Disney characters and you're up to serious numbers. Manuel Noriega had a certain bias for Austrian banking, as did Imelda Marcos. The only problem is that anyone using these accounts cannot deposit foreign currency – it's strictly for schillings – so arriving in Vienna with sacks of used £20 notes won't work.

But it will in Switzerland.

Despite the new legislation, depositing mountains of used

£20 notes is not a crime. All you have to do is convince the bank that the money is not the proceeds of crime.

Where you might have a bit of worry is in the pronounced tendency of the Swiss, nowadays, to assist foreign states in certain, very specific, types of criminal investigations.

Provided that a foreign government can substantiate, to the complete satisfaction of exceptionally sceptical Swiss judicial authorities, that funds in an account there are the object of a fraud – including tax fraud but excluding tax evasion – and that criminal proceedings have already been initiated in that foreign state against the beneficial owner of those funds, the Swiss are willing to seize assets.

Along similar lines, the Swiss were the first nation to sign a treaty with the United States to expose drug-related wealth. If the DEA is on a witchhunt, they won't cooperate. But if the US Justice Department can identify drug money held in a Swiss account, and, again, can substantiate those claims in accordance with dreadfully strict guidelines, the Swiss will intervene.

A controversial matter, to say the least, cooperation with foreign governments has been vehemently opposed by most Swiss bankers, who emphasize that every breach of banking secrecy contributes to a lack of confidence in the Swiss banking system. As an example of what invariably happens, they point to the Marcos case. By forcing banks to reveal the existence of Ferdinand's and Imelda's accounts, and by then freezing the money in them, the government gave the impression that banking secrecy would no longer be adequately safeguarded. The immediate result was a rush of funds out of Switzerland in favour of Luxembourg, Liechtenstein and the Caribbean.

However, it appears as if the gnomes haven't drawn a lot of sympathy with that argument. On a request from the Haitians, the authorities in Bern identified and froze private accounts held by Baby Doc Duvalier. When the

Americans requested that they look into Manuel Noriega's affairs, the Swiss were accommodating enough to padlock his funds. It was the same story when the new Romanian government asked about Nicolai Ceausescu's assets, when the Indonesian government sought help identifying funds stashed there by President Sukarno, and when the Americans came up with proof that a huge amount of money had been deposited in Switzerland by the Colombian drug cartels.

This is not a cross-roads they've come to easily, and at times they have been noticably less than forthright with the truth. The recent episode of Nazi gold having been hidden in Switzerland, despite strenuous Swiss denials of having hidden Nazi gold, puts a serious dent in their credibility. Denying that there were any remaining dormant Jewish bank accounts, when there plainly were, puts another question mark against their candour. Still, over recent years they've begun, gradually, to cooperate with foreign governments, proving that, at least to some extent, they will no longer protect monies which have come into the country as a result of drug trafficking and other types of criminal activity.

But that only applies to Swiss banks in Switzerland.

Swiss banks operating offshore in, say, the Cayman Islands, can deliver the same services that they used to in Switzerland, and with even greater protection.

'So,' the Gentleman makes his point, 'you can plainly see how, and I hope can appreciate why, we are not interested in harbouring criminal funds.'

'Most definitely,' Signor nods. 'But that's not my case.'

The Gentleman is too polite to disagree. 'Of course not.'

Signor puts on his most reassuring expression, 'Let's say, I'm looking to invest some capital quietly. You understand. Without wanting to involve myself in various . . . let's call them, international hassles.'

For some odd reason, he immediately assumes that 'international hassles' means tax avoidance. 'If you don't pay your taxes in the United States, that's hardly a problem for the Swiss government to worry about. Although I'm certain that I don't need to remind you how some countries, the United States and Great Britain among them, have written laws which make undeclared bank accounts illegal. But it goes without saying, those laws are not binding in Switzerland.'

Not wanting to worry him with minor details – like how 'international hassles' could also mean an arrest warrant issued by the FBI – Signor settles on, 'Just how would someone go about opening such an account? How would you propose to fill the void left by the Form B?'

'For the sort of private facility you're alluding to, I think it would be fair to say that sufficiently large sums are required.'

'What would you say to . . .' Signor picks a figure off the top of his head . . . 'two point five?'

Taking for granted that we are talking seven figure numbers, he wonders, 'Swiss francs?'

With enormous confidence Signor informs him, 'Dollars.'

'Hmmmm.' He likes that. 'Yes, it is definitely in the range of business we would be willing to consider.'

Now, here comes the not so subtle hint, 'There may be a certain amount of cash involved.'

'Ah.' His eyebrows raise. 'I see.' Long pause. 'Cash can present certain hurdles.'

'Oh . . .' Signor reacts matter-of-factly. 'But they're not necessarily insurmountable hurdles.'

He thinks for a moment. 'We are required to exercise due diligence. Now, I don't take that to mean that we must insult dozens of new clients simply to identify a villain who will, when we refuse his business here, merely take his business somewhere else. But cash is, I'm sorry to say, often inconvenient. And large amounts of cash are, frankly, not very desirable.'

'I understand.' Signor leans forward. 'Yet Switzerland is one of the world's largest bank-note trading centres. I read somewhere that a ton and a half of foreign currency arrives every day at the airport in Zurich. Surely a few extra bank notes aren't going to cause anyone a problem.'

With two and a half million dollars being dangled as an opening deposit, and the prospect of more to come, he doesn't want to see his prospective client walk across the street. 'If we could be completely satisfied . . .'

'You mean, if the cash was coming from, say, various business ventures in the Middle East? Or, a rather lucky evening at the gaming tables across the lake?' Signor hides his grin. 'Would that make things more . . . convenient?'

Well aware that other bankers in town will gladly take Signor's deposit – although, little does he know that four have already shown Signor to the door – he proposes, 'If we could somehow satisfy ourselves as to where the cash came from, I'm certain that we can come to an arrangement.'

'And this can be done verbally?'

He gazes at Signor for a very long time. 'We might require some written evidence, depending on the nature of the verbal statement. Invoices, perhaps. Or contracts. Letters of agreement. Paperwork is good. And it might happen that discreet inquiries will then be made. But please allow me to assure you, whatever is discussed between us remains in the strictest confidence. We may ask questions. However, once we're satisfied with the origin of the money and the integrity of our client, we never repeat any of the answers.'

How comforting to know that, with little more than a passport, well-prepared answers to the obvious questions, a handful of faxes for backup and a hefty pile of dough, almost anyone can avail themselves of the most famous laundromat in the world, despite the fact that some Swiss would have you believe such facilities no longer exist.

CHAPTER TEN

Eli Pinkas –
A Mystery Story

*col.lec.tor (ke-lek'-ter) n. A person employed to collect taxes,
duties, or other payments.*

The American Heritage Dictionary
of the English Language

Just after dawn on Tuesday, 10 June 1980, the Lausanne
police received an emergency call from an hysterical maid
at the Villa Gentilhomiere, the luxury estate of a local
businessman named Eli Pinkas. She kept babbling on about
a dog being murdered and intruders. Several cars were
dispatched. Arriving at the large gates that guarded the
villa, the police found them unlocked, so they hurried inside
the grounds. There was a Jaguar coupé in the garage and
when one of the officers routinely touched the hood, he
noticed that it was hot. Not simply warm, he later wrote
in his report, but hot. The car had obviously been driven
for a long time during the night.

The villa seemed otherwise quiet.

Almost as soon as the officer in charge rang the bell at the
front door, the maid threw it open, insisted the dog had been

murdered by intruders and brought the officers inside. They found a German shepherd dead in the hallway at the bottom of the stairs. Later, the police were able to determine that the cause of death had been cyanide.

Now fanning out, making their way through the house to search for intruders, one officer went upstairs. In the master bedroom he found Pinkas's body. On the nightstand next to the bed there was a handwritten note. In it, Pinkas asked that his friends forgive him. Later, the police were able to determine that the cause of death had been cyanide.

No intruders were found. There were no signs of a break-in. As far as the police were concerned, it was obvious that Pinkas had killed the dog then taken his own life.

Normally, an autopsy confirmation of suicide would have closed the case. Except, sometime that very same morning – but definitely before the Lausanne police went to La Gentilhomiere – an anonymous phone call to the police in Cannes, France, summoned them to a penthouse apartment at the Grand Hotel.

The front door to the apartment had a whole series of locks but when the police got there, none of them were bolted. Nothing in the apartment led them to believe there had been intruders. But in the master bedroom they found a woman's body. Later they were able to determine that the cause of death had been cyanide.

On the floor at the foot of the bed they found a note ripped into small pieces. 'Flo, m'amour, I give you some last advice because I love you. Open these two packages and swallow these four capsules which operate very quickly so that you can join me.' It went on to warn that if she stayed alive she would suffer great difficulties and dishonour. 'I've tried for years to re-establish my financial situation but without success.' It was signed, 'I love you always and until the last breath of my life, your Eli.'

At first glance, the matching suicides of two lovers,

208 miles apart, had a Romeo and Juliet quality about it.

But first glances are often deceptive.

Eli Pinkas was a cultured man who spoke French, English, German, Italian and Bulgarian. Of average build but with heavy features – he had extremely large hands and a very large forehead – he always dressed in a traditional, conservative manner. His thinning dark hair was just on the verge of turning white.

Born in 1920, his family had settled in Lausanne in 1941, war refugees from Bulgaria. He earned a degree in chemistry from the local university and over the next 39 years enjoyed the trappings of a successful and respected businessman. His home was aptly named, translating to mean 'The Gentleman's Manor' and he spent a great deal of time there, much of it in his garden tending to his roses. He was a private person, although some people preferred to think of him as aloof and slightly distant. His personal annual income would have been in the range of $1.5 million, yet he showed very little outward sign of extravagance, except perhaps for his love of Jaguars. He had several.

His business life was a multi-layered series of interests almost all revolving around his background as a chemist. Being a serious man, other serious businessmen invited him to serve on their corporate boards and one of the boards he sat on was the very conservative Banque Vaudoise de Credit.

The company he ran was called Socsil and his factory in Lausanne was a large, heavily-guarded, fully mechanized plant operating in three distinct fields: first, there was the manufacturing of mechanical pumps, a process that Pinkas had patented; next, there was the chemical testing of raw materials being used to make a certain soft drink, the name of which was kept secret. Pinkas, however, once confided in a few close friends that it was Coca-Cola and that he was the only person outside the United States to possess the secret Coke formula. Finally, the most important and by far biggest share of his business, was the production and sale of the highly explosive gas, nitrous oxide, popularly known as laughing gas.

Complementing that side of his business, Pinkas had many years before invented a chemical process that rendered the gas inert. Understanding the potential of non-explosive nitrous oxide, he designed a medical kit for use in battlefield hospitals. Accordingly, he sold these kits to dozens of militaries around the world. Among his clients were the NATO armies and the armed forces of several Arab nations. A lucrative enterprise, it brought him into contact with people in the Middle East. Because a military build-up somewhere in the world was clearly reflected in increased orders for his battlefield kit, Pinkas was privy, albeit as an incidental party, to certain military intelligence and information that might otherwise be considered classified.

Not that classified information was something he was unaccustomed to. He saw a lot of it because in his spare time he was a major in the Swiss Army Reserve.

Or maybe he wasn't.

In Switzerland, just about every male citizen has a commitment to the military for a good part of his life. That's why it was hardly surprising when friends spotted Eli Pinkas walking through the streets of Lausanne wearing his reserve officer's uniform. Nor did any of those friends ever doubt him when he admitted to being the Swiss Army's Reserve Chief of Gas Warfare. After all, he was a chemist with a thorough knowledge of gases.

The Swiss, who are not a nuclear force, have historically depended on gas warfare as a last line of defence. When attacked, their battle plan is to retreat into the mountains and fill the valleys with gas. They believe it makes the country just about impregnable, at least to an army advancing on foot.

So Major Eli Pinkas, Reserve Chief of Gas Warfare for the Swiss Army seemed totally plausible. What's more, Lausanne is a small town where everyone knows everyone else and if Pinkas wasn't who he said he was, word would have got around very quickly.

These days, however, the Swiss Ministry of Defence says Pinkas never had anything to do with the Army Gas Warfare Department. In fact, they claim he wasn't even a reserve officer.

In addition to the three main parts of Socsil, Pinkas had his fingers in a few other pies. In the mid-1960s he bought a 283-acre tract of land outside Lausanne with the intention of developing it into a resort area. He had intended to enlist the help of an American consortium but Swiss laws discourage foreign ownership of property and as a result, the Americans shied away. Instead, he used the land as collateral with the banks when he wanted to swing other deals.

Then, quite ingeniously, he also seemed to be in the scrap steel business.

While selling nitrous oxide to the US Army – at least this is what he told friends – he stumbled across the curious fact that where the Americans were concerned, there was a difference between gas bottles that were 'full' and gas bottles that were 'almost full.'

When he shipped the bottles to them, they were checked and certified full. But as the valves on those huge steel cylinders often leaked, not all of them were 100 per cent full by the time the US Army got around to using them. Through some eccentric accounting regulation, bottles that were not 100 per cent full, Pinkas explained, were written off by the Americans as unusable and discarded as scrap steel.

When he discovered this, he immediately started buying

the scrapped bottles, repainting them, topping them up with gas – he said there was usually no more than 15–20 per cent missing – and selling them back to the Americans for the full price.

He used to brag to friends that it was a truly wonderful business, and even let some of them in on it. Every now and then, he'd invite a few pals to invest. He'd even show them their gas cylinders whenever they visited the factory. And he did send them regular dividend cheques. Because those friends were making money with him, none of them bothered looking any deeper into it. Although an official report later claimed Socsil was only doing $4.2 million a year worldwide in nitrous oxide sales, Pinkas flaunted records which showed he was doing $27 million a year just with the Sanitary Division of the United States Army.

As a contractor to the United States Government, Pinkas was in a position to discount US paper. It's a standard procedure. When a company invoices the government for say, a million dollars, and the government acknowledges the debt, promising to pay in 60–90 days, a businessman can take the invoice to a bank and get $1 million right away, minus whatever small commission he's negotiated with the bank for taking over the 60–90 day debt. It goes without saying that Uncle Sam's signature on US Army invoices meant that any bank in the world would welcome Pinkas and his US paper.

Except, Pinkas didn't actually discount the paper. Instead he borrowed against it. He put the invoices down as security for loans. It was a slightly quirky thing to do, but most of the bankers he dealt with figured he was just trying to save a little money. So they went along with it. They couldn't know that Pinkas never intended to give a bank the opportunity to collect on this paper.

When a bank wanted to see balance sheets for Socsil, Pinkas showed them balance sheets. When they wanted to see his personal accounts, he showed them his personal accounts. Everyone who asked for paperwork got paperwork. And in every case, the bank looking at his accounts was listed in those reports as Pinkas's only creditor.

Pinkas's borrowing against US government paper has now been traced as far back as 1948.

So banks gave him money against that paper as collateral. By backing it up with his balance sheets and, wherever necessary, his personal guarantee, the bankers with whom he dealt conveniently forgot the most basic lesson of the lending business: always check with the originator of a collateral note.

Astonishingly, not one bank – not even American banks – ever bothered checking with the United States Army Sanitary Division.

Enter now the former Mrs Pinkas.

Her name was Florence, she was two years older than Pinkas and a hopeless alcoholic.

Before she and Eli were married in 1943, she appeared on the scene as a dark-haired lady from Argentina who spoke beautiful Spanish and French with a heavy accent. After they split-up in 1964 she left Lausanne, preferring to live in the south of France and only rarely came to Switzerland. They never had children, which some people felt accounted for the touch of melancholy that often surrounded her. Or maybe she loved him and just didn't want to live apart.

Although they divorced, their affair continued on a regular weekend basis. He would openly tell anyone who asked that he was totally devoted to her. And the proof of it was that every Thursday night he flew to Nice, telling anyone who asked that he always spent the weekend with her.

Oddly, it now turns out that she was not from Argentina. Instead she was born near Lausanne – she still has family there – and met Pinkas when she was working as a barmaid in a local hangout. Why the masquerade about being from Argentina, no one seems to understand. The important thing is that everyone either believed it or was at least willing to play along with it.

The first week of June 1980 is one which, in the scheme of world history, probably doesn't mean much. It wasn't as remarkable as the first week of June 1900 when the Boxer Rebellion engulfed the southern provinces of China. Or the first week of June 1920 when the Treaty of Trianon redrew the map of Europe. Or even the first week of June 1960 when President Eisenhower sent 120 USAF planes to Southeast Asia, marking America's toe testing of the waters that would become the war in Vietnam.

However Henry Miller died during that first week of June 1980. And it was the final week of Eli and Florence Pinkas's lives.

It was also the week that a clerk in the Banque de Paris et des Pays-Bas in Geneva was auditing the lending portfolio and noticed that ink had rubbed off his hands. Curious, he sorted back through the stack of paperwork on his desk until he found some smudged letterheads from the United States Army Sanitary Division.

How bizarre, he thought, imagining that the Americans ought to have better printing facilities. He'd never seen anything like that. So he studied the letters more closely, reminded himself that ink on US government forms wasn't supposed to rub off, then sent a memo to his superior to report the matter. The only thing his superior could think to do was wire the bank's office in Washington DC and have them inform the Sanitary Division of the United States Army that there was a minor problem with their letterhead. Accordingly, someone in the bank's office in Washington phoned the Pentagon and asked to speak with the US Army's Sanitary Division.

The operator on the other end wanted to know, 'What's a Sanitary Division?'

For the price of better ink, the world was about to cave in on Eli Pinkas.

A telex went back from Washington to Geneva. The smudged paperwork was sent to a senior officer at the bank who inspected it, then studied the rest of the file. He was inclined to phone Pinkas, to ask him what this was all about, but just to be prudent, he decided first to show the entire dossier to his lawyers.

They demanded he call the police.

Being so well connected, Pinkas must have learned what was happening because by the middle of that week he began paying back a number of small loans that were then outstanding. A few thousand dollars here. A few thousand francs there. And in every case, he paid cash. He also wrote letters to at least six people asking that they forgive him, although he never spelled out what for.

On Friday 6 June, the public prosecutor in Lausanne saw for the first time a document charging Eli Pinkas with fraud. And he was absolutely stunned. The thought of someone as reputable as Pinkas being involved in such a crime was so worrying that he rang Pinkas to say, 'I must see you.'

Pinkas laughed, then agreed to meet with the man later the following week. Hanging up on the public prosecutor, Pinkas now called two friends in the hierarchy of a local bank, asking them to meet him at his factory first thing Monday.

Almost as soon as they stepped into his office that morning, he informed them, 'I'm being indicted.'

They too were stunned.

Without going into detail, he admitted to 'a few wrong doings'. He assured them, 'It's very little. But it's so embarrassing.'

Back at the bank, they decided they both liked Pinkas

enough to want to do something for him. So while one checked the bank's records to establish the extent of Pinkas's borrowings there, the other approached the public prosecutor to see if their personal intervention might help Pinkas save face.

By Monday afternoon, everyone concerned was quickly coming to the conclusion that 'a few wrong doings' and 'very little' was hardly the case.

Before dawn on Tuesday, Eli Pinkas was dead at La Gentilhomiere and Florence Pinkas was dead in Cannes.

The Swiss press announced the Pinkas affair with headlines labelling him a 'Fraudster Bulgarian Jew'.

But he wasn't a Bulgarian. He'd taken Swiss citizenship and carried a Swiss passport for nearly 40 years.

Nor was he still a Jew. He'd become a Protestant in the 1950s. Whether he did that for business reasons, or because he particularly believed, no one knows. The point is, he did not openly acknowledge Judaism for at least the last 25 years of his life.

That he was a fraudster, however, is another matter.

When the police went to the Socsil offices after his death, they found that a large number of documents had been destroyed. They merely assumed that Pinkas had got to them first. Yet from what remained, they were able to determine that he'd used United States Army Sanitary Division invoices, plus similar invoices from the German army, plus a guarantee for $30 million from the Swiss bank UBS as collateral for loans that totalled a staggering $300 million.

When the police established that the bogus invoices were printed in Cannes, the French were called in. The printer who did the work for Pinkas later claimed that he didn't know what he was printing. He said he didn't speak English and besides, it wasn't any of his business what a client wanted printed on a form. All he'd say was that Pinkas paid for his work on time and in cash. In the end, the printer was the only person to go to gaol in connection with the affair, doing two years for not declaring that cash to the French tax authorities.

As investigators got deeper into his affairs, it became obvious that Pinkas had somehow managed to convince American banks to make wire transfers to Switzerland by order of the US Army Sanitary Division. He needed to do that in order to make everything look absolutely official. He needed to have payments coming in to Switzerland from the US Government. After all, if he was supposed to be doing business with the Army, he couldn't deposit money in Switzerland and simply ask his bankers to believe that it was from the Army. But they were never able to figure out exactly how he managed that.

Over the course of the next two years, the Swiss tried to trace the money Pinkas brought into the system. Believing at first that the sums involved were perhaps 'as much as' $300 million, they located hundreds of companies around the world that Pinkas was using to launder money and were forced to revise their estimate. 'As much as' $300 million was changed to 'perhaps as high as' $800 million.

Yet the grand total of liquid assets attributable to Eli Pinkas once every book was examined came to only $1.5 million.

At that point, bizarrely, the case was officially closed. It was as if the Swiss suddenly didn't want anyone to know exactly how much was missing or where it might have gone.

Six weeks after Pinkas's death, the *Washington Post* reported that Pinkas had effectively stolen $140 million. Just over $112 million of it came from 18 banks around the world: eight in Switzerland, four in France, one in Britain, one in Israel, and four in the US, including Citibank and

First National of Minneapolis. The rest of whatever money Pinkas had, at least according to the *Washington Post*, came from his friends and business associates.

Other newspapers have since suggested that, on top of the $140 million, there might be as much as $20 million more that's been written off by creditors who, for legal or personal reasons, cannot publicly admit to having been involved.

Within two months of Pinkas's death, the *Wall Street Journal* quoted someone inside the Swiss banking authority as saying that the $140 million originally estimated was being revised down to $108.7 million. What's more, the Federal Banking Commission seemed content to write off the scandal as a bit of temporary craziness. They said that because Pinkas was so heavily in debt, he had to keep borrowing just to pay the interest. That created more debt which in turn created the need for more borrowing. In other words, it was a Ponzi scheme. They noted that Pinkas was all right as long as interest rates were low. But when he had to borrow at 19 per cent to pay off loans that had been made at 12 per cent, that strangled him.

Except that temporary craziness does not answer the question, where did the money go?

Finding someone in authority these days who'll speak about Pinkas isn't easy. Their first reaction is, it was a long time ago. They suggest you just forget it. If you persist, they tell you in a whisper – as if they're doing you a favour and finally letting you in on a genuine secret – that the money went to pay for his lifestyle. They tell you, he lost it gambling. They insist, there's nothing else to say.

The only problem is that Pinkas clearly lived within his own income and he was not a gambler.

He was, however, an extraordinarily talented laundrymen.

The mechanics of his sink revolved around three companies. First there was Socsil. Next there was an investment company he'd founded in 1970 called Vilro. And finally there was a land development company, Villas La Roche, which owned that property outside Lausanne he'd once hoped to develop with American partners. Like spokes on a wheel, they branched out to those hundreds of companies he'd scattered around the world. To create cash flow he over-subscribed the three main holdings, selling each share three and four times. Because every share is numbered, he needed to keep his creditors from comparing notes, so he skilfully used the 'he's got a big mouth' technique.

It worked like this: Pinkas would strike up a relationship with Monsieur A. They would be discussing a business possibility when, by chance, Monsieur B's name came up. Immediately Pinkas would say to Monsieur A, 'Listen, B is a great guy and I really like him, but this deal has got to be just between us. You see, the problem is that B has a big mouth. He talks too much. If you mention our business to him it will be all over Lausanne in an hour,' Naturally, Monsieur A would then make a point of shying away from Monsieur B. However, when Pinkas brought Monsieur B into his confidence, which he invariably would, and offered him a piece of the deal, he'd tell Monsieur B the same story about Monsieur A. 'He's got a big mouth.'

As simple as it was, it played on a common human trait, that most people don't want other people to know the details of their business. And it wasn't until long after his death that all sorts of people who otherwise knew each other's business, or at least thought they did, started comparing notes and realized that Pinkas had successfully kept them apart.

They also started to understand Pinkas's apparent aloofness. Some of his friends noted that he was a man with extraordinary control, a man who didn't seem to have a temper, who never seemed to get into an argument with anyone. They once thought it was just his nature. Now, they admit, considering the glass house where his finances lived it's obvious why he never threw stones.

Spinning money through the three main companies, sending it out to the others, then bringing more in when he needed to, made the three main assets seem that much more liquid. And as capital built up from his borrowing schemes, he moved that money out.

But where to? All those companies on the outside rim of the wheel were empty shells.

Sometime around 1975 there was a terrible accident at the Socsil factory. At six in the morning, while doing some sort of experiment with a gas that couldn't explode, it did explode and the laboratory's chief engineer was killed. There was an official investigation and the coroner's report settled on misadventure. No one thought again about that conclusion until Pinkas died. Some people began to wonder if perhaps the chief engineer had stumbled onto something odd at the factory, and for whatever reason, had been eliminated.

Although some dark conspiracy remains nothing more than conjecture, with hindsight, it's plausible. Consider this: some months before his death, Pinkas had added a clause to his will specifically to provide for his own funeral. He wanted a Valkyrie-like affair where his ashes would be sprinkled across Lake Geneva. Perhaps it was just a coincidence that he wrote the provision when he did. Or perhaps it wasn't. And what about the woman he loved so much that he asked to die with him? Could he possibly have forgotten to provide for her? He was by anyone's accounting a wealthy man. The apartment in Cannes was filled with antiques, paintings and Oriental carpets. Florence had jewels. She also had 470 pairs of shoes in her closet. Yet she was buried in a commoner's grave because there wasn't enough money to pay for a funeral.

Did Florence actually take her own life? When the police got to Pinkas's home on the morning of his death, his car was hot. Could he have driven to Cannes the night before and killed her, trying to make it look like a suicide? Could he have murdered her then raced back to Lausanne and taken his own life?

Or maybe he drove somewhere else to meet someone else. Or maybe he didn't take his own life. The note next to Florence's body looked as if it had been written by Pinkas, but it was never officially checked by experts. Why was it ripped up? Perhaps he failed to provide for her funeral because he didn't know she needed one. The door of Florence's apartment had so many locks that friends who visited there joked that it looked like a fortress. Pinkas had keys to her apartment. So why, when the police arrived, were all of those bolts unlocked. Could she have let someone in who didn't have any keys to lock up on the way out?

Pinkas was a very proud man, someone who would have been incapable of suffering the torture of a public trial or coping with a jail sentence. For those people who knew him well, suicide seems logical, a fast and simple way out of the problem. Negotiating a discreet settlement seems equally logical, at least it does if he still had any of the money. There's nothing a jilted banker wants more than to see his money returned. Especially in Switzerland, bankers genetically avoid the sort of adverse publicity that would have certainly followed the arrest and trial of a man like Eli Pinkas. And he would have understood that.

The most logical reason that he didn't try to return the money is because he didn't have it. If the money didn't go to any visible private causes, is it possible then that it went to a public cause? Could there have been a circuit somewhere in Pinkas's brain labelled fanatic?

Consider this: having had access to certain military information, it was not surprising that the Swiss authorities found some classified military documents stored in his factory office safe. There was the Cold War with the super powers, the Gulf War with Iran and Iraq, heightened tensions throughout the Middle East and brush fire wars throughout the rest of the world. Perhaps there were also people on one side of the fence or the other – or someone sitting in the middle of that fence who wanted to know whatever he knew.

The most obvious contact he might have had was Bulgaria. After all, he was 21 when he came to Switzerland and there were all sorts of people he would have befriended while growing up there. The possibility exists that he was selling them information. If nothing else, it would be a source of cash to help in times of financial difficulties. But that would have brought money in, not made $300–800 million disappear. Unless he was buying something from the Bulgarians. But they didn't have much to sell, except perhaps drugs and Pinkas wasn't a drug trafficker. Although they did have access to Russian weaponry. They might also have access to certain Russian nuclear secrets.

If he was dealing with the Bulgarians, whatever he was buying wasn't coming back to Switzerland.

Now the plot thickens.

Every Thursday evening, Eli Pinkas drove to Geneva Airport for the short flight to Nice, France. He returned to Switzerland on Monday morning. He always said he was going to Cannes to spend the weekend with Florence.

Except he didn't.

The reason he flew to Nice on Thursday nights, instead of, say, Friday evening like so many people who regularly spent weekends in the south of France, was because he could change flights there on Thursday nights and not on Friday nights.

El Al didn't fly on Fridays after sundown.

The inconvenience of spending a few hours waiting in the tiny airport at Nice for the late night flight to Tel Aviv was outweighed by the benefit that no one in Switzerland knew where he was going and no one in France cared. On those very limited occasions when he bumped into someone he knew in Nice airport, Pinkas quietly confessed that he kept an apartment in Israel and had installed a lady friend. It seemed plausible enough.

Israeli law required that foreigners owning property, even if it was only a weekend residence, register it. Since Pinkas's death, the Israelis have categorically denied knowing anything about him, claim to have no record of his supposed apartment, or any information about his supposed lady friend. Nor does Israeli Immigration admit to his frequent visits.

Now consider this: it is known that the Israelis were only able to fully develop and maintain their nuclear capability with help from several sources. The United States was one. But Washington didn't foot the entire bill and couldn't be depended on for unhindered support. So the Israelis raised some money on their own, selling high-tech military equipment to low-tech nations, such as Iran, South Africa and Chile. They raised the rest with 'Collectors'.

Since independence in 1948, they have actively courted prominent people scattered around the world who address themselves to selected sources of wealth in order to make those sources available when a need arises. This is nothing like an organized appeal by conscientious Jewish organizations who throw massive dinners, or doorstep charities that plant trees.

This is done very quietly and very discreetly.

For example, in 1960 the Israelis put together their so-called 'Group of 30' – an ad hoc brotherhood of two and a half dozen American millionaires quietly united by a common cause. The $40 million they collected helped to pay for Israel's first nuclear reactor and the neighbouring plutonium separation plant.

But Eli Pinkas never spoke about Israel. He wasn't even a Jew any more. Yet he kept a residence there. Except, the Israelis insist he didn't. But he was a man who knew how to launder money, how to make the paper trail disappear to obscure its source or, even better, how to obscure its destination. The Israelis built their bomb with other people's money. Did they spend any of it inside the Iron Curtain, perhaps buying secrets or expertise or designs or perhaps weapons grade plutonium that the Bulgarians might have stolen from the Russians?

The Israelis don't talk about their nuclear weapons programme any more than they talk about their Collectors.

And, $300–800 million later, why should they?

CHAPTER ELEVEN

Brinks-Mat Meltdown

'Gold has no conscience.'
> Detective Chief Superintendent Brian Boyce,
> Scotland Yard

Shortly before dawn on Saturday 26 November, 1983, between six and eight armed hoodlums broke into the heavily fortressed Brinks-Mat warehouse at Unit 7 of the International Trading Estate, less than a mile from the main runway at Heathrow airport.

With great expertise, they neutralized the guards – handcuffing them, hooding them and binding their feet with masking tape. Then, with gruesome brutality, they terrorized the guards – beating them, threatening to shoot them, pouring petrol over them and holding lit matches close enough to make the guards believe that they were going to be torched.

The gang threatened carnage unless the guards barked out the numbers they'd memorized for the combination locks that would open the underground vaults.

One hour and forty-five minutes later, the gang was gone. With them went 6,400 gold bars – three and a half tons worth. As the price of gold on the London market had closed the night before at around $258 an ounce, the haul was valued at £26,369,778.

Within two weeks, Scotland Yard had four of the men in custody. A year later, three of the four were in jail. One was Mickey McAvoy, a 38-year-old professional thug known in the milieu as 'The Bully'. Another was 41-year-old Brian Robinson, a professional criminal whose organizational abilities had earned him the nickname 'The Colonel'. They were sent away for 25 years. The only thing they still had going for them was that they knew where the gold was.

A year after the largest heist in British history, the police hadn't found a single ounce.

McAvoy was not without friends.

Brian Perry ran a mini-cab agency in East London. Although he'd been known to associate with villains for most of his adult life, he'd never run seriously foul of the law.

John Lloyd also dwelt on the periphery of the East London crime world. He was even living with an archetypal gangster's moll – a woman named Jeannie Savage – whose first husband had been sent down for 22 years for armed robbery.

They were the ones McAvoy turned to. They were the ones he trusted to make sure that his share of the take would be waiting for him when he got out.

To help them, Perry and Lloyd brought in a crony of theirs called Kenneth Noye.

Stocky, 36 years old, with a boxer's build and a broken nose, Noye pretended to be a self-made success – a respectable Kent businessman with interests in haulage and building. As a sideline, he dealt in watches and jewellery. But, unlike Perry and Lloyd, Noye had 'a sheet' – a criminal record – having done time, at various times, for receiving stolen goods, shoplifting, assaulting a police officer, smuggling a pistol into Britain and violation of the gun licensing laws. At the time of the robbery – but unrelated to it – Noye was the object of an investigation by British Customs and Excise officers who were looking into a gold smuggling and tax fraud scheme.

Perry and Lloyd also knew all about Noye's talents in this area, which is why they sought his expertise. And with so much money up for grabs, Noye didn't need much convincing.

One of his contacts was John Palmer, a 34-year-old jeweller. Some years before, the playboy-style Palmer had set up a gold bullion dealership in Bristol called Scadlynn Ltd. His partner was his chum Garth Chappell – also in his mid-30s – who'd previously been convicted of conspiracy to defraud and fined by Customs and Excise for VAT offences. By 1984, however, Palmer had purportedly left the business exclusively to Chappell so that he could oversee a small chain of jewellery stores which he owned in Bristol, Bath and Cardiff.

Noye quickly surmised that the Brinks-Mat gold could easily be laundered through Bristol – the same path used by fraudsters in those Customs and Excise inquiries that had previously targeted him. But he felt it wasn't safe to take the Brinks-Mat gold to Scadlynn as long as each bar carried its original serial numbers. So Noye recruited Palmer – who owned his own smelter – to begin the laborious process of melting down McAvoy's gold and recasting it.

The idea was to send this recast gold – without serial numbers – to Scadlynn where it would be melted again, now mixed with copper and silver coins, and made to look like scrap. From there, it would be forwarded to the official government Assay Office in Sheffield where each bar would be weighed, taxed and legitimized. Scadlynn would then be free to sell it to licensed bullion dealers who would, as middle middle men, melt the impurities out and market it to the British jewellery trade.

As long as everything went according to plan, it would be absolutely impossible to link any of the gold showing up in London's Hatton Garden jewellery district with gold bars stolen from the Brinks-Mat warehouse.

Planning the venture down to the minutest details – Noye's experience told him he had to protect himself at every turn – he flew to Jersey, in the Channel Islands, on Tuesday 22 May, 1984, with £50,000 in fresh £50 notes. He met with officials of the Charterhouse Japhet Bank on Bath Street in St Helier, and discussed with them the possibility of purchasing 11 one-kilo gold bars. They said they could oblige him.

To the bank officials, it appeared to be a straightforward deal.

But Noye was extremely cautious. He kept saying how concerned he was that the certificates issued for the gold might include the serial numbers of each bar. He kept saying, if that's the case, I'm not interested.

It was only after the bank officials assured him, and reassured him, that the certificates did not contain any such information, that he left the £50,000 with them as a deposit. He returned to London and arranged for the outstanding balance to be forwarded to Jersey.

Eight days later, Noye flew back to St Helier to pick up his gold and the non-serial-numbered certificates. From Charterhouse, he carried the gold for the five-minute walk to the New Street branch of the TSB (the Trustee Savings Bank) where he rented a large safe deposit box and stored all 11 bars.

He came home to England that afternoon with only the certificates.

It was no accident that, in size and gold content, his purchase matched the gold that had been stolen.

Nor was it happenstance that he bought 11 gold bars.

He chose that number for two well thought out reasons:

First, because 11 kilos – just over 24 pounds – is still light enough that it can be carried in an attaché case without much strain; and, second, because the value was close enough to £100,000 to be a neat, round figure.

Now, with the proper paperwork to substantiate his purchase of 11 gold bars, Noye intended to transport exactly that number of Palmer's resmelted gold bars per journey from London to Scadlynn. For Noye, the Jersey paperwork was nothing more than an insurance policy, something to show the police if they ever stopped him and wondered where he got the gold.

But without realizing it, in his caution, he'd been a bit clumsy. He'd aroused some suspicions during that initial visit to Jersey when he showed how worried he was with serial numbers on the certificates. The people he was dealing with at Charterhouse Japhet discussed it among themselves and, following routine practice, quietly notified the local police. On Noye's second visit, he was followed. Long before his plane landed in England, the Jersey police had alerted their British counterparts.

Once Palmer had melted the gold, and Noye brought it to Bristol, Scadlynn charged the going scrap rate per ounce plus value added tax, which then stood at 15 per cent. The deal was that, for their trouble, Scadlynn could keep the undeclared VAT. The rest would be deposited into one of their company accounts at the local Bedminster branch of Barclay's Bank. When it came time to pay Noye and the others, the money was withdrawn in cash, stuffed into black garbage bags and trucked to London. Over the next five months, Scadlynn would deposit, withdraw and send to Noye, Perry and Lloyd over £10 million.

If anyone at the bank was in the least suspicious of all this cash coming in and going out, they apparently weren't troubled enough to tell the police about it.

Using a false passport, showing his name as Sydney

Harris, Noye deposited his share of this cash at the Bank of Ireland in Croydon, where he had a standing arrangement that it was to be wire transferred immediately to the bank's Dublin office. McAvoy's girlfriend, Kathy Meacock, used the same branch and the same wire transfer system, on alternate days. So did Jeannie Savage.

Here again, if anyone at the bank was at all suspicious, they never shared those suspicions with the police.

Enter now a few more players.

Brian Perry had a mate named Gordon John Parry, a thick-set ex-convict who was trying to make a living in the property business. A perfect example of how clothes make the man, when Parry was wearing a tie and jacket he looked the part of a businessman. When he was dressed casually, it was easy to tell that this was a very tough character who had learned the hard way how to survive.

Perry brought in Parry, and Parry brought in Michael Relton, a bent solicitor who'd unsuccessfully defended him some years before on a drug trafficking charge. Parry wound up doing three years. With Relton's help, Gordon Parry deposited £793,500 of the cash coming from Scadlynn into the Bank of Ireland in Balham, southwest London, which was instantly wired offshore to the bank's branch in Douglas, on the Isle of Man. Parry, it turns out, had also managed to convince his wife's cousin to help them and she too used the bank in Balham to send nearly £500,000 to the Isle of Man.

In all, £1.5 million in cash was washed through Balham.

To confuse anyone who might attempt to follow the paper trail, Gordon Parry brought some of that money back from the Isle of Man and put it into a second account at the Bank of Ireland in Balham. He subsequently withdrew those funds, in drips and drabs, and sent them offshore to yet another bank.

And all the time, Noye delivered gold to Scadlynn and

Scadlynn kept melting it down, selling it as scrap and sending the cash to London.

In early August 1984, using a solicitor's introduction from Relton, Gordon Parry opened an account at the Hongkong and Shanghai Bank in Zurich where he deposited £840,435 in cash. A week later, an unidentified man showed up at that bank's Bishopsgate headquarters in the City of London with £500,000 cash jammed into a sports bag. He instructed the bank to forward it to Zurich and walked out saying nothing more. He even left the sports bag.

Two weeks after that – over the three-day period from Wednesday through Friday, 29–31 August – Perry, Parry, Relton, a jeweller named John Elcombe who was Parry's friend, and Elcombe's wife Ann, all found themselves in Zurich. It was, of course – as they later claimed in court – nothing more than a coincidence. To substantiate the claim that they hadn't planned to meet, they pointed to the fact that they'd stayed in different hotels.

It was an even greater coincidence that they all opened accounts at the very same branch of the Hongkong and Shanghai bank. A total of £490,000 in cash was deposited between them, bringing their Zurich holdings to just under £1 million.

And the coincidences continued.

On that Thursday, 30 August, Perry and Parry went to nearby Vaduz, Liechtenstein, where they each opened an account with £45,000 cash at The Bank of Liechtenstein. What's more, they co-signed for each other's account. But here, instead of numbers, the accounts were given names. Parry called his 'Glad,' supposedly after his mother, Gladys. Perry called his 'Como,' a play on the name of the popular singer.

Parry now purchased an off-the-shelf company in Jersey called Selective Estates. He then opened an account for the company at Barclay's in Guernsey and had money from the

Isle of Man transferred to Guernsey. From there, Selective Estates wired it on to the Hongkong and Shanghai in Zurich, where Parry opened a second account, this one called 'Burton,' as a tribute of sorts to the actor Richard Burton who'd just passed away.

The following month, John Elcombe deposited £65,000 in cash into his Zurich account, for which Gordon John Parry was a co-signatory. The same day, Parry walked into The Bank of Liechtenstein with a case that he believed to contain £400,000 in cash. When it was counted, he was surprised to find that the actual amount was £500,000. Then, on 24 September, Elcombe put £435,000 in cash into his account, topping it up on 4 December with an additional £640,000 in cash.

Scadlynn was proving to be a cash cow beyond anyone's wildest imagination. They were selling gold as fast as they could melt it. It soon got to the point where the company was moving so much money in and out of Barclay's, the branch had to bring in extra tellers just to deal with Scadlynn's business.

But if this was Mickey McAvoy's money, you couldn't prove it by the way everyone else was suddenly living on it.

Having been tipped off by the Jersey police about Noye's couple of visits to St Helier, Scotland Yard decided to keep an occasional eye on him. When they spotted him in the frequent company of Brian Reader – a wanted criminal whom they believed to be hiding in Spain – they moved in for a closer look. Not liking what they saw, they abandoned routine surveillance and brought in the Metropolitan Police's C-11 team – a specialist unit used exclusively for top secret reconnaissance and close-target surveillance.

Early on a cold and dark Saturday evening – 26 January 1985 – two officers scaled the perimeter wall of Noye's house and positioned themselves to spend the night in the grounds. One of those officers was John Fordham, a nine-year veteran of C-11.

But sometime around 6.25 p.m., one of the three rottweiler dogs that constantly patrolled the grounds discovered Fordham. Two more dogs joined the commotion. They cornered Fordham. That's when Noye arrived, possibly with Reader. And Noye was carrying a four inch knife.

Fordham's body was discovered by police with 11 stab wounds, mostly in his back. Noye was immediately arrested. Reader was picked up a few miles away. The two were charged with murder. The police claimed that Reader had held Fordham down while Noye killed him. Both Noye and Reader denied that allegation. Noye pleaded self-defence. Reader claimed he wasn't involved at all. And to the utter astonishment of the police, 10 months later an Old Bailey jury acquitted both of them.

There was however, enough evidence to link them with the laundering of the Brinks-Mat gold – a small cache of gold bars was found at Noye's house – and they were subsequently charged with conspiracy to handle stolen goods.

Within three days, the police had also arrested Palmer and Chappell and moved in on Scadlynn.

John Elcombe knew nothing about Fordham's killing.

On that Saturday, he and his wife left London for Switzerland in Gordon Parry's Mercedes with £710,000 in fresh £50 notes stashed in the trunk. They'd already made one trip to Zurich that year – on 7 January – to deposit £453,000 in cash. They knew the route well and figured they could simply breeze through it again.

For the Elcombes, this was turning out to be a very easy way to earn some money.

However, a few days later, crossing into Germany from the southern tip of Holland, a guard on the Aachen side of the border stopped them and asked if they had anything to declare. Elcombe and his wife said no, nothing except £45,000 in cash – they said it was their life's savings – which they were taking to Switzerland.

The guard's sixth sense told him something was not quite right. He studied the Elcombes' passports, lingered for a long time with the vehicle registration papers, then announced he wanted to search the car.

John and Ann Elcombe had little choice but to stand there and hope the money was well hidden.

It wasn't.

The guard opened the trunk, automatically pulled up the carpeting on the floor and found the £710,000. The Elcombes now tried to bluff it out, stating that they were antique dealers working out of Belgium and this was indeed their life savings. But they'd already been trapped by their first lie, and the two were officially detained for questioning.

The money was removed from the car, piled on top of a desk inside the shack at the border crossing, and counted. For some reason, the guard took it upon himself to write down the serial numbers of random bank notes. Then he notified his headquarters in Wiesbaden, telling them what he'd found, asking them what they wanted him to do. Wiesbaden debated that point for a while before someone there decided to notify the German Interpol office. They, in turn, concluded that the proper course of action would be to inform the British authorities.

So German Interpol sent a telex to British Interpol to ask: are you looking for either John or Ann Elcombe? Have large amounts of currency recently been stolen? Is the Mercedes being held at the Aachen border on the stolen car register?

British Interpol passed the query along to Scotland Yard and a fast check was done. The answer to all three questions came back, no. So Scotland Yard duly informed British Interpol, who duly informed German Interpol, who passed the information along to German Customs and Immigration, who finally rang the border guard near Aachen. The money was loaded back into the trunk of the Mercedes and the Elcombes were allowed to drive away.

That might well have been the end of that, had someone at Scotland Yard not taken a second look at all the various telexes. He noticed that the car John Elcombe was driving was registered to one Gordon John Parry. And for some odd reason, the name Gordon John Parry rang a vague bell. It was a name he'd seen before, but he wasn't quite sure where.

He thought about it for a long time, until late that evening, when he realized it was a name that was somehow associated with the Brinks-Mat inquiry. Immediately, he phoned the Brinks-Mat situation room. When officers there heard the name Elcombe, they couldn't believe it and begged British Interpol to ask German Interpol to arrest him.

But by now, the Elcombes were long gone.

Clearly shaken by the close call at the border, the Elcombes took their time getting to Zurich. It wasn't until the following Friday, 1 February, that John Elcombe deposited £100,000 in his own account and £608,000 in a new account, this one known solely by the number 720.3. The £2,000 difference between what they took out of England and what they deposited was written off to expenses, including one night to settle their nerves in the royal suite of the Dolder Grand Hotel – in the bed that had hosted, among other international personalities, Dr Henry Kissinger.

Three days later, on Monday 4 February, someone deposited £493,970 into Parry's 'Glad' account. One week after that – as a direct result of John Fordham's killing and the border scare at Aachen – John Elcombe transferred £1.6 million from his account into 720.3. Next, Parry closed his 'Glad' account and moved that money into 720.3, bringing the total there to over £2.6 million.

Not surprisingly, Michael Relton was just as busy as

everyone else. On Friday 26 April, he arrived in Liechtenstein to create what is usually known as a 'Red Cross account'.

Formally referred to by attorneys and tax specialists as a 'foundation account', the idea is that the monies are controlled by an organization – often one with the name of a charity, as if to suggest that the money in the account is destined to go to some good cause – and under the administration of an attorney.

While it's customarily written into the foundation's charter that a charity is to be named beneficiary, the beneficiary is not necessarily the beneficial owner of the account. No one is supposed to know who that is, not even the bank's directors. The true identity of the beneficial owner is protected by the double layer of bank secrecy and attorney–client privilege.

This is precisely the type of account that Robert Maxwell used in Liechtenstein, enabling him to claim that neither he nor his family controlled any of the monies he'd deposited there and that neither he nor his family would subsequently benefit from them.

In the strictest sense, that's true. But controlling funds and being the ultimate beneficial owner of them are two different matters. And such is the iron-clad nature of a Red Cross or foundation account that anyone lying about their beneficial ownership will get away with it every time because it is impossible to prove otherwise.

Being a lawyer, Relton knew the ins-and-outs of Red Cross accounts and opened his in the name of the Moet Foundation, a reference to his favourite champagne. However, either the attorneys acting for him or the bank misunderstood his instructions, and when the account was processed they spelled it Moyet.

In any case, Relton and Parry put £3,167,409.25 into the Moyet Foundation's account. Unfortunately for them, Parry had just bought some property – Gowles Barn Farm, near Sevenoaks in Kent – which he paid for with a Credit Suisse draft drawn against the 720.3 account. And, in their haste to move funds from 720.3 to the Moyet Foundation, Parry hadn't bothered to find out if his draft for £152,126 had cleared.

As a matter of fact, it hadn't.

So when Credit Suisse presented it to The Bank of Liechtenstein, there were no funds left in the account. Normally the bank would have refused the cheque. But because the managers knew where the money was, they took it upon themselves to transfer the necessary funds back from the Moyet Foundation account into 720.3.

Had Parry not bounced that cheque, the police would never have been able to penetrate the secrecy of the foundation account and associate the Brinks-Mat hoodlums with that money.

In the 15 months that separated the robbery and the killing of John Fordham, the gang now controlling the gold had gotten through most of it. The police estimate that less than £5 million remained. What none of the gang members knew was that the Metropolitan Police had, by this point, assigned 200 officers to the Brinks-Mat inquiry. The largest heist in British criminal history was being matched by one of the largest manhunts in British police history.

Unaware of just how close the police were getting to them, Gordon Parry and Michael Relton began thinking that they should provide for their old age, for that day in the distant future when the gold supply would eventually dry up. So they embarked on a series of hefty real estate investments.

With the Selective Estates shell company as their umbrella, they formed a wholly owned subsidiary called Blackheath Ltd. Parry and Relton – now as Blackheath – made their first purchase in Cheltenham, picking up a residential development project for £350,000.

To finance it, Relton had the Hongkong and Shanghai

Bank in Zurich send $300,000 to the Southeast Bank in Sarasota, Florida, where he maintained an account. Southeast then forwarded $200,000 to his personal account at Midland Bank in London. Next, he sent £104,000 of the £174,029 that he was credited with to the British Bank of the Middle East, a London subsidiary of the Hongkong and Shanghai, which in turn wired £103,700 to the solicitors acting for the sellers of the Cheltenham property. Finally, Blackheath 'borrowed' £250,000 from the British Bank of the Middle East, guaranteeing the loan with monies still sitting in the 'Burton' account.

Because the first deal in Cheltenham worked like a charm, they did it again, this time adding Jersey, Guernsey and the Isle of Man to the washing cycle. In all, they invested £2.1 million, smugly believing that anyone trying to crack their maze would constantly find themselves running up against brick walls. After all, they were spinning money around six countries. Relton knew that even if the police somehow stumbled onto what they were doing, it would take years to obtain court orders in six different jurisdictions to open nearly a dozen bank accounts. And, even if they managed to get their cases heard, there was no guarantee that their requests would be granted.

In fact, Relton was so utterly convinced that they were beyond the reach of the law that he and Parry headed south, to London Docklands, which was considered, at the time, one of the hottest property development projects in Europe.

They bought New Caledonian Wharf, Upper Globe Wharf, Globe Wharf, Cyclops Wharf and Lower Kings and Queens Wharf. In each case, their laundry cycle was basically the same. They would borrow money from one bank, securing it with money in other accounts, then move that money through various banks, bringing it out to look like legitimate loans secured by the property they were buying. In all, they spent just over £5.4 million in Docklands. By selling most of it at the height of the property boom – at least on paper – they more than doubled their money.

Intellectually equipped to play such lucrative games, Relton and Parry now formed a Panamanian company – Melchester Holdings – and contrived to sell a nightclub that Parry owned back to himself.

First they took just over £300,000 out of the 'Burton' account and gave it to a London solicitor acting for Melchester Holdings. He put it in his client account. When the paperwork was ready, that solicitor sent the money to Relton, for his client account. When the papers were signed, Relton passed the money along to Parry to complete the sale.

As if they hadn't already made enough on the deal, Melchester sold the club to a friend of Parry's for £100,000, which wound up back in the 'Burton' account.

On Tuesday 7 February, 1984, a man – whose identity is as yet unknown to the police – walked into a small merchant bank in the City of London and, on the understanding that it acted as agents for Mercantile Overseas Bank on the Isle of Man, handed a manager there £304,000 in cash. His instructions were to send the money to the bank's headquarters in Douglas.

Confirmation of the transfer was put onto Mercantile's books the following day. But, according to the bank, as no one there knew anything about this, the money was stored in a settlement account – a temporary account for monies that have no other home, monies that are waiting to be claimed. In this case, Mercantile Overseas identified the money as Mangrove Settlement Account #691,343.

On 2 March, a man calling himself Patrick Clarke purchased a £300,000 draft with cash at the Bank of Ireland in Ilford, made out to John Lloyd. That same day, a Mercantile

Overseas Bank officer in London received a phone call from an as yet unidentified man, asking him to fetch an envelope from a man he didn't know at the Tower Hotel, near the Tower of London on the River Thames. The bank officer later told police that he walked into the lobby where a total stranger came up to him, handed him an envelope, told him it was to be forwarded to Douglas, then walked away.

Even though it was now more than three weeks after that first anonymous deposit, and even though there was apparently nothing to suggest that these two deposits were in any way related, and even though other monies totally unrelated to the Brinks-Mat laundering operation had come into Mercantile, and even though they'd assigned new numbers to those unrelated deposits, this £300,000 draft made out to John Lloyd was – by sheer coincidence – held for safe keeping as Mangrove Settlement Account #691,343-B.

Twelve days later, on Wednesday 14 March, Kenneth Noye paid £300,000 into the Mercantile Bank, where it was assigned the name Belleplaine Settlement Account #690,227.

On Monday 30 April – a full 47 days after Noye's first £300,000 deposit – he sent another £300,000. Again, by coincidence, the bank credited it to Belleplaine Settlement Account #690,227-B. A further £200,000 that Noye transferred to Mercantile Overseas wound up in Belleplaine Settlement Account #690,227-C.

And all this time, the bank maintained, it didn't know who any of this money belonged to.

That's when an even more curious thing happened. Money sitting in those accounts – supposedly owned by someone unknown to the bank – was transferred, apparently at the bank's own initiative. On Wednesday 4 July, £104,366 was moved out of the Belleplaine Settlement Account into Mangrove Settlement Account #691-343-C. On that Friday, the bank took a further £200,000 from

Belleplaine and put it into Mangrove Settlement Account #691,343-D. Seventeen days later, an interbank transfer for £105,000 found its way into Mangrove Settlement Account #691,343-C2.

Again, all this took place without any instructions from any client.

The next day, Tuesday 24 July, Noye handed £200,000 in cash to the Royal Bank of Canada in London, which was acting as agents for Mercantile Overseas and not otherwise involved with this matter. He wanted it sent to Douglas. And the bank in the Isle of Man automatically stored those funds in Belleplaine Settlement Account #690,227.

On Friday 10 August, a man as yet unknown to the police put another £200,000 through the Royal Bank of Canada and that became Mangrove Settlement Account #691,343-E.

The final transfer – from an as yet unknown man in London – for £112,223 came into Mercantile Overseas in Douglas and became Mangrove Settlement Account #691,343-F.

When the police finally managed to unravel all these transfers at the end of 1986, they were able to get their hands on most of that money which, they decided, belonged to Noye.

But £975,000 was missing.

The bank's explanation was that, one day in November 1986 – a month after Relton was arrested – a man with a German accent calling himself Captain Schultz walked into the Douglas branch and demanded his money. Bank officials insisted they didn't know what he was talking about until he mentioned the dates that he supposedly deposited the funds, the sums involved and the bank transfers he'd arranged. Because he was able to satisfy the bank that the money sitting in the #691,343 series of Mangrove Settlement Accounts was his, they took his instructions and, just like that, forwarded £975,000 to Germany.

By that time the police had also arrested Parry and Noye,

had frozen accounts in four countries, plus the Channel Islands and the Isle of Man, had found £1.5 million stashed in Noye's Dublin account, but had somehow missed the £2.5 million Jeannie Savage had hidden there too. Her money stayed dormant for five years. She left it there, accruing interest, watching her original £2.5 million cozily turn into £4.1 million – which is when the police grabbed her stash. They also eventually found and seized additional accounts for Brian Perry, Gordon John Parry, the Elcombes and John Lloyd, among others.

Assets totalling close to £21 million of the original £26 million have now been recovered.

Everything changed the night John Fordham died.

A cop had been killed.

The Commissioner of the Metropolitan Police said that he wanted the Brinks-Mat investigation to be given an even higher priority and it noticeably clicked into a higher gear. In addition, he ordered a team of officers split away from the main task force and put on the trail of the international money launderers.

One of the men suspected of having taken part in the burglary was a professional criminal named John Fleming who was on the lam in Spain. He'd been spotted there and, with the cooperation of the Spanish authorities, British undercover officers were keeping him under surveillance. They'd planted themselves close enough to his house to watch his every move. They'd also tapped his phones. But in those days there was no extradition treaty with the UK. So all they could do was watch, and continue to build a case against him.

For all intents and purposes, Fleming could have stayed right where he was – safe in the knowledge that he was untouchable – had his passport not expired.

Because there was an arrest warrant waiting for him in

London, getting his passport renewed at his local British consulate was out of the question. And, without a valid passport, Fleming knew he couldn't stay in Spain. So he fled the country.

He headed for the Caribbean – with British detectives in tow – and when he learned he couldn't hide there he tried Latin America. When that failed, he made a big mistake and wound up in the United States.

Promptly arrested by the Americans, acting on a request from the British, extradition proceedings began. Fleming sat in a Florida jail for the next several months, fighting that process. He lost. And within hours of the judgment against him, he was handcuffed and on a plane to London.

This time, luck was on Fleming's side.

His expired passport had forced Scotland Yard to act too soon. They now believe that, had Fleming stayed in Spain, they would have had all the time they needed to build a solid case against him. Unfortunately, they had to take him when the Americans deported him and base their entire case against him – and his alleged part in the Brinks-Mat robbery – solely on what they had available at the time. Because that wasn't enough to convince a judge and jury, John Fleming walked free.

However, while eavesdropping on his phone calls in Spain, the police were able to learn about Fleming's relationship with a man named Patrick Bernard Arthur Diamond, who ran an Isle of Man company formation service called Comprehensive Company Management (Manx). On several occasions, the police heard Fleming ask Diamond to wire money to Spain. So now Scotland Yard turned their attention to Diamond and, with the cooperation of the Manx police, they tapped his phone too.

Although none of the other people involved in the inquiry appeared to have any ties with Diamond, the Isle of Man was too small to write off the connection as a mere coincidence.

What's more, Diamond's sense of humour had a certain black tone to it. He'd recently formed companies – which were ultimately tied directly to the Brinks-Mat money – with names such as 'G. Reedy Holdings' and 'Inventive Inventories, Inc.'.

Keeping him under close surveillance, Scotland Yard learned that Diamond was a man who liked to party and came to London almost every weekend. So now, whenever he landed in London, officers tracked him. Most evenings, they followed him to nightclubs frequented by the underworld.

Each of his contacts was carefully noted.

On one particular Friday night, Diamond checked into the Westbury Hotel on Conduit Street in London's West End, and met with a young American who'd registered there under the name of Stephen Marzovilla.

Curious about this possible new player, officers moved into the hotel, expanding their surveillance to cover him – although a quick check with the FBI failed to turn up any information about anyone called Marzovilla. The phones in both rooms were tapped.

That Saturday night, when Diamond and Marzovilla left for the evening, one surveillance team followed them while a second team gained access to Marzovilla's room.

Sorting through the American's possessions, two interesting – albeit minor – items were found: the first was a family tree, showing Marzovilla's occupation as a plumber and listing information about his wife and children, including their dates of birth. The other, hidden inside a secret compartment of his toilet kit, was a pair of switchblade knives.

For the police, a family tree is a dead giveaway that a suspect is learning a new identity. They could now reasonably assume that Marzovilla wasn't his real name.

As for the switchblade knives, they decided those might come in handy later.

On that Monday, before Diamond left for home, the wire taps recorded a phone call from him to Fleming in which the two spoke about a visit later in the week from 'The Pizza Man'. As Diamond was clearly referring to Marzovilla, it meant that Fleming knew him as well.

Undercover officers spent the next five days tailing Marzovilla, and as a result of that surveillance were able to establish a pair of significant facts: that he kept an apartment in Chelsea, on the fashionable and expensive Cheyne Walk; and that he maintained several safe deposit boxes in vaults around Central London.

The decision was now made to arrest him.

But that had to be done with extreme caution. They didn't want to alert him to their interest in Diamond, in Fleming or in his safe deposit boxes. Nor did they want to admit that they suspected Marzovilla was not his real name. So they settled on a scenario that proved to be as unusual as their interest in him.

Marzovilla checked out of the Westbury on Friday and took a taxi to the airport for his flight to Spain. He was allowed to check in and proceed to security. There, airport police – acting on instructions – waited until his carry-on luggage went through the X-ray machine. And that's when they pulled him aside. They claimed something had shown up on the screen that didn't look quite right. He said he didn't know what they were talking about. They hand-searched his carry-on. He waited. When they got to his toilet bag, they uncovered the switchblades.

While he was held at Heathrow for attempting to carry dangerous weapons on board a plane, the Metropolitan Police obtained a warrant to open his safe deposit boxes. Among the things they found were $100,000 in cash, plus a US passport and corroborating identification – including a driver's licence and other papers – in the name of Craig Jacobs. That name was promptly wired to the FBI and the response came back that Craig Jacobs was a known alias of Scott Nicholas Errico, a man who'd been convicted on two counts of drug smuggling but had jumped bail awaiting sentencing. An FBI warrant had been issued for his arrest in that matter.

But that wasn't all.

Menacingly, Errico was also wanted by the FBI on three counts of murder.

Still playing their cards close to the chest, the police formally charged him with possession of offensive weapons at an airport. To move their prisoner from Heathrow to Cannon Row police station in London, they strapped him in chains and provided an uncharacteristically huge armed escort. In fact, there was so much fire power visible, even Marzovilla remarked that there were an awful lot of armed guards just for one guy with two small knives.

By this point, he plainly suspected that they were on to him because, when the convoy arrived at Cannon Row and he was taken to be fingerprinted, he refused to cooperate. As he was well within his rights to reject fingerprinting, there was little the police could do about it.

And over the next two days, he resolutely stuck to his lie – I'm a plumber named Marzovilla.

His refusal to budge from that story put the police in a minor quandary. They needed to prove beyond any doubt what they already knew, that Marzovilla was Errico. The best way to make their case was through fingerprints, but they couldn't force him to cooperate without tainting their evidence.

That's when one of the officers suggested a gag so simple-minded – the undisputed, oldest trick in the book – that the others on the case with him thought he was totally out of his mind. It's a stunt cops pull in bad movies, and even then it doesn't usually work.

Yet the officer insisted he be allowed to give it a try. And with great amusement – not to mention a heavy dose of utter scepticism – permission was granted.

After a particularly long interrogation session, that officer asked Marzovilla if he wanted a cup of coffee. Marzovilla said he did. But a few seconds later the officer reappeared to apologize that the kettle wasn't working. I'm sorry, he said, how about a glass of water instead? Marzovilla said thanks. He took the glass, drank from it and put it down on the table. The instant he did, the officer grabbed it.

Even Marzovilla was willing to admit that he'd been had.

Forensics lifted a perfect set of fingerprints off the glass and the FBI now confirmed Stephen Marzovilla, alias Craig Jacobs, was in fact Scott Nicholas Errico. Hardly a plumber, he was a professional killer.

Although Errico fought extradition for more than 18 months, claiming that the murders he'd been accused of had taken place on a boat outside US territorial waters, the courts didn't see it that way and he was shipped back to the States. There, he was found guilty and sentenced to life in prison.

Errico's business dealings helped the police establish a sure link to Diamond. The two had a company together called Castlewood Investments. As the British police had proof that Diamond was in business with a convicted drug smuggler, Isle of Man magistrates ordered Diamond to produce all his Castlewood Investment files. Those files, together with evidence Diamond gave to police when he was finally arrested, led to Miami attorney Michael Levine. Scotland Yard tipped off the DEA, which got into Levine's bank accounts and discovered that Diamond had helped to launder $10 million through that connection.

A lot of the money Diamond washed for Levine – who had direct ties to the Colombian drug cartels – was done in classically simple ways. For example, US Customs require anyone coming into the country with cash or bearer instruments worth more than $10,000 to report it. So Diamond would fly to Miami carrying a bearer cheque, drawn on one of his many companies for the sum of $250,000, fill in the proper forms and declare the cheque. Once he had a copy of the form to prove that he'd brought that much money into the country, he'd destroy the cheque. Levine would then give him $250,000 in cash, which Diamond would take out of the country. On the odd chance that US Customs stopped him, he had the proper paperwork to back it up.

Over the course of several years, Diamond set up 90 companies for Levine. He also purchased Strangers Key, a small Bahamian Island, on Levine's behalf. However, when Levine discovered it was not large enough for an airstrip – in other words, too small to be used for smuggling drugs – he sold it.

Diamond was arrested in March 1986 and admitted his involvement with Fleming. He also admitted to having laundered a total of $19 million for Levine. Cornered, Diamond decided to cooperate with the DEA and testify against Levine.

For his role in the Brinks-Mat affair, Diamond was sued in the American civil courts under the anti-racketeering statutes – RICO – which allow for treble damages. Because the Brinks-Mat gold was worth £26 million, the claim set by the court against him was £78 million.

A dozen separate cases fell under the auspices of the Brinks-Mat investigation, which has resulted in 29 people standing in the dock. The trials were, however, marred by jury tampering and death threats. In one case, four separate trials needed to be convened, and in all four the jury had to be protected.

Most of the gang went to jail. Despite being found not guilty of the murder of John Fordham, Kenneth Noye was sentenced to 14 years for handling the gold. Parry got ten years, Perry got nine, Relton got 12 and Jeannie Savage got five. The Elcombes were acquitted. The mysterious German, Captain Schultz, remains free, although he has been located and is under surveillance. The money he took from the Isle of Man has now been traced to Germany – first to a bank in Kiel, then to a bank in Hamburg – and finally back to a National Westminster branch in East London.

Relton is now out and Noye is too, although he has since disappeared, suspected of an alleged involvement in a road rage killing. It is believed he's hiding in Cyprus. Some of the smaller players are out as well.

The two who will stay where they are for a long time to come are Mickey McAvoy and Brian Robinson. They're not due out until 2011, although there is a possibility they could be up for parole in 2004.

In the meantime, their money is gone.

So the two guys who pulled off the greatest robbery in the history of British crime – two guys who went down for 25 years – have had to sit tight while a whole bunch of minor crooks plundered their booty.

It's a good bet that they're both very bitter.

And the police are certain it's an equally good bet that, when they do finally get out, they're going be looking for £26 million worth of flesh from the laundrymen who did them wrong.

There is a very odd postscript to this story.

By the time the American aspect of this case was finally wrapped up, the Drug Enforcement Administration had seized $380 million in drug trafficking assets. So the US government made out a cheque for half of that to say thank you to the Metropolitan Police.

It's called 'asset sharing', and the Americans do it to encourage international cooperation in the war against drugs. But the money is given with a string attached. Although it can be spent on anything – equipment, weapons, training, ongoing operations – whatever it is spent on must, in some way, contribute to the war effort.

Here, the British balked. As one senior official put it, 'The Metropolitan Police mustn't be seen to be bounty hunters.' The ruling came down from somewhere in Whitehall, it must go to the Treasury.

No, the Americans said, that's not the way the deal works. It goes to the police and they have to spend on the war against drugs.

Frantic meetings were held at the Home Office.

Come on, the Americans urged, we've set a very broad criterion. You're free to interpret it in lots of different ways. You can do whatever you want with the money, as long as it satisfies the single objective of the asset sharing programme.

After months of bandying about, the government said they could not accept the gift unless it was given unconditionally.

So the Americans said, sorry, and kept their $190 million.

CHAPTER TWELVE

The Coke Connection

'He doesn't look so dangerous.'
'You never saw him smile!'
Whispered behind the back of Pablo Escobar

The link between money and drugs is absolute.

That the bulk of dirty money spinning around the world comes from the illicit drugs trade is indisputable. It is equally certain that the whopping success of international drug traffickers – the ones primarily dealing in heroin, cocaine and crack – is directly contingent on their ability to launder their profits.

As in any business, a certain percentage of turnover must be recycled into the costs of production and distribution. But where drugs are concerned it's a very small percentage because drugs are a business where the wholesale markup is anywhere from 500 per cent to 1,000 per cent. That puts leviathan sums in the accounts of the dealers, who – by being able to scour that money – can invest in legitimate business in order to finance further criminal activity.

With a momentum and force that might surpass any singular element of the legitimate economy, drugs are a tidal wave, overwhelming fragile economies. In small, dusty towns like Atoka, Oklahoma, and Roma, Texas, property values shot up astronomically when cash-bearing Mexicans arrived, ready to buy. They literally broke the back of the local economy. In small countries like Bolivia, Peru, Ecuador and Colombia, drug money has become a cancer, subverting both the political and the judicial systems.

There are some people who maintain that this narco-economy is so all-powerful it has made traffickers the most influential special-interest group in the world. The money generated and controlled by them has reached such monstrous totals that dozens of Third World countries could not possibly maintain their own economic existence if it were not for the input of drug money. The stupendous amount of dollars that the cocaine industry has brought into Colombia is the sole reason the local peso is one of the most stable currencies in the Americas.

For such nations, narco-economics has become an unofficial form of US foreign aid. If there was some way to put a permanent halt to their income from drug trafficking, the only method then to keep Colombia, Bolivia, Ecuador and Peru afloat would be to continue the massive importation of hard currencies – now in the form of outright charity from the west. Not even an oil-producing nation like Venezuela would necessarily survive without aid.

Following the Cartagena Summit in early 1990, the US government offered to pay $1.5 billion over a five-year period to a group of countries to underpin crop substitution programmes. Colombia, Bolivia and Peru all rejected the gift as inadequate. The Bolivian government said it would need at least half that to make such a scheme work. The Peruvians stated they alone would require in excess of $1 billion, and if they got the entire $1.5 billion they still couldn't guarantee success.

And yet, even if America paid it and even if Bolivia and Peru did destroy all the coca and did wipe out all of the trafficking that takes place inside their borders, the impact on the world market would be negligible. The demand would be met instantly by any of a dozen producing nations.

The sums involved are way beyond anything that is easily comprehensible. A few years ago, the late Colombian cocaine cartel boss Pablo Escobar had to write off $40 million in cash because it rotted in a California basement. He couldn't get it into the washing cycle fast enough. He was already laundering so much that the machinery overheated and the system blew a fuse.

When he was caught the first time, and word spread that he might be extradited to the United States, Escobar offered to barter for his freedom by personally paying off Colombia's national debt.

Policies aimed at attempting to curtail, or even, somehow, just to control, the spread of international narcotics consumption have failed – and failed miserably.

US Customs, in a combined effort with the US Coast Guard, and backed up by the US Navy – fully armed guided missile cruisers were on constant patrol in the Gulf of Mexico and the Caribbean to provide early warning detection of planes and boats that might be bringing drugs into the country – spent $1.1 billion in 1992–93 trying to inderdict the smugglers. The result, according to a classified National Security Council document, was abject failure. Confronted with that report, Attorney General Janet Reno was forced to admit, 'General interdiction, which has been very costly, does not work. I've not seen anything since I've been in office which would indicate to me that it's been a cost-effective effort.'

With more drugs on the streets than ever before, it's little wonder that so many policemen feel they're fighting a losing battle. How do you convince a 12-year-old black or

Hispanic kid in Harlem that if he comes to school he'll learn a trade and someday earn $10 an hour when for the past two years he's been selling crack to his friends and pulling down $1,000 a day?

The roots of the problem get straight back to Third World economics. There's more money in opium poppies or the coca bush than in oranges, cotton, bananas or coffee.

Sugar cane, for example, is harvested, refined, packaged, shipped, marketed and finally retailed in supermarkets for $1–1.50 a kilo. Heroin goes through much the same process – harvesting, refining, packaging, shipping, marketing and finally retailing – except there's no supermarket overhead calculated into the price. And heroin can wholesale for $30,000–35,000 a kilo. Given a choice – and a rudimentary knowledge of simple arithmetic – why would anyone in their right mind want to be in the sugar business?

What's more, narco-dollars are exogenous – they derive from outside the native economy to bolster the balance of trade, to relieve pressures on a country's dollar reserves and to provide a hefty, short-term fix to the local standard of living.

The Third World is filled with people who can't see how putting an end to drug trafficking is in their interest, while the industrial west is filled with well-meaning souls who don't have the slightest clue of what life is like in the rest of the world.

Some years ago, a bunch of do-gooders tried to promote a crop substitution plan along the Afghan borders where opium poppy is the main cash crop. They wanted local farmers to grow orchids instead. Not only were the Afghans against the plan for fundamental economic reasons, but the western missionaries never fathomed that orchids couldn't grow there anyway.

Even if orchids could grow on the moon, a peasant doesn't need a degree from the London School of Economics to know that if he harvests opium poppy to satisfy a booming market he'll feed his family and if he harvests sorghum or sugar or tobacco leaf for a shrinking market, they'll starve.

Legitimate commodity prices have plummeted in the past 20 years, at a time when Third World debt has skyrocketed. There might once have been a sensible argument for pro- grammes designed to replace Third World drug crops with maize, alfalfa or tomatoes, that is, as long as there was a flourishing world market for maize, alfalfa or tomatoes. But those days are over. Preaching to some Bolivian – or his compatriots in Colombia or Peru, Thailand or Cambodia – on the joys of the simple life in the beetroot trade is an exercise in futility. As pointless as selling that New York City street kid on the benefits of going to plumbing school.

One Washington source professes that the foundation of today's crisis lies in the aggressive lending by American and European banks to the developing economies during the 1970s and 1980s. Defaults on those loans derailed the entire western banking system. As the cocaine industry is the major employer in Bolivia, Colombia and Peru, it's hardly surprising that the proceeds of drug trafficking are returning to the west in the form of loan repayments from Latin America.

Those funds – now washed – are the same funds that have begun to buoy up the liquidity of western banks.

How ironic that drug money should now stretch from the valleys of Peru, through several Latin American finance ministries, directly back to the boardrooms of major west- ern banks.

As coca production in countries like Peru has increased seven and eight fold over the past five years, assets from the drug trade – at least those finding their way into nations belonging to the Bank for International Settlements – have grown from $350 billion to $500 billion.

Something approximating one half of that is said to belong

to the major drug cartels. A 1990 report to the leaders of the seven largest industrial nations lays bare the fact that 50–70% of the proceeds from drug trafficking around the world is laundered through the western banking system. Drug traffickers operating only in America and Europe are estimated to be washing upwards of $100 billion a year – a figure that exceeds the GNP of 90% of all the countries currently represented in the United Nations.

Officially proclaimed sums must always be taken with a grain of salt because it's standard operating procedure for government agencies throughout the world to exaggerate a threat in order to keep a straight face when asking for an exaggerated budget increase. But, as the global assets from the drug trade continue to rise, two facts undeniably stand out:

First – shockingly – more money is being spent today, worldwide, on illicit drugs than on food.

And, second, random forensic testing in the United States has revealed that practically every bank note in circulation throughout the entire country bears microscopic traces of cocaine. In other words, practically every US bank note in circulation has at some point been used in a drug deal.

Drugs in general and cocaine in particular have become the backbone of several Latin American economies.

The Medellin and Cali cartels were often referred to as the region's only successful multinational enterprises. But then, they were in a business where the production–profit ratio is staggeringly high. Approximately 20 per cent of the wholesale price, as imported into the west, goes towards expenses – cultivation, bribes, smuggling, handling and write-offs for drugs that are confiscated or stolen along the way. The rest – an astonishing 80 per cent – is pure profit.

If you accept one US government estimate that as much as $200 billion worth of narcotics is coming into the United

States alone – roughly equivalent to one-third of all US imports – then the lion's share of $160 billion filters back to the drug barons, putting them at the top of the list of the world's wealthiest people. At least three Colombian cartel members are purported to be among the five richest men in the world, surpassed only by the Sultan of Brunei and King Fahd of Saudi Arabia. Even their lieutenants are said to be worth more than the Queen of England.

A very small portion of the world's cocaine is actually grown in Colombia – only about 10 per cent. The cartels purchase most of their product from Peru and Bolivia. They then buy their processing chemicals in Germany, Brazil and, surprisingly, the United States. As approximately 10 per cent of Colombia's workforce is somehow tied to the narcotics trade, Pablo Escobar Gaviria – founder of the Medellin drug cartel – was, for a time, the nation's largest and most important employer.

The city of Medellin, capital of Antioquia Province in west central Colombia, is 155 miles from Bogotá. Dating back to 1675, it sits in a mountain valley 5,000 feet above sea level, is the country's second largest city – population 1.6 million – and is its principal industrial centre. Local manufacturers produce steel, textiles, rubber, electrical goods and tobacco.

For much of the 1980s and into the first few years of the 1990s, it was the most dangerous city in the western hemisphere. Many crimes in Medellin did not then – and still do not – get investigated because the police have been intimidated. Even the DEA, which once had an office there, left town for safety reasons. They wanted to keep their operatives alive.

Escobar was plump, stood five feet six inches tall, had curly black hair and occasionally sported a black mustache. Hardly menacing in appearance, he was a ruthless, cold-blooded murderer who'd spent years building a Robin Hood image. He told people he'd grown up in abject poverty. It isn't true. He was born in Rionegro in December 1949, and raised in Envigado, a working-class suburb of Medellin. His mother was a schoolteacher. His father was a mildly successful farmer.

Beginning his own career as a teenaged petty crook, Escobar's first job after high school was as an apprentice to a minor smuggler, dealing in small electronic goods stolen from warehouses along the Panama Canal. He worked his way up into heavier crimes, but didn't make any real money until the early 1970s when he orchestrated the kidnapping of a local industrialist. From there, he drifted into the drug business.

Arrested and convicted in September 1974 for trafficking 39 kilos of cocaine, he bribed enough people to be released after three months and all charges against him were soon dropped. Over the next five years, he continued to be arrested for drug dealing, and he continued to be let off.

At first, it was the evidence that disappeared.

Then it was the witnesses, the arresting officers and the judges.

When Carlos Mauro Hoyos, Colombia's Attorney General, first advocated extraditing drug traffickers to the US, he was machine gunned in the centre of Medellin by three car loads of Escobar's soldiers. In 1989, Escobar planned and carried out the bombing of an Avianca airliner, which took 107 lives. He was implicated in the murder of a Supreme Court judge and almost two dozen lower court judges. He orchestrated a 1992 bombing campaign against government officials and rival gangs in Medellin, setting off 300 devices, which killed as many people. And, at the beginning of 1993, his men went on a rampage and murdered 178 local policemen. In all, Escobar was directly responsible for several thousand assassinations.

His conquest of the world of major league drug dealing began with one old friend and one new cohort.

Jorge Luis Ochoa Vasquez was Escobar's childhood companion.

Along with his brothers Juan and Fabio, Ochoa had pioneered a smuggling route into the US while managing an import–export company called Sea-8 Trading in Miami. Sent there to take charge of a cocaine ring set up by one of his uncles, by 1978 Ochoa was independently bringing 100 kilos of drugs into the US every week. But the DEA was soon wise to Jorge and sprung a trap to arrest him. He escaped – literally within inches of his life – and hurried home to Colombia. His younger brother Fabio took over the Miami interests.

Back in Medellin, Jorge manifested his own ambitions. He ordered the murder of his uncle and stepped into his place as head of the family business. For Escobar, an association with Ochoa was a natural way to expand both of their businesses – although, until this point, the two were comparatively small-time operators.

Carlos Enrique Lehder Rivas was Escobar's newest acquaintance.

Born in Quinido Province, 180 miles south of Medellin – the same age as Escobar and Ochoa – he'd moved with his mother to the United States when he was 15. Ten years later, he was sitting in a federal penitentiary for trafficking 100 kilos of marijuana. His cell mate was a convicted dealer from Massachusetts named George Jung. Seven years older than Lehder, it was Jung who taught him the ins and outs of the marijuana business. When Lehder heard that Jung had been smuggling thousands of kilos into the country from Mexico, he wondered why anyone would bother with marijuana when cocaine was easier to smuggle and offered greater markups.

In 1976, Lehder was released and deported to Colombia. He settled in Medellin, opened a car dealership and contacted Jung, who was already out. As Jung's parole conditions denied him a passport, he sent his friend and fellow trafficker Frank Shea to Medellin. The result of that visit was a deal whereby Lehder would supply cocaine to Jung and Shea, who would then distribute it through Jung's old marijuana network.

Lehder turned to Escobar and Ochoa for product and the Medellin cartel was in business.

Theorizing that the way to conquer the lucrative North American and European markets was to bombard them, non-stop, with drugs, Escobar accepted that a percentage of his shipments would be stopped. But he was cocksure that a larger percentage would get through. As he was taking a big chunk of that larger percentage, he saw himself in a no-lose situation.

To ensure that he stayed that way, he concocted an image. He opened the doors to his ranch in Puerto Triunfo, along the Magdalena River, and brought the public in to see 'Pablo's Zoo' – a couple of giraffes, some camels and a kangaroo. Mounted on the gates was a light airplane which, he bragged, was the very one he used to smuggle his first shipment of coke into the US.

Riding around in a car once owned by Al Capone, he set off on a mission of benevolence, straddling drug trafficking with right-wing populist politics. For every plane-load of merchandise he sold, Escobar mandated a two kilo kickback to feed, clothe and house Medellin's poor. He supported local football teams and built hundreds of homes. In 1982, the people of Medellin elected him an Alternate Member of Colombia's House of Representatives.

Jorge Ochoa fled to Madrid in June 1984, after being accused of murdering the Minister of Justice. He lived with his family on a false passport in a huge suburban villa, paying for a luxurious lifestyle with money he'd laundered in Europe. He bought a fleet of cars and land for development. But five months after he settled down, the Spanish police captured him.

An arrest warrant had been issued against Ochoa in the US on narcotics charges, so an official request was made for his extradition. Over the next 20 months, Ochoa – easily able to afford the best attorneys in Madrid – fought it. When it became apparent that he would not be handed over immediately, the Americans offered a secret deal. The DEA told Ochoa's lawyers they wanted him to testify that Nicaragua's Sandinista government countenanced drug trafficking. If he'd agree to do it, the United States government promised, their extradition request would be rejected by the Spanish foreign office.

Ochoa's response was that he didn't know anything about that particular connection. Of course he was lying, and the Americans knew it, because they had evidence that Ochoa had personally negotiated with a high-level Sandinista official to build a cocaine processing lab in Nicaragua. Now, because he wouldn't play ball, they renewed their call for Ochoa's deportation. But the Spanish courts learned of the DEA's covert offer and ruled in favour of Ochoa. They said that the Americans were interested in him only for political reasons – to discredit the Sandinistas – and refused the request. Ochoa was deported to Colombia in July 1986 and held in jail for six weeks.

As extradition to the States is perhaps the only thing that the so-called *los extraditables* actually fear, Ochoa's friends in the cartel threatened to eliminate political leaders one by one if he was handed over to the Americans. The government refused to bow to threats and pledged to prosecute Ochoa. Instead, he was 'mistakenly' released.

On the run for another five years, Ochao was captured again in 1991. By this time, Ochoa had finally had enough. While awaiting trial, he accepted a Colombian deal and negotiated a nine-year jail sentence. He also agreed to surrender some of his property and pay a fine of $9,500 – probably less than a day's interest on his laundered wealth.

Carlos Lehder fared considerably less well.

The man who prophetically described cocaine as 'the Third World's atomic bomb' was captured in a shoot-out with Colombian government troops at his jungle mansion in 1987 and almost instantaneously extradited to the United States.

His trial in Florida was billed as one of the most important prosecutions in the history of American law enforcement. Dubbed by the broadsheet press as the embodiment of a narco-terrorist, the tabloids called him *el loquito Carlos* – crazy Charlie. The media covered every facet of his life, real and imagined, in great detail. Special play was made of the fact that he'd once founded his own political party – the anti-Semitic, neo-Nazi Latin National Movement – which had some minor successes in local Colombian elections. Like Escobar, Lehder had also endowed low-cost housing for slum dwellers.

The prosecution claimed that, in 1978, Lehder purchased the tiny island of Norman's Cay in the Bahamas, rebuilt the airstrip there and used it to transship cocaine from Colombia to the States. His former pilot testified that they'd fly drugs into Ft Lauderdale's Executive Airport, offload them without any interference from US Customs, take on suitcases filled with cash – again, no one asked questions – and head straight back to Norman's Cay for the next load. Another witness described how Fidel Castro had introduced Lehder to Robert Vesco and how Vesco had taught Lehder the business of money laundering.

Lehder's defence team tried to make the jury believe that the 39-year-old coke addict – who owned a yacht, had 19 cars, bragged about his endless supply of women and kept a naked, helmeted statue of John Lennon in his private discotheque – was nothing more than misunderstood. They asserted that he was an otherwise innocent businessman who hoped to build a resort on Norman's Cay but backed off when he found it overpopulated with drug traffickers.

He was convicted and sentenced to life imprisonment plus 135 years.

Next came Escobar's surrender.

The government wanted him enough that it was willing to take him any way he'd agree to be taken. Early in the summer of 1991, he said he'd submit himself to protective custody while waiting to stand trial for murder and drug trafficking, but only on two conditions: they had to guarantee that he wouldn't be extradited to the United States; and, he had to be held in a prison designed expressly for him.

The government accepted his terms.

So it denied the Americans' request for him and built the Envigado jail to his specifications in the hills overlooking Medellin. *Hacienda* style, it came complete with a swimming pool, a tennis court and a sauna. Complying with his every wish, it was also stocked with telephones and fax machines. He was even permitted to bring his own plastic surgeon into the compound and have his face lifted.

For Escobar, prison was going to be business as usual.

Ensconced along with 50 of his own armed guards, he cost the Colombian government half a million dollars a year – including the security system that not only kept Escobar in, but kept possible assassins out.

A year later, with his trial slated to open, he was told he'd have to be transferred to an ordinary cell. He refused. Negotiators came to see him and a hostage situation developed. The army arrived and, in the confusion, Escobar escaped. A dramatic military and police manhunt searched 15,000 homes for him to no avail. The US State Department now considered Escobar so dangerous that it put a $2 million price on his head. Coupled with the $1.4 million the Colombian government had already tagged on him, Pablo Escobar became the world's most wanted man.

After 17 months in hiding, Pablo Escobar died the way he'd lived much of the past 20 years – violently.

On 2 December 1993, the day after his forty-fourth birthday, the Bloque de Bosqueda – the elite, CIA-trained and DEA-funded 'search unit' of the Colombian security police – located him in a residential neighbourhood on the edges of Medellin. He was talking on the phone to his 16-year-old son. They burst in on him and showed no mercy. In a hail of bullets, they promptly and efficiently gunned him down.

His ego was such that he might have liked to be remembered as a businessman who once controlled an 80 per cent market share of all the cocaine sold in the US. He crowed when he found himself on both the *Forbes* and *Fortune* magazines' lists of the world's richest men.

His personal wealth was put at over $3 billion, prompting William Bennett – 'Drug Czar' to the Bush administration – to remark, 'He was richer than Ross Perot and more powerful than Genghis Khan. They said he was invincible.'

Pablo Escobar thought so, too.

But Pablo Escobar was dead wrong!

He wasn't invincible, any more than he was Robin Hood.

Wanted internationally on numerous charges of drug trafficking, kidnapping and murder, among others, his legacy is of a man who ridiculed the Colombian justice system, killed his enemies, slaughtered innocent people, threw his country into a long and horribly debilitating political crisis and wreaked havoc throughout the rest of the world, destroying untold numbers of lives with the drugs he sold. But then, when they killed him, very little changed.

Cali is the heart of Colombia's agricultural region.

A city that pre-dates Medellin by a century – although

slightly smaller, with 1.4 million people – it lies in the western part of the country, in the heart of the Cauca Valley, on the Cali River not far from where it feeds into the Pacific Ocean. It is a major distribution point for coffee, livestock, minerals, textiles, chemicals, tobacco and paper products.

By all reports, the drug trafficking cartel operating out of there wasn't actually a cartel, at least not in the same sense as Escobar's group. Run more along the lines of a franchise with a main holding company doling out small parcels to a network of independently owned outlets, the federation was the brain-child of Gilberto Rodriguez Orejuela who himself once owned the Chrysler Motors franchise for Colombia. Born in 1939, he got his first job in a Cali drugstore at the age of 15. Five years later, he was the store manager. Five years after that he opened his own drugstore and from there, at least according to him, he built his considerable fortune. Known to his friends as 'The Chess Player', he is the father of seven children, one of whom has an engineering degree from the University of Tulsa.

When Ochoa was sent back from Spain, he and Gilberto were put on trial and very quickly found not guilty. He just as quickly consolidated his position as chairman of the Cali cartel and used his laundered money to create an aura of legitimate affluence. He built Drogas La Rebaja into a national chain of drug stores, owned a bank in Colombia and another in Panama plus a consortium that ran 30 radio stations.

His partner was his attorney brother, Miguel. Five years younger, four times married with eight children, he was an obsessive soccer fan who bought Cali's America team and poured so much money into it, paying outrageous salaries to the best players in Latin America, that he inadvertently capsized the entire league because none of the other teams could compete. Sometimes called 'Patricio', sometimes called 'Manolo', but mostly called 'El Señor', he ran the day-to-day affairs and managed the various groups they did business with around the world.

The number three man was the very violent José Santacruz Londono. A year older than Miguel and nicknamed 'Don Chepe', Londono preferred the more macho handle '07'. Before joining up with the Orejuelas, he'd earned a reputation in the business shipping cocaine from Guatemala to Miami hidden in crates of frozen vegetables. It was his expertise in smuggling that completed the inner circle.

An engineer by trade, Londono had been on the DEA's most wanted list since 1980. One of the aliases he'd used was Victor Crespo but in 1981 the DEA hadn't yet associated the two. On a tip that Crespo was coming to New York, agents stopped a fellow who'd gotten off a flight from Latin America. They checked his passport and because the name in it wasn't Crespo, they allowed him to go about his business.

In 1990, two of his laundrymen were arrested in Luxembourg. One of them, José Franklin Jurado Rodriguez, was a professional money manager with a degree from Harvard. He and his partner, Edgar Alberto Garcia Montilla, spent four years in jail in Luxembourg fighting extradition, but lost and were sent to the US to stand trial. According to them, Londono's money laundering cycle began in Panama, where cash was deposited in the bank owned by Gilberto. From there, it was wired around the world to banks in Britain, France, Holland, Italy, Germany, Monaco, Hungary, Finland and Luxembourg before being sent back to Colombian companies owned by Londono, his family and his friends.

At times considered the most dangerous man in Latin America, Londono was also thought to be the wealthiest of the Cali bunch. Legend had it that in the 1980s, he was refused admittance to the Club Colombia, an exclusive address for local industrialists, so he built an exact replica of it. Among his assets are thousands of apartments in Colombia. Along with the extradition of Jurado and Garcia, $30 million belonging to Londono were frozen in banks around the world. There could be anywhere from three to fifteen times as much still hiding in European banks.

Besides drug trafficking and money laundering, Londono ordered the 1992 murder in New York of Cuban-born journalist Manuel de Dios Unanue who'd been writing about him. Constantly fearing for his own life, carrying a $600,000 price on his head, Londono lived in bedrooms with bulletproof windows.

Gilberto started by moving cocaine into New York in the early 1970s, then expanding to LA and Miami. He and Miguel first came to prominence in November 1975 when Police at Cali's airport discovered 1400 pounds of powder hidden in a small plane that had just landed. The pilot and co-pilot were arrested. That weekend, 40 people were murdered. Some few years later, Escobar was told that Ochoa's near-arrest Miami had come as a result of a tip-off from the Cali cartel. A wave of murders followed. The Orejuelas and their camp immediately sought revenge. Escobar and his cronies might have been the most famous traffickers in Colombia but the Cali bunch were without doubt the most dangerous. Their taste for gratuitous violence even surpassed Escobar's and for a while Colombia's cartel cities averaged 10–15 murders a day.

Eventually Gilberto got smart and started spending more money on bribes than bullets. That's when US officials quietly dubbed the Cali cartel the most sophisticated criminal organization in the world. That's also when Gilberto funded the vigilante group PEPES, People Persecuted by Pablo Escobar. Although the group killed more than 60 of Escobar's relatives and associates, they vindictively helped the authorities hunt him down. In return, Colombian prosecutors took a more live-and-let-live attitude towards the

Cali faction, rationalizing their stance by saying that the Orejuelas were not terrorists the way Escobar was. In fact, it was the Orejuelas who supplied the critical information on Escobar's whereabouts that led the Bloque de Bosqueda to him. They'd already taken away a giant share of his business, now seeing him dead merely handed them the rest of it.

In those days, the Cali cartel's annual profits were estimated at around $7 billion, more than three times as much as General Motors.

At one point, they were moving $50 million monthly out of New York. Computer logs impounded after a 19-month covert operation led to the arrest of their top guy there, Ramiro Herrera, whose brother Pacho worked for the Orejuelas back home. In addition to apprehending 37 other cartel soldiers stationed in the States, the police grabbed 1.3 tons of cocaine and confiscated $16 million in cash. But it turned out to be little more than a hiccup on the cartel's ledgers.

By 1990, the Chess Player, El Señor and Don Chepe were the world's dominant cocaine traffickers.

Long before they'd plundered Escobar's market share, they'd already begun to distance themselves from the retail side of the drug business. They'd lost interest in smuggling. They'd recognized that their future was in wholesale.

Because anybody with collateral in Colombia can become a drug dealer, the Orejuelas offered to subcontract to the mini-cartels. All an aspiring trafficker had to fill out was a very detailed form which listed all his relatives so that the Orejuela brothers knew who to kill if someone tried to betray them, then come up with enough cash or collateral to pay for the shipment up front. The brothers continued to buy directly from the producers but they sold on to these smaller groups, letting other people worry about the transport, marketing, sales and money laundering. If cargoes were intercepted, it wasn't the Orejuela's product. If cash was confiscated, it wasn't the Orejuela's money. The deck was stacked in their favour, structured to guarantee that they couldn't lose. And yet as many as 300 mini-cartels rushed into business with them.

Further diversifying, they nurtured a Mexican connection and franchised out some of their US markets, unsuspectingly designating their own heir apparent.

Suddenly the Feds were faced with a new problem. They would seize a ton of cocaine knowing that the drugs originated with the Orejuelas, but the seizure did no damage to them because there was a broker in the middle. The one or two or three guys making up a mini-cartel might have had to give up ranches and other property to pay for the lost drugs, but the Orejuelas were still alive and well in Cali.

As wealthy as Escobar ever was, the Orejuelas proved themselves more resourceful. For example, just to keep the CIA from intercepting their phone or fax communications, Gilberto almost got away with buying his own satellite. They were also better educated and spent a fortune on pragmatic matters, such as friends in high places.

One of their friends was Gustavo Enrique Pastrana Gomez, an attaché at the Colombian Embassy in Uruguay. Arrested at the end of 1993 as the result of a DEA sting operation in Miami, he'd been washing Orejuelas' money through the purchase of polo ponies and automatic car washes in Argentina. The cousin of a nationally prominent Colombian politician, he bragged to an American undercover agent that he could launder $2 million a week through his network of banking contacts in Montevideo.

The Orejuela brothers spent money successfully to lobby for a constitutional ban on extraditing traffickers to the United States. They spent money successfully to lobby for a law which allows traffickers to turn themselves in, to exchange guilty pleas for light sentence, to demand the outright dismissal of more serious charges and to be sent to prisons where they had whatever they needed to continue doing business. They spent money building police stations in poor neighbourhoods to help reduce street crime and spent money paying off the judiciary.

One of their judges in Bogotá released three Cali laundry-men, saying there were no charges to answer because the prosecutor never showed up. He'd been told to appear in one courtroom after the cartel's lawyers had moved the case.

Another judge, this one in Cali, ordered the release of a trafficker who'd been caught red handed. It created such an outrage that an appeal was rushed into the Supreme Court which promptly overthrew the acquittal. But no one ever bothered re-arresting the man.

A third judge even smuggled drugs for them. Esperanza Rodriguez-Arevalo was arrested in Miami when she flew in with a couple of pounds of uncut heroin in her luggage. The Orejuelas had convinced her she could net upwards of $250,000 wholesaling the drugs, which was more than she could expect to earn on the bench in her entire lifetime.

The Colombian government half-heartedly moved against the cartels in 1992 by levying a 10 per cent tax on any cash imported into the country and deposited locally. It also permitted banks to increase their fees by about one-third for handling cash. In response, the cartels took a side-step and turned Venezuela into their newest amusement park. Eighteen months later, it appeared that 75 per cent of all Colombian cocaine was being exported through Venezuela, that Venezuelan banks were holding upwards of $14 billion for the drug dealers and that more money was being washed through Venezuela than the country earned in oil revenues.

Law enforcement officials in Caracas accused Colombian drug traffickers of having washed $1 billion in Venezuela over a ten-year period, most of the money coming from the US in cash and cheques and through bank transfers, washed through foreign exchange houses along the Colombian border.

A formal request was made to the Clinton administration, asking the Americans to look into allegations of possible drug money laundering at Chase Manhattan Bank, Bank of America, International Bank, Bank Atlantic and Bank of New York. Also named were four major Venezuelan banks – Banco Provincial, Banco Internacional, Banco de Maracaibo and Bancor – in addition to a branch of Colombia's Banco Tequendama.

Sharing a long, rugged and thoroughly porous border with Colombia, Venezuela is a cocaine smuggler's heaven. From mountains in the north to flatlands and jungles in the south, the boundary is just about impossible to patrol. Venezuela and Colombia are active trading partners and banks from one country have branches in the other. Communications between the two are also good, making wire transfers easy. The financial markets were also relatively sophisticated. Currency brokers boomed. So did the Caracas stock exchange, which found itself transformed by narco-economics into an oversized sink. Likewise, banks have done a booming business in short-term treasury bills.

Until recently, there were no prescribed penalties in Venezuela for failing to report large cash transactions, even if banks and brokers had good reason to suspect the money was derived from drug trafficking.

The laws in Venezuela have since been amended. But the laissez faire attitude that continues to characterize sections of Venezuela's financial community remains prevalent throughout Latin America.

Argentina, for example, is making ready to pick up any slack left by the Venezuelans. Once thought of as too far off the beaten path, drug traffickers are starting to take another look at Argentina and use the country's newly won economic stability to wash money. Access in and out, for both product and funds, is easy. The border with Bolivia presents few difficulties for smugglers. And the booming markets of Buenos Aires present almost unlimited opportunities for turning cash into investments. Under the old regime, wealthy Argentines kept their money hidden overseas. They're now bringing much of it back. That influx, coupled with foreign investments – sparked off by the privatization of formerly state-owned enterprises – means that whatever drug money gets shuffled into the deck is virtually impossible to spot. Furthermore, Argentina's cultural ties to Europe – Spain, because of its shared language, and Italy, because nearly half of all Argentines are of Italian extraction – make for near-unencumbered access to European markets, money and criminal expertise.

Peru is the world's largest producer of coca, and a working agreement that binds drug barons to local Maoist guerrillas has made the cocaine trade there bigger than ever. It's estimated that 10 per cent of the entire population – that represents more than two million people – are regular coca chewers. The most important producing region is the Upper Huallaga Valley, where today there are just as many banks doing business in dollars as there are in many small American cities. On any given day along Ocona Street – the heart of Lima's informal foreign exchange market – $3–5 million in cash changes hands.

Across the border in Bolivia, the market in coca and coca paste makes up a whopping 80 per cent of that nation's source of dollars. And, for many years, Bolivian drug baron Jorge Roca Suarez was Pablo Escobar's primary source of cocaine paste.

Roca directed his worldwide operations from a 19-room mansion in San Marino, California. The Escobar gang converted his paste into powder, smuggled it into the United States, sold it and used part of that money to pay Roca. For supplying more than a ton of paste a week over the course of a couple of years, Roca earned $50 million.

In the beginning he shipped the money back to Bolivia with couriers. Later, his housekeeper and his sister found that they could get cash to Bolivia by hiding it inside appliances. Apparently they could stuff as much as $200,000 in a stereo speaker, $400,000 in a vacuum cleaner and $2 million in a freezer. Roca was eventually arrested and convicted of conspiracy to manufacture cocaine, conspiracy to export currency, conspiracy to evade taxes, tax evasion and money laundering. He was sentenced to 35 years hard labour.

Sadly, Roca is not the real problem, and putting guys like him away for a very long time doesn't solve the problem.

Under Bolivian law, it is perfectly legal to grow coca. The Bolivians chew it, smoke it and use it in cooking. And they've done so since before the Inca culture took hold.

Although coca derivatives are forbidden, to keep the tradition alive the government has designated that coca may be grown in the Yunga region of La Paz.

To keep the tradition under control, it has set about trying to destroy coca bushes everywhere else in the country. But herbicide spraying renders large areas of the country barren and it's years before other crops can take hold. The CIA has been happy to provide satellite intelligence to help locate farms. But there are limitations to what satellite surveys can do and then they work only in certain areas. Coca bushes will show up when they're covering very large areas. Smaller plantations can't always be spotted. So, for every big farm that is put out of business, half a dozen smaller ones take its place.

The Bolivians have also set about trying to locate and destroy the thousands of chemical labs scattered around the country where the leaf is converted into cocaine.

Needles in haystacks are easier to find.

*   *   *

Colombian President Ernesto Samper came into office in August 1994 riding on a law and order platform. However his election was met with some scepticism in Washington. Narco-dollars had already undermined much of the legal infrastructure, heavily influencing the Colombian Congress, politicians, prosecutors, jurists and penal-code reform. For instance, a 1993 act stipulated that a trafficker who turns himself in can have his sentence reduced by as much as two-thirds and any additional pending charges will be dismissed. Under that law, the Orejuela brothers had been trying to negotiate their surrender in exchange for a 3–4 year term. It's believed that the deal would have gone through under Samper had Washington not strenuously objected.

He was long on rhetoric but dogged by persistent rumours that the Cali cartel had contributed money to his campaign. The day after his election, a weekly news magazine revealed that the Orejuela brothers had contributed $3.7 million. Although he strenuously denied those rumours, Samper didn't allay American supporters when he transferred General Rosso Serrano, head of the national police's anti-narcotics division and a relentless enemy of the cartels, to Washington as a military attaché. He was also quick to emphasize that Colombia would not extradite drug traffickers to the US.

Samper followed that with a call to the Orejuela family. A Colombian army unit had received a tip-off that Miguel Orejuela planned to attend his daughter's communion party at a Cali hotel, so they raided it. When they came up empty handed, Samper personally apologized to the Orejuelas for having disrupted the celebrations and ordered Colombia's defence minister to stop 'arbitrary operations'.

Understandably concerned, the Clinton administration worried about the growing acreage of coca plantations in Colombia and the sentence reductions granted to confessed drug traffickers. A secret memorandum was sent from the

State Department to Colombia's Foreign Minister. Because it was so highly critical, the Foreign Minister took the unprecedented step of publicly rebuking the State Department for the communiqué, although the details of the letter were not released.

Fighting back with sound bites, Samper vowed to prevent the United States turning Colombia into 'a kind of Vietnam in the fight against drugs'. He added, 'It is unacceptable that some consumer countries come here and wage a war that they haven't been able to win inside their own borders.'

It's true that the Colombians had seized two Boeing 727s that were being used by the cartel for transporting drugs. But one estimate put their aviation fleet at 40 long-range passenger jets, some of which could carry nearly $2 billion worth of cocaine. Two planes out of 40 wasn't a very good percentage. So Clinton indicated that if Samper didn't act more decisively, Colombia risked losing a portion of its $40 million aid programme unrelated to counter-narcotics efforts, as well as certain trade benefits plus future membership in the North American Free Trade Agreement. A pair of Republican Senators on the Foreign Relations Committee – Jesse Helms of North Carolina and Connie Mack of Florida – upped the stakes by threatening to shut down relations with Colombia within a year unless Samper implemented a series of very ambitious anti-narcotics programmes.

Although the committee softened the measure, making the provisions discretionary rather than mandatory, by January 1995 Serrano was brought back to Bogotá to be chief of the Colombian national police. Fearing that certain units had been infiltrated, he fired more than 3000 policemen, including 500 in Cali. He also ordered that the offensive against the cartel be commanded from Bogotá and that it be kept so highly secret that the police in Cali would never know when a raid was coming down.

Next, Samper appointed Alfonso Valdivieso, a tough-talking

prosecutor who would refuse to negotiate with the traffickers, to be attorney general. He also permitted the CIA and the DEA to bolster their intelligence operations in-country and move into Cali.

To support Serrano, the CIA bugged the traffickers' cellular phones and flew surveillance flights to track their movements. They also helped to decipher nearly 600 computer floppy-disks that the Colombian police had seized in various raids. The DEA handled the shoe-leather part of the operation, gathering on-the-ground intelligence, helping to plant operatives in offices, staking out safe houses and following suspects.

Still under pressure from Washington, Samper agreed to offer cash rewards on national television for information leading to the capture and arrest of named traffickers. That triggered a purge. Fearing for their own lives, some lesser cartel members went on a killing spree, trying to eliminate other cartel members whom they believed could not be trusted. In turn, some of those lesser cartel members started coming forward. The walls that had protected the Cali bunch were starting to crumble.

In mid-1995, around the same time that the Colombians finally got around to outlawing money laundering, they caught up with Gilberto. Serrano's men, with help from the DEA, had been monitoring the offices of the Orejuelas' lawyers. Contacts there helped to narrow the search for both brothers. On 9 June, the police raided a house in Cali, arrested four people and discovered Gilberto hiding behind a false wall.

The likelihood that he would now try to barter a lighter sentence plainly worried some of his cronies. Within ten days, Henry 'The Scorpion' Loaiza Ceballos, the cartel's military leader turned himself in at an army base in Bogotá. One of the most hard-line members, he is known to have ordered violent revenge attacks and now stands accused of the chainsaw slaughter of 107 peasants in southwestern Colombia who'd refused to cooperate with the cartel. On 24 June, Victor 'The Chemist' Patino Fomeque, a former policeman and head of the cartel's naval smuggling operation came out of hiding. He'd once commanded a mini-fleet of ships, including three submarines, which the cartel had used to smuggle drugs into the US.

Others soon followed. Julio Fabio Urdinola and Jonier Ospina Montoya, men whose names were not widely known outside Colombia but who were already the object of international arrest warrants, negotiated surrenders.

Then, on 4 July, the police scored another major victory by capturing Londono. The search for him had intensified around Cali. Instead, a man fitting his general description was spotted by an off-duty cop dining at a restaurant in Bogotá. It was known that Londono had a skin condition and because of that never wore socks. But it wasn't until the suspect stood up that the policeman noticed he wasn't wearing socks. Serrano was called and without any fanfare Londono was taken into custody. One newspaper later reported that before he left with the police, he insisted on paying for his dinner.

Four days after that, Phanor Arizabaleta Arzayuz surrendered. A former cattle rancher, the 67-year-old was responsible for purchasing the chemicals the cartel used to process cocaine. A warrant had been issued against him for the murder of a police chief.

Still on the run were Helmer 'Pacho' Herrera Buitrago, a 43-year-old smuggler from a long family of smugglers who headed up the cartel's military wing, and Miguel Orejuela. But their days were numbered.

Miguel was known to sleep during the day and work at night. So Serrano began looking for apartments in some of Cali's more luxurious neighbourhoods where lights were on all night. After watching one for several nights, at four o'clock on the afternoon of 6 August, Serrano and his men broke through the door.

Startled out of a sound sleep, Miguel dashed for the safety of a secret closet. They arrested him in his underpants.

While all this was going on, Santiago Medina, President Samper's campaign treasurer, was also arrested. And Medina swore that it was Samper's campaign manager who knew all about the Cali cartel's $3.7 million gift, having laundered most of the money in American banks.

There must have been ironic sneers on the faces of jailed cartel bosses when they heard that Samper's campaign manager had been arrested. He was Serrano's boss, Defence Minister Fernando Botero.

Faced with a fight for political survival, Samper fired 51 senior police officials in Cali after their names were discovered on a cartel payroll. He suspended eight senators from his own party who'd been accused of having ties to the cartels, then froze bank accounts owned by three Orejuela family businesses.

To remind Samper that America took this seriously, President Clinton ordered all US-based assets belonging to 33 companies thought to be owned by the Cali cartel to be frozen and forbade American companies to do business with them. He also froze the assets of 47 US citizens identified as shareholders in those companies, and the Botero bank accounts in the States.

Coinciding with that, US Customs announced an investigation into 105 American companies that had accepted money from the Cali cartel for electronics, auto parts and other goods shipped to Colombia. A separate inquiry was launched into small costume jewellery exporters in midtown Manhattan who were suspected of accepting drug cash.

Next, the Samper administration identified some of the mini-cartel bosses, naming cousins Raul and Luis Grajales as the most powerful of the new leaders in the Cali region.

Other stars waiting in the wings are Archangel Henao, Diego Montoya and Luis Gomez. And while Samper seemed willing to bet that the mini-cartels haven't yet secured the international contacts or the political clout that could put them into the big leagues, the key word becomes 'yet'.

Londono escaped from jail but was eventually caught again, shot and killed. The Orejeulas are said to be still trafficking from their prison cells, although if they are, their business has clearly been hampered by Mexican drug cartels who have moved in to fill the vacuum they left. And if the Mexican drug traffickers have their way, it's a good bet that they will one day try to do to Colombia's mini-cartels what the Orejuela brothers did to Pablo Escobar.

So the game is not over.

Nor is it likely to end soon.

It's like putting out brush fires. You get one and two more start. Then again, just because the Orejuelas and their pals might be spending the rest of their lives in gaol, it doesn't mean they're necessarily out of business. There are people in America who run some pretty significant criminal organizations from gaol and it's fair to assume that if it's possible in the States, it's probable in Colombia. Yet, even if they have grown too old for any more of this and have finally decided to hang up their spikes, there's a long list of people who have been waiting for their turn at the plate. Many of them are just as good as the Orejuelas, know the business just as well, and are smart enough to have learned from the Orejuelas' mistakes.

No, the game is not over.

In 1990 opium poppies were planted in the Andes mountains. Five years later, Colombia was the world's fourth biggest producer of heroin.

In 1994 the DEA targeted the Cali cartel, seized over $100 million in cash and property and arrested 116 people. It changed the course of the river a little, but only a little. It didn't dam it up.

Carlos Lehder's arrest was once hailed as a major victory in the war on drugs, and yet the drugs continued to flow.

When Pablo Escobar was shot, the good guys boasted that the worst of the bad guys was permanently out of business, and yet the drugs continued to flow.

Now they've busted the Cali gang.

And still the drugs continue to flow.

CHAPTER THIRTEEN

Factories South –
Maytag North

'The most efficient means of battling organized crime is to act against money laundering.'

Louis J. Freeh, Director of the FBI

The Mexicans have picked up where the Colombians left off.

Today, 50–70 per cent of all the cocaine smuggled into the United States comes through Mexico. The country is also the primary source for opium gum, which is the base product that gets refined into the kind of heroin used in the US. At the same time, Mexico is America's largest supplier of marijuana.

With a 2000-mile common border that is at best badly patrolled, at worst unpatrollable, it's easy to understand how Mexico has become the front door to the world's most important drug market.

Mexican police forces are inefficient, bribery is rampant, a large part of the judiciary is totally crooked – literally thousands of Justice Ministry officials and federal judicial police have been fired in the past few years for conspiring with drugs traffickers – and the government has proved to be otherwise helpless. These days around Washington, especially at the DEA, the feeling is that the Mexicans are the worst.

In tandem with their new found trafficking successes has come the problem of washing all this money. At first they settled for the obvious ways. Where the Colombians favoured cashier's cheques, the Mexicans showed a preference for traveller's cheques because Mexico does not require records be kept for them. Laundrymen used to brag of buying them in $1000 units, stuffing 500 in their left pocket, 500 in their right pocket and crossing the border with $1 million. The money would then be wired from a *cambio* – currency exchange house – to banks in the Caribbean before being brought back to the States as a real estate deal, the way it was done by Ricardo Aguirre Villagomez through the American Express Bank International.

On at least one occasion, Mexican laundrymen seized an opportunity to spend it all in Mexico. Following a 40 per cent devaluation of the peso, they simply went on a buying spree, turning dirty dollars into pesos to buy cars, vacation homes and yachts which they then marketed through shell companies to Americans for apparently clean dollars.

Still, they weren't prepared at first to handle such vast amounts of cash. The Colombians were a lot more savvy about wiring things around. They'd taken the time to develop the proper contacts. When the Mexicans moved in on the remains of the Cali cartel they took the core business but didn't secure, or perhaps couldn't secure, the logistical support. So for the most part they still bulk their money out of the country. They run around southern California and Texas with truck loads of cash and often get their money taken away.

Once they got their cash out of the States and safely into Mexico, at least until a couple of years ago, they didn't have much difficulty putting it into banks. That's changing now because of the volume involved and the pressure Washington is trying to bring to bear on Mexico City. But they're still susceptible to anyone with a good way of handling cash.

Back at the end of the 1980s, a three-year sting operation run by the DEA and known as Green Ice baited the Colombians with a phony leather goods company through which they could conceal international money transfers. It led to 192 arrests in the United States, Italy, Canada, England, Spain and Costa Rica, seized more than $50 million and revealed well developed links between Colombian and Italian crime gangs.

The sequel known as Green Ice II was run out of San Diego. It was aimed at the currency exchange houses that litter the US border with Mexico. By setting up a *cambio* in Coronado, California, the DEA managed to lure some Cali cartel representatives to wash their money there. When it came time to pull the plug, 50 people were arrested in five states, Colombia and Canada. Seven tons of cocaine, 16 pounds of heroin, various weapons and $12.8 million were seized. An additional 30 people were named in the indictments and sought. Among those caught in the net were Mexican nationals living in the United States, confirming the link between Mexican dealers and the Colombian cartels.

Evidence then surfaced of other joint ventures between Colombian and Mexican traffickers. Together they bought cement companies, construction firms and factories specifically to launder money in Mexico. Further evidence suggests that drug traffickers are the largest single group of investors in the Mexican stock exchange.

Although the border with Mexico has for years been pockmarked with currency exchange houses, now that the Mexicans have so much cash it has turned into a plague. They are not required by Mexican law to keep thorough records or identify customers making large cash transactions. But then, neither are Mexican banks. There are no effective controls on cash being brought in or transferred out of the country. What's more, Mexico's laws do not necessarily render illegal any profits from drug sales and the authorities cannot ordinarily confiscate drug-derived property. If they catch a dealer flying drugs in his plane, they can claim the plane as a prize. But if that dealer uses his drug money to buy a fancy hotel in Puerto Vallarta, even if he's convicted of trafficking, he gets to keep the hotel. The situation has become so extreme that some people believe the US needed the North American Free Trade Agreement simply to repatriate the drug money heading south.

Mexicans ship drugs across the border any way they can. They have planes, they have boats, they have tractor-trailers, they have cars with hidden compartments, they have people sneaking through holes in chain fences. It comes in colossal waves. When the Colombians owned the game, at least in the beginning, drug seizures from Mexico were measured in pounds. Today they are measured in tons. The Mexican Attorney General's office recently estimated that traffickers there are making roughly $30 billion a year. If that's true, it's four times more than the combined annual income of the Cali and Medellin cartels.

The 'Colombianization' of Mexico is in full swing.

With the demise of Escobar and the apparent ruin of the Orejuelas, and while the mini-cartels are still playing in the minors, at least three Mexican groups have gained international influence.

The Tiajuana cartel is run by Ramón and Benjamin Arellano Felix, brothers who are now suspected of murdering Cardinal Juan Jesús Posadas Ocampo. A third brother, Francisco Rafael, was arrested in 1993 for drug trafficking and is already in prison.

The Juarez cartel is divided into two factions. One was originally controlled by the Fonseca Carrillo family, the head of it having been 39-year-old Amado Carrillo Fuentes. Wanted for drug-related crimes in the US, he operated with apparent immunity from his ranch across the border from El Paso, having only ever been charged there with a weapons misdemeanour. Nicknamed 'Lord of the Skies' he became famous in drug smuggling circles for buying Boeing 727s to fly his cocaine into the States. The other faction is under the thumb of Rafael Aguilar, a former federal police commander.

The third, and by far the most dangerous, was run by Juan Garcia Abrego, heir apparent to the Cali cartel. Based in Tamaulipas, he and members of his family controlled Mexico's Gulf coast region. Standing six feet tall and weighing 200 pounds, it's not clear if Abrego was born in Soliseno, just outside Matamoros, across the Mexican border from Brownsville, Texas, or in La Paloma, Texas. That confusion became his downfall.

Abrego got into the drug business by floating bales of marijuana across the Rio Grande. He soon graduated with honours, becoming the first international drug dealer to make it onto the FBI's 'Ten Most Wanted' list.

Additions to the roster are usually announced by the FBI in a press release, but Attorney General Janet Reno showed her determination to put an end to Abrego's reign by personally announcing his inclusion. Although, in an aside, she wondered why drug traffickers had not historically been considered worthy of the FBI's 10 Most Wanted.

Like Escobar and the Orejuelas, Abrego also allowed the press to glamorize him. He claimed to have fathered several children by different women – in keeping with a macho Mexican image –. and was apparently so superstitious that he had witch doctors on permanent call to help protect him. Less glamorously, he was responsible for dozens of killings on both sides of the border. In fact, it was Abrego's massacre of six rivals in 1984 that made him Mexico's principal cocaine trafficker.

Also like the Colombians, he set up distribution units around America. The main ones were in San Antonio, Houston and New York. But others have flourished all along the border, across the Gulf in Florida and as far north as Milwaukee and Seattle.

Nicknamed 'La Muñeca' – the doll – for a time there was as much as $2 million on his head. He was wanted in both the United States and Mexico for trafficking multi-ton quantities of cocaine and was first indicted in Houston in 1993 for drug trafficking and money laundering. But it wasn't until the Americans began to exert real pressure that the Mexican authorities gave in and decided to do something about him.

Because they needed to, they managed it. Until then, Abrego was shelling out $50 million a month in bribes to keep the authorities off his track.

In January 1996, fifteen hand-picked agents from Mexico's National Institute for Combating Drugs surrounded Abrego's fortified ranch in the northern Mexican city of Monterey. Camouflaged as shrubs, they got so close that when they finally spotted him, it only took a foot race to snare him.

As a show of good faith, the President of Mexico – 'Because his [Abrego's] continued presence in the country is judged to be undesirable' – extradited him. This is where his birth certificate beat him. Had he been a Mexican, he would most likely still be in Mexico. But the government ruled he was either an American, or had dual nationality, and because he could then be considered a foreigner, he should be handed over to the Americans. So, heavily armed FBI agents bundled the then 51-year-old onto a private jet at Mexico City airport and brought him back to Texas.

During his heyday, much of Abrego's drug money was

laundered through Texas, brought there from a *casa de cambio* in Monterey Texas, about 140 miles south. The First City Bank of McAllen wire transferred the funds to Banker's Trust in New York. From there, Antonio Geraldi, an officer in Banker's Trust's private banking branch, deposited Abrego's money in two locations – a Swiss bank and a private investment corporation in the Cayman Islands.

After a few years, during which time more than $22 million is said to have gone through Banker's Trust, Geraldi and his assistant, Maria Lauitus Riadigi, took new jobs at American Express Bank International in Beverly Hills. Abrego and others in his cartel duly followed. Geraldi and Riadigi now invested the drug lord's money in a new set of Cayman companies which began to make very large real estate purchases and other investments. But the authorities were soon onto the two bankers and the case against them resulted in forfeitures to the United States government – made up of fines to the various banks, the drug lord's money and civil penalties – of approximately $44 million. Geraldi was sentenced to ten years for money laundering, while Riadigi was given three and a half years. Abrego, facing 26 counts of drug trafficking, money laundering and murder, was prosecuted in Houston and, in January 1997, received nine life sentences.

The inevitable slack created by Abrego's deportation was quickly taken up by Abrego's former associates who battled for succession and control. After much blood was spilled, it appeared as if 37-year-old Oscar Malherbe had seized command of the cartel. But not before the Juarez cartel and Amado Carrillo Fuentes tried to strong-arm their way in.

At this point, in a truly bizarre twist of events, Fuentas – possibly panicked by the sentence to Abrego and the similar fate awaiting him – seems to have decided to change his identity. He is said to have hired a plastic surgeon to give him a new face. But he died on the operating table. Or, at least, someone did. The local Mexican District Attorney says it was Fuentas. The FBI says so too. They took the dead man's fingerprints and matched them with those on file for Fuentas. A few weeks later the plastic surgeon was murdered, and the Fuentas organization went through turmoil sorting out succession. So there is good reason to believe the dead man was Fuentas. But then again, with all the money these men have at their command, it's not inconceivable that a drug lord could buy himself both a cadaver and freedom.

Abrego's brother Humberto was also arrested for money laundering, as the result of a massive investigation into the 1994 assassination of José Francisco Ruiz Massieu, secretary-general of Mexico's ruling Institutional Revolutionary Party. The Ruiz murder and the Abrego family involvement in it was an example of why any serious attempt at putting the Mexico cartels out of business is destined to fail.

In Mexico today, along with drug trafficking and money laundering, corruption is a fact of daily life.

Ruiz's own brother, Mario Ruiz Massieu, once the nation's chief drug prosecutor, has been accused of covering up the plot to kill his brother. Stopped at Newark Airport in 1995 on his way to Madrid for failing to declare the $40,000 in cash he was carrying, US Customs has since located $9 million in one of his Texas bank accounts. Officials now suggest that some of that money came from Abrego who kept the assistant attorney general on his payroll.

The plot thickens when you add in Raul Salinas de Gortari, brother of former president Carlos Salinas de Gortari, who's been arrested on charges of murdering José Francisco Ruiz Massieu. Then, in June 1995 it was announced that the former president himself was being investigated on suspicion that he knew his brother Raul had masterminded the Ruiz Massieu assassination. Shortly thereafter, Raul's wife Paulina Castanon was arrested in Geneva. She'd apparently gone there to make a simple $84 million withdrawal from Raul's account. The Swiss froze that one and others in six cantons that they believed to have been owned by Raul using false names. The total is said to exceed $100 million. Mexican authorities then turned up an account apparently owned by Raul in London with $20 million. While all this was going on, Carlos Salinas was on an extended vacation. Rumoured at various times to be in sunny Cuba, he wound up spending six months in snowy Canada.

When last seen, he was living quietly in Ireland.

Described by US Customs officials as 'The Maytag of the money laundering industry', it's amazing how precisely Canada fits the offshore gospel according to Lansky.

A firmly established democracy, Canada has a sound banking infrastructure, highly advanced communications and easy access to the world's most important drug market. The US–Canadian border, nearly 5000 miles worth, happens to be the longest undefended border in the world. Also mostly unpatrolled, where there are checkpoints traffic in both directions, at least for American and Canadian citizens, passes largely unhindered. The only thing that unequivocally stops at the border is US federal jurisdiction.

Every now and then, when luck is on their side, Canadian Customs do catch someone trying to smuggle something. A few years ago they nabbed some Mexican laundrymen crossing the border at Surrey, British Colombia. Because these two were such a long way from home and didn't look like your average tourists, they were asked to open the trunk of their car. When they did, an especially alert officer happened to notice that the spare tire did not fit the car. He ripped it open and found $800,000.

But that's the exception.

A spare tyre that does fit, in a well-maintained car with New York State licence plates and skis lashed to the roof, driven by a well-dressed young American couple heading for northern Ontario late on a Friday afternoon might attract someone's attention in July, but never in a month of late Friday afternoons would anyone think twice about it during the winter.

Before 1989, when money laundering finally became a criminal offence in Canada, hardly anyone thought twice about cash at all. The Mulroney government attempted to change that by introducing currency transaction reporting. But it's not mandatory. Banks voluntarily agree to ask depositors about cash. And because no one will prosecute them if they don't, they sometimes 'forget'.

Combining the kind of laxity that is built into all voluntary systems with a modern, internationally networked financial services industry, it's no surprise to discover that Canadian banks have for years maintained a major commercial presence in tax havens such as the Caribbean.

Bruce 'Peewee' Griffin, a convicted drug smuggler from Florida, had a well-established relationship with one of Canada's largest financial institutions, the Bank of Nova Scotia in the Bahamas. According to the FBI, from 1975 to 1981 he laundered more than $100 million through the Scotiabank branch in Nassau, almost a quarter of it during one hectic four-month stretch in 1979. He kept several accounts there in the names of Bahamas-registered shell companies. To consolidate his holdings, he wired money to Scotiabank Cayman Islands and into an account it held for a Cayman-registered shell, Cobalt Ltd. From there, the money travelled through Scotiabank New York before being dispersed into several US companies controlled by Griffin. When Griffin was finally indicted in 1983, along with 100 associates, his assets included racing cars, racing boats and a Texas ranch where he bred horses.

In those days, the Bank of Nova Scotia was famous for not asking questions about large cash deposits and also for ignoring normal banking practices. Among other things, it purposely kept minimal records to hide the identity of its depositors. What's more, some Scotiabank employees in the Caribbean actually received tips in the thousands of dollars from their clients for their help in washing drug money. In 1984, a US federal court in Miami fined Scotiabank $1.8 million for refusing to turn over to a federal grand jury records which they'd subpoenaed.

One of Griffin's associates was a Bahamian lawyer named Nigel Bowe. It was Bowe who introduced Griffin to Bahamian Prime Minister Lynden Oscar Pindling. Hardly a coincidence, the Bank of Nova Scotia was also where Mr Pindling washed his money. Then under investigation for allegedly receiving $100,000 in monthly drug bribes, Pindling owed much of his success to his old friend and mentor, Meyer Lansky.

Having the right friends can yield dividends. If you can get a politician, a lawyer and a bank manager on your side, you can launder any amount with ease. But then, many laundrymen work wonders with only one of out three.

The Canadian–Caribbean connection made the front pages in September 1988 when sprinter Ben Johnson won his Olympic gold medal. Accused of using steroids and later deprived of his medal, Johnson's pusher turned out to be a doctor from St Kitts with a licence to practise medicine in Canada, named George Jamie Astaphan.

Politically well connected on the island, Astaphan became the object of a separate drugs and money laundering investigation in both the US and Canada. In late 1991 and early 1992, he delivered steroids to two men in Buffalo, New York, who claimed to be running a chain of weightlifting clubs. Around the same time he conspired with undercover agents in Florida where he tried to purchase 100 pounds of cocaine.

But the investigation into Astaphan's dealings go way beyond those two incidents. One source puts Astaphan in the middle of a St Kitts money laundering ring which uses casinos throughout the Caribbean to wash money. It is then sent through a company in Montreal, before being reinvested in drugs. That investigation never got very far in St Kitts but is apparently ongoing in Canada. Whether or not Astaphan himself is cooperating, no one will say. Although the answer is probably not. He has very little incentive to do so and his life wouldn't be worth much if he did.

He boarded a BWIA flight in Antigua bound for Toronto on Saturday 8 January 1994. The weather had supposedly closed in Toronto – at least that's what the airline still claims – and the plane was forced to land at JFK in New York. Knowing that Astaphan was on board, FBI agents met the plane and arrested him.

It's a moot point whether or not the FBI somehow managed to coerce BWIA into making a stop in New York. Had Astaphan made it to Toronto, the RCMP was waiting to arrest him there.

Arraigned in Buffalo and tried in Tampa, he was not prosecuted for money laundering. However, he was convicted of possession of steroids and possession of cocaine with intent to distribute both. He was sentenced to two years.

Instead of going after small fry like Astaphan, the Canadians have frequently taken a more long-term view.

In 1990, the RCMP in Montreal had a lot of evidence that drug money was being exchanged in Montreal. They'd also received information from the DEA and US Customs about cheques being issued by money exchanges in Montreal that were showing up as part of a laundry cycle in Panama. So a few RCMP officer decided they could do something about it by going into business and opening their own currency exchange bureau.

They decided to call it le Centre International Monétaire de Montréal – the International Monetary Centre of Montreal – or CIM for short. RCMP undercover agent Yvon Gagnon assumed the identity of Yvon Richard, President of CIM.

'We set up the business exactly the same way that any Canadian or Quebecois business would be. That is, we went through all the required steps for incorporation. But at every step, we made certain that fewer than 30 people ever knew the CIM was an RCMP sting.'

The location they chose – right on the corner of Peel and Maisonneuve in the heart of Montreal – was an area surrounded by about eight or nine other bureaux de change. It was ideal because Gagnon's intelligence was that the others had long been frequented by drug traffickers.

He then installed a second office – this one an observation post from which they could secretly film people going in and out – just across the street. It afforded a perfect camera angle with the front door, so that every time someone came into the centre, the client's visit was, unbeknownst to him, recorded for posterity. RCMP photos and videotape eventually identified players from 20 different drug trafficking groups using the exchange.

Because the CIM would be a business that handled large sums of cash, it stood to reason that there should be security cameras there too. So they put in a lot of security cameras which taped everyone inside the offices, and made for a permanent record of their faces and their transactions. Amazingly, during the entire time that the CIM was laundering drug money, not one single trafficker or laundryman ever objected to being on camera.

The undercover agents who worked there were RCMP officers brought in from other parts of Canada. They were given some actual bank training so that they knew how to exchange money, keep books, and handle wire transfers.

With everything in place, the CIM opened its doors for

business on Sunday morning, 30 September 1990. The very next day, the first of a long succession of money launderers stopped in to do business.

Most of it was to change Canadian dollars into American dollars. Some of it was to wire cash – huge sacks filled with money were carried into the CIM – to Venezuela, Florida, New York, Liechtenstein, Panama and Switzerland. But Gagnon and his team offered other services too. He'd established an American dollar account for the CIM in New York, specifically so that the office could supply cashier's cheques which might give them a lead into how the cartels were laundering money through Panama. Over the course of four years, some $40 million worth of CIM's checks were cashed in more than 200 different banks, 150 of them in Panama.

'They would deposit cash with us, then have us write cheques payable to fictitious names, which were passed on to businesses in Panama. It didn't matter who we made the cheques payable to, and at one point we were asked to make the cheques payable to players on the Montreal Expo baseball team. It didn't matter at all to them whose name we put on the cheques.'

Once they were received in Panama, the cheques would either be used to pay the business's suppliers elsewhere in the world, or deposited there. Now sufficiently washed, the funds would then be shipped to the traffickers in Colombia.

As the sting continued, three specific groups emerged.

The first was run by Joseph Lagana, an attorney whose client was Vito Rizzuto, the suspected head of the Canadian-Italian Mafia. The second was run by Dominic Tozzi who worked for a rival gang headed by Vincenzo di Maulo. The third was run by Samy Nicolucci, who not only shared an office with Tozzi but worked with several people in the Rizzuto mob.

Associated with Lagana in this operation were a pair of attorneys from his office, Vincenzo Vecchio and Richard Judd. Two other men stand out – Norman Rosenblum, who dealt with logistics for the first group's drugs and had the ill fortune of being present when half a ton of cocaine was delivered in the middle of the Caribbean to a ship manned by undercover RCMP and US Customs agents; and David Rouleau, whose job it was to collect money from the group's primary drug distributors, a chapter of the Hell's Angels motorcycle gang.

Branching out and asking for help from America, Italy, Switzerland, France and Panama, the RCMP was able to follow money into the Italian–Panama gold connection. They were able to identify back-to-back loans made through Switzerland for the purchase of real estate in Canada. They were also able to locate more property held by the suspects in the south of France and Florida.

The CIM stayed in business until 30 August 1994.

'The day we decided to go out of business,' Gagnon continues, 'we arrested 52 people. During those four years, we laundered C$160 million. That doesn't include the legal business we did, such as the money we changed for tourists. What's more, we ran the business at a profit, making around C$2 million. So this operation didn't cost the Canadian taxpayer anything.'

The takedown netted those 52 arrests in Montreal – including all the major players – plus four in England. The RCMP also seized a lot of property, in addition to 558 kilos of cocaine. They also froze over 200 accounts in 29 banking institutions.

It was Canada's biggest money laundering bust to date.

But it's a record that won't stand long. Because the United States, in its infinite wisdom, decided that border crossings north and south take too long. So they instituted a programme called Line Release, which reduces regular cargo inspections of trucks crossing into and out of the United States to spot checks. And pre-approved transport companies will be granted totally free access.

The Mexican drug barons no longer need to invest in 727s and super-fast speed boats. All they have to do is throw thousands of trucks at the border. They simply have to hire approved transporters who will unknowingly allow them to mix narcotics with legitimate cargo.

Forced to institute a policy that many inspectors know gives the Mexicans a free hand, Customs came up with Hard Line, which is supposed to supplement spot checks at heavily trafficked border crossings with increased intelligence and sniffer dogs.

Even then, pre-approved trucking companies will still enjoy priorities. One of them, Hipodromo de Agua Caliente, is a race-track-owned horse van company in Tijuana. They have approval to transport race horses across the border. Except the Aqua Caliente track is out of business. And a few years ago the track's owner was apparently investigated by US Customs on money laundering suspicions. And that was known when the truck was given Line Release approval.

In the name of progress, the factories in the south are now linked by road with the laundromat in the north. Call it the super-highway for smugglers. It's an advantage the Colombians would have killed for. It's a convenience to the traffickers and the laundrymen that American and Canadian kids will end up dying for.

CHAPTER FOURTEEN

La Mina

'Drug money freely mingles with the life force of the world
economy, like a virus in the bloodstream.'

Time Magazine

March 1986.

They knew they could trust him.

He was an Argentinian living in Uruguay, a precious
metals dealer who did business with the jewellery trade in
Los Angeles, respectable enough on the surface, in his early
40s, with a good reputation and all the proper contacts. And
greedy.

He was the perfect partner.

So the Colombians approached Raul Vivas with a straightforward deal. They wanted to turn him into their personal
laundryman. His share would be a flat 5%.

Five per cent of $500 million a year is a lot of money.
Vivas didn't have to think about it for very long. Five
per cent of $500 million a year was more money than he'd
ever dreamed of.

He said, cut me in.

And they did.

Because he knew that the simplest way is often the best,

he created a pair of front companies in Montevideo. The first, Letra SA, would deal in gold. The second, Cambio Italia SA, was to be a currency exchange business. Once the two were in place, Vivas flew to Los Angeles, where he opened an office in the West Coast Jewelry Center – 610 South Broadway, overlooking Pershing Square – in the heart of the city's diamond district.

The way he and his new friends planned it, whatever money the Colombians collected from coke and crack deals around the US was to be funnelled through a front company in New York's jewellery district, transported by courier to Los Angeles and delivered to the LA office. There it would be counted and bundled. Vivas would then use that money to buy gold in all its various forms – scrap, bars and shot – paying over the odds to any dealer willing to handle substantial cash purchases.

Knowing the business as well as he did, he never had any doubts that more than a few would be more than willing.

Once he had his gold, he would melt it down and mix it with silver, giving it the look and feel and weight of South American gold, which is traditionally of a lower quality than American gold.

Letra in Montevideo would then ship lead-plated gold bars from Uruguay to California, invoicing the consignment as South American gold. When those shipments arrived, the lead-plated bars would be destroyed, while Raul's gold – complete with this apparently authentic documentation – would be sent to New York to be sold on the open market there. The money from those sales would then be wired to Cambio Italia, which would pay Letra, which would then hand the money over to the Colombians.

It was the perfect scheme.

And, for a while, it worked like a charm.

* * *

October 1987.

Eduardo Martinez Romero was a sleaze.

But he was a very rich sleaze – like all of his friends – and he lived on a huge, heavily fortified ranch outside Medellin.

Like all of his very rich, very sleazy friends, protection was one of Eduardo's biggest expenses.

He didn't usually tell people much about himself, but when he did – when he felt like he wanted to or felt as if he had to – he'd say that he was an international economist. You know, one of those globe-trotting businessmen who make money with money. Sometimes he even bragged about having an advanced degree in marketing.

Not that he handed out business cards.

But if he had been that sort of fellow, if he had been one of those glad-handing guys you sometimes get stuck next to on a plane – the ones who say, call me next time you're in town and we'll do lunch – then his business card would have read, Chief Financial Consultant to the Medellin Cocaine Cartel.

He was the main laundryman for Pablo Escobar and Jorge Ochoa and José Rodriguez Gocha.

Which is why Jimmy Brown came to see him.

A stocky, middle-aged New York drug trafficker who claimed to have all the right Mafia connections, Jimmy swung himself an appointment with Eduardo at his ranch – not an easy feat to manage – and flew to Colombia.

When they finally sat down, face to face, Eduardo challenged him. He wanted to know, what's this all about? Jimmy told him, I'm looking for some action. Eduardo asked, what are you selling? Jimmy said, I'm a laundryman. Eduardo shrugged, we don't have any laundry to be done. Jimmy insisted, there's always laundry to be done. Eduardo told him, you're too late. And then, just like that, Eduardo told Jimmy all about Raul's operation in Los Angeles.

He revealed how it centred on fake gold imports from South America. He revealed how it turned on various jewellery businesses in New York and LA. He even went as far as to explain that, from New York, the money was wired to the Banco de Occidente in Panama City, Panama.

Jimmy let him babble away.

Eduardo boasted that this was the best, most efficient sink in the US. He claimed that Raul had washed $12 million in just the past 30 days.

Then he joked, it's like owning a gold mine.

And he dubbed it 'the mine' – *La Mina*.

Undeterred, Jimmy kept pitching Eduardo. He argued that it was unwise for the cartel to put all their eggs in one basket. He said he wanted them to know that he had something different to offer. He disclosed his plan to move drugs through Atlanta, Georgia, and wash the profits through sinks he'd already established there.

Eduardo continued to insist that they weren't interested.

And when Jimmy left Eduardo that night, there was no deal.

But something Jimmy said must have hit a nerve, something he said must have started Eduardo thinking, because, two days later, Eduardo phoned Jimmy to say he wanted another meeting.

This time Jimmy was driven to an even more elaborately fortified ranch. It was like Fort Knox.

This time he was taken to meet the boss – Pablo Escobar.

Jimmy went through his spiel again.

Escobar listened intently.

Jimmy figured he had a sale.

That's when one of Escobar's people suddenly jumped up and screamed that he smelled a rat. He accused Jimmy of being an undercover agent for the Drug Enforcement Administration.

Instantly, the mood at the ranch turned sour.

Jimmy stuck to his story. No one had to tell him that he was facing certain death.

The cartel members argued among themselves, debating Jimmy's fate.

With his life literally hanging in the balance, Jimmy tried to tough it out. He dug in his heels. There wasn't anything else he could do. He had to convince Escobar that he was who he said he was. He stuck to his story. And waited for the verdict. Just like that, Escobar ruled, you're okay. Escobar told him, we'll work a deal.

So Jimmy and the Medellin cartel went into business and by January 1988 their joint venture in Atlanta had already put $12 million into the washing cycle, cleaned it and gotten it into a cartel account in Panama.

But then there was a hiccup.

A cash shipment out of Atlanta for $1 million was intercepted by the American authorities. Who knows how they found it. But they did. They spotted it and grabbed it, and Eduardo was furious. He demanded that Jimmy come up with a suitable explanation. So Jimmy answered that he could indeed explain it all and arranged a meeting with Eduardo for 17 January in Panama City. They agreed to meet at the main offices of the Banco de Occidente.

Jimmy arrived with his partner, a Cuban-born, Miami-raised hustler who called himself Alex Carrera.

Eduardo arrived with his army of bodyguards.

Jimmy and Alex had to wait while Eduardo strutted around the bank as if he owned the place. He played the star and flaunted his power and crowed with enjoyment at being treated with great reverence by the employees.

But once they were alone – once it was just Eduardo and Jimmy and Alex – the mood changed. Eduardo turned on them. He was angry about Jimmy's million dollar blunder.

Jimmy tried to argue it was the price of doing business.

Eduardo wasn't having it.

Jimmy said he knew the cartel had already written it off. Eduardo kept saying, no way, no way. He persisted, that's not the way we operate. He warned, we expect you to pay it all back.

Jimmy said they could work it out.

Sure, Eduardo said, then scolded Jimmy and Alex for not running their laundromat fast enough. You're too slow. La Mina is much faster. So tell me, he demanded, tell me precisely how the Atlanta laundromat works.

Alex managed to sidestep the question, arguing that this was neither the time nor the place to be handing out such sensitive details.

Eduardo kept pressing for details.

Now Jimmy agreed with Alex, this isn't the right moment.

For whatever reason, Eduardo backed down. He said, okay, later. And the three of them arranged a second meeting.

That discussion took place some seven weeks later, on 8 March, in a $500 a night hotel suite on Aruba. Eduardo, Jimmy, Alex and someone they introduced as the man in charge of their Atlanta operation, all sat down to talk.

Eduardo should have known better than to accept a stranger at the meeting. But there was plenty to drink and the more Eduardo got into the bottle the more he boasted about La Mina's success.

'It may not be good business to be moving money around in the street, but it's not illegal,' he said. 'If they caught me, I'd say I'm sorry. I'd pay the tax, walk away and that's good, that's my cost of protecting that money and there's a lot of good ways to do it.'

In the past 45 days, he went on, Raul had washed $28 million. Best of all, the money went through the laundry cycle in only 48 hours.

That's two days, he reminded Jimmy and Alex and their partner. And two days is twice as fast as you can do it.

Jimmy and Alex agreed that was pretty fast.

Damn right it is, Eduardo maintained. So here's the way

it's going to be. You're going to match La Mina and get our money to us in two days. And, you're also going to take a one point cut in commission. You're going to come down from 7 per cent to 6 per cent because of the money you lost for us.

Jimmy and Alex objected. This isn't the way our deal works. They said, count us out. They said, no way.

Eduardo told them flatly, like it or not, this is the way it's going to be.

Jimmy and Alex tried their best to get Eduardo to compromise. But he wouldn't budge. He kept repeating, in a menacing tone, 'It's not negotiable.'

So the round went to Eduardo.

Jimmy and Alex both knew, in the end, there wasn't much they could do about it.

In the end, Jimmy and Alex managed to console themselves, it was cheaper than getting killed.

January 1988.

By this time, Raul Vivas had a serious problem.

There was so much cash being fed into the system that the gold brokers he'd been using simply couldn't handle it all. He needed to expand. So he brought a few more people into the game.

One of them was a 47-year-old Syrian named Wanis Koyomejian – Joe to his friends – who'd moved to the States in 1980. He owned a company called Ropex and worked out of a pair of fancy suites on the ninth floor of the International Jewelry Center.

Raul also brought in the Andonian brothers – Nazareth and Vahe – who ran a brokerage nearby, on the third floor of one of the original jewellery district buildings at 220 West 5th Street. Beirut born, the two brothers had moved to the US at about the same time as Koyomejian.

These three, Raul figured, would be able to take up the

slack on the additional cash. But he also felt he needed someone to handle all the extra gold coming into the LA office. So he farmed some of that work out to a couple of friends who'd set up in Miami.

And all the time, the money kept pouring in.

Before long, Raul needed to expand again, so he farmed out more of the operation to friends in New York and Houston.

And still he couldn't catch up.

To say the least, La Mina was flourishing.

March 1988.

Eduardo was suffering from verbal diarrhoea.

He loved to brag. And now, whenever he was with Jimmy and Alex, it was as if he couldn't shut up. He was telling them just about everything. He'd grown to trust them and apparently even thought of them as his pals.

In exchange, they were telling him very little.

But then, there was no way they could have confessed to him that Jimmy's real name was John Featherly and that Alex's real name was Cesar Diaz and that the laundry they were running for Eduardo was entirely financed by the DEA.

June 1988.

A senior officer of the Wells Fargo Banking Corporation in San Francisco had been assigned the less-than-glamorous task of monitoring the bank's currency deposits.

He sat in his office, robot-like, going through page after page of computer print-outs. It seemed like a never-ending stream. Page after page, each looking like the previous one. At least until one caught his eye.

Cash deposits.

A Los Angeles gold broker – someone called Andonian Brothers – had, in just under three months, put nearly $25 million in cash into an account at one of the Wells Fargo branches.

This was precisely the sort of thing he'd been asked to look for. So he did precisely what he'd been asked to do if he spotted something like this. He picked up the phone and notified the Internal Revenue Service.

September 1988.

A shipping clerk from the Loomis Armored Car Company in Los Angeles was checking a cargo that had just come in on a United Parcel Service plane from New York.

It was all routine stuff. Matching cartons and boxes and packages against his manifest. Checking waybill numbers. Making certain everything that should be there was there.

Then he noticed that one box had accidentally ripped open.

According to the waybill, this shipment was supposed to contain scrap gold, sent by a jeweller in New York to a gold dealer called Ropex, whose office was Suite 970 of the International Jewelry Center, 550 South Hill Street in downtown Los Angeles.

The stated content didn't impress him because Loomis dealt with high-value shipments all the time. What did bother him was, for such a valuable cargo, this stuff has been pretty badly packed.

He bent down to inspect the damage and noticed what was inside.

Instead of gold, the box was filled with money. Stacks of it. Piles of greenbacks, all neatly bundled together.

Because the bill of lading said it was supposed to be gold, he reported it to his superiors, and they phoned Ropex to ask why the paperwork accompanying the shipment said one thing when the shipment contained something else.

Ropex answered, there was a mix-up. They said, it's not a problem because we know all about it. They said, a guy we know in New York, a jeweller we do business with, is sending it to us because he's hoping to find better short-term interest rates in LA.

The management at Loomis said okay, mix-ups happen. And they forwarded the shipment to LA, just the way they were obliged to do. But the excuse they got from Ropex made no sense whatsoever. So they took it upon themselves to notify the FBI.

December 1988.

The Feds moved in on La Mina.

They installed hidden video cameras in buildings all over the Los Angeles jewellery district, and at very specific locations in New York. They put wire taps on phones. They shadowed people in LA, New York, Florida and Houston. They draped the neighbourhood around Pershing Square with undercover agents disguised as maintenance men and garbage collectors, delivery boys and gold brokers, jewellers and even homeless people living on the streets.

They recorded hundreds of hours of audio and video tapes and dug thousands of documents out of office garbage cans. They collected invoices that revealed names and addresses of contacts as far afield as Canada, Mexico and Great Britain; they found paperwork naming friendly bullion dealers; they gathered documents outlining all sorts of transactions; they got cancelled cheques and from those they were able to identify bank accounts.

The Feds code-named their La Mina investigation, Polar Cap.

And Polar Cap soon became the biggest surveillance operation in the history of American law enforcement.

February 1989.

The task force assigned to shut down La Mina consisted of agents from the FBI, Customs, DEA, IRS, the Bureau of

Alcohol, Tobacco and Firearms, plus the US Immigration and Naturalization Service. It was placed under the direct supervision of a senior, experienced Assistant US Attorney. Once he was convinced he'd seen enough, he ordered the task force to swoop down and arrest everyone.

When the end came, the Feds found evidence of 1,035 bank accounts in 179 different banks around the world – banks located in Central, South and North America and throughout most of Europe.

The work begun by Jimmy and Alex culminated in 127 indictments, including the extradition to the United States of Raul and Eduardo. Both stood trial, were convicted on numerous charges – including money laundering – and are both still serving prison sentences.

In just over two years, Raul and Eduardo had supervised the laundering of $1.2 billion.

Capitalizing on information obtained during Polar Cap, the US government was able to seize assets and freeze bank accounts all over the world. Additionally, it was able to impose heavy civil fines on foreign banks with US branches for their wilful participation in La Mina.

The government's clear intention was to send a chilling signal to the cartel's drug barons that America had declared open war on the laundrymen.

Unfortunately – like that fable of the little Dutch boy who stuck his finger in the dike to hold back the tides – just five years after Polar Cap scored such a heavy broadside hit on the laundrymen, the tides have grown too strong and the little Dutch boy has run out of fingers.

CHAPTER FIFTEEN

The Mobs

*'Today's criminals make the Capone crowd and the old Mafia
look like small time crooks.'*
Former US Secretary of State George Shultz

Once awash with oil, Nigeria is today the focus of the
continent's drug trade. A unit of heroin – about 700 grams –
is easily imported from Southeast Asia for under $6,000 and
just as easily resold to distributors supplying the European
market for around $120,000. With prices in Europe more
than twice what they are in drug-saturated North America,
organized crime is booming.

So too are the laundrymen.

For anyone confident enough to trust his cash to the
evolving nations of Africa, the dark continent offers a legion
of possibilities. Hard currency is king. Yet unlike many
other fragile economies – for example, Eastern Europe – the
Africans haven't just discovered it. They've known of the
potency of cash for decades and are very sophisticated when
it comes to separating less sophisticated people from it.

And nowhere in Africa has money laundering acquired
the same state-of-the-art trademark as in the Nigerian
capital. In a world where international fraud is an expedient

source of foreign income, organized criminals in Lagos understand the sex appeal of dirty money so well that they've built around it highly lucrative scams.

An official-looking letter, usually with a return address in the United States or Europe, is sent to a prominent gentleman – at home, never his office – with the promise of a huge commission for his help. It's signed by someone with a vaguely serious title – often pretending to be an attorney, and, in one well-documented case, by a man claiming to be Nigerian royalty who is affiliated with something oddly familiar called 'Shell BP'.

The text begins by saying that the prominent gentleman has been approached on the advice of an unnamed mutual friend. The sender points out that he's acting as an agent for an official entity – Nigeria's national oil company is a favourite – which has a particular problem with owed funds. A large sum due the company is blocked in a Swiss account and, as the result of some muddled legal complication, the money cannot be released directly to the company.

'The reason for my writing you,' the letter goes on, 'is to establish a communication link and possible means of exploring business avenues together. We are anxiously looking forward to securing a foreign partner who can offer us the benefit of having some money remitted into any company's or personal buoyant account. This money runs in millions of US dollars.'

The agent explains, if the prominent gentleman will allow the money to pass through his bank account – in other words, to launder it – he will be paid handsomely for the service. The deal is that the third party will wire the monies due – for example, $10 million – into the prominent gentleman's bank account, without the prominent gentleman assuming any liability. All he has to do – once the money clears – is forward $7 million to the agent. The prominent gentleman is welcome to the difference – that is, $3 million – as his share.

Reassured that he's not being asked to do anything illegal – just to step into the middle of a legitimate commercial transaction – the agent offers to meet the prominent gentleman, being more than happy to show him references and all the background paperwork. However, as there is always some sort of fast-approaching deadline when this money must be paid, the agent suggests – to save time – that the prominent gentleman immediately furnish his banking details, plus his personal authorization for the transfer, written on his own letterhead and signed by him.

Needless to say, once the prominent gentleman supplies the agent with the information, that's the last he ever hears of the deal. The letterhead, signature and banking details are sent to Nigeria, where a second letter is forged, this one ordering the prominent gentleman's bank to wire out the balance of his account.

Instances of these swindles have become so prevalent – and have so deeply embarrassed honest factions in the Nigerian government – that the Central Bank of Lagos has taken out ads in the *International Herald Tribune* warning businesses to stay clear of home-grown money laundering schemes. In response, highly organized Nigerian conmen – world-class innovators when it comes to ensnaring even the most cynical amateur laundryman – have created all sorts of 'advance fee fraud' variations on the theme.

For example, they bait their wealthy target with piles of background paperwork – fabricated letters and contracts from companies and banks explaining why and how the money must be paid into the account of a disinterested person. Tempted by a huge commission, the prominent gentleman agrees to get involved. But this time, at the very last minute, there's an awkward hold-up. The prominent gentleman is bombarded with telexes, faxes and phone calls from very embarrassed bankers and very embarrassed lawyers, explaining that the party due those funds is suddenly insisting the money must be simultaneously transferred. So a conference call is hastily arranged to ensure that, as the prominent gentleman authorizes his bank to wire out $7 million, lawyers representing the party paying the money will authorize their bank to transfer in $10 million.

By sheer coincidence, as soon as the prominent gentleman instructs his bank to send the $7 million, the conference call goes dead.

The Yakuza – Japan's equivalent of the Mafia – is said to consist of 165,000 members. Although there are some organized crime authorities who argue that figure is on the low side, at least according to Britain's *Guardian* newspaper, it must have a sizeable workforce because its annual turnover exceeds £6 billion.

One of their more effective tactics has been company extortion. They approach publicly held corporations and threaten that, unless the company comes up with protection money, they'll disrupt the shareholders' next annual general meeting. This type of harassment had become so widespread that in 1991 some 2,000 Japanese corporations conspired among themselves to nullify the Yakuza's menace by holding their AGMs on the same day and at the same time.

At the beginning of the 1970s, the Yakuza discovered that stockbroking was a terrific way to launder money, so, with the help of Malaysian Chinese gangs, they opened brokerages in Malaysia and Singapore. As their business grew, they moved quickly into Hong Kong, Australia, New Zealand, Indonesia and the Philippines. It is alleged that they've now opened shop in the United States. Cash is funnelled in one end, shares in legitimate companies that pay legitimate dividends come out the other.

When one Yakuza stock market ring was shut down by the authorities in Malaysia – without charges ever being lodged against anyone – the gang showed up intact in London.

Most of the time they launder their money by sticking to tried and true methods. For example, they wash hundreds of millions of dollars annually through Tokyo real estate, buying and selling the same buildings to themselves. They artificially run up prices, then back loans on those buildings with US Treasury bonds bought in the freewheeling, unregulated Hong Kong market.

Occasionally, however, they display typical Japanese flair and venture into something new. In mid-1985, having generated enormous amounts of cash through their drug dealing networks, one Yakuza syndicate turned its attention to the thriving trade in French designer luxury goods.

The first hurdle was getting their cash to Paris. Some of it was wired in, using Asian banks that routed it via Luxembourg, Switzerland and the Channel Islands. The rest was smuggled in, using well-dressed Japanese businessmen as couriers – unlikely suspects to have their attaché cases searched and seized by French Customs.

Next, the ring leaders rented an apartment near the Madeleine, in central Paris, took out classified ads in Asian-language newspapers and recruited some 300 Chinese, Vietnamese and Japanese 'customers'. Every morning, each customer reported to the apartment, was given a bankroll of 500 franc notes and directed to shops – primarily Vuitton and Hermes but also Chanel and Lancel – where they bought handbags and scarves by the dozen. Every afternoon, the purchases were deposited at the flat and packed for shipment. Having successfully bribed a French Customs official, the goods were exported with forged documents back to Japan where they were wholesaled by a Yakuza shell company.

It wasn't until the operation had been in business for six years that anyone became even slightly suspicious of it. And then, it was down to employees at Vuitton to wonder about the increasing number of shabbily dressed Asian clients all of whom paid for expensive purchases with brand-new, crisp, 500 franc notes. The management at Vuitton tipped off the police, who soon discovered that although these goods were being shipped out of France – and, therefore, were normally exempt from value added tax – no one had ever bothered to apply for a VAT rebate. Subsequently, the police began noticing long queues of shabbily dressed Asians waiting to get into an apartment near the Madeleine. And all of them were carrying shopping bags filled with French designer goods.

The authorities started making arrests in spring 1992 and quickly pulled in nearly 100 people. The stores themselves were not implicated. When the French police raided the apartment, they found $450,000 in cash and nearly $1.3 million in goods – including 2,500 Vuitton and Hermes products waiting for shipment to Japan. They also found bank statements detailing $2.7 million in local accounts.

No one can say for sure how much the syndicate had laundered since 1985, but French Customs were able to determine that in 1991 alone, the gang managed to wash Fr 400 million – about £48 million.

The Triads are the most notorious of the Chinese mobs – a blood brotherhood that materialized in the seventeenth century to overthrow the Ching Dynasty. When their rebellion ultimately failed two centuries later, many of their members fled to Hong Kong, Indochina and North America.

Independent units linked through an oath of fraternity, the gangs deal in everything from drug trafficking and money laundering to business extortion and burglary. They are the primary force behind Southeast Asia's 'Golden Triangle'.

Spanning the mountains and valleys that cut across the borders of Laos, Thailand and Myanmar – which used to be called Burma – the region produces anywhere from 60 to 120 tons of heroin annually. A kilo of this Triad-distributed drug wholesales at $400,000–600,000. Cut to 6 per cent purity, the street value can easily top $6–10 million.

Unquestionably the most influential power in the world's heroin trade, Triad predominance in the marketplace is growing and expected to thrive. In 1997, Great Britain acknowledged the end of 150 years of colonial rule by returning the sovereignty of Hong Kong to the People's Republic of China. Uncertain as to what economic system would materialize in the new Hong Kong – and in genuine fear of an oppressive Communist regime – many of the capitalist-inclined crime lords have long sought greener pastures, naturally favouring cities with indigenous Chinese populations.

In late 1992, the *Toronto Globe and Mail* reported that 17 senior Triad leaders applied to emigrate to Canada. All of them were barred, as were the 14 who applied in the first months of 1993. The seriousness of the problem is documented by a classified report of the Royal Canadian Mounted Police, which describes the Triads as 'heavily involved' in drug trafficking, gambling, extortion, smuggling, counterfeiting, armed robbery and money laundering.

Similarly, a top-secret evaluation by a combined task force of Australian law enforcement agencies – including the National Crime Authority, the Federal Police, Customs and various state police forces – divulged that 85–90 per cent of all the heroin coming into the country was owned by Chinese groups directly linked to organized crime in Hong Kong and China. These gangs were additionally associated with groups operating out of Vietnam, the Lebanon, Italy, Turkey, Romania, and New Zealand and with a network of motorcycle gangs in Australia, which they use as the backbone of their marketing operation.

The report – never intended for publication – identified hundreds of Chinese criminals operating in the country, many of them otherwise known as influential members of their local community. It warned that these people, along with their associates, had built an underground Chinese banking system to launder drug money and abet widespread extortion rackets. The report concluded that Australia was ill-prepared to deal with this threat, having totally failed to understand the nature of Chinese organized crime.

Today, Chinese gangs are already securely established in many cities around the world – not just Hong Kong, Sydney, Toronto and Vancouver, but San Francisco, Los Angeles, New York and London. They are also beginning to show up in places where the Chinese don't have traditional ties, such as Germany. Police there recently raided 90 Chinese restaurants, questioned 653 people, arrested 102 of them, and seized 24 false passports, more than $1 million in cash, large amounts of cocaine and heroin, and several weapons. They also uncovered evidence of what the police described as 'Mafia-type' money laundering schemes.

In certain respects, organized crime throughout the world is similar. Drug trafficking comes arm in arm with money laundering and the two are an integral generator of terrorism.

Except for their claim to be fighting political wars, groups such as the Irish Republican Army, the Basques' ETA and the PLO are just as skilled at law-breaking as the Yakuza and the Triads.

The Metropolitan Police in London – through their Special Branch – have often said that the IRA do not deal drugs. The Irish police openly contradict them and insist they do, pointing to instances where the IRA have been involved in trafficking marijuana. There's probably every reason to believe that the IRA deal in whatever they need to in order to finance their struggle. It is known that they ride shotgun on shipments for international traffickers. And drug dealing is now a conventional means of turning dirty money into guns. So the betting line must be on the Irish police.

Everyone agrees that the IRA are skilled armed robbers – they've definitely got a track record to back up that claim – and that building societies, banks and post offices on mainland Britain are their preferred targets. The IRA are said to be responsible for anywhere from 800 to 2,500 armed heists a year.

They also run protection rackets, offering insurance against fire and bomb damage. Several British newspapers have identified large business in Northern Ireland paying as much as £2 million a year for a policy with the IRA. The common belief among the security agencies monitoring such things is that any large British-owned company in Northern Ireland which is not regularly bombed is somehow insuring itself against that eventuality.

To top up their reserves, the IRA own pubs and drinking clubs in Northern Ireland – some licensed, some not – all of which have slot machines and jukeboxes.

Cash rich, they wash some of their money through legitimate business fronts such as construction firms, taxi companies and private security services, all of which help to generate more revenue. Once it's laundered, they've even been known to invest their money on the London Stock Exchange. Evidence surfaced a few years ago that, during the early 1980s, the IRA bought shares in a quoted British company – said to have been worth £200 million at the time – using offshore brokers to take it over. They permitted most of the company to be legitimately run, but kept a corner of it to themselves to wash £30 million over an eight-year period.

Donations are a secondary source of IRA funding. Macabrely, contributions increase with each well-publicized death. When Bobby Sands died on a hunger strike and when IRA members were shot by the SAS in Gibraltar, sympathy offerings flooded in. Recruitment increases too, helping the IRA maintain manpower for diverse smurfing operations. They run small frauds with their stalwart band of sympathizers – 50 different people can easily use 50 different names to defraud the UK government out of social security benefits of £75 per week. This is small enough to go undetected for a long time, but important enough to add up quickly – 2,500 accounts milking the system can be worth £187,500 a week or £9.75 million a year. The same numbers come up when those same smurfs launder money through banks and building societies around the UK. In the case of the IRA, smurfs don't think of themselves as money launderers. They do what they do for the cause, which means they're more strongly motivated.

A good part of the IRA's overseas income arrives from the US through NORAID. That source is estimated to be worth anywhere from £1 million to £3 million a year. Considering the large Irish population in Boston, it's hardly surprising that the Bank of Boston – which figured so prominently in 1985 when the US government finally took direct action to put all American financial institutions in line with cash transaction reporting – had been for some years a prime sink for the Boston cell of the Provisional IRA.

As far back as the early 1970s, an ad hoc coalition had been formed between active members of the IRA cell in Boston and local Mafia dons. Organized crime wanted marijuana, the Provo sympathizers became the importers. The middle-man, Joe Murray, was a large, ill-tempered Boston-born chap who ran a towing company in nearby Charlestown. Trusted by his Italian benefactors and dedicated to the cause of the British defeat in Ulster, Murray smuggled tons of drugs into the Boston area on fishing boats. The cash he received for his efforts – laundered through the Bank of Boston – was spent on arms, which those same boats then transported to Northern Ireland.

The Basques' ETA follow the same general pattern as the IRA, dealing in anything they can to further their cause. One main difference is, instead of running clandestine extortion rackets, ETA openly charge Spanish-owned businesses – as opposed to Basque-owned businesses – a 10 per cent 'liberation tax'. Any company in the Basque country refusing to pay is quickly and efficiently shut down.

Protection by any other name, it's hardly any different from the second stamp you have to buy in support of the PLO in order to mail a letter in Beirut.

Folding money remains the key. And these days that can go a long way in the black markets of Eastern Europe. Russian middlemen have been flooding arms bazaars in Poland and Hungary, with everything from surface-to-air missiles to Kalashnikov rifles. The laws of supply and demand being what they are, the going price for a slightly used Russian automatic weapon is down to £2.

That the terrorists have structured themselves along the same lines as organized criminals is hardly surprising because the terrorists wind up being sent to the same jails as organized criminals. It's only natural that, with no other way to bide their time, they compare notes.

It's just as natural that, when they get out, they join forces.

In Russia, where reported crimes are increasing now at nearly 40 per cent a year, Mafia-style groups abound. Besides murdering bankers who refuse to cooperate with them, they're heavily into protection rackets, extracting money from westerners who think they can waltz into the former Soviet Union and make a killing. One estimate suggests that as many as 98 per cent of all businesses in Moscow pay some sort of 'insurance' to the Russian mobs. They've also found their way into the auto trade, stealing tens of thousands of new and late-model used cars in Germany, which they drive back to Russia and sell for hard currency.

But automobiles are only a small part of this game. German police sources insist that more than 300 variously organized Russian crime gangs have invaded Germany since the break-up of the Soviet Union. And that figure has been confirmed by Russian intelligence sources. They are professional criminals who have taken advantage of their newly opened borders to deal in anything and everything – from nuclear materials, which they flog to the highest bidders in the Third World, to drugs, radioactive materials and extortion.

When pressed, the German police admit they are finding themselves unable to cope with the threat. What's more, there's hardly anyone they can call on in Russia for help. The police there have no equipment, no motivation, nothing left of an organization. Whatever infrastructure the Communists had imposed has long since fallen to pieces.

Further afield, Russian gangs have created a market in refugees from the poorer, former Soviet republics in the south whom they sail across the Baltic and deposit in Scandinavia. Those same Baltic trading routes are then used to wash money through Scandinavian banks.

Until recently, it was thought that Russian mobs were operating independently of the more established international syndicates. But that view has begun to change. A gang of Russian emigrés were indicted in New Jersey along with seven members of the Gambino crime family in May 1993, after police broke up a huge petrol and diesel fuel smuggling racket. The 101 counts against them included racketeering, extortion, mail and wire fraud, plus state and federal tax evasion. They also stand accused of having laundered more than $66 million. Of particular concern to the police was the $6.7 million 'mob tax' paid made by the Russians to the Gambino family who allow them to operate. It's one of the first indications that there is a working agreement between Russians and the Mafia.

Although they couldn't link the Russian emigrés in New Jersey directly back to organized crime in Moscow, American law enforcement authorities have always believed that the Russian immigrant community in Brooklyn had those connections. Those fears proved true when a ton of cocaine was confiscated near St Petersburg.

The biggest drug bust to date in Russia – 1,100 kilos were hidden in cans marked 'meat' and 'potatoes' and trucked in from Finland – has led law enforcement officers in Europe and America to believe that Russia has become a key marketplace, a back door for Colombians needing to get product into Europe.

It's all the more worrying that the middlemen lived in New York.

Cocaine use was almost unknown in Russia, but opium poppies grow throughout the ex-Soviet republics. So far, they are being converted only into inexpensive opium-based compounds and are not yet being refined into heroin. But the Colombia–New York–St Petersburg–Europe trade route signals two distressing trends: the beginning of a joint venture between the Colombian and Russian crime cartels; and that it's only a matter of time before heroin is produced, on a grand scale, throughout the region.

There is also reason to be concerned that gargantuan fields of wild marijuana will soon be harvested. The southern republics of the Commonwealth of Independent States are covered with the weed. So are huge tracts of Siberia, where wild marijuana blankets an area of several million acres, roughly the size of Connecticut.

The Russians realize the enormous possibilities that the drug trade offers and Washington sources reveal that certain Russian emigrés sought contacts with the Colombian cartels as early as 1990, around the same time that Colombian laundryman Franklin Jurado was arrested on his way to Moscow. But trying to establish a network is one thing. Actually finding cocaine in St Petersburg destined for Europe has been an enormous shock.

It's difficult enough for western authorities to come to terms with the breakdown in law and order in the former Soviet republics; with the easy availability of raw materials that will get the Russians into the narcotics trade; with their need for hard currency; with the large pool of well-trained chemists who have found themselves out of work as the economy transitions from controlled to market related; and with the opening of Russia's borders. It will be that much more difficult to stop Russia from becoming another Colombia.

According to Assistant Commissioner of Police David Vaness, a former head of Scotland Yard's specialist organized crime unit, 'The level of contempt for the law and the random violence of these criminals is immense. We need to revise our estimates of the threat every three months. And the more you learn, the more discouraging it is. Russian crime syndicates are expected to be Britain's major supplier of drugs and illegal weapons within five years.'

To put the size of the growing threat into some perspective, Swiss authorities now admit that in the three years 1992–1995, at least $54 billion has been deposited in Swiss banks from Russia.

Russia is destined to become a jungle in the snow.

Former KGB agents, no longer in the spying business, are currently using the remnants of the state police network to deal in currency and money laundering. Eventually, these professionally trained, highly qualified ex-spooks will get their drug trafficking act together. After all, something like 40 per cent of the arable land in the former Soviet Union is ideally suited for the heroin poppy. The Mafia won't like it and neither will the Colombians. But there's very little they'll be able to do about it. If they can't beat them, they'll almost certainly want to join them.

Italian police intelligence sources claim to have uncovered evidence that two summits have already been held – one in Warsaw in March 1991 and another in Prague in October 1992 – hosted by Russian organized crime bosses. The guests of honour were representatives of Sicilian, Neapolitan and Calabrian crime organizations. The topics of discussion were money laundering, narcotics and the sale of nuclear material.

Drug trafficking, as practised by the Colombian cartels, is basically a one-product industry. By comparison, the Mafia is a multinational conglomerate with a wide array of commercial interests – prostitution, arms dealing, protection, extortion, gambling and drug dealing.

Especially when it comes to drugs, the Mafia has a big advantage. The Triads deal heroin and the Colombians deal coke, but the Mafia is long on experience with both.

It also dabbles in government. Until recently, it was the single most consistent political force in Italy since 1945.

Known inside the country as 'La Piovra' – the octopus – the Mafia is today made up of three tightly entwined groups. There is the traditional bunch out of Sicily, there is the Camorra in Naples and there is the Ndrangheta from Calabria. Despite recent crackdowns – at least according to the chief prosecutor at the Italian Supreme Court – the Mafia's tentacles continue to reach into every aspect of national life, wielding influence in every town throughout the country. In the major cities like Rome, Milan and Naples, nearly 60 per cent of the shops, bars and restaurants pay protection money to the Mafia. In Sicily – especially in the capital city of Palermo – it's 100 per cent.

It was the Sicilian branch that set up the first overseas subsidiaries. They arrived in the United States steerage class, in the first quarter of the century, along with great waves of other Italian immigrants looking to escape war and famine. Banded together by family, village and a common dialect, the Sicilians worked their way through prohibition and into racketeering, gambling and infiltration of the labour unions. Their children went into the family business but they had enough money to see that the third generation – Don Corleone's grandchildren – got a good education. Pushed to be better than their parents, they became lawyers who could protect the family interests. Or they got themselves MBAs from respectable business schools, and showed their elders how to transform cash into legitimate, tax-paying concerns.

Referred to in the States as the Cosa Nostra, at the very height of their influence – back in the 1950s and the 1960s, when policing methods were much less effective than they are today – they numbered around 7,000. More dispersed and considerably smaller these days, there are still well-entrenched pockets of influence. For instance, it's said that the families who run New York have been, for at least 40 years, the single largest commercial landlord in the city.

The Mafia is also the major heroin dealer in the United States.

For five years, from 1979 to 1984, a Mafia clique franchised the distribution of their heroin through a network of pizzerias that stretched across the industrial northeast and into the midwest. The original idea was to use the restaurants to distribute the drug – heroin to go – as well as to launder money by mixing narcotics receipts with pizza sales. But heroin soon became the main item on the menu and there was simply too much money to put into the tills. They needed to find other ways to wash their profits.

One of the men who took on that task was fish broker Sal Amendolito. Years before he'd been involved with a financial consultancy in Milan that illegally moved currency to Switzerland for wealthy Italians. When that dried up, he imported fish into Italy. After a while, he moved to the States to export fish back to Europe. Around 1980, he was contacted by his former associate in Milan – Sal Miniati – who said he sought his help on behalf of a Sicilian construction firm. Miniati's story was that they were building a large resort with American investors who all happened to run pizzerias. He explained that they had a lot of cash that needed to get to Switzerland – to pay for the shares in the investment – without attracting any attention. At the moment, Miniati revealed, $9 million was waiting to be moved. For his services, Miniati offered his old friend $90,000.

Amendolito agreed and the first instalment – an even $100,000 – was delivered to him that July. To keep deposits under the $10,000 cash transaction reporting limit, he opened accounts in a dozen banks. A few days later he bought cashier's cheques for the amount on deposit, minus his 1 per cent commission, and consolidated the stash in new accounts, which he opened in four different banks. From there the money was wired to Switzerland where Miniati took over.

This laundry service was rudimentary to say the least – the paper trail was broad enough for a child to follow – but Amendolito decided it would work fine as long as the payments stayed relatively small. He ran the washing cycle a few more times with $100,000 amounts. Towards the end of July, however, Amendolito was handed $550,000 in small bills. And now he had a problem. It was too much to feed into his established banking network.

Through a contact at the Swiss investment house Finagest, he was told that Conti Commodity Services in the World Trade Center could accommodate him. However, when he arrived at Conti's offices carrying four small suitcases packed with cash, they said they didn't have the facilities for that much and referred him to the Chase Manhattan Bank downstairs. That branch repeated Conti's excuse and suggested Amendolita find a bigger Chase branch. The bank's headquarters were only a few blocks away, but by the time he got there they were closing. He was invited to come back in the morning. The following day Chase did, in fact, take the money from him and credited it to a Finagest account held at Credit Suisse in Lugano.

Refusing to subject himself to that again, he decided to find a better way to wash very large quantities of cash. He settled on smuggling funds out of the States and depositing them in the Bahamas. Before long, as the amounts increased with each transaction, Amendolito worked out a deal with Miniati that some of the money would be taken by couriers direct from New York to Switzerland.

At this point, Miniati mentioned how a friend of a friend in Sicily was interested in using Amendolito's services. To handle his growing business, Amendolito opened an office on Madison Avenue, installed a cash-counting machine and added a newly opened contact – a bank in Bermuda – to his list for cash deposits. But Amendolito had the nasty little habit of sticking his fingers into the cookie jar. When some of those recent clients in Sicily discovered he was helping himself to a few pennies more on each deal – quietly topping up the 4 per cent commission they'd already negotiated – they weren't especially pleased, and politely suggested it might be healthier if he paid them back. Instead, he decided it was healthier to disappear.

The mob replaced Amendolito with an Italian banker – Antonio Cavalleri – who managed a Credit Suisse office in the alpine village of Bellinzona. He was instrumental in creating a company called Traex which, on paper, dealt in property and raw materials. In reality it didn't do anything except wash pizza connection money. With the help of a Swissair employee, nearly $10 million was flown out of

New York for deposit into the Traex account at Cavalleri's branch.

As far as the mob knew, no one was yet on to them. But they were mistaken. Early in 1979 – just as the pizza connection was really getting started – Italian Customs stumbled across a suitcase at Palermo Airport containing $497,000. Their investigation led to the discovery of five working heroin laboratories in Sicily. The Americans heard about it and wanted to know more. Thanks to the information the Italians were willing to share with them, by the time Cavalleri's Swissair shuttle was up and running the FBI had identified Amendolito, had followed some of his transactions and located his office on Madison Avenue. From there, it was easy to get phone records and, from that, their interest broadened to a wider group of players.

Ironically, it was the as-yet-unsuspected Swissair employee who first started getting cold feet about all this smuggling. The mob replaced him with Franco Della Torre, a laundry-man who'd worked for them in Switzerland. He came to New York with his credentials in place – a representative of Traex – opened an account with stockbrokers Merrill Lynch and, during the first four months of 1982, washed $5 million there. Towards the end of April, he opened a Traex account with brokers EF Hutton and in 11 cash deposits in under ten weeks washed $7.4 million.

Worrying that such an enterprise could attract attention, he opened a second EF Hutton account – this one in the name of Acacias Development Company – and over the following ten weeks laundered a further $8.2 million through Hutton.

Della Torre's concerns were well founded. Like Amendolito, he too was leaving a broad paper trail. Merrill Lynch and Hutton both kept records of all these transactions.

In 1983, Amendolito resurfaced. He'd been arrested for fraud in New Orleans. By that time, the FBI were onto Della

Torre. A joint task force was formed – modelled roughly on Operation Greenback – to work out of the office of Rudolph Giuliani, then a brash young US Attorney for the Southern District of New York. He attacked from two sides – the drug dealers and, separately, the laundrymen. Because none of his targets had yet developed very good money laundering skills, the second trail proved relatively easy to follow.

Agents from the FBI, Customs, the DEA, the IRS and the Bureau of Alcohol, Tobacco and Firearms put a case together that brought grand jury indictments against 39 members of the ring for their participation in drug trafficking and money laundering. Sal Amendolito became a government witness, testified against the others and was never charged. Because some were hiding in Italy – among them Della Torre – only 22 actually stood trial in New York. After 17 months of hearings, endless FBI wire taps – 55,000 to be exact, most of them in Italian – plus the murder of one suspect, 21 defendants were found guilty. The judge sentenced the five Mafia ring leaders to terms of 20–45 years. He also ordered four defendants to pay $2.5 million to help pay for treatment of heroin addicts.

The group had smuggled 750 kilos of heroin into the States – with an estimated street value of $1.6 billion. In taking them to task, some major financial institutions had also been embarrassed – Merrill Lynch, EF Hutton and Chemical Bank in New York, Handelsbank in Zurich and, especially, Credit Suisse in Bellinzona. One of the accounts at Credit Suisse was secretly called 'Wall Street 651'. The owner was Oliviero Tognoli, a well-known industrialist to whom the Mafia chieftains secretly turned for financial advice. Nearly $20 million had passed through his account.

Some powerful men were locked away for a long time and the case was widely publicized as a major victory for the good guys.

With hindsight, it was something more. The bad guys had

washed over $50 million. But this time – for the very first time in a major drugs case – the Feds had been able to follow the money.

Suddenly both sides realized that the rules of engagement had been changed.

Suddenly, the stakes were higher than ever.

Italian mobsters have had a physical presence in Latin America for many years – notably through the maritally linked Cuntrera and Caruana clans, which have overseen their heroin empire from a once-secure base in Venezuela.

However, little by little, the authorities have been able to chip away at their sovereignty. In 1985, British and Canadian police seized a $300 million shipment of heroin sent from London to Montreal and convicted one of the Caruanas for it. Two years later they put a dent in the families' budgets by grabbing a monstrous hashish cargo in Newfoundland. Another relative went down for that one. The following year the Venezuelans arrested yet another of the kinfolk for conspiring to traffic cocaine.

That particular bust was significant because, until then, the authorities suspected, but could never prove, that the two families had ties to the Colombians. Now they understood that there was no way they could operate next door to the cartels without permission.

A major break came that same year when John Galatolo, a south Florida businessman, was convicted of smuggling cocaine. He told the DEA that he'd personally brokered a recent deal for the Mafia to buy 600 kilos of cocaine from the Cali cartel. According to Galatolo, that deal firmly established the Mafia's cocaine franchise for Italy.

Originally, the Colombians had restricted the Mafia to their home base, hoping to distribute their own powder throughout the rest of Europe. But Europe is a long way from Latin America and although the Cali mob could function easily in Spain – they spoke the language – northern Europe proved to be a more difficult market. Transactions started going wrong and shipments were seized. It finally came to a head in February 1990 when the Dutch police found three tons of cocaine hidden inside a consignment of fruit juice.

Pragmatists that they are, the Colombians acknowledged defeat. They needed the Mafia's established distribution networks throughout Europe, and turned to the experts. Together they set up front companies to handle the drugs and bank accounts to wash the money.

Stopping them would take the kind of international cooperation that was, until this point, unprecedented.

The first hint that such an exploit might be possible came in April 1992 when the FBI arrested 14 people in Florida for trafficking and money laundering. In and of itself, the bust was just one of several that month. What made it unique was that the evidence found linked these people to the Colombian cartels and a Calabrian Mafia cell in Toronto.

Five months later, on Monday 28 September, police from eight nations – America, Great Britain, Canada, Colombia, Costa Rica, Spain, Holland and the Cayman Islands – launched what can only be described as an all-out nuclear attack against the Mafia–cartel connection.

It was called Green Ice and it represented the first time that an operational international task force had been formed specifically to take on the money launderers.

Undercover agents posed as laundrymen, starting first in San Diego in 1989, then slowly building up contacts in Texas, Florida, Illinois and New York. They ran a chain of leather goods stores – subsidiaries of Trans Americas Ventures Associates, a DEA front company that imported merchandise from Colombia. Each ton of imported leather was listed as 20 tons, creating enough false invoices to wash drug profits back to the cartel's banks in Colombia and Panama.

In fact, the Cali bunch were so happy with the way Trans Americas ran their sink, they asked them to expand overseas – originally into Canada and the Caribbean, then into Europe. The agents working the scam – DEA, FBI, IRS and Customs – were only too pleased, as were the various foreign law enforcement agencies that came into the operation as the money laundering sting expanded.

After nearly three years of ground work – in one momentous, simultaneous swoop on three continents – more than 200 people were arrested worldwide. They included 112 in the States, three in Britain, four in Spain and 34 in Italy. Among the people nabbed were seven primary targets – the top-ranking financial managers of the Cali cartel.

They got Rodrigo Carlos Polania, a former inspector of Colombia's national bank, and they got Jose 'Tony the Pope' Duran, described by the Italian police as the world's most important cocaine distributor. A subsequent request by Interpol for fingerprint files on him revealed dossiers on him in 20 different countries under 20 different names. He had gone to Rome to introduce Pedro Felipe Villaquiran, his chief European representative, to the Mafia bosses, and also to meet Bettein Martens, a major Dutch money launderer. They too were arrested.

The police also confiscated 750 kilos of cocaine and over $54 million in cash.

When the trap was snapped shut, 15 money laundering front companies were raided. Besides a pan-European animal protection society and a Sicilian wine exporter, there was a sink in Mantua, Italy, managed by an 80-year-old woman with no business experience who laundered tens of millions of dollars for her nephew.

Thousands of files were confiscated on both sides of the Atlantic. One truly outstanding prize was a wealth of computerized records found in the Cali offices of drug baron Rodriguez Orejuela, which detailed the cartel's world-wide money laundering. Other documents pointed to several Mafia–cartel joint ventures, including drug trafficking along the French Riviera and money laundering in Germany.

Since Green Ice – and largely as a result of it – the Italian police, through the Central Operational Service, and the Interior Ministry, through its Internal Security Service, have arrested Giuseppe Madonia, the Mafia's number two man in Sicily; Carmine Alfieri, a *capo* in the Camorra; three Sicilian brothers who've come to be called the Mafia's private bankers; Antonio Sarnataro, who is believed to be the Camorra's chief laundryman; and, in May 1993, Michele 'The Crazy One' Zaza, the alleged overall leader of the gang. Ten more Camorra members were arrested with Zaza on the French Riviera, where a Camorra money laundering network had invested $1.3 billion in hotels, stores and small industry. At the same time, 40 additional suspects, all tied to Alfieri, Sarnataro and Zaza, were taken into custody in Italy, Belgium and Germany.

When the initial success of Green Ice was reported in the press, the then US Deputy Attorney General, George Terwilliger, declared the operation 'a stake through the heart of the illegal drug business'.

In Colombia, at least one senior Cali cartel member conceded that it had been 'a disruption'.

CHAPTER SIXTEEN

The Adventurers

*'Laundering methods keep changing to stay ahead of the
authorities and the good guys are overwhelmed by the size of
the problem.'*

US News and World Report

The poor bastard used to have a real name, but in November
1986, after he showed up at the Drug Enforcement Administration office in Seattle, Washington, with a story to tell,
they christened him CI-#1. And, once the DEA awards you
Confidential Informant status, you are forever known by
your number.

CI-#1's story began: over the three-day period – from Monday 25 August 1986 through Wednesday 27 – two brothers
from Los Angeles were running a gang that smuggled 23
tons of high-quality Thai marijuana into the United States.

CI-#1 said: two local fishing vessels, escorted by a surveillance plane loaded with radar equipment to protect them
from intervention by US Customs, rendezvoused with the
mother ship several hundred miles off southwestern Alaska,
and brought the product ashore in Anacortes, a commercial
salmon port 60 miles north of Seattle. The shipment was so
large it filled two tractor-trailers and the same brothers were
now planning a much bigger haul for summer 1987.

CI-#1's story ended: I didn't get paid what they promised me and I'm looking to get even.

So Special Agent Gary Annunziata gave him his chance. He wired CI-#1 for sound and sent him back into the smuggling business.

Bill and Chris Shaffer were in search of adventure.

As kids, they'd lived in London – their old man worked for the US Navy – but after high school, in 1963, Bill went back to America, got himself a degree from Penn State University and a job teaching school in New Jersey.

Chris stayed in Europe for a while, running around with a girlfriend. When they were able to put some money together, they bought a sail boat and headed for Australia. There they worked charters until they could buy an 80 foot sloop. Slowly but surely, their charter business turned into amateur smuggling. They made a few runs, brought in some dope and picked up some fast money. It worked well the first few times so they kept doing it, fetching bigger loads each time.

In the meantime, Bill gave up his teaching job, dealt a little cocaine in Florida and wound up in Los Angeles, where he dealt a little dope. It was fast money with very little risk, an easy way to get through life while trying to manoeuvre his way past the periphery of the film world.

By the time Chris came back to the States in 1983 – and joined up with big brother in LA – they both knew a lot about the drug business.

They told people they were treasure hunters, marine salvage experts who went in search of sunken galleons. Chris even set up a company in London – China Pacific Films – to fund their salvage work. In reality, all it did was finance a ship for smuggling. By January 1985 the Shaffers had raised enough money to pay $1 million for a fishing vessel out of Hawaii called the *Six Pac*. Along with the boat came its captain, a former British merchant mariner named Terry Restall.

It was a fortuitous encounter. Restall had been smuggling hashish for years and was savvy to the ways of the drug world.

Within two months, the Shaffers sent Restall into the Gulf of Thailand, where he was met by two Vietnamese fishing boats and took on board seven tons of marijuana. Restall brought the product to a rendezvous point 600 miles off the coast of San Diego, California, where it was transferred to a fishing vessel called the *Pacific Rose* and eventually brought ashore near Santa Cruz.

On his next trip, Restall brought back eight tons.

Early in 1986, the Shaffers invested in a shipment that they weren't transporting – five tons of product – which was seized by US Customs near Hawaii. It shook the brothers into realizing just how vulnerable they were.

Suddenly worried that the authorities might be watching them, Bill and Chris went looking for a vessel that had never before been used in any American smuggling operation. They found the *Niki Maru*, a 110 foot oil supply ship, sitting in Japan. They bought it, then immediately spent $300,000 converting it to look like a Japanese fishing boat.

It was the *Niki Maru* that brought in the 23-ton shipment.

In February 1987, thanks to CI-#1, Gary Annunziata learned that the Shaffers had purchased a big fishing boat in Seward, Alaska – the *Stormbird* – which they brought to Seattle where it was to be converted for smuggling.

In September of that year, the DEA watched the refitted *Stormbird* slip out of port heading for Alaska. They were now ready to arrest the entire gang.

But Bill Shaffer had developed a sixth sense – acute paranoia – and something told him he was being watched. He hastily acquired a new boat, the *Blue Fin*, then he put out the word that the load was coming ashore in Mexico.

Gullibly, CI-#1 relayed that story to Annunziata.

A Shaffer boat called the *Manuia* delivered the product to the *Six Pac* south of Hawaii, the *Six Pac* brought it to the *Stormbird* in the northern Pacific and the *Blue Fin* met the *Stormbird* south of Alaska. By the time the *Stormbird* arrived back in Anacortes on 21 September, empty, the *Blue Fin* had already docked at Bellingham, 25 miles north, and unloaded 42 tons of marijuana.

And all the time, the DEA were looking towards Mexico.

Because the drug business functions through its subculture, successful dealers move through the underworld, finding the people they need to know – people with access to the product, people with access to the boats, people with access to the distributors. And specialists – people who have expertise in areas like buying, offloading and money laundering.

The Shaffers worked their way inside this subculture. While Bill was clearly the man in charge – he conducted the planning and handled the financial side – Chris was the one who dealt with the logistics and the transportation. But they couldn't do everything themselves and over the years they put together a large organization, mainly friends, and then friends of friends.

The larger the group, the more vulnerable they became.

The product they were buying in Southeast Asia was being supplied by two of the world's largest dealers.

Tony the Thai was somewhere in his 40s. He spoke good English and knew his way around the murky world of international drug dealing. At this time, no one knew what his real name is. Or, if they knew, no one seemed willing to say.

An entrepreneur who, rumour had it, fronted his drug dealing with a small but successful empire in real estate and hotels, he was definitely the right man to know if you wanted to buy high-grade Thai marijuana, because Tony the Thai was seriously connected.

At one point he invited Restall to meet him in Bangkok so that he could show the Shaffers what they were buying. When Restall arrived, Tony personally took him into the jungle, north towards Chang Mai, and across the border into Laos.

No one asked who they were or what they were doing there.

When they arrived in Laos, they were met by a senior, uniformed Laotian police officer who escorted them to a heavily guarded warehouse where Tony had stashed 200 tons of high-quality dope.

The second guy – for a while, Tony's largest competitor – was Brian Peter Daniels, an ex-pat American. The Shaffers bought their 1987 shipment from him.

The same age as Bill, with the same taste for adventure and the same appetite for flashy women, Daniels lived in Thailand and for a time actively challenged Tony for the title of world's most important marijuana supplier. In just four years – between 1984 and 1988 – Daniels is known to have smuggled several hundred tons of marijuana into the United States.

Each bale of Daniels' marijuana was tightly wrapped in heavy, dark blue nylon canvas, and bore the Eagle Brand sticker – a white tag, with a crudely drawn blue eagle and the bold red words 'Passed Inspection'. Whether it was his way of saying, 'This belongs to Brian Daniels', or just a bit of bravado on his part, the US Justice Department isn't sure. There is also some evidence to suggest that the Eagle Brand was never exclusive to Daniels.

What the Justice Department does know for certain is that Daniels – like Tony the Thai – couldn't possibly have operated on the scale he did without a lot of help.

Insiders maintained that the governments of Thailand, Laos and Vietnam consistently turned a blind eye to people like Tony and Daniels, because Tony and Daniels were always willing to pay handsome amounts of much-needed hard currency for the service. In some instances, men like Daniels – and in this case, certainly, Tony the Thai – got into bed with those governments. They were partners, apportioned shares in the action to command the allegiance of high officials, local warlords, police chiefs and provincial governors. The military were in on it, too. One of Daniels' shipments to the Shaffers was guarded by uniformed Vietnamese Army officers during the offloading in the Gulf of Tonkin.

Marijuana coming out of Thailand and Laos, crossing Vietnam and being shipped from Da Nang still gets waved through when it bears the right label.

At the US Department of Justice, they read 'Passed Inspection' to mean, everyone will get a slice.

As the money rolled in, the brothers set themselves up in several places around LA. They hung out in Malibu but rented houses all over town. Two of Bill's pals from his New Jersey days were Ed and Eileen Brown. She produced porn films and called herself Summer. At Bill's request, the Browns rented a big house on Helena Drive in fashionable Brentwood so that the Shaffers had a place to count their money. The Browns also rented a second house in the Hollywood hills – far enough away from the counting house – so that the Shaffers had a place to hide their money.

As wholesalers, Bill and Chris limited their dealings to two distribution groups – one in California, the other in New York.

The LA distributors were an odd couple who came to be known as Greater and Lesser. Greater was a husky, ex-football player named Kenneth Tarlow. Lesser was his more diminutive pal named Dennis Specht.

In New York, their distributor was known simply as Sonny. At the time, no one knew anything more about him than that.

Just because the Shaffers did business with Greater and Lesser and Sonny, that was no reason to trust them. So, whenever a payment was due, they sent their own people to pick it up and – once assured that they weren't being followed – deliver it back to Brentwood. The money was counted and boxed there, then taken to the safe house in the hills. When enough boxes were piled high, the Shaffers would ask friends like the Browns to take the money to Switzerland.

Characteristically, Bill planned and compartmentalized everything down to the minutest details. People who worked for him knew only what they had to know to get their job done.

On 20 October 1986, he personally packed a motor home with 40 cartons from the safe house – containing $20 million in cash – and drove it to Salt Lake City, Utah. There, he was met by a small group of friends, including the Browns, in a chartered Gulfstream II jet.

He'd already gone to the trouble of forming a shell company called Bi-Continental Computers and printing business cards – complete with official titles – for each of those friends. He also handed out tiny lapel pins – which looked like company logos – so that no one could show up at the last minute and claim they'd been invited along.

Each of the 40 cartons was labeled 'Computer Related Equipment', and the pilot's manifest reflected that. The next morning, when Shaffer's friends landed in Zurich, the pilot passed his manifest along to Swiss Customs. The boxes were taken off the plane and one of them was randomly opened.

To the utter shock of the Swiss authorities, instead of computer related equipment, they found neatly tied stacks of $20 and $50 bills.

The customs officer in charge went wild. He summoned the pilot and screamed, 'You've declared computer equipment and we've find that your cargo is banknotes. Why did you make a false declaration?'

The pilot had no answer, so the Swiss authorities turned to the passengers and accused them of filing a false declaration.

There was little the Browns could do but admit that they'd lied.

At which point the Swiss Customs officer explained, 'We don't have any problem with bank notes but we do have a problem with computer equipment. Never, ever, ever file a false declaration like that again.'

In a state of shock, the Browns and the others promised they wouldn't do that again.

Swiss Customs allowed them to pile the cartons into a van and leave with it, as planned, for Liechtenstein.

The DEA had been caught looking the wrong way.

The case against the Shaffers ground to a halt.

The dope had come through and most of the suspects had long since left the area. Anyway, Annunziata had plenty of other bad guys to deal with – in particular, Brian Daniels.

During the DEA investigation of him, Annunziata learned how the Shaffers had beaten him with an end run. Incensed, he went to Assistant US Attorney Mark Bartlett, determined to reopen the case.

Then in his early 30s, the 5 foot 10 inch, dark-haired, weight-lifting Bartlett was not what cops call 'an ivory tower lawyer'. He didn't hide in his plush office. He went on busts. He got his hands dirty. When Annunziata told him how much he wanted the Shaffers, Bartlett said okay and assigned it OCDEF status – creating an Organized Crime Drug Enforcement task force.

To run it, Bartlett brought in Fran Dyer.

At 48, Dyer had already been in law enforcement 25 years. Boston born, with blond hair, about the same height as Bartlett but slimmer, he'd served with the US Air Force in counter-intelligence during Vietnam. He then spent five years as a Seattle detective before joining the Internal Revenue Service, Criminal Investigation Division.

Because they didn't have any of the smuggled goods to use as evidence, Bartlett and Dyer – and Gary Annunziata until he was transferred to Malaysia – needed to put together what the textbooks call 'a no-dope conspiracy' case. To secure convictions, they'd have to build everything on testimony and support it with documents.

In textbooks, it's easy.

In the real world, it took more than three years.

For the Shaffers, this adventure was turning out to be a very good one.

Their 1987 operation netted them in excess of $35 million. In all, they'd earned somewhere around $60 million.

And they'd managed to get most of it out of the country.

After the Zurich episode in October 1986, Bill arranged the flights to Switzerland in a different manner. He met a fellow named Alex Major who ran a small chartered jet operation, and used Major to make the runs to Europe.

By design, neither Bill nor Chris ever flew with the money.

On 9 November 1987, Major flew $11 million in one of his own planes to Zurich. A month later, on 8 December, Major flew his own plane again, this time with $8 million on board, to Switzerland.

Changing the routine, to avoid arousing suspicion, on 24 January 1988, Major leased a Canadair 600 jet to take $6 million to Zurich. It turned out to be a seven-day charter, which cost the Shaffers $130,000. Five friends accepted Bill's offer to eat, drink and be merry, and their in-flight food bill alone – caviar, smoked salmon and champagne – came to $18,000.

Major's fourth trip to Switzerland, on 27 February, was to transport another $6 million.

The Shaffers were using brokers to set up shell companies in Liechtenstein and Switzerland, so whenever money arrived it was delivered to those brokers. They made the actual deposits because Bill had decreed that neither he nor Chris should ever go to the banks themselves.

Through those brokers, the brothers operated at least 17 different shell companies in Liechtenstein alone, with accounts in seven different banks. Other accounts were eventually located in England, France, Germany, Switzerland, Ireland and Austria.

They used those shells to pay for stocks and shares and a mansion that Bill bought in Santa Barbara, California. The shells paid for their art and their jewellery and the sports cars that they started racing around Europe. They owned property in England and covered their walls with expensive paintings – Picassos and Warhols. Bill also bought himself an ocean-going yacht, for $1.2 million, through a shell company set up in the Isle of Man.

Spending the money was the greatest adventure of all.

Ironically, the boat was named for the pirate Henry Morgan.

With the Shaffers living high on the hog in Europe, Dyer, Annunziata and Bartlett got together for the first time, 8,000 miles away in Seattle, in November 1989.

After sorting through the information that Annunziata and the DEA had already compiled, Dyer and Annunziata decided to start by rolling over the little guys – the boat crews – hoping to work their way up the ladder.

By April 1990, Mark Bartlett had compiled a long list of participants and took his fledgling case to a grand jury. It returned an indictment, charging Bill and Chris Shaffer, plus 27 others – including Terry Restall and the Browns – with conspiracy to import marijuana, the importation of marijuana and conspiracy to distribute marijuana. He also resurrected an earlier indictment in northern California that implicated Chris in a 1983 marijuana shipment.

The Shaffers were now officially fugitives from justice.

Within a few months, Bartlett returned to the grand jury, adding more names to the list. Before the end of 1990, he'd indicted a total of 47 people. At that point, he received a phone call from lawyers in Boston indicating that they were under instructions from two Shaffer associates – one of them being Restall – to strike a deal.

Dyer and Bartlett knew they had a highly prosecutable case against the Shaffers, but having Restall to testify would be a major bonus. So the negotiatons began. Restall surrendered to Fran Dyer in January 1991 and, on the strength of the testimony he was willing to provide, Bartlett agreed to ask the courts for a minimum of five but not more than ten years.

Restall took the deal, knowing that, without it, he was facing 25 years.

Dyer and Bartlett now closed in on the others.

Passionate about cars, Dennis 'Lesser' Specht drove a very special turbo-charged Ferrari Testarossa. One of only three ever made, it appeared on the cover of *Road and Track Magazine*. When it did, a source recognized it and Dyer was able to trace him through the magazine. Once he'd found Specht, it was easy to get Kenneth 'Greater' Tarlow.

Dyer then learned that Sonny – a man in his mid-to-late

50s – once confessed to a Shaffer messenger how he always wanted to be in the movies. He said he never could make it in Hollywood, but had come close because a girlfriend who worked for an ad agency had gotten him a job acting in a television commercial. Dyer found out what the product was, contacted the company and discovered that Sonny's real name was Irwin Kletter. A warrant for his arrest was issued immediately.

The Shaffers didn't know it yet, but their days were definitely numbered.

When CBS News went to Geneva in April 1987 to cover the Sotheby sale of the Duchess of Windsor's jewellery, they interviewed some of the people present. At one point they turned their cameras on a blond guy in an expensive suit, drinking champagne with a gorgeous woman. When they asked his name, he seemed startled, and replied, 'Bill Ryan.' When they asked him if he was going to buy something, he told them 'There are times when you just have to go for it.'

It turned out that Bill and Chris were going for it in London, now carrying British passports.

At least one of their passports was falsely obtained by someone who went to Somerset House and copied a birth certificate of an individual who'd passed away. Another was stolen. A third – this one a German passport – was purchased by Bill, in broad daylight, for $50,000 cash, over lunch with a self-proclaimed CIA operative, at the Serpentine Restaurant in Hyde Park.

The instant he had reason to believe that there might be a UK connection, Fran Dyer turned for help to Scotland Yard.

Working through the Justice Department Attaché at the US Embassy in Grosvenor Square, Dyer was put in touch with the Metropolitan Police International and Organized Crimes Branch in April 1990. Within a matter of hours, Detective Sergeants Rick Reynolds and Graham Saltmarsh were on the case. And, for much of the next three years, the London–Seattle phone connection would be in use for several hours every day.

It was Reynolds and Saltmarsh who tracked down and seized Terry Restall's assets – among them, an English country estate in Fareham, Hampshire. It was Reynolds and Saltmarsh who went to see Bill Shaffer at his house in Alexander Square in South Kensington, only to find it empty. It was Reynolds and Saltmarsh who came within hours of arresting Shaffer less than half a mile from Scotland Yard.

In March 1991, Shaffer checked into a suite at Dukes Hotel, in the heart of Mayfair, using the name Alan Abill. Typically, playing the big spender, he was flashing a lot of money. Foolishly, for a fugitive on the run, his money was attracting attention. One afternoon, he asked the concierge to put some roses in his suite – a lot of roses – £500 worth. The concierge accommodated him. That night, Shaffer returned to the hotel with the British actress Cherie Lunghi on his arm.

Suspicious that their client might not be who he said he was, someone in hotel security decided to make a discreet phone call to a friend at Scotland Yard. But the officer was on a stake-out and didn't return the call for two days. By that time, Shaffer had checked out.

By now, Reynolds and Saltmarsh had proof that false passports were involved. To help identify the names in those false passports, they turned to the BBC.

Phoning the 'Crimewatch' production office, Reynolds explained that he had something the programme might be interested in. The producer promised to take a look at it. Until then, the show had concentrated almost exclusively on British bad guys. On Thursday evening, 12 September, 1991, 'Crimewatch' broke new ground by asking for help to locate a pair of American bad guys and showed viewers their photos.

More than 70 people rang with varying degrees of information.

Ten of the calls made some sense. Two of the ten came from the Continent. One of those two placed Bill Shaffer in Germany.

Although Bill now claims that life as a fugitive was a terrible experience, the search for him lasted another four months. It ended on 15 January 1992, in the bar of the Sheraton Hotel near Frankfurt Airport, where he was arrested by the Bavarian state police. When they grabbed him, he shrugged, 'Congratulations. Today is your lucky day. You've won the big one.'

Dyer and Bartlett hoped that they could bring him back to Seattle within a week. But Shaffer had other plans. He hired a local lawyer to fight his extradition – or at least somehow to delay extradition long enough to strike a deal. His problem turned out to be that neither Bartlett nor Dyer was in the mood to haggle. Shaffer held out as long as he could and wound up spending the next nine months under maximum security in a filthy, outmoded German prison. He was confined to his cell 23 hours a day. The only hour out was for recreation in a garbage-filled courtyard. The window to his cell was barred and there was no glass, which allowed in both the weather and odours from the courtyard. A single, 25-watt lightbulb burned continuously day and night.

When his appeals ran out, the Germans bundled him onto a plane, accompanied by US marshals. On the evening of 16 September 1992, the plane set down at Seattle's Sea-Tac International Airport.

By this time, Dyer and Bartlett had indicted more than

45 people and obtained more than 40 convictions, most of them on guilty pleas. Bill was safely tucked away for the time being, dressed in the tatty red coveralls of the Kent Corrections Facility, near Seattle.

But Chris was still free.

Scotland Yard had tracked him to Ireland. The Garda were asked to arrest him but, by the time they got to the house where he was believed to be staying, he was gone. However, they discovered that someone known to be helping him had rented a van and taken it, along with Chris Shaffer, to France. Now Dyer, Reynolds and Saltmarsh turned to the French police.

Aware that Bill was in custody, Chris later admitted that he lived in a constant state of panic. He changed hotels every few days and was forever looking over his shoulder.

In September 1992, Dyer discovered that the Browns were in Paris, living just off the Luxembourg Gardens. Convinced they were in touch with Chris, he asked the French police to arrest them.

At 9 o'clock one morning, a police officer dressed as a workman knocked on the Brown's front door. Summer Brown couldn't figure out what he wanted, so she turned to her husband. At that very moment Ed was on the phone with Chris, who was hiding in a small hotel five blocks away.

Ed said to Summer, 'Let me get it,' told Chris, 'I'll call you right back,' and hung up. When he opened the door, the workman stepped in, followed by several armed officers.

The Browns were handcuffed and the police began a thorough search of the apartment. That's when the phone started ringing.

Chris had grown impatient waiting for Ed to call him back, so he dialled the flat. For whatever reason, the police chose not to answer the phone. Totally unnerved, Chris immediately checked out of his hotel.

Stressed beyond breaking point, now changing rooms every night, afraid even of his own shadow, Chris soon got in touch with an attorney in the States and asked him to negotiate a surrender. Dyer and Bartlett agreed in principle to work out a plea bargain with him and on 16 December 1992 – almost three months to the day after his older brother was taken into custody – Chris made his way to Amsterdam and then on to Seattle where he surrendered to Dyer.

Under the agreement, both brothers pleaded guilty to all charges. They also agreed to make a full and honest accounting of all the currency and assets they possessed or controlled, which would then be seized. In exchange, Bartlett promised to ask for a sentence of 'no more than 15 years for Bill Shaffer and no more than 13 years for Chris Shaffer'.

While Dyer and Bartlett have admitted that they couldn't have brought the Shaffers to justice without Reynolds, Saltmarsh and Scotland Yard, there were still a few matters that need to be cleaned up.

One was the business of Tony the Thai.

His real name was Thanong Siriprechapong and he happened to have been a member of the Thai Parliament. Secretly indicted by a Federal grand jury in San Francisco in November 1991, he was wanted in the United States on charges of smuggling into the country 45 tons of marijuana, conspiracy and operating a continuing criminal enterprise over a 14-year period, between 1973 and 1987. That indictment remained sealed for three years, without his true identity being revealed, while the Feds looked for ways to lure him to the States so that they could arrest him. When he failed to take the bait, they bandied about several plots, including kidnapping. In one, they manoeuvred to lure him into a friendly place, such as Hong Kong, where US agents intended to bang him on the head and then bundle him onto a waiting plane.

Three years after the indictment, a newspaper in Bangkok broke the story that Siriprechapong had been formally incriminated in the States. So the decision was made to unseal the indictment, publicly acknowledge that Tony was Siriprechapong, and seize whatever assets they could find in the States, including a $1 million Beverly Hills home and a Mercedes-Benz.

Of course, Siriprechapong protested his innocence. But the evidence against him was strong enough for Washington to demand his extradition. It took a while, but eventually the Thai government decided he was enough of an embarrassment and gave him up.

It now appears that Siriprechapong was not the only Thai politician to be accused of moonlighting in drugs. The deputy leader of the Chart Thai party and the Deputy Finance Minister have also been named as suspects in drug cases by Washington. And just like Tony before them, they too deny the charges.

Next came the matter of the Shaffers' money.

To everyone's enormous chagrin – despite four years of work, 550 interviews, 15,000 man hours and the cooperation of law enforcement agencies in eight countries – the task force confiscated only around $12 million of the Shaffers' assets.

The Shaffers have insisted there is no more.

Bartlett had warned them that if more was ever found, the deal was off – even after they get out – and that could mean they wind up serving 25–30 years.

Philosophical to the end, the Shaffers both claimed they'll still be young enough when they get out to lead fruit-ful lives.

If that means there is money hidden away – if they've

washed it so clean that no one can find it – and if the money is still there after 13–15 years, then the Shaffers might well reckon that the best adventure of all is not in fact over, just unavoidably postponed.

CHAPTER SEVENTEEN

Funny Money

> '"Funny money" is a highly sophisticated, logically alternative
> economic system used by a long list of international criminals,
> tax evaders, drug traffickers, arms dealers, terrorists and
> governments. The difficulty is often to decide which is which.'
> Former British Fraud Squad detective,
> Rowan Bosworth-Davies

When he raped Kuwait, Saddam Hussein ordered his soldiers to commandeer whatever automobiles they could
drive away. A few of the more expensive cars – Rolls,
Mercedes, Lamborghinis, Porsches, BMWs and Ferraris –
were given to Ba'ath Party officials as a gift from Saddam,
or appropriated for use by the government. When he
visited Baghdad during the Gulf Crisis, former British
prime minister Edward Heath was chauffeured about in
a stolen Kuwaiti Mercedes.

However, 50 of the choicest cars – including an armour-
plated Mercedes and an armour-plated BMW – were sent
overseas. They were driven from Baghdad to Amman, then
flown to Geneva by Royal Jordanian Airline cargo planes,
under the protection accorded diplomatic shipments. Once
in Switzerland, they were put on the market and, within
hours of their arrival, turned into cash.

Months later, after their country was liberated, the Kuwaitis discovered what they'd always suspected – that the Iraqis had stormed across the border with shopping lists. Not only had they come looking for cars, but the invading army had pillaged with a very elaborate, predetermined agenda. They were under orders to plunder machinery – entire factories were emptied out – computers, construction cranes, plus parts and supplies from ports and airports. They were told to steal 200,000 books from the central library in Kuwait City, as well as books, furniture and even blackboards from schools. They had instructions to take hospital fixtures and furnishings and every piece of medical equipment they could find. They were directed to drive away with 3,500 school buses and most of the nation's public transport system.

One obvious Iraqi target was Kuwait's central bank, where Saddam looted gold and currency. After the war, however, he was forced to repatriate all of that money because the exact amount of the bank's reserves was known. But the invading army also raided private homes and offices – tens of thousands of them – and pilfered a fortune in cash and jewels, and none of that was ever returned. Some of the ransacked gold was melted down and sold by Saddam in the amenable markets of Yemen, the Sudan and Mauritania. Most of the jewels were broken up and sold in the *souks*. The cash is still being used to pay the hoards of smugglers from Iran and Turkey who have successfully broken the embargo ever since it was imposed.

Although incidental shipments of Iraqi oil continue to turn up in Turkey and Jordan – in direct violation of the boycott – the country's primary source of revenue has been cut off. It's reckoned that, without his oil income, Saddam has been feeding his people with those Kuwaiti assets – that he's managed to launder enough money to keep the country alive. It is known, for instance, that, in order to soak up whatever precious metals or stones appeared in Baghdad after the Gulf War, Saddam merely printed more banknotes. The inflationary effect on the economy was of little significance as far as he was concerned because he needed those Kuwaiti assets to survive the coalition embargo. Still, the money he stole from Kuwait turns out to be small potatoes compared with the money he's systematically stolen – and successfully laundered – from his own country.

In June 1972, Iraq nationalized its petroleum interests. Saddam, who was then Deputy President, convinced the ruling revolutionary council that the commissions they'd been paying to westerners under long-standing agreements should instead go to the Ba'ath Party. So he took a page out of the life of Calouste Sarkis Gulbenkian.

A Turk of Armenian descent, Gulbenkian was the founding power behind what came to be known as the Iraqi Petroleum Company. For his efforts, he laid claim to a royalty on every drop of its oil. His fee gave birth to his nickname, Mr Five-Percent. When he died in Lisbon in 1955, the royalty was passed on to his son Nubar. Some 17 years later, Saddam confiscated Nubar's 5 per cent in the name of the Ba'ath Party. Saddam personally assumed joint custody of the funds, sharing signature authority with Defense Minister Adnan Khairallah and Petroleum Minister Adnan Hamdani.

According to a document claiming to be a true accounting of those funds, $51 million was deposited in a major Swiss bank in Geneva in 1972. With interest, the balance in the account climbed to $92 million the following year and – as the price of oil quadrupled during the Yom Kippur War – to $327 million in 1974. By the time the Iran–Iraq war broke out – with Saddam now firmly in control of the country – the account held in excess of $1.69 billion. Today, it is reliably believed that Saddam controls funds worth some $32 billion.

As his power base has always been his grip on the nation's only political organization – today, he and the Iraqi Ba'ath Party are, for all intents and purposes, one and the same – some of this money has gone to buying continued reverence. He pays handsomely for loyalty. And on those occasions when devotion has proved less than unremitting, he's stopped writing cheques and has had people killed. In 1979, he ordered the execution of his old friend, and co-signatory, Adnan Hamdani. Ten years later, his pal Adnan Khairallah died in a mysterious helicopter crash. The full extent of Saddam's early interests in Swiss banking went to the graves with them.

Some of the money has also been spent on whims and fancies. When the Empress Faradiba – wife of the late Shah of Iran – wanted to sell a few of her jewels, Saddam pulled $352 million out of Switzerland to buy them for his wife. Faradiba denies it, for obvious reasons. But two sources – both reliable and both independent of the other – confirm the story.

For the most part, though, Saddam has converted the 5 per cent into a giant safety net for himself, his family and his closest Ba'ath Party associates. It is supposed to keep them in the game, no matter what cards Fate hands out. To protect his nest egg, he's moved a lot of the money out of Geneva, washing it through a network of companies he's set up around the world. One of them, Montana Management, a holding company registered in Panama, is controlled by Midco Financial, a Geneva shell. In 1981, Midco – through Montana – began buying into the French broadcasting and publishing conglomerate, Hachette SA. At one point, Saddam is said to have owned as much as 8.4 per cent of Hachette's shares.

Another Saddam company is Al-Arabi Trading, head-quartered in Baghdad, which purchased a large stake in the British-based Technology and Development Group. In 1987,

TDG bought a precision engineering firm called Matrix-Churchill. A few years later, UK Customs and Excise became aware of the connection, took a closer look at Matrix-Churchill, moved in on them, and wound up confiscating parts of an alleged super-gun that was destined for Iraq.

The Americans also took a closer look at Saddam's dealings and, by April 1991, the US Treasury's Office of Foreign Asset Control had identified 52 businesses and 37 individuals with direct financial links to him and/or his Ba'ath Party. Of those 52 companies, 24 were based in the UK – a number of them using the same address, No 3 Mandeville Place, in London's West End. Of the 37 named individuals, a dozen also had addresses in Britain.

American sources quickly determined that 'Saddam International Inc.' was run by his half-brother Barazan al-Takriti. Now officially Iraq's Special Ambassador-at-Large, he lived for years in Switzerland – always protected by diplomatic status – where he is known regularly to have received currency, gold and jewels by diplomatic pouch that he easily washed through Swiss banks. But his main contribution to Saddam's retirement fund was to have sought the best western legal advice that money could buy, and to have used that counsel to design a fabulously intricate laundromat. This is not about 52 companies and 37 people supplying Iraq with super-guns, this is about 500 shell companies and as many people who are paid handsomely to wash Saddam's money.

Intelligently and with enormous patience, Barazan spent the better part of two decades setting up a worldwide network of friendly businessmen, taking most of what's accumulated from the 5 per cent royalty – a healthy chunk of that estimated $32 billion – and bedding it down for safe keeping with them. There are some Iraqis in on this, but for the most part they're mainly Jordanians and Palestinians.

The money is in their name – washed by Barazan via bank loans and investments – so that it shows up on the books of legitimate businesses in Spain, France, Brazil, Indonesia, Hong Kong, Britain and the US.

Although the funds are ultimately administered by Barazan, they are so skilfully disguised that none of the money can possibly be traced back to Saddam Hussein or the Ba'ath Party. Obviously, those friendly businessmen know who owns the money and are, in any case, constantly reminded what the penalty is should they ever think it's theirs. But thanks entirely to Barazan and this network of docile custodians, when the western allies set out to seize Iraqi assets to punish Saddam for his foray into Kuwait, the lion's share of Saddam's money had been scrubbed so clean it was virtually invisible.

Perhaps Manuel Antonio Noriega should have taken lessons from Saddam Hussein.

In the early 1970s, as chief of Panama's military intelligence, Noriega discovered how to play both ends against the middle by turning himself into a CIA spy, a DEA informant, a staunch American ally, a Panamanian diplomat and an international drug trafficker. He also dabbled in gun running, supplying arms to leftist guerrillas in El Salvador and right-wing guerrillas in Nicaragua. In his spare time, he became commander of the Panamanian Defence Forces – which made him de facto ruler of the country – and, for good measure, a major league laundryman.

Unlike Saddam, he wasn't clever enough.

The heart of Panama's money laundering industry is the Colon Free Zone – a 500-acre site on the Atlantic end of the Panama Canal. Established in the 1950s, it is today the second-largest duty-free trading centre in the world after Hong Kong. With minimal government regulation, hundreds of ships carrying tens of thousands of containers move in and out of the Free Zone daily, carrying everything imaginable – from Japanese electronic goods, Scotch whisky and French perfumes to German precision widgets, American running shoes and Colombian cocaine.

Nearly $10 billion worth of duty-free goods were traded in the Free Zone in 1992, not counting the 19 tons of narcotics that the Panamanian authorities managed to uncover. Almost a quarter of that haul was a single shipment of cocaine stuffed inside containers of Brazilian tiles destined for Maryland. More recently, federal agents in Miami inspected a shipment of 318 coffee boxes that had come in from a warehouse in the Free Zone, only to discover that they contained 5.2 tons of cocaine.

One company that had been operating freely there, Celeste International, turned out to be a front for the Cali cartel. The authorities got wise to Celeste only when they stumbled across a multi-ton shipment of cocaine sitting in its warehouse. Until then, Celeste had spent years issuing false invoices for consumer goods, against which it deposited tens of millions of drug dollars in Panamanian banks.

Unfortunately, Panamanian officials quietly recognize, for every company like Celeste that they find, there may be 10 or 20 or 50 that they never hear about.

Under the terms of a 1904 treaty with the United States, the dollar is legal tender in Panama. In compliance with that treaty, whenever there is a shortfall in the supply, the US Treasury ships dollars to the Panamanian National Bank, which acts exactly like a Federal Reserve for the local banking system. But it seems that cash transactions over the past few years in the Free Zone have been so enormous that the US Treasury Department has demanded a formal investigation.

In one instance, it was discovered that 12,000 US money orders had been sent in a container from New York to Panama. They were cashed by 13 companies – mainly jewellery stores set up for the sole purpose of laundering these money orders – then deposited in accounts held at the Hongkong Bank of Panama. Mostly in the $500–700 range – well under the US reporting limit – each cancelled money order was stamped on the back with tiny seals used by the Colombian cocaine cartels – the same ones that often appear on shipments of Colombian cocaine – to help compliant banks identify the correct account to which the deposit should be credited. Once deposited, the money was wired back to the States – to an account at the Marine Midland Bank of New York, maintained there by the drug traffickers who originally bought the money orders.

Although the US authorities managed to seize the account in New York – it contained $7.7 million – they admit it represents probably only about 10 per cent of the money these particular traffickers had laundered in this way over a two-year period. And when US agents handed their Panamanian counterparts detailed information on those 13 local money laundering enterprises, the Panamanians said thank you, but made no effort to do anything about them.

Panama has always been the perfect stage for someone like Noriega.

Born in 1934, he seized the reins of the government at the age of 39 and held on to them for five years. One of the traditional perks of high office in Panama is a cut of the various rackets that go on just beneath the surface of local officialdom, including regular handouts from all sorts of traffickers.

Noriega had personally been in touch with the Colombian cartels for several years. In the mid-1970s, he'd met and helped to protect Ramon Millan, a Miami accountant who shuffled money out of the States to Panama for drug baron Carlos Lehder Rivas. In 1979, along with Pablo Escobar and Jorge Ochoa, Lehder asked Millan to set up a deal with the Panamanian strong man, Omar Torrijos. Noriega – as

Torrijos' main henchman – was assigned by his boss to negotiate a standard protection racket contract, whereby the Panamanian government would safeguard Lehder's drug trafficking and money laundering in exchange for a slice of the action.

When Torrijos was killed in a July 1981 plane crash, command of the Guardia – the real power in Panama – passed first to Florencio Florez, who was betrayed and unseated by Ruben Paredes, who was then betrayed and unseated by Noriega. He renamed the Guardia, calling it the Panamanian Defence Forces, reassured his old pals at the CIA – who were reportedly paying him $200,000 a year – that he was still America's man, and picked up where Torrijos left off, banking Lehder's protection money.

But then Noriega went Torrijos one better. He set up a series of well-hidden airstrips and allowed Lehder to transship cocaine bound for the US. Noriega reportedly charged the cartel $500,000 per flight – 1 per cent of the cargo's wholesale value – and apparently by the end of 1983 was pulling down $10 million a month.

The DEA came to Noriega, concerned about drug trafficking and money laundering that might be coming through Panama. So Noriega handed them Ramon Millan. Thanks to evidence provided by Noriega, Millan was convicted by a US court and sentenced in 1983 to 43 years, and the DEA reckoned Noriega was their best friend.

He reinforced that notion two years later when he ordered the closure of the First Interamericas Bank. A few of his Colombian chums had been a little too obvious this time. It wasn't just that they were using the bank to wash dirty money, they owned it outright. The majority shareholder was Gilberto Rodriguez Orejuela, one of the honchos of the Cali cartel. Also on the board were Rodriguez's brother, Miguel Angel Rodriguez Orejuela, and Edgar Alberto Garcia

Montilla, the cartel's main financial adviser and the brains behind their international money laundering activities.

Shutting down First Interamericas might have endeared Noriega to the DEA but it didn't do much for his relationship with the cartels. Insult was added to injury when Noriega ordered a raid on a drug lab he'd personally allowed the cartel to set up in Panama. The Colombians felt that for $10 million a month he might be a little more sensitive to their business needs. Their response was to order Noriega's murder.

One source says they asked the Basque separatists to kill Noriega next time he came to Europe. And ETA was certainly in a position to do so. The claim is supported by the fact that Noriega never accepted Spanish asylum when it was offered, preferring to take his chances with the American courts.

The story goes that Mossad agents got wind of the contract – the Israeli secret service maintains an active interest in all terrorist groups around the world – and alerted Noriega. Knowing first hand that Colombian drug dealers have no sense of humour, the Panamanian turned to the one man who could have some influence over them, Fidel Castro. Noriega begged for help and the Cuban dictator intervened, negotiating a truce with the cartels.

Not that there was any love lost between the two men, but Noriega and Castro were also in business together and Castro felt it made good economic sense to keep his partner alive. With the US still enforcing an embargo on Cuban goods, Castro had been sending produce – mainly shrimp and lobster – to the Colon Free Zone, where Noriega's people repackaged it as Panamanian produce and shipped it to the States. In return, Noriega paid Castro with embargoed US high-tech merchandise, which Castro sold to the Russians.

In the beginning, Noriega used Panamanian banks to hide his money. When he hit the big time, he branched out and began laundering his money around the world. He used a large network of banks, among them BCCI, Banque Nationale de Paris, First American and the Algemene Bank Nederland. In some cases, he kept accounts in his own name. But a number of his larger accounts were in the name of the Panamanian Defence Forces (PDF), with his signature being the only one that could authorize the use of funds. Records confiscated from BCCI show that Noriega had, at one time, as much as $50 million on deposit, much of it in a PDF account in London. BCCI not only hired Noriega's daughter to work in its Miami branch, it issued him and his family with Visa cards – against a PDF account – with which the Noriegas ran up monthly bills in excess of $25,000, shopping at Gucci in Paris, Bloomingdales in New York and K-Mart in Miami.

With his share of the cartels' money, Noriega bought houses all over Panama, an apartment in Paris, a chateau outside Paris, a home in Spain, two houses in Israel and one in Japan. He also had places in the Dominican Republic and Venezuela. He invested in local cable TV companies, a newspaper, an explosives manufacturer and four retail stores in Panama City. He owned commercial real estate in Panama, Florida and New Orleans.

And all this time the DEA thought of their pal 'Tony' – that's how he signed hundreds of photos of himself that wound up hanging proudly on office walls across Washington – as a swell guy.

Noriega's troubles began in the mid-1980s. They stemmed from a routine investigation into a laundryman working out of a warehouse on the perimeter of Miami International Airport. DEA agents infiltrated the place and identified one man as Floyd Carlton Caceres, who turned out to be Noriega's personal pilot. When they arrested him, Caceres immediately asked if there was any way to make a deal.

Amidst much embarrassment in 1988 – suddenly, a lot of

those autographed pictures were taken down – Noriega was indicted by a pair of US grand juries. He was charged with drug trafficking – including conspiracy to smuggle more than one ton of cocaine and more than 520 tons of marijuana into the US – racketeering and money laundering.

As quickly as they could, the Americans froze some $26 million of his assets – it was all they could find at the time – although they were required eventually to turn $2 million of that back to him so that he could pay for attorneys.

The evidence presented to the grand juries was largely circumstantial. A mountain of paperwork – fuel receipts from private airplane rides, records from visits to hotels, sales slips from whatever he bought and phone logs of whatever calls he made – none of which actually proved that Noriega was drug trafficking and money laundering. But it did help to substantiate the government's case for his double-dealing. It also backed up the testimony of a whole slew of less-than-respectable witnesses – convicted smugglers, drug dealers, laundrymen and other Noriega associates – who, in exchange for lighter sentences, were willing to testify.

Obviously, Noriega wasn't in much of a hurry to answer any of those accusation so, in December 1989, George Bush sent an expeditionary force to Panama to kidnap him. When Noriega sought refuge in the Vatican Embassy, the Americans smoked him out with their secret weapon – non-stop rock 'n roll! The Army delivered him to Florida, and into the hands of the Justice Department, which held him without possibility of bail, in a suite of cells, as Federal Prisoner # 41586. When his legal appeals ran out, he was put on trial. Convicted in 1992 on eight of the 11 counts lodged against him, Noriega was sentenced to 40 years in prison.

As one of Noriega's supporters said at the time, 'This is no way to treat a friend.'

Amidst much official blushing, it was revealed that on

14 December 1978, DEA administrator Peter Bensinger wrote to Noriega to thank him for his 'excellent efforts which have contributed substantially to the on going battle against drugs'. Such praise was repeated six years later by DEA administrator Francis Mullen, Jr, who assured Noriega, 'Your long-standing support of the Drug Enforcement Administration is greatly appreciated.'

Two years after that, in May 1986, DEA administrator John Lawn echoed those sentiments. 'I would like to take this opportunity to reiterate my deep appreciation for the vigorous anti-drug trafficking policy that you have adopted, which is reflected in the numerous expulsions from Panama of accused traffickers, the large seizures of cocaine and precursor chemicals that have occurred in Panama and the eradication of marijuana cultivations in Panamanian territory.'

Ironically, Lawn added, 'I look forward to the day when all governments develop the means to systematically identify and seize those illegal profits and drug trafficking starts becoming a self-defeating enterprise.'

The following year Lawn heaped even more praise on Noriega, this time for his assistance with a multinational drug bust called Operation Pisces. 'Many millions of dollars and many thousands of pounds of drugs have been taken from the drug traffickers and international money launderers. Your personal commitment to Operation Pisces and the competent, professional, and tireless efforts of other officials in the Republic of Panama were essential to the final positive outcome of this investigation. Drug traffickers around the world are now on notice that the proceeds and profits of their illegal ventures are not welcome in Panama.'

Little did anyone at the DEA realize that Noriega was simply helping them eliminate the competition.

In addition to taking out Noriega, the American invasion of Panama unearthed a huge cache of bank records, tapes and documents – five tons in all that helped make money laundering cases against a group of major players – plus 100 pounds of cocaine and $6 million in cash. However, it did not necessarily end the problem. Panama is still struggling to clean up its reputation as a major international cocaine market and sink.

In early 1992, two containers were confiscated in the Colon Free Zone when they were found to be holding $7 million in cash. No one ever claimed the money and some of it has since disappeared. At the end of that year, Panama's Attorney General, Rogelio Cruz, was charged with illegally releasing $37 million in previously frozen bank accounts that were believed to belong to the Colombian cartels. His Deputy Attorney General for Drug Prosecution, Ariel Alvarado, was also arrested. It's hardly a coincidence that Cruz once served on the board of First Interamericas Bank.

In the end, very little seems to have changed since Noriega's ouster.

The Colon Free Zone is alive and well, and – despite rhetoric aimed at pacifying anyone in Washington who still believes in the tooth fairy – every indication is that it's going to stay that way. It's a pipe dream to think that any Panamanian leader is going to risk 13,000 jobs and $10 billion worth of business by cooking up regulations that might make the place less attractive than it already is.

The secret banks are wide open. Cash is the commodity of the day. The cartels are still there. And everyone agrees that asking too many questions is bad for business.

What's more, officials in Panama City have restored one of Noriega's million dollar mansions and turned it into a tourist attraction.

There is a disturbing postscript to the Noriega story.

After his conviction in Miami, he met with certain French officials who wanted to know about whatever business he might have been doing in France. Based on their interviews with him, since hidden away in a top secret report – and this story is based on first-hand private conversations with someone directly involved in those interviews and that report – it turns out that Noriega was doing quite a lot of business in France. Over a period of several years, he purchased arms in France which he, in turn, sold to the Contras in Nicaragua in their fight against the Sandinistas. In other words, he was not only doing the same thing Colonel Oliver North was doing for the CIA, but was doing it with Colombian drug money, washed for him by the French.

When Harry Truman signed the 1947 National Security Act, creating the Central Intelligence Agency, he seriously believed its mission was nothing more sinister than the collection and collation of foreign intelligence information. He seriously believed that it was strictly an 'overt' operation.

His mistake was to staff it with highly motivated men – like Allen Dulles – who'd learned the old-fashioned spying trade during the war in the Office of Special Operations at the knees of the famous General William 'Wild Bill' Donavan. To a man, they believed that 'overt' was not the way this game should be played.

Right from the beginning, the Agency's more consequential role would be 'covert'. Officially included in that category have always been: subsidies to individuals; financial support and 'technical assistance' to political parties; support of private organizations, which includes labour unions, business firms, cooperatives, and so forth; economic operations; and para-military or political actions designed either to overthrow or to support a regime.

As the CIA could never finance any of these things publicly – the idea of the nation's primary espionage service going to Congress to ask for funds to kick the Mossadegh regime out of Iran was a non-starter – they operated their own laundry. The director maintains a top-secret slush fund – a huge pile of invisible money that Congress knows nothing about – for which he's accountable directly, and only, to the President. What's more, Dwight Eisenhower created – and every President since has followed suit – a top-secret group to advise the CIA on the best use of those funds and, when necessary, to procure additional monies for specific covert operations. In Ike's day, the group was called the 5412 Committee, named for the National Security Council paper that authorized it.

It was then, and remains today, the most secret organization in the United States of America.

A sub-cabinet level organization, it's charged with reviewing and approving all of the nation's clandestine operations in order to protect the President from any clandestine operation gone wrong. Considered so ultra-sensitive that not even the National Security Council is kept informed of its activities, those few men who know about it refer to it simply as 'The Special Group'.

For whatever reason, various administrations have changed the name from 5412 to such obscurely derived numbers as 'The 303' and 'The 40 Committee'. But the concept behind it remains the same: that it must be the Special Group, and not the President, who officially approves certain plans – such as illegal interventions into the internal affairs of another sovereign state.

Traditionally, the cabal consists of a chairman – most often, that job goes to the President's National Security Advisor – the Secretaries of State and Defence and the Director of Central Intelligence. For obvious reasons, the President is not a member.

There's no denying that the buck stops at the Oval Office and it is ultimately the President who must authorize such projects, but his approval of a Special Group proposal is only ever given verbally. The members of the group work it out among themselves, then brief the President. Nothing is written down with his name on it. Nothing is ever signed by him. That way, should something go wrong, the CIA can rightfully claim they acted on the authority of the Special Group, which means the President can ostensibly deny that he has ever approved of such an activity.

It was the 5412 Committee that approved the CIA's building of and subsequent use of the U-2 spy plane – which Allen Dulles and his assistant Richard Bissell financed entirely out of the director's slush fund. If, as it has been alleged, the CIA murdered Salvador Allende in Chile in 1973, it would have been Richard Nixon's Special Group discussing that. And if, as has often been suggested, Ronald Reagan knew anything at all about Iran–Contra affair, that would have been down to his administration's equivalent of the 5412 Committee.

Iran–Contra is, in fact, a perfect example of what the committee is supposed to do. If you accept the premise that William Casey, as Director of Central Intelligence, committed the CIA to engage in the illegal activities for which Oliver North was tried, then the plan would almost certainly have been brought up in a Special Group meeting. The Secretaries of State and Defence would have known about it, agreed to it, and presented it for final approval to the President. But because nothing is written down and therefore nothing can ever be traced back to the President, Ronald Reagan's denial of any knowledge of the affair is an impenetrable defence.

During those years, Reagan's Special Group empowered the CIA to funnel money to right-wing forces that were trying to overthrow the leftist government of Mauritius, to spend millions trying to destabilize Colonel Qadhafi's regime in Libya and to bankroll the Afghan rebels with hundreds of millions of dollars. White House and CIA records now suggest that in the first six years of his administration, Reagan knew of and/or approved of at least 60 money laundering plots to finance CIA covert activities.

One of the greatest CIA-financed covert operations came out of John Kennedy's Special Group. It was Operation Mongoose, a White House sanctioned plot to assassinate Fidel Castro.

When the Bay of Pigs invasion failed, Bobby Kennedy – who was then the Attorney General – managed to convince his brother that getting rid of Castro had to be a priority of the administration. The President agreed and turned to the CIA.

They were already manning a huge command post on the campus of the University of Miami. Code-named JM/WAVE, operatives there directed the activities of a reported 3,000 Cuban agents whom they'd set up in false businesses – known in the vernacular as cut-outs. The CIA not only paid the bills for these business, but washed money through them to pay for all sorts of covert activities. They poisoned the cargo of a Russian ship that had docked in Puerto Rico, counterfeited Cuban money, broadcast propaganda to the island, and regularly financed anti-Castro guerrilla warfare. They paid for planes, speedboats and arms.

In one particular case, a CIA operator found that he could make more money running an Agency cut-out than he could by staying on the payroll. According to the rules, he was required to turn over the extra money to the government. So he simply resigned from the CIA, kept the business and kept the profits. The CIA never said a word, because they couldn't admit they'd owned the business in the first place.

They have, however, since admitted to eight different plots to murder Castro. In one early attempt, they shipped poison pills to Cuba, but the operative in Havana failed to get anywhere near his target. In another, several devices were sent to a Cuban dissident in Havana who was believed to have access to Castro. Included in this box of toys were:

a poison pen, pills, bacterial powders, an exploding cigar and a cigar deeply impregnated with bolulinium toxin, a poison so potent that it would kill Castro the moment he put the cigar to his lips. This too failed.

In a third plot, organized crime was recruited and professional hitmen were dispatched.

The roots of that attempt were planted in the summer of 1960, under Eisenhower, when ex-FBI agent Robert Maheu was instructed by Richard Bissell to find some men who might be willing to do the CIA's bidding. The first one to sign up was Johnny Rosselli, a Las Vegas gangster who'd previously been connected to gambling interests in Havana. Next was the man who ran the mob in Chicago – he called himself Sam Gold but his real name was Momo Salvatore Giancana. Then there was the ex-pat, Cuban Mafia don living in Miami, who was known as Joe to his friends and Santos Trafficante to everyone else.

Together, the three located a Cuban who worked at a restaurant frequented by Castro and convinced him to drop pills into Castro's food. They even supplied the pills. But by the early spring 1961, when the plan was scheduled to come to fruition, it seems that Castro had changed restaurants.

A year later – post Bay of Pigs – the poison pill plan was resurrected. With Kennedy in the White House, the gangsters were asked to try again. This time they retained a Cuban who was willing to carry out the murder but, as payment, demanded a small cache of weapons and communications equipment. The Mafia trio turned to Bissell and the CIA agreed to fund the operation through their cut-outs in Miami. The assassin failed, but by then the CIA's front companies had already financed the purchase of explosives, boat radar, radios and handguns, and shipped them off to Cuba. Years later, it would be revealed that some of the people who dealt with the CIA at JM/WAVE – or who were involved with the washing of funds through cut-outs for Operation Mongoose – also had links to the assassination of John Kennedy in Dallas in 1963. Circumstantially related or otherwise, included in that bunch are Lee Harvey Oswald, Jack Ruby, the Mayor of Dallas – who changed the parade route at the very last minute so that it would pass directly in front of the Texas School Book Depository – Sam Giancana and Santos Trafficante.

Conspiracy theories being what they are, it should be noted that the five guys who broke into the Watergate building to do Richard Nixon's bidding in 1972 also had links – in this case very direct links – to Operation Mongoose.

No conclusions here, just food for thought!

The point is that, with the tacit approval of the White House, the CIA might well be the greatest laundrymen of all time.

In the name of national security, they continue to run more businesses than most Fortune 500 conglomerates. None of these cut-outs are in any obvious way associated with the US government. Often staffed by retired military officers and former CIA operatives, they tend to employ Cuban exiles, Vietnam veterans, Israeli agents, soldiers of fortune, Middle Eastern businessmen and, on some occasions, international drug traffickers. Services on offer can be anything from air cargo to money laundering. At least 30 cut-outs were created just to back up Iran–Contra.

Under the auspices of George Bush's presidency, the CIA went into the coke smuggling business. Using a cut-out in Venezuela, in 1990, the Agency adroitly smuggled a ton of pure cocaine into the United States. It was supposed to help snare traffickers. Instead, it wound up being sold on the streets. It came to light only three years later, thanks to the investigative skills of the CBS television programme '60 Minutes,' which later revealed that when that CIA cut-out tried to work its routine as a joint venture with the Drug Enforcement Administration, the DEA refused to take part. They argued that the plan was unworkable. The CIA eventually admitted it was 'most regrettable'.

However, the classic CIA cut-out had to have been Air America. Based in Southeast Asia throughout the Vietnam War, the airline was hardly what might be considered a thriving masquerade, in that every peasant in every rice paddy from Saigon to Hanoi knew that Air America was the CIA.

At other times, in spite of their natural tendency towards clumsiness, they have shown an occasional touch of subtlety.

In 1973, two young men went into the banking business. One was Michael Hand, a 31-year-old former CIA operative from the Bronx. The other was Frank Nugan, 30-year-old Australian playboy and heir to a fruit-processing fortune that had been built on Mafia connections. The Nugan Hand Bank was headquartered in Sydney and survived seven years.

It collapsed when Frank Nugan was found sitting in his Mercedes with a rifle in one hand, a bible in the other and a hole through his head. Stuck into the pages of the bible was a list of names, including Bob Wilson, then the ranking Republican on the House Armed Services Committee, and William E. Colby, former director of the CIA. Also on the list were the names of known international drug dealers, plus personalities from politics, business, sports, films and television. Next to those names were five- and six-figure dollar amounts.

Shortly after Nugan's body was found, Michael Hand made a hasty exit from Australia and supposedly hasn't been seen since.

A precursor of BCCI, Nugan and Hand were running a con game, bilking investors, cutting themselves in on arms dealing, handling drug deals and laundering cash. Oddly, the bank's president was retired US Rear Admiral Earl

Yates, who'd once been in charge of the Navy's strategic planning; Colby was its legal counsel; Walter McDonald, a former deputy director of the CIA, was a consultant; Richard Secord, of Iran–Contra fame, had a business connection with the bank; while one of the banks in-house commodity traders was also one of Australia's major heroin importers.

In February 1977, Nugan Hand opened a branch in the unlikely outpost of Chiang Mai, Thailand – unlikely, that is, until you know that's where most of the opium produced in the Golden Triangle gets turned into money. The bank's office was next door – apparently with connecting doors – to offices used by the US Drug Enforcement Agency, with which the CIA shares, as one DEA officer put it, 'a warm working relationship'.

The US Senate investigated the Nugan Hand Bank and its connections with the CIA, heard sworn testimony from the Agency behind closed doors, then promptly locked that testimony away.

It's a typical pattern.

In 1980, a company called Associated Traders Corporation went into business in Baltimore, Maryland. At first sight, ATC appeared to be involved with import or export or general trading – something vague like that. At least they must have had some international connections because from 1980 to 1985 they deposited millions of dollars in an account at the First National Bank of Maryland, then wired the money on to other companies in the Cayman Islands and Panama. Compounding the vagaries of their business dealings, every now and then ATC asked their Maryland bankers if they wouldn't mind making certain that the name ATC was removed from, and could therefore never be associated with, these transfers.

Over those five years, ATC laundered at least $20 million through First National. In one particular deal, $5.2 million was wired to Associated Traders Grand Cayman, moved from there to a dummy company account in Panama and then transferred on to Switzerland. In another, $2.25 million followed the usual route through Grand Cayman and Panama, before making its way to India, where it financed the purchase of 60,000 Enfield rifles for the Mujaheddin rebels in Afghanistan.

By 1986, ATC had folded its tent and gone out of business. It was no coincidence that ATC's demise corresponded with the unravelling of Iran–Contra.

None of this would have come to light had a young banker at First National not discovered who his client was, stressed-out on the thought that he might be breaking the law, suffered a nervous breakdown and then sued both the bank and the CIA for putting him under enough pressure to endanger his health.

But then, this is nothing new.

In the late 1970s, the Junta ruling Argentina decided to help General Luis Garcia Meza Tejada – a known cohort of South American drug traffickers – to launch a coup to take over Bolivia. To help finance it, the Argentine intelligence service planned to open a laundromat in Florida. To help them do that, they approached their contacts in the CIA. In fact, two businesses were opened in Miami. One was called Argenshow, which was supposed to be a booking agency to bring music groups to Argentina. The second was a pawnshop called The Silver Dollar. Deliberately opened next to a gun shop – clearly hoping to pick up some business in illegal weapons – it was to be the operations centre for Argentinian intelligence activities throughout Latin America.

Serving US interests, the CIA believed it was safer to have Argentinean military advisers in El Salvador, Costa Rica and Honduras than Americans stationed there. So, Argenshow and The Silver Dollar arranged weapons shipments to Central America, laundering the necessary funds from Switzerland, the Bahamas, the Cayman Islands and Liechtenstein, through Panama, to wherever they were needed in Central America. In just 18 months, one shell company in the Bahamas facilitated the transfer of $30 million for the pawnshop.

To fulfill its original mission, Argenshow and The Silver Dollar handled a multi million dollar deal between the Junta generals and Roberto Suarez Levy, a prominent Bolivian drug dealer. Funds from the drug dealer were washed through Florida. In exchange, Argentina shipped ambulances to Bolivia – every one of them loaded with weapons to overthrow a centre–left coalition and restore the military to power in what came to be known as 'the cocaine coup'.

Later that same year, it was Argenshow that first recruited the Nicaraguan Contras to attack a shortwave radio station in Costa Rica. It's not clear whether that contact was made through an already established CIA channel, or whether that contact became the original CIA channel, but it turned out to be at the heart of Iran–Contra. A few months later, Argenshow was dissolved, The Silver Dollar was sold and the CIA moved on to the next gig.

CHAPTER EIGHTEEN

A Tale of Two Banks

'Money launderers bridge the gap between the underworld and
the rest of society.'

Michele Sindona

Roberto Calvi, a 62-year-old Italian with mournful eyes and
a distinctive black moustache, was found hanging under
Blackfriars Bridge in London on 18 June 1982. At first
glance, his death appeared to be suicide. Today, hardly
anyone believes it was.

Known as 'God's Banker' because of his close associations
with the Vatican, Calvi had been chairman and president of
the Milan headquartered Banco Ambrosiano. Having started
work there in a very junior position in 1946, he rose slowly
through the ranks until the mid-1960s, when he met the
Sicilian financier, Michele Sindona. Six years later – thanks
to Sindona's encouragement, friends and backing – Calvi
was not just running the bank, he was well on his way to
owning a good chunk of it.

Banco Ambrosiano soon became Italy's largest private
banking group. But, for a bank with that sort of prestige,
it seemed odd that there were no offices in the City of
London or on Wall Street. Instead, there were branches in
the Bahamas, Luxembourg and Nicaragua.

Furthermore, there were all sorts of strange dealings going on. In June 1979, the Nicaragua branch loaned $9 million to Nordeurop, a Liechtenstein shell company set up by Calvi in the United States. Immediately, Nordeurop sent the money to another Calvi-created shell, this one in Panama, where it was recorded as a fee. No proper explanations for the movement of this money have ever been located – no paperwork to support the original loan, no paperwork to substantiate the payment of a fee.

By May 1982, it was reported that $1.3 billion of the bank's money was unaccounted for. Three weeks later, Calvi was dead.

The mystery surrounding his hanging unquestionably revolves around that missing money, much of which turns out to have been washed through shell companies registered in Panama and Liechtenstein – shell companies that had affiliations, direct or otherwise, with the Vatican's private bank, the Istituto per le Opere di Religione, which translates as the Institute for the Works of Religion. Referred to as the IOR, it functioned as an offshore merchant bank in the heart of Rome. The Vatican was its principal client. And, by design, the bank's directors were never answerable to anyone outside the hierarchy of the Roman Catholic Church.

Suitably beyond the reach of the Italian banking authorities, the IOR could send currency anywhere in the world without contravening any currency control laws. For Calvi – who needed to fund the web of shell companies he was establishing around the globe – the IOR was a perfect sink.

To make it even better, he brought the IOR in as his partner on several offshore deals. One of them was Cisalpine, Banco Ambrosiano's subsidiary in the Bahamas. The chairman of the IOR sat next to Calvi on Cisalpine's board. Together they used that bank to loan each other money, creating an elaborately tangled paper trail. By 1978, the IOR reportedly had $114 million on deposit with Cisalpine, while Cisalpine – in other words, Calvi – had $236 million on deposit with the IOR.

The chairman of the IOR in those days was the athletic, American-born Archbishop Paul Marcinkus. Sindona had been influential in his appointment to the bank. Marcinkus later claimed not to have any knowledge of Calvi's machinations and maintained that the IOR was the real victim, having lost a fortune when it was naively lured into an elaborate fraud – enticed with attractively high interest rates – by the villain Calvi. Never admitted, but now known to be true, is that as a result of the Calvi–Marcinkus relationship – whatever form that took – the IOR skated on the brink of bankruptcy.

When the Banco Ambrosiano scandal broke, Marcinkus sequestered himself in his offices at St Peter's, protected from questioning and any threat of prosecution by the sovereignty afforded to the Vatican City as a foreign state.

Another key figure was Tuscan businessman Licio Gelli. An admirer of Mussolini and Juan Perón, he was Grandmaster of the Masonic-like lodge *Propaganda Due*. A secret Italian society. The 923 members of 'P-2' – cabinet officers, leading parliamentarians, financiers, high-ranking military officers, the heads of all three secret services and the nation's most influential jurists – functioned very much as a parallel government. They were all about real influence and enormous power. Yet it has since been revealed that P-2 received financial support from various factions involved with organized crime in Italy and that these monies were laundered by Gelli through Switzerland. Gelli knew Swiss banking well, having spent much of his life circulating through the murky world of illicit arms dealing.

When the Banco Ambrosiano scandal broke, he fled the country, was arrested in Switzerland, bribed his way out and spent the next five years hiding in South America, where he had heavyweight contacts, especially in Argentina.

A third player was Calvi's mentor, Sindona. Born in 1920, he was by his 50th birthday generally considered to be one of the wealthiest, most important businessmen in Italy. He claimed to be personally worth $500 million. A devotee of Mussolini and Machiavelli, he advised Pope Paul VI on financial matters – which accounted for his nickname, 'The Pope's Banker' – controlled half a dozen banks in four countries, in addition to owning the CIGA hotel chain and nearly 500 other corporations. One of them was Moneyrex, a currency brokerage in Milan and a major conduit for Mafia money laundering. Another – ironically, for a money launderer – owned the Watergate complex in Washington.

In Italy, Sindona's financial muscle was such that he was the predominant force in the Milan stock exchange and could, literally, hold it to ransom. Less visibly, he was Gelli's partner in P-2, and the Mafia's foremost financial *consigliere*. In 1980, Sindona had been convicted and sentenced to 25 years by an American court for fraud and perjury, having used $15 million of misappropriated funds to buy shares in two American banks illegally – one of them, Franklin National, crashed spectacularly in 1974.

Coinciding with that bankruptcy, Finabank, a private bank in Geneva, also went under. This was a funnel for Mafia and P-2 funds destined for the United States and Sindona maintained a numbered account, code-named MANI-1125. His co-signatory was the IOR.

When the Banco Ambrosiano scandal broke, he was in prison in the States. But two years later he was extradited to Italy to face fraud charges and sent to prison there. In 1986, the man who knew where all the skeletons were buried, was found dead on the floor of his cell after someone laced his coffee with cyanide.

It was Sindona who taught Calvi the ins and outs of

laundering money through offshore companies. Quick study that he was, Calvi formed several offshore shells over the years, using many of them for his work with Marcinkus and the IOR. They supported Banco Ambrosiano's share price, bought companies with questionably exported lira and – with or without Marcinkus – defrauded Banco Ambrosiano's investors.

When the Italian parliament passed a law in 1976 that made it a criminal offence to export lira illegally – it had formerly been only a civil offence – Calvi faced a massive investigation into the way he'd been using the bank's funds. To cover his tracks, he devised a restructuring scheme that would increase the Banco Ambrosiano's share capital by 50 per cent. But to pull this off – and, at the same time, support the bank's delicate share price on the Milan exchange – he had to bring funds into Italy from those shell companies.

Frantically juggling his assets, he moved money in and out of shells to create – he hoped, at least on paper – the aura of stability. But his timing was off and his creditors were nervous.

Worse still, his luck had by now run out.

In June 1980, one of Banco Ambrosiano's biggest clients – a leading Italian construction company – went bankrupt, leaving a huge dent in the Calvi's treasury. In January 1981, the government clamped down on all Italian banks that owned non-bank foreign holding companies. Three months later, the Milan stock exchange changed the dealing rules for Banco Ambrosiano. Previously, its shares were traded only weekly, over the counter. The exchange ordered that they now be traded daily on the main floor. Calvi could no longer support his own shares.

The following month Calvi was arrested for illegal currency transactions.

Although many people expected Banco Ambrosiano to go down with him, it somehow managed to stay in business.

One very good reason might have been that Marcinkus was handing out letters on IOR stationery confirming that his bank was the beneficial owner of 11 shell companies registered in Panama and Liechtenstein that were now holding Banco Ambrosiano shares and assets. Suddenly it appeared as if the IOR was covering Calvi's debts.

Hoping to salvage the situation, Calvi – on bail awaiting an appeal hearing – managed to interest the entrepreneur Carlo de Benedetti in becoming deputy chairman and purchasing 2 per cent of the bank's shares. But de Benedetti – who'd been chairman of the Olivetti group – resigned after three months when he couldn't get past the bureaucratic brick walls Calvi had built to protect his own fraudulent activities. De Benedetti later claimed that he received phone calls at home threatening his life if he maintained a presence at the bank.

For the rest of 1981, the pressures on Calvi grew to the point of being intolerable. The Bank of Italy was closing in on him. Utterly desperate by early 1982, Calvi turned to Marcinkus, asking him to confirm that the IOR was indeed responsible for those shell companies and, therefore, would back up Banco Ambrosiano's outstanding loans.

Now Marcinkus refused.

Apparently, the Vatican was on his back about money missing from the IOR – various 'guestimates' put the total anywhere from $100 million to $500 million – and he gave Calvi a 30 June 1982 deadline to pay it back. When Calvi realized he couldn't meet it, he begged for more time.

Again Marcinkus balked.

That's when it was discovered that the Banco Ambrosiano had a gaping $1.3 billion hole right through the middle.

Some time later, Marcinkus would conveniently produce a secret letter – seemingly signed by Calvi – absolving the IOR from any debts incurred by those 11 shell companies. He used this letter as the basis for his argument that the

IOR had no financial obligations whatsoever in the Banco Ambrosiano bankruptcy.

The liquidators and the Italian banking authorities weren't so sure, and, although Marcinkus never gave evidence about the affair, the Vatican did eventually agree to a relatively minor settlement.

Just as intriguingly, the authorities soon uncovered evidence that something in excess of $100 million had been paid by Calvi to Licio Gelli and one of his henchmen, Umberto Ortolani. Those funds were washed by the Banco Ambrosiano through the complex web of Calvi shells and – at least some of it – into a secret account controlled by Gelli on the Caribbean island of St Vincent. This money was sent, according to the Italian authorities, 'without any commercial justification'.

Yet, there might well have been a very good reason – specifically, Calvi's health. It's known he'd been paying Gelli and the P-2 – and therefore the Mafia as well – since 1975 to protect him from the Italian authorities. He apparently laundered as much as $10 million just to hand out as bribes. They might have done what they could – although that's not certain, either – until it was too late and Calvi had become too much of an embarrassment. But, having shelled out all that money, Calvi might have thought they owed him something. In 1981 alone, he purportedly paid $163 million to the P-2.

No one knows for sure whom Calvi might have threatened – or what threats he indeed made – to buy time with Marcinkus, or to extort money from P-2, or to expose Gelli and his links to the Mafia, or any variation of those possibilities. He must have felt that, if he could save the bank, he would be saving himself.

By now he was desperate. And that also made him dangerous.

What is known is that he left Italy on Friday 11 June

1982 with his briefcase, going first to Austria, then to London. On Monday, Banco Ambrosiano's shares crashed. On Wednesday, the bank's board was dissolved. On Friday, Calvi was dead.

The rumour that now floats around the back halls of certain intelligence services is that Calvi was murdered for the contents of his briefcase.

There is a strong belief – shared by some people with inside knowledge of the saga – that Calvi had come to London to meet with certain bankers in the hopes of blackmailing them into a support scheme that would bolster his bank. To convince them that he was serious, he'd brought with him documents showing how those particular bankers – who were not necessarily British – had knowingly laundered money for Licio Gelli.

Calvi's papers conclusively proved that Gelli's money had been washed through the heart of the British capital – with the knowledge and compliance of certain City bankers – and then used by Gelli, who was at the time acting for the Argentinians, to buy Exocet missiles, which were fired at British forces during the Falklands War.

Banco Ambrosiano was the greatest banking collapse in Europe since World War II. It was shortly to be followed by the greatest banking collapse – and outright fraud – in the history of banking.

The American invasion of Panama was supposed to have sent a message to the rest of the world that the United States wasn't going to sit around and allow men like Manuel Noriega to stay in business.

But at home, word had already gone out. In 1988, the Feds launched Operation C-Chase – the letter 'C' standing for currency.

Posing as drug dealers, undercover agents put out the bait that they had loads of currency to launder. And the Bank of Credit and Commerce International (BCCI) fell for it.

A costly and complicated five-year operation under the auspices of an Organized Crime Drug Enforcement task force – this time a joint effort of Customs, the IRS, the DEA and the FBI – produced evidence that included more than 1,200 secretly recorded conversations and nearly 400 hours of clandestinely recorded video tape. Having assisted drug dealers to wash $34 million, the Justice Department was able to indict – and in 1990 to convict – several BCCI bankers plus dozens of other individuals for drug trafficking and laundering $14 million. In one effective blow, the Americans had unknowingly pulled the bottom out from under a gargantuan house of cards.

The man who built that house was Agha Hasan Abedi. Born in 1922 in Lucknow, India – heart of the former Mughal Empire – he always claimed to be the son of a wealthy landowner. And he might well have been, except that a lot of what Abedi said over the years hasn't necessarily been true. What is known about him is that, from 1959 to 1972, he was president of Pakistan's United Bank Limited. But in 1972, Pakistan nationalized its banking industry. Abedi, who'd spent those years building up a network of wealthy Arab clients and friends, appealed directly to them. Thanks to their deep pockets, he was able to start his own bank – initially capitalized at $2.5 million.

Abedi's backers included Sheikh Zayed Bin Sultan Al-Nahayan – ruler of Abu Dhabi and President of the United Arab Emirates – various members of the Saudi royal family and the Bank of America, then the largest bank in the world. Bringing it on board was one of his greatest coups because it gave Abedi's venture instant credibility. Needless to say, he shamelessly capitalized on that association. When the bank got smart to him and pulled out in 1980, Abedi was cool-headed enough to play it down so that at least some people actually believed he was the one who ended the marriage.

His skill in setting up what he claimed would be the first multinational bank for the Third World was stunning. To begin with, he deliberately registered the main BCCI holding company in Luxembourg, so that he could hide behind the Grand Duchy's strict banking secrecy codes. A year later, Abedi opened branches of BCCI in four Gulf states and in several Asian communities throughout the UK. Then, in 1975, he registered the bank in the Cayman Islands, but moved his top management to London, where the Bank of England could – and did – add another heavy dose of credibility by giving BCCI a sound bill of health for the next 15 years.

As set out by Parliament, the Bank of England authorizes and oversees all banking activities in the UK. To make certain that everyone complies with the rules, it sends accountants into banks to spot irregularities. It is therefore the direct responsibility of the Governors of the Bank of England to ensure that all irregularities are properly dealt with before they trigger a crisis. If, on the other hand, a bank operating in the UK can convince a Bank of England accountant that it is doing business by the book, that's the end of the matter until the next audit. The Bank of England does not have agents who pretend to be potential customers to check on how effectively the bank in question is indeed complying with the statutes.

Until a few years ago, there were two types of bank in the UK. There were full status banks, which, having complied with a set of very orthodox requirements, were empowered by the Bank of England to offer a complete range of financial services. And there were Licensed Deposit Takers, a technical term intended to categorize smaller banks that offered a limited range of services.

The public often mistook them for being much the same thing.

In reality, authorized banks were the genuine article and Licensed Deposit Takers were not. Because they were not supervised as thoroughly, License Deposit Takers were therefore considered – off the record – to be businesses which did not enjoy the full confidence of the Bank of England.

BCCI was a Licensed Deposit Taker.

By 1977 Abedi was bragging that BCCI was the world's fastest-growing bank, with 146 branches in 32 countries and total assets of $2.2 billion. Although he had 45 offices in the UK, the grand prize, as Abedi saw it, was a banking network in America. To help him get that, he turned to Bert Lance, friend – and, by then, the slightly disgraced former Budget Director – of President Jimmy Carter.

First, Abedi hired Lance as a BCCI consultant. Then he arranged to assist Lance, who needed to sell his shares in a Georgia bank. Abedi came forth with a willing buyer – a preferred BCCI client – named Gaith Pharaon.

A Saudi businessman whose father had once been a court physician in Riyadh, Pharaon fancied himself a young Khashoggi and tried to do flashy deals throughout the west. Some of them went right. But many of them didn't. Still, when Abedi needed a front man, Pharaon was available.

After seeing Lance get rid of his bank, Abedi arranged for a facility for Lance to help pay back a $3.4 million loan. Such kindness gave Abedi access to Carter, whom he proudly declared to be one of his closest friends. While Carter has, these days, tried to explain away the relationship in a very different vein, there's no denying that Abedi was extremely generous when it came to his support for Carter's pet charity, Global 2000, and the Carter Presidential Center in Atlanta.

Three years after that initial foray into the US, Abedi expanded into Panama, where General Noriega soon became one of his largest clients. A year later, Abu Nidal – the Middle Eastern terrorist – began channelling funds through BCCI. And he was soon followed by members of the Medellin cartel.

By 1988, Abedi controlled 417 branches in 73 countries and reported assets of $20 billion.

And, all this time, the Bank of England maintained that everything was just dandy.

Clearly, it had somehow missed a few vital points.

To begin with, as BCCI's principal place of business was the UK – the bank's treasury was there – under the act that established Licensed Deposit Takers, BCCI should never have been allowed to use the word bank in its name.

In 1976, when BCCI attempted to buy the Chelsea National Bank in New York, state regulators weren't happy with what they saw and turned down the request. Two years later, an affidavit lodged in a US court showed that Bank of America – then holding a 30 per cent share in BCCI – wasn't pleased with the way Abedi's managers were lending money. The Bank of England was aware of all this, but apparently didn't feel that any of it affected BCCI's status in the UK – although, to give the Bank of England some credit, in 1980 it did refuse a BCCI petition for full status.

By this time, many of BCCI's Gulf shipping clients were so seriously in default that Abedi had to steal money from other accounts to plug leaks in these. It was a typical Ponzi scheme – robbing Peter to pay Paul – bringing in new cash to pay off old debts. With great aplomb, Abedi managed to keep his troubles out of sight of the auditors.

In 1985, when banking regulators in Luxembourg tried to get the Bank of England to assume full responsibility for BCCI, the Governors flatly refused. It was around this time that the Bank of England received an anonymous letter outlining massive fraud at BCCI, and took no formal action. It was also around this time that BCCI's treasury posted such huge losses due to irregular practices that Abedi became desperate to find fresh cash and turned to Latin America.

He'd already opened an outpost in Colombia. Now he added seven branches – five in Medellin alone – and increased his assets there to over $200 million. It's hardly surprising that the Medellin offices were constantly awash with cash. One of their major depositors was José Gonzalo Rodriguez Gocha, known internationally even in those days as a cartel kingpin.

Taking an important position in Colombia was a logical extension of BCCI's corporate culture, which became one of 'Get the money'. Abedi exerted such severe pressure on his employees to bring in deposits – constantly putting jobs and lifestyles on the line – that no one much cared where those deposits were coming from.

BCCI Miami was an especially good operation, accepting cash deposits in excess of $10,000 that went unreported to the IRS. In some cases, the bank's private jets would fly the cash to branches in Panama or the Caymans, deposit it there, then wire it to BCCI in Luxembourg, from where it disappeared. In other cases, to get around the reporting regulations, large cash deposits made in Miami were receipted as if they'd been deposited at BCCI Bahamas – this at a time when BCCI did not have a bank in the Bahamas.

On the heels of the Bank of Boston affair in 1985, when it seemed as if the Americans were starting to crack down on reporting irregularities, BCCI turned its attention to Canada and shifted a lot of laundry work there.

Always going where the action was, Abedi opened extensive networks in the United Arab Emirates (UAE) and Hong Kong, expanding at a time when other foreign banks operating there were contracting because of political and economic turmoil. Abedi's explanation for BCCI's success was that they'd found small, lucrative niches that they were willing to exploit. Many people thought he was talking about foreign exchange dealing. He was instead talking about money laundering.

The UAE operation was put in place to serve drug traffickers who dealt in heroin from the Golden Crescent. The Hong Kong operation catered to the Golden Triangle crowd. BCCI also did remarkable business in Nigeria – at a time when the world oil glut had depressed the local economy – and became the most important sink for the massive heroin trade coming through black Africa.

Knowing his clients, Abedi quickly expanded throughout the Caribbean, opening branches in marijuana-rich Jamaica, Barbados, Curaçao and Trinidad and in the Bahamas, where he also set up strings of shell companies to facilitate the movement of dirty money.

With leaks springing up everywhere, Abedi stole $150 million from a staff pension fund in 1986 to plug more holes in his balance sheet. Now afraid that the Bank of England was on to him, he decided to take the treasury out of Britain.

International banking supervisors in Basle had by this time looked at BCCI – specifically at how Abedi was managing his assets – and duly reported their concerns. Yet the Bank of England's auditors still did not cotton on to what Abedi was doing. They categorically failed to uncover any fraudulent practices at BCCI. And so the Governors approved Abedi's request to move the treasury to the sanctuary of Abu Dhabi.

In 1987, auditors Ernst & Young – who reviewed the books of the holding company – informed Abedi they were worried about 'excessive management power' and serious weaknesses in BCCI's systems and controls. Meanwhile in Basle, those bank supervisors were still so unhappy with BCCI that they forced Abedi to appoint a single auditor for the entire international network.

Then came the indictments in Florida.

BCCI was fined $15.3 million for its money laundering activities. Abedi insisted that it was an isolated incident. But suddenly everybody started asking questions about BCCI. Official investigations were launched in Canada, France, Luxembourg, Brazil, Singapore, Bermuda, the Caymans, Cyprus and even Nigeria. While several of these investigations involved currency control violations, a number of them uncovered evidence of more sinister endeavours.

At the Bank of England, the Governors were shown two reports – one from the City of London Fraud Squad, the other from a Middle Eastern accountant – indicating fraudulent practices at BCCI.

Nothing was done about either report.

A year later, the Governors were shown a Price Waterhouse audit that revealed a series of false and deceitful practices.

Now, finally convinced they needed to act, the Governors approved a bail-out scheme that had been proposed by BCCI investors in Abu Dhabi who claimed they were ready to save the bank from total collapse. Yet again, despite the incontestable discovery of fraud, no official inquiry was requested by the Bank of England.

In the States, one investigation took a look back ten years, to the time when BCCI romanced Bert Lance and wound up owning Financial General Bankshares, a financial holding company in Washington DC.

Under American law, anyone controlling more than 5 per cent of the shares in a public company must file a disclosure form with the Securities and Exchange Commission. But in late 1977 and early 1978, Abedi believed he'd found a way around the law. He convinced a group of BCCI clients each to buy less than 5 per cent. When the SEC ultimately sussed out what was happening, they filed suit against 11 people, including Abedi. Faced with the prospect of going to jail, the defendants worked out a deal, part of which included the right of the defendants to make a tender offer to all of Financial General's shareholders.

The takeover took several years to complete and when it finally happened, in 1982, it was done on the basis that Financial General would be renamed First American Bankshares and that the new entity would be totally independent of BCCI. The reason the Americans demanded that it be operated by management autonomous of BCCI was because the US Office of the Comptroller of the Currency didn't trust BCCI and said as much in a letter to the Federal Reserve Bank. Couched in polite terms, the exact wording was, 'BCCI is not subject to regulation and supervision on a consolidated basis by a single bank-supervisory authority.' In other words, they weren't going to permit a rogue like BCCI to run a bank in the United States.

In the meantime, it turned out that Bert Lance's National Bank of Georgia and the Independence Bank of Encino in California, which had been bought by Gaith Pharaon, had been surreptitiously funded by Abedi through a $500 million loan from BCCI. As collateral, Pharaon had signed over the shares of the two banks. And, while Abedi later arranged for First American Bankshares to buy the National Bank of Georgia, he in effect – but illegally – had gained control of three US banks.

Being a staunch believer in the doctrine that 'credibility is contagious,' Abedi and his cronies installed prominent Americans on First American's board. Clark Clifford, one of the most exalted attorneys in Washington – an elder statesman who served as an adviser to and/or personal friend of almost every President since Harry Truman – was named chairman. His law partner and protégé, Robert Altman – best known for being married to TV's 'Wonder Woman,' Lynda Carter – became the bank's president.

But, then, friends in high places had long since become something of an Abedi speciality. He charmed Robert

Mugabe and BCCI became the first foreign bank permitted to operate in Zimbabwe in 1980. He made friends with the Chinese Communist rulers and BCCI was permitted to open in Shenzhen, the special economic zone across the border from Hong Kong. In 1982, when the United Arab Emirates announced that no foreign bank could have more than eight branches on its territory, Abedi formed the Bank of Credit and Commerce (Emirates), cut in the ruling families of the UAE, and bought BCCI's excess branches.

By the time C-Chase indicted BCCI, the dossier on Abedi had become pretty weighty. US Senator John Kerry had already opened subcommittee hearings on BCCI and its relationship with Manuel Noriega. Under oath, a pair of convicted drug dealers claimed they'd laundered funds through BCCI in Panama and that their introduction to the bank had come from none other than Manuel Noriega. A further Senate inquiry revealed that Noriega had used BCCI since 1982 to wash millions of dollars.

Concurrent with Senator Kerry's inquiry, New York County District Attorney Robert Morgenthau also took an interest in BCCI's activities, specifically in Abedi's manipulation of First America.

At 73, Morgenthau's half-century of legal experience – more than 30 of those years as a prosecutor – had produced sharply honed instincts where financial crime is concerned. A major political force in New York since the days when Jack Kennedy asked him to serve as the US Attorney there, it was Morgenthau who went after the local Mafia – winning convictions against 52 members of the Luchese, Bonanno, Gambino and Genovese families. It was Morgenthau who brought indictments against lawyer Roy Cohn – Joe McCarthy's partner in the Communist witch hunts of the early 1950s. And it was Morgenthau who attempted to shut the door on Americans hiding funds in Swiss bank accounts.

Because First America had branches in New York, Morgenthau claimed jurisdiction. On several occasions, attorneys and investigators from his office travelled to London, hoping for assistance from the Bank of England. It was, for the most part, steadfastly refused.

Undaunted by either the Bank of England's obstructive attitude or the lethargy displayed by US federal prosecutors – Morgenthau announced that the Bank of England had been 'wholly inadequate' when it came to regulation of BCCI and believed that the Justice Department had seriously dragged its heels – he now took aim with his biggest guns. Knowing that the way to nab the white-collar bad guys was, as he put it, 'to follow the money', he tenaciously went after Abedi and everyone involved with the takeover of First American – including Clifford and Altman. He aimed to punish those who might have conspired with BCCI to create a presence illegally in America.

By March 1990, the Governors at the Bank of England had been briefed by the British intelligence services that Abu Nidal was among the many dubious account holders at BCCI. He maintained 42 accounts at various BCCI branches around London.

Eight months later, a report to the Governors compiled from private files seized from Abedi's right-hand man – BCCI's chief executive, Swaleh Naqvi – detailed extensive fraud throughout the bank. Included in the practices outlined by the Naqvi files were diverted deposits, phantom loans – money sent to Abedi's friends without any intention of seeing it repaid – and totally fictitious loans that were laundered through other banks to obliterate the money trail.

Two months after that, in January 1991, the Governors were informed that BCCI had amassed some $600 million in unrecorded deposits.

In response, on 4 March 1991 – almost as if they had at

last run out of excuses – the Governors ordered an audit of the bank, using the independent accounting firm of Price Waterhouse instead of their own inspectors. It was only when that report was done, in July, that the Governors took direct action and shut down BCCI.

Morgenthau indicted several people – Clifford, Altman, Abedi and Naqvi. The first two were ordered to stand trial, although the case against them subsequently petered out. The second two became the subject of extradition warrants. Naqvi was brought to the United States, where he plea-bargained an 11-year sentence which could see him released in less than half that time. Abedi died in August 1995 at the age of 73. His extradiction had been requested but the Pakistan government refused.

It seems that among the unanswered questions is how, in 1989, when Abedi realized First American was not properly situated to expand his money laundering activities in Miami, he conspired with Gaith Pharaon to buy CenTrust. So, the Americans allege, Pharaon secretly acquired 5 per cent of CenTrust – as usual – on behalf of BCCI. By the time federal banking regulators closed down CenTrust, Abedi and/or Pharaon and/or BCCI owned, and never declared, at least 28 per cent of it. Abedi and Pharaon, the government continued, not only used CenTrust to launder BCCI funds, but they also funnelled various political donations through CenTrust – mainly to Democratic campaign funds – including a $50,000 gift from Pharaon to the Carter Presidential Center.

With as much as $9.5 billion missing worldwide from BCCI's books – seven times more than disappeared at the Banco Ambrosiano – it's fair to say that it took a lot of people a lot of time – plus a lot of people turning blind eyes – to make that much money disappear.

It's true that the CIA had damning information about Abedi and BCCI that should have been passed along to other federal agencies, and wasn't. It's also true that various US law enforcement agencies made bad decisions which severely delayed any direct action against BCCI. So, it's only right that blame for allowing the bank to continue doing business long after doubts arose, must be spread wide. But if one finger is to be pointed, it has got to be towards the Bank of England – after all, BCCI operated since the beginning out of the UK.

A House of Commons Treasury and Civil Service Select Committee felt it should be incumbent on the Bank to accept responsibility for its failure as the supervisor of BCCI. The committee believed that the Bank probably could have prevented such a fiasco had it not subjected itself to a tragedy of errors, misunderstandings and failures of communication. In his 1992 report to Parliament – *Inquiry into the Supervision of the Bank of Credit and Commerce International* – the Lord Justice Bingham wrote, 'The Bank of England failed to discharge its supervisory duties in respect of BCCI.'

Wrongdoings were brought to the attention of the Governors on several occasions, over the course of several years, and by virtue of their mandate from Parliament they could have been expected to have taken appropriate action to straighten out inefficient or non-satisfactory practices. Where money laundering is concerned, the Bank of England must meet the same conditions as all other banks and report to the police any suspicions that its auditors might have when it comes to the washing of drug or terrorist funds. It seems reasonable to conclude that, if the Governors knew that BCCI was handling drug- or terrorist-related monies, then they were clearly delinquent, and in violation of the law. If they didn't know, then they were incompetent because it was their obligation to know.

Yet, as if they were impervious to criticism, the Governors arrogantly maintained then – and arrogantly continue to insist now – that the Bank of England did nothing wrong.

Of course, if they didn't bother reading the reports they were being sent about BCCI, it is wholly believable they haven't read the newspapers either since the scandal broke. Facing a Select Committee of Parliament, the then Governor of the Bank of England, Robin Leigh-Pemberton, actually made the astonishing statement, 'If we closed down a bank every time we found an incidence of fraud, we would have rather fewer banks than we do at the moment.'

One would have thought that was exactly what he was supposed to do.

In the end, BCCI unravelled, not because the Bank of England was doing its job, or even because Abedi had grown so greedy for so long. It fell apart because Robert Morgenthau wouldn't be placated. If there are any heroes in this story, the New York County District Attorney must be first in line.

BCCI is a perfect example of how the offshore system is a Godsend to the laundrymen.

One of their branches was the world's first non-existent bank. To facilitate drug money laundering in Florida, they created a bank in the Bahamas that only existed on the hard drive of a computer. Drug dealers arrived at a Miami office with bags full of money and their deposits were credited to the phantom branch. It simply required one clerk who understood how to log the deposit into the computer. Bank officials in Miami then filed forms with US Customs to say that they were shipping money in from the Bahamas. Once the forms were stamped, they'd take the cash and deposit it in another Miami bank saying here's a legally imported shipment from our Bahamas branch.

A scam that started with BCCI is now indicative of the world we are living in. Any banker anywhere on the globe can book any transaction to any bank in any other part of the globe. No one actually ever has to go there. It merely takes a few seconds, some e-mail addresses and the proper passwords.

Now consider those 50–60 jurisdictions around the world offering banking secrecy and privacy protection.

It's easy to see how the world has become a buyer's market for the laundrymen.

Since BCCI's closure on 5 July 1991, banking authorities around the world have tried to jam plastic wood into the holes that permitted such a thing to happen. There are those who believe that the full facts will never be known. The most interesting of blanks in the Bingham Report is Appendix No 8, headed: 'The Intelligence Services.'

The role of the intelligence services in the BCCI will not be revealed in Britain for at least 30 years – if ever – although it should eventually come to light in the US thanks to the Freedom of Information Act. When it does, both the American and British intelligence services are expected to have a lot of questions to answer.

One of them might be, why did the UK security services insist that the Bank of England delay closure of BCCI for perhaps as much as 15 months? Another might be, why did the Bank of England comply?

The answer might lie in the fact that BCCI had a working relationship with Saddam Hussein. It is known that the US National Security Council used BCCI to launder funds for the Iran–Contra affair. It is known that the CIA maintained accounts with BCCI, and used it to wash money destined for Afghan rebels. It is believed that the US Defense Intelligence Agency kept a slush fund with BCCI. It is known that one of Abedi's front men in the US was Kamal Adham – the former chief of Saudi intelligence – who was allowed to bargain a $105 million fine to avoid a jail sentence. It has been suggested that MI6 found BCCI to be convenient as well. It is known that BCCI was influential in the transfer of North Korean Scud-B missiles to Syria. It is known that

BCCI helped to broker and then finance the sale of Chinese Silkworm missiles to Saudi Arabia. It is known that BCCI stepped in as the middleman when the Saudis needed Israeli guidance systems for those missiles.

Whether or not the Bank of England was doing the bidding of the intelligence services: (a) to protect an ongoing intelligence operation, (b) to allow the intelligence services time to cover themselves, or (c) both, it is important to stress that people living in a democracy have an inalienable right to know what has been done in their name, and why.

Appendix No 8 is guaranteed to make interesting reading. But because the red faces that would result are certainly not confined to the Board of Governors at the Bank of England, don't hold your breath until the public is permitted to see it.

What's more, there's no reason to believe that the lessons of BCCI have been learned by any of the banking regulatory bodies around the world. Although, there's little doubt that the lessons of BCCI have been learned by those bankers who are running other BCCIs.

After all – in the words of the legendary bank robber Willy Sutton – 'Banks is where the money is.'

BCCI was one that got caught.

CHAPTER NINETEEN

The 40 Day Bank

'We became too popular, too fast.'
DEA Undercover Agent Bill Malarney

Anguilla is 91 square kilometers of sand, houses and small hotels floating quietly in the middle of the West Indies, a short bumpy plane ride from San Juan, Puerto Rico. Fishing and tourism are the economic mainstays, but only just. This is not one of the wealthier hangouts in paradise. There are, however, several banks on the island. Although there was never a bank in Anguilla – or anywhere else in the Caribbean – quite like RHM. This one was a door, a plaque, a phone and six clients.

In 1994, a group of DEA agents in Atlanta, Georgia, were sitting in an apartment, working a surveillance as part of an undercover operation, waiting for something to happen. With time on their hands, they talked about all sorts of things, but especially about the people they were dealing with and the methods those people were using. One of the agents expressed his opinion that the Achilles heel of the drug cartels was moving money. The others agreed. Then someone made the casual remark, 'You know, if we had an inroad with a bank, we could jump a few of layers and deal with the actual financial people of the cartel.'

And someone else said, 'Why not?'

The next day they talked about all sorts of things again, but especially about what they needed to do to go into the banking business.

Bill Malarney, a tall, smiling, soft-spoken fellow in his late 40s – whose premature white hair makes him look more like a kindly high school maths teacher than a hardened narc – was one of them.

'Nothing like this had ever been done before, but that was no reason not to try. We knew that if we could make it work, we could do some real damage to the cartels. If we could make it work, get all the permissions we'd need, get through all the red tape, we'd be in the banking business and that would mean we'd be inside the cartels.'

To help formulate a workable plan, the agents turned to Wilmer 'Buddy' Parker III, the 6 foot 2 inch Alabama-born former college football player who was then an Assistant US Attorney in Atlanta. They'd worked well together in the past and now phoned him to say they needed to talk.

'The idea of establishing a bank intrigued me,' Parker recalls, 'because I knew it would be the ultimate honey pot. But none of us had much knowledge about banking. Not only were we faced with the dilemma of how to go about setting up a bank, but we obviously needed to have other individuals involved who could run it. So while the idea was intriguing, it was a daunting idea in terms of the logistics of how to put something like this together.'

Working inside the US Government, they understood they could not be seen to be cutting corners. And yet, they needed to keep this as secret as possible, which meant they wouldn't always be able to use regular channels. So the first step was to get the idea approved inside the DEA. After that, they had to go up the chain of command and get the idea approved at the Treasury and Justice Departments. In the end, because these were federal agents planning, essentially, to violate all sorts of US statutes, final permission had to come from the Attorney General.

Once that happened, the way was clear for the group in Atlanta to begin focusing on specific details.

It quickly became evident that in order to make this work – especially to keep the traffickers from suspecting anything – they'd have to establish the bank in a jurisdiction other than one controlled by the United States.

'None of us were bankers,' Malarney explains, 'or knew anything about banking, so we had a pretty steep learning curve. We knew we needed a Class B bank, a type of private bank that sells secrecy. But you just can't pick up the *Wall Street Journal* and take out a want-ad. We had to find out how to get one. We also had to think about where we wanted it. It had to be somewhere convenient for both the Colombian narcotics traffickers and us.'

Anguilla looked to be ideal. The island not only had a reputation as a banking haven, it was close enough to Venezuela and Colombia that a trafficker could jet there in an hour or so. Anguilla had the additional benefit of being a largely self-governing British crown colony, which meant that the agents could turn to British colleagues – people they knew they could trust with their secret – to help them go into business. That immediately brought to mind a previous investigation where this same group had established a good working relationship with someone in the Foreign Office. They invited him to come from London to Atlanta to discuss the proposal. He paved the way for them.

They now put out feelers to a contact in the British West Indies who warned that Class B banks weren't necessarily as easy to come by in Anguilla as they'd once been and, that if they tried to purchase one off the shelf, there was a two-year waiting list. None of them cared to sit around that long, but knew that if they pulled strings to jump the queue, they'd raise suspicions. The next best thing seemed to buy a bank that was already licensed, but that meant finding someone willing to sell.

Their contact in the West Indies now came up with a man in California who'd bought a bank in Anguilla but hadn't yet got around to using it. One version of the story goes that he was a legitimate businessman who, when made an offer by the DEA that he couldn't refuse, turned over his bank. The truth is that he was anything but legitimate, so Malarney and Parker went to see him intending to play good guy/bad guy with him – Malarney insists, 'Quite naturally, I was to be the good guy' – but the man knew what they wanted and gave in before they could even start their routine.

Malarney again. 'As you can imagine, all of our strategy and planning came to a grinding halt. Buddy drafted the paperwork and it was signed.'

Once the DEA paid the activation fees for the bank, they were technically in business. But it took another year to set up everything so that it looked like a legitimate bank. They needed an office. They needed properly trained personnel. They needed brochures. They needed stationery. The Colombians have a problem dealing with any US entity because they're paranoid about American law enforcement, so the bank had to be appropriately packaged. Right from the beginning it had to act like a Caribbean bank. That meant paying attention to very minor details. For example, a legitimate bank operating in a British territory uses A4 size paper which is 8" x 11½" and not US size stationery which is 8½" x 11". A little mistake like that could bring down the entire operation.

They also had to maintain the highest level of secrecy because any leak could put their lives in jeopardy.

'Getting that banking license,' Malarney goes on, 'turned out to be a very involved process. We had to list our assets, our backgrounds and our credit references. The authorities then looked into everything. They verified that we had a minimum deposit to put up and a banking relationship with a Class A bank somewhere in the world. We needed to set all of that up in advance, including getting a real bank to vouch for us.'

So, over the next several months, that's exactly what they did. They arranged for certified financial statements, and $500,000 to be placed on deposit in a location that the licensing authority could certify. They made up names and histories for themselves, all of which had to be suitably manufactured so that if anyone in Anguilla – or even more menacingly, Colombia – ran a check, everything would ring true.

A special office inside the Justice Department in Washington procured passports for them. Through contacts in Georgia's Department of Motor Vehicles, they were each issued with new driver's licences.

'I became William L. Rice,' says Malarney, 'a bank executive who lived in Covington, Georgia, a rural part of the state approximately 40 miles outside of Atlanta.'

The address he used was a house set far back into the woods off a quiet country road. All that anyone could see from the road was the mailbox, which is one of the reasons Malarney chose it. There was no way to see if anybody was home without going up the driveway, and there was no way to get up the driveway without attracting attention from the house next door. What's more, if someone drove by at night, they'd see lights. But unless they knew there were two houses hidden in the woods, no one would realize the lights were coming from the house next door.

Knowing that people in small towns talk to each other and will often repeat what they hear – whether it's accurate or not – Malarney protected his identity by getting a few rumours spread through town. One was that the house had been sub-let to a divorced businessmen, which explained why there were no children living there. The other was that the businessman travelled a lot in Europe, which explained why he wasn't around very often.

Finally, to make certain that he got plenty of mail, whenever he travelled, wherever he went, Malarney filled out coupons in inflight-magazines and hotel brochures which meant that for months, the mailbox at Covington was inundated with junk mail all addressed to William L. Rice.

Three days a week, a local law enforcement officer stopped by the mailbox to empty it.

In the end, it was one of those little details that paid off.

Late in the investigation, Malarney learned that a private investigator had driven up from Miami, gone to the mailbox, found letters addressed to Rice and verified to his employers that William Rice did live there.

Ironically, Malarney himself never set foot in the house.

Armed with new names, each of the agents created histories for themselves, including old addresses. They knew from experience that whatever they claimed had to be real enough to allay the suspicions of anyone with doubts, but still be vague enough so that no one could determine it wasn't true. For example, one of the addresses Malarney gave was a road in Connecticut, where he's originally from, that is 30 miles long and has no numbers.

Each of the agents was also equipped with bank accounts and credit cards in their new names.

Where did all the background information come from?

Malarney is totally frank. 'We made it up, we lied. The thing is, we needed to make certain that if anybody had access to a data bank and checked on, say, William Rice, they'd find out he did exist and had a past. The photo on William Rice's driver's licence was my photo. It was my signature, my weight, my height, everything was verifiable.

The same went for the credit cards. The same went for various clubs around town. William Rice was a member of a private eating club, very exclusive, very hard to get into, which gave him a cachet. It allowed people to see that we ran in a circle of people who had a lot of money. It also provided us a secure place for undercover meetings.'

His business card identified William Rice as vice president of the bank because Malarney found it easier to be vice president. That way, he could always shrug decisions off and say, I need to speak with the president. It gave him the opportunity to stall for time, which almost always comes in handy in an undercover capacity. It gave him time to think and weigh the various options.

Fluent in Spanish, Rice's background was in sales and finance, although his previous position was listed as a consultant, a nebulous enough claim that allowed Malarney to answer questions such as 'Who did you consult for?' with answers like 'People who made me sign confidentiality agreements which forbid me from discussing that'.

Exactly the sort of thing that a laundrymen would understand and appreciate.

In all, there were four banking officers. President, vice president, secretary and treasurer, and to make the ruse seem even more believable, all of them were highly visible. They went to Anguilla and made certain that everyone saw them, got to know them and would remember them.

'As our aircraft approached the island it made a lot of noise so people would notice a private plane coming in. When we landed we made sure we made a lot of noise, tipped very generously and were boisterous, so if later on anybody wanted to check our background and say, do you remember these people, they would. People always remember private aircraft and guys who tip very well. We did the same thing with the hotel. We were loud and obnoxious. We went out of our way to be sure that everyone we met spotted our gold credit cards. We left them lying around in sight when contacts were nearby. We also made sure to leave our passports and other ID in places where they could be seen. We needed people to say, I remember them, God they were terrible, they were rude, they were obnoxious, but they were dripping with money. It was all done for a purpose.'

They rented a tiny office on the first floor of what turned out to be Anguilla's only shopping mall – a two-storey collection of little stores and a Canadian bank – then returned to Atlanta, setting up a fancy office in a part of town where, unless a company had big bucks, they didn't rent space.

'We did it the same way any legitimate business sets up an office. We went to a business supply store, bought desks and filing cabinets, bought pictures for the walls, bought plants and telephones and computers. When you're undercover, you have to make the place looked lived in, like you're working there and doing business there, but you stay away from personal objects. We didn't put pictures up of anyone's family because that could open up a discussion, you know, tell me about your wife, tell me about your children. We needed to keep them out of it. So we decorated with very nebulous things. Baseball souvenirs. Football items. Sporting stuff is always good. We also made sure that there were cigarette butts in the ashtrays and coffee in the coffee dispenser.'

At the same time, they designed the bank's brochure to look right and to say all the right things. It took more than a month simply to collect brochures from dozens of financial institutions, to tack them up on a wall and study them. With the help of a trained psychologist, they tried to establish what attracted their eyes, what looked expensive, what sent out the proper signals. And they printed several dummy versions before they settled on the one they finally used.

They called the company, RHM Trust Bank – they later joked that it stood for 'Registered with Her Majesty' – and used a lot of blue with gold, silver and red in the logo to create a positive association with money and wealth. The brochure's text, in English, French and Spanish, spoke about a 'banking relationship', and 'confidentiality', promising potential customers that the officials would be readily available 'at your request' and 'at your convenience'.

On the psychologist's advice, they never used more than six words per line, keeping their message crisp and to the point. And, at the back of the brochure, they printed a little map of the Caribbean, showing Anguilla and the coast of South America, but including only one small part of the United States – South Florida – the drug capital.

Besides Anguilla and Atlanta, the bank's letterhead listed offices in the British Virgin Islands, London, Monte Carlo and Singapore. Permission to do that had to be secured from 'friends' in those places – that, too, took time – but the message they wanted to send out was clear – this bank is equipped to operate worldwide and prepared to satisfy all its clients' needs.

The notepads they used – headed RHM Investment Company – showed their downtown Atlanta address, just in case one of their customers wanted to stop by to check if they really existed. And while the bank's official address was that one room in Anguilla, the phone number they used was a freephone 1-800 number, which rang in Atlanta.

The idea was that someone would man the Atlanta office during regular banking hours, 9–3, but Malarney and the others would only go there when it was necessary. And then, they would rarely stay very long. 'You don't want to be available full-time because if you are, then your clients think they can drop in on you any time. You always want to present the fact that you're travelling. To look very busy.'

Once everything was in place, they convinced a Colombian

contact to get their brochures distributed to several of the 'right people' in Cali. In all, the scam took just 15 months to set up.

'You'd think you could do it a lot faster,' Malarney says, 'like in 20-30 days. But you don't become a bank overnight.'

RHM opened its doors at the end of August 1995 and proved very popular from the first day. That same morning, they received correspondence from someone known to be associated with a drug cartel concerning money pick-ups. Within 24 hours RHM had accepted cashier's cheques for half a million dollars with instructions to wire the money around the world.

Within a week, they'd laundered over $3 million.

To discourage legitimate business, the bank's fees were astronomically high. For instance, checking accounts cost 18 per cent per transaction. But RHM's clients accepted this as simply the cost of doing business.

Obviously, the fewer people who know about such an undercover operation, the better. In this case, there were only three people in the banking community who knew what the DEA was doing, and not many more at the Department of Justice. Ironically, their secrecy created a problem.

Sometime around early October, the Georgia Banking Association began to take an interest in the workings of RHM. Not knowing that this was a sting, they voiced their suspicions to the Internal Revenue Service and the Controller of Currency at the Treasury. As soon as the undercover team in Atlanta got wind of this, they rushed to Washington to meet with the chief investigator for the Controller of the Currency. Before they could let him in on the secret, the Treasury investigator actually said to Malarney, 'I like to meet this guy, William Rice. I don't think he's legit.' So Malarney reached across the table, shook his hand and admitted, 'That's me.'

Without spilling the secret, the Georgia Banking Association's request for information was temporarily lost in the bureaucratic shuffle.

Only once, as far as Malarney knows, did anyone from Colombia have similar suspicions. 'One individual, who was very much involved in the trade, showed up at our office. I think he wanted to see four walls, to hear the phones ring, to see the receptionist, to talk to someone face to face, to see if we existed. That's why every minute detail in planning pays off.'

The bank only ever had six clients, and sometime in late October, one of the six contacted Malarney to ask if the bank might be able to broker the sale of three paintings. According to the client, one was Peter Paul Reubens' 'St Paul', one was a Joshua Reynolds portrait of a man, the third was Pablo Picasso's 'Head of a Beggar'. Malarney promised to look into it and, after a reasonable amount of time, went back to the client with the assurance that buyers could be found.

Not all of the agents' time during those 40 days was spent investigating their clients. Some of it actually had to be spent on running a financial institution. There was also a constant round of travelling, back and forth to Europe – mainly the UK, France and Italy – and to Mexico also, where on one trip, Malarney and an associate picked up $400,000 in cashier's cheques to be deposited in their bank. They also returned to Anguilla a couple of times, to reinforce their rich businessmen persona.

When they weren't undercover, they were DEA agents doing mounds of paperwork – 'Everything had to get written down,' Malarney says, 'because memories fade, reports don't' – and what seemed to be a never-ending amount of accounting. 'We needed a set of books for the bank and another set of books for our operation. Being accountable to the taxpayer, we had to justify how we spent our money. We had to keep expense accounts, and arrange authorizations for our trips. We had to do monthly statements, to show our cash flow. And at the end of the investigation, we had to show what money was left over so that it could be forfeited to the United States government. We generated a lot of paperwork. But it was very important to keep track of everything.'

Most of the money that came into the bank was routed through Europe – mainly France and Italy – before being brought back to Colombia or Panama. But that didn't surprise anyone on the undercover team, because Europe has always been a favourite place for drug traffickers.

'Especially in the last 20 years,' Malarney points out. 'There are no more border crossings, Europeans traditionally speak several languages and it's not uncommon to discover that your astute trafficker today was educated in the United Kingdom or in France. They also speak several languages and they easily blend into Europe where they can claim they're Spanish or come from somewhere else in South America besides Colombia.'

Interestingly enough, the agents very quickly got pretty good at being bankers. 'We found that if we could delay a trafficker's money in our system for, say, a weekend, we could make the interest on it. So we floated funds for the weekend, using their money to earn interest. It meant we had to put up with the calls from the people in Colombia saying, where is our money? What's the delay? When are we gonna get it? Obviously, they wanted to earn the interest on it too. It became a big chess game. We really did play at banking just like real banks.'

While Malarney and the other agents were doing their thing, Parker stayed busy monitoring what was going on and was in regular consultation with the Department of Justice. 'Washington's concern, and it was a legitimate one, was that we were in a position of laundering a substantial amount of money and needed somehow to justify this.

They kept asking, are you going to be able to arrest very significant violators and seize very significant amounts of money? The debate became, when does an operation like this become part of the problem. And that was, quite frankly, a heated debate. If you're knowingly involved, then you're an accomplice to this conduct. And if you're the government, then you're violating your own laws. You've got to have a justification for that. That's where you have to come up with the arrests and the seizures.'

Needless to say, long before they shut RHM down, they started talking about how they were going to shut it down. And that required international coordination.

Earlier in November 1995, the Atlanta bankers and Parker met in Washington with colleagues from Great Britain, Spain and Italy, as well as from various DEA offices around the world. They wanted to plan every detail of the bank's final day, to anticipate every possible problem that could arise with the 'take down'. They needed to be certain that everyone executed arrests at the same time, which would not necessarily be easy with Europe being five and six hours ahead of the United States. They needed to factor in time delays. It was absolutely vital, because without arrests the sting would have failed.

Parker explains, 'If you go about your efforts in investigating the world of criminals, and wind up not being able to do anything with the information because those criminals remain outside your jurisdiction or the jurisdiction of any country in which you have a treaty, then all you've done with your undercover operation is further the interests of those criminals. You haven't received any benefit from it by way of bringing them to justice. Our problem with Colombia has always been that they refuse to recognize extradition. Unless we could find the defendants outside Colombian jurisdiction, it would be almost impossible to prosecute. We needed to work on a scenario of getting certain defendants into the United States so we could arrest them.'

That included the client with the three paintings.

As November wore on, the agents elected to play on the upcoming Christmas holidays. They knew that the traffickers would take their traditional vacations and that there wouldn't be a lot of currency transactions going on. So they settled on a take-down date for mid-morning on Friday, 8 December.

All six RHM clients were informed that, in expectation of Christmas, the bank would be accepting money through that date. Then, as it came in, Malarney and the others began cooking up excuses why funds currently in the system were delayed in getting wired out. They mis-sent faxes, purposely put the wrong numbers on them, told clients the phone lines were down, and sometimes simply didn't answer calls. Whatever it took to make sure that when they did close down, they'd still be holding onto several million dollars.

In all, the bank was only in business for 40 working days.

The official story is that they'd accomplished their mission – they'd gotten inside the Cali cartel's financial network – and that the Department of Justice felt it could not afford to allow the sting to operate any longer. But Parker now admits that he was slightly startled at the links they stumbled across between organized crime and what he refers to as 'threats to national security'.

'Through a law enforcement initiative, we were beginning to run into activities of investigative agencies on behalf of nations that dealt with national security issues. I knew then that we were obviously tapping in at the highest levels of criminal conduct. I'm afraid I'm not able to explain any more about the national security issues, although I might say that a loose definition would involve the CIA and Department of Defense agencies who are dealing with security issues involving narcotics trafficking. We began getting indications from Washington that some of the people or some of the activities we were looking at might also be activities or people being reviewed or considered or analyzed by intelligence agencies. Now, in our country, law enforcement and intelligence do not work in tandem. And although no one in Washington told me what they were, it was obvious that there were concerns that we might inadvertently or imprudently or improperly or whatever you want to say, compromise an intelligence-gathering operation. So that was another issue we had to deal with.'

Parker will not say that they were called off by Washington because of the national security implications and instead, contends that the reason the bank was shut down was the ongoing concern Justice Department authorities had continuously expressed to him, that they would wind up with a situation in which they had effectively laundered so much money that they would not then be able to justify the results of that activity.

So, after spending 15 months to set it up, 40 banking days later it was all over.

'We became too popular, too fast,' Malarney insists. 'We had the ability to launder vast amounts of money but that was not the purpose of the bank. The purpose of the bank was to locate cartel bank accounts throughout the world. We were not in business just to launder money for the cartel, we were in business to dismantle cartel financial structures.'

The bottom line was that the DEA laundered a total of about $12 million. In exchange, they seized in excess of $110 million in assets throughout the world and arrested well over a hundred individuals. Many of them were significant players. They did get the three paintings – although there is some doubt about the authenticity of the Picasso – and also confiscated grocery stores, a car rental agency and various other businesses, in addition to the usual collection of homes and boats. They are still looking for an ocean-going yacht which, when they find it, they intend to seize as well.

Perhaps as important as the arrests and seizures, the DEA scored big points in having established themselves as players in the undercover world. No one in the history of US law enforcement had ever pulled off a sting like this.

'After us,' Malarney says, 'the banking industry will never know who they're dealing with, whether the people sitting on the other side of the desk are criminals or good guys. Because we were there once, there will always be some doubt as to whether or not we're still there.'

Parker agrees. 'The message sent to the cartel was simple, you can't trust anybody. I'm not sure the cartels ever imagined that Great Britain and the United States would cooperate like that in an undercover activity that included the Italians, the Canadians and the French. I think we gave them an indication as to where law enforcement is heading, that we're no longer going to investigate and prosecute from a territorial perspective but from an international perspective.'

And here Malarney grins, 'Hopefully, those individuals who are wavering whether to follow the law or not will think twice. Is there another bank on the horizon?'

Long pause.

Then a shrug.

'One never knows.'

With each deposit and each wire transfer, the DEA collected names of players and started to build evidence against them. At one point, the investigation came across the name, Pasquale Locatelli.

The intelligence the DEA had on Locatelli in Atlanta was sent to John Costanzo, the DEA attaché in Rome. He passed it along to the proper Italian authorities, and a subsidiary sting operation began there.

Costanzo says, 'We were able to tap into the Locatelli operation and at one point we were requested to pick up money in Rome and transfer it to banks in the Caribbean for subsequent transfer to traffickers in Colombia. So we supplied a cellphone number to Malarney, who passed it off to an individual in Colombia, with instructions to call and ask for Vincenzo. That was me. A week later I got a call from a guy who identified himself as Mario. He asked if I had someone who could take delivery of approximately $760,000 in Italian lira. So we arranged for two police officers of the Servizio Centrale Opportivo of the Italian National Police to meet undercover with Mario's contact in Rome. The contact showed up, brought the two undercover officers to a vehicle and showed them how the money was hidden in an electronically controlled trap. That money was subsequently transferred via the Caribbean to the traffickers in Colombia.'

With this lead, the Italian police began investigating the man who'd delivered the money to them, Mario da Jacomo. Through surveillance, wire intercepts and good old street work, they were able to link him to a certain Pasquale Locatelli.

A fugitive from justice on the lam in Spain, he'd escaped from a French prison where he was serving 20 years for drug distribution and had also once been in a shootout with the Carabinieri. He was known to specialize in transporting cocaine from Colombia to France, Romania, Croatia, Spain, Greece and Canada. At one point, one of his ships was intercepted by NATO trying to evade the UN arms embargo of Croatia and found to be carrying containers with small arms and ammunition. The Italians now located him living in Malaga, Spain, and after contacting the authorities there, an ad hoc task force was put together allowing the Italians to base two officers in southern Spain for three months.

Those officers were able to establish that Locatelli had

25–30 people working for him in Spain, plus others in Italy and Montreal.

Enter again, Yvon Gagnon of the RCMP and his Centre Internationalé Montaire de Montréal.

'We were also very interested in Monsieur Locatelli because we'd already identified him as the main supplier to the da Vito family, a father and his sons, who were traffickers in Montreal. The family was using our bureau de change, having their money deposited with us by Sabatino Nicolucci and Dominique Tozzi. We'd also identified Locatelli as the owner of a shipment that had been lost off the coast of Nova Scotia. He'd air-dropped nine tons of cocaine onto a ship and five of those tons sank to the bottom of the ocean.'

Accordingly, the RCMP was now brought into the Locatelli intelligence circuit.

The way the man operated was typical of international drug traffickers. All his communications were done on cellphones, and to keep them secure, he used 30–40 different phones at any given time. After three or four days, he'd disconnect the number and give the phone to someone else. That made it difficult to keep an eye on him.

Being based in Malaga made it particularly tough. A tourist area, anyone who was neither a tourist nor working there became the object of local curiosity, especially if they stayed too long. There was also the fact that Locatelli had been allowed to live in Spain, even though there were international arrest warrants issued against him, which meant he was doing more than simply taking advantage of antiquated extradiction treaties. It meant he, quite obviously, had connections. Requests for his arrest were never effected. That worried the Italians and the DEA because it reminded them that they didn't necessarily know who to trust.

It took several months to build a case against him, but the Italians managed it and along with some help from the DEA, they convinced the Spanish authorities it was time to act.

When the RHM take down came, the Spanish grabbed Locatelli along with five of his people. The Italians arrested 15 others. Locatelli now sits in a Spanish jail, and is expected to be there for the next 25–30 years. At that point, if he does walk out, there are extradiction requests with his name on them from Italy, France and Canada.

All this, just because a bunch of guys in Atlanta, sitting around talking, started wondering, what would happen if they opened a bank.

CHAPTER TWENTY

Hanging out the Wash

"Money laundering is the crime of the '90s."

Business Week

In the summer of 1969, Richard Nixon pledged to formulate a new national policy in the fight against drugs. He might even have elevated that fight to a full-blown war had it not been for America's ongoing 'police action' in Southeast Asia.

Colombian cartel cocaine was just beginning its infiltration of American culture. Nixon, naively unaware of how complex the problem was, arrived at the conclusion that marijuana and cocaine were equally dangerous. Needing a culprit, he settled on Mexico. Accordingly, he stepped up surveillance of America's southern border and coerced the Mexican government into herbiciding marijuana fields. He succeeded in putting amateur, freelance smugglers out of business – kids who dealt home-grown marijuana. But he left the field wide open for professionals – grown-ups flogging cocaine. Because coke is a powder, it's easier to smuggle than bales of marijuana and is therefore less risky. It is also a higher-profit product. So Nixon's new national policy did little more than create a huge competitive advantage for the deadlier drug.

By the time Jimmy Carter moved into the White House, things were getting out of hand. Dozens of American cities were being transformed from wholesale marijuana markets to major cocaine trading centres. It was party time for street pushers, pimps, pilots, speedboat captains and any federal agent who could be bought.

For the laundrymen, it was the Second Coming.

When the television programme *60 Minutes* brought the depth of the problem into the nation's living rooms, exposing how otherwise respectable businessmen were jumping on this profit bandwagon, Carter approved an inter-agency task force that called itself 'Operation Greenback'. Customs officers and IRS agents identified and approached individuals who'd banked large amounts of cash. Their question was, where did you get the money? If the suspect answered, that it was US-generated income, then the IRS would mention the words, 'tax evasion'. If the suspect answered that it was imported, then Customs would define the word 'smuggling'. If he wouldn't answer, or couldn't answer without admitting it was drug money, then he was slapped with charges of drug trafficking, conspiracy and money laundering. The success of Operation Greenback – 215 indictments, the seizure of $38.8 million in currency and $14.6 million in property plus $120 million in fines – formed the model for other multi-agency joint ventures, including the creation in 1984 of Organized Crime Drug Enforcement Task Forces.

Ronald Reagan appointed George Bush to vanguard the nation's combat against drugs but the then-Vice President, for all his good intentions, never displayed much of a stomach for severe financial prosecution. Within a year, he downgraded Operation Greenback from an inter-agency effort directed out of Washington to a small unit working out of the US Attorney's Office in Miami.

One gauge of Bush's failure to grasp the problem was

reflected in the cash surplus figures. The federal government monitors the amount of currency in the banking system. A cash surplus represents money that wouldn't be found in a particular area under normal banking conditions. When Bush de-emphasized Operation Greenback, the cash surplus in Jacksonville and Miami alone shot up by $5.2 billion. Like Nixon's targeting of the Mexican border, the moment Washington concentrated its forces in south Florida the laundrymen headed for healthier climates. In this case they went to southern California where the cash surplus quickly topped $3 billion.

In spite of evidence to the contrary, the Reagan administration seemed convinced that money launderers didn't bother with cash any more. They even went on record saying that professional criminal financial managers did their banking electronically. As for the cash-filled garbage bags shown on the evening news with every drug bust, they shrugged, all entrepreneurs keep petty cash on hand.

While Reagan and Bush weren't looking, along came crack.

A crystallized form of cocaine, cheaper than heroin or coke, it can be smoked like hashish. With the North American coke market saturated and prices falling, the cartels saw crack as a financial Godsend. One ounce of cocaine could become 300–400 crack vials and their profits would soar. By the mid-80s, both of Colombia's main cartels were shipping crack by the ton.

The nickel and dime bags, $5 and $10 worth, widened the cartels' market by attracting middle-class white consumers who gave it a certain social status. Because this business didn't require more than a few dollars start-up money, it also brought a new category of seller onto the street, black teenagers.

There was a time when sports offered the main hope for any black kid who wanted to escape from the inner-city ghetto. If he could play baseball or football or, even better, could play great basketball, there were people who'd back him through high school and college. Only a tiny percentage of those kids ever got to the pros but at least sports held out hope. And, in some cases, hope was enough.

Crack changed that.

When George Bush moved into the Oval Office, Customs and DEA officials tried to persuade him that a full-scale attempt to eradicate the production of illicit drugs around the world would be costly and futile. In some countries, government officials were openly cooperating with drug producers. A top-secret State Department document noted, for instance, that the narcotics trade in Laos had become such an integral part of the local economy that supporting it was 'de facto government policy.'

The President was also advised that there was direct involvement by Syria in the growing, refining and trafficking of drugs. The CIA repeatedly told Bush that Damascus was earning up to $1 billion a year, about 20 per cent of its national income, by subsidizing the opium and hashish industry in the Bekka Valley of Lebanon. The main market was then, and is still, the United States. Named as the main culprits by the CIA were the Syrian President's brother, the Defence Minister and the commander of Syrian military intelligence. But Bush needed the Syrians during Operation Desert Storm and later to stay at the tables during the Middle Eastern peace talks. So, at least in the short term, it suited American foreign policy to turn a blind eye to international heroin trafficking.

Those officials who understood what the war on drugs was really all about urged Bush to put his resources into the battle on the financial front. The President's response was two-pronged: at home, he planned to wipe out street dealers by discouraging demand through education. Overseas, he plotted to send US troops into the mountains of Colombia, making a massive wave of arrests their top priority.

The massive wave turned out to be nothing more than a brief high tide. Between 1989 and 1991, a total of 26 cartel members were captured and sent to the United States. For a while it appeared as if Bogotá was willing to appease Washington. But the Colombians made extradition unconstitutional and Saddam Hussein invaded Kuwait. The President's attention turned back to foreign policy.

His Gulf War was still to be fought.

His drug war had already been lost.

Bill Clinton didn't have to inhale to understand something his immediate predecessors did not. That 90 per cent of all crime is financially motivated and therefore the most effective way to fight criminals is to go after their money.

He put money laundering on the agenda at the celebrations for the fiftieth anniversary of the United Nations by warning drug traffickers, terrorists and the world's organized criminals, 'Your dirty laundry is no longer welcome.'

Congress had mandated a certification process which requires the President to assess foreign cooperation in counter-narcotics efforts on a yearly basis. Consequently, the State Department named 11 nations that were seen to be aiding and abetting the laundrymen. However, six of them – Bolivia, Colombia, Lebanon, Pakistan, Paraguay and Peru – were considered vital enough to US national interests to justify continued support from Washington. The remaining five are Afghanistan, Burma, Iran, Nigeria and Syria. An additional State Department roster, not publicly released, added to the usual suspects Antigua, the Cayman Islands, Venezuela, Thailand, Austria and Cyprus.

The certification process is a report card where the grades are pass, fail and still thinking about it. But countries who care about passing have long since started doing something about money laundering whereas countries that couldn't care less about failing have sufficient income from drug dealing that only the most severe economic sanctions could grab their attention. However, to make sanctions effective requires a global effort and it is clear from the way recent embargoes have been violated in Iraq and Bosnia that many offending countries couldn't care less about most of the globe. It is equally clear that most of the globe doesn't care a hell of a lot about America's drug problem.

If the list had been compiled under the same criteria by another country, the United States would be cited as the world's biggest per capita user of illegal drugs, and therefore wouldn't pass. That brings the argument straight back to the Third World contention: before you tell us how to live, clean up your own streets.

Clinton plainly hoped to do just that by putting more policemen on the beat. But that negates the fact that once drugs reach the streets it's probably too late. What's more, arresting, convicting and imprisoning traffickers does not always prevent them from running their cartels. And then, for every trafficker taken out of circulation, a dozen more seem willing to take his place.

For the first time, the money laundering statutes have been used to prosecute a trafficker for a drug deal conducted outside the United States. A Pakistani man, Asif Ali Khan, was indicted in 1995 in Louisiana after purportedly smuggling 10 tons of the hashish between Australia and Pakistan. The Justice Department claimed jurisdiction because $300,000 worth of the $67 million deal was washed through the Pioneer Bank and Trust Co of Shreveport, Louisiana.

By concentrating on the laundrymen, by following the money trail and going after that money, the government continues to drive up the traffickers' cost of doing business. He's now paying anywhere between 6 and 25 per cent to get his money collected, washed and into his pocket.

The downside is that the added expenses are reflected in the street price, and there is a direct correlation between increased street prices and increased street crime.

From the middle of the last decade to the middle of this one, the war on drugs has cost more than $100 billion. It is fair to ask, what has America got for its money? The answer is, probably not a lot. Doing nothing would have created anarchy but in that same ten-year period drug-related deaths have doubled and drug-related murders have tripled. And now, $100 billion later, the problem has become so very drastic that perhaps only very drastic solutions can even attempt to solve it.

Because the underground economy functions almost exclusively with dollars, one of the more radical proposals has been to render the traffickers' dollar mountains useless by changing the colour of money. The United States is the only country in the world whose currency is both the same size and the same colour in all denominations. Paper money has been green throughout the nation's history. Under the Reagan administration a proposal was floated around the Senate to end that same-colour/same-size tradition. Supported by Treasury Secretary Donald Regan, the plan was to announce on a Monday morning that within seven days green $20, $50 and $100 bills would no longer be considered legal tender. Instead the government would be issuing newly designed banknotes – perhaps bigger, perhaps smaller, perhaps yellow, red or blue. All anyone would have had to do was walk into a bank and exchange the old notes for the new notes. But any cash transaction over $1,000 would be recorded and the information would be passed on to the IRS and the DEA. For the average person it wouldn't have been anything more than a minor nuisance. Even if someone always carried a few thousand dollars in his pocket, making the switch would take only a few minutes. But it could cripple a drug dealer with several million in cash hidden under his mattress. Swapping thousands of old $20s, $50s and $100s for the new money in such a short period of time, even using an army of smurfs, would be out of the question. And once the week was up, his cash mountain would be worthless.

The DEA then suggested that the government might print two types of currency. One would be legal tender exclusively inside the country, the other would be legal tender exclusively outside the country. The only place the two would be interchangeable would be at specially controlled financial institutions. At least in theory, that should put an end to dollar smuggling.

Going one better, there have been calls to do away with all paper money, to turn the American economy into one that functions solely with cheques and plastic. Although there might have to be some coins left in circulation, if for no other reason than to keep the vending machine industry happy, by relegating folding money to history the government would be delivering a fatal blow to drug dealers. It would also be a positive step towards putting loan-sharks, tax evaders, protection racketeers and kidnappers out of business.

To date, none of these plans has got very far. The legislators who could make any or all of them happen have written them off as unrealistic. They claim that such a stunt would be too disruptive and cause too much of an inconvenience for tens of millions of Americans. The truth is probably closer to the fact that tampering with the currency to knock out the laundrymen is too abstruse an issue to win re-election votes.

In 1989, the heads of state of the seven leading industrial nations, known as the G-7, officially recognized for the first time that money laundering was a runaway global problem. Acting in unison, they formed the Financial Action Task Force (FATF) to coordinate a multinational approach to dealing with this crisis. Membership was promptly opened beyond the G-7 nations and now consists of all the OECD countries, plus Hong Kong, Singapore, the Gulf Cooperation Council and the European Commission. Every member has loudly endorsed a proposed blueprint consisting of 40 specific measures intended to deal a lethal blow to the laundrymen but, to date, not one single member has incorporated the entire blueprint into law.

FATF does what it can. They have gone from a group whose special interest seemed, in the beginning, to hold meetings in fancy holiday locales, to an important special interest group who has made enormous strides in focusing attention on money laundering. Based largely on FATF's efforts, all sorts of other groups have put money laundering on the top of their annual general meeting agenda. Their intentions are good and most of the time the delegates' hearts are in the right place. In one recent twelve month period: experts from 40 nations met in France to recommended measures to halt money laundering in Russia and Eastern Europe; representatives from 140 governments met in Italy to plot a strategy against the world's criminal organizations; delegates from 180 governments convened in Egypt to mount a global front against organized crime; American lawyers met in Washington to discuss their responsibilities vis-à-vis money laundering; ministers from 25 nations met in Argentina, committing their administrations to fight money laundering; and 600 international law enforcement professionals assembled in England to call for the easing of banking secrecy laws.

And while, all too often, conclusions are published and generally disregarded, it must be said that conferences bring together people who might not have otherwise met and allow them to network. It helps create a web of experts from member states working in various fields – customs, drug enforcement, banking and financial supervision. After all, the bad guys know the other bad guys. The good guys are finally getting to know the other good guys.

Even if every member of FATF complied fully with the organization's 40 directives, they still wouldn't work.

Money is at the root of the problem and money is also at the root of the solution but wherever such huge sums are bandied about, common sense is often given a back-seat ride.

Start with the genius who wrote the manual for administrative budgeting. Government accountants set annual budgets with two factors in mind: how much is needed next year; how much was spent this year. If an agency was handed $10 billion last year and only spent $9 billion this year, it risks getting only $9 billion next year. So bureaucrats rush around in the final month of the fiscal year to make certain that all of their allocated money is used up. Then, to justify an increase for their next budget, they naturally inflate the threat they're battling to defeat. They may know that $250 billion a year is being laundered but they find an expert to swear it's $350 billion and warn that if they don't get increased funding they'll never be able to do their job. Given more than they previously got, they now have to spend it all or they'll lose it the following year. So waste is factored into the equation and annually re-creates itself. So are egos. Like the company chairman who brags that he heads a $10 billion organization, in government too there's a tendency to confuse real importance with allocated revenue.

Nowhere is that more visible than in asset-sharing programmes which offer law enforcement agencies a portion of the bounty they confiscate. Battle lines are drawn for the right to claim a goal and not just to be credited with an assist. Law enforcement agencies pull together but only up to a point. Then it's a free-for-all to grab the prize. Customs, the DEA, the FBI and the IRS run operations together and often with great success, but each agency fights for control of the task force because being chief pays better than being just another Indian.

With cash dangled like an apple on a stick to motivate a mule, some agencies go after cases that produce big cash rewards instead of pursuing more difficult and often more important cases where the prize is nothing but a conviction.

Human temptation also gets in the way.

Four federal agents in south Florida, three from the FBI and one from Customs, were caught by undercover officers in a sting operation and charged with stealing a total of $200,000 from drug dealers. One of the four happened to have a girlfriend who managed a Great Western Savings Bank branch in suburban Miami and she washed their cash. No sooner had that case broken, when another Customs agent in Florida was arrested on charges of trafficking and money laundering in a separate case. This man was approached to help launder cash derived from the sale of counterfeit goods. The agent, who held down a second job at a financial investment firm, had no trouble laundering his money there in his spare time.

The headlines are never short of similar stories. Three sheriff's deputies in LA were convicted of stealing $750,000 in confiscated drug money and laundering it through a gun store. A Tampa police 'Officer of the Year' pleaded guilty to five federal drug-related charges. And Rene De La Cova, the DEA agent who personally served Manuel Noriega with his arrest warrant, admitted stealing $700,000 while working on an unrelated money-laundering sting.

It's naive to expect that there won't always be rotten apples. Fortunately, the overwhelming majority of law enforcement officers involved with this sort of work do it because they sincerely believe it's a job that needs to be done. And the various sacrifices they're called upon to make in order to accomplish that mission are made unselfishly, honourably and with justifiable pride.

There are some people who believe that drugs represent less than 10 per cent of the total amount of money hiding in off-shore tax havens and nations offering secret banking. One estimate has it that nearly $5 trillion is currently placed in jurisdictions willing to use their sovereignty to take money out of the legal tax systems of other countries. In some parts of the world, the consequences of a citizenry who do not support the infrastructure of the country where they live can be disastrous. In Mexico, for example, there are several dollar billionaires, virtually every one of whom houses his assets offshore. The Mexican treasury estimates it collects only a fraction of the tax due and as a result may never be able to solve its social and economic problems. The problem is mirrored in Europe. German tax evasion is big business for neighbouring Liechtenstein and Austria. Switzerland caters to French tax evasion. The Channel Islands offer respite for British citizens. A major worry is that somewhere down the road, perhaps as soon as the next few years, the piper will have to be paid.

In a world of 24-hour-a-day global markets and of integrated financial systems, having a mass of dirty money floating around the world threatens not just the markets but also western democracy.

Suddenly, huge chunks of the world's wealth are being traded outside the sphere of supervision. It puts into question many companies' books. It puts into question many companies' assets. The Barings Bank fiasco might well be the tip of a titanic-sized iceberg. Operating largely unregulated and unsupervised in Singapore, here was a financial institution that the Bank of England believed it was supervising. And just like that, one day, it evaporated.

It seems obvious, then, that continued non-supervision will eventually transform global financial markets. That was the case in 1929. The question now becomes, must a melt-down of the world's economic system – a global version of the Great Depression – happen before western governments decide it's time to rein in the dirty money?

The answer is anyone's guess.

Compounding the problem in Europe, according to Washington-based attorney Jack Blum – he's a former staff member to the Senate Foreign Relations Committee and was counsel to Senator John Kerry's hearings on international drug trafficking and money laundering – is that the nations who have formed the EU are at a cross-roads in terms of their various legal systems.

'You have an integrated Western European economy, but no integration of criminal law or law enforcement. Officials in Brussels have told me that they're losing around $5 billion a year in cigarette and alcohol tax revenue and have no way of going after the people who are doing the tax evasion. They have to rely on the law enforcement authorities in each of the member countries. And, of course, when these cases come to individual countries they're given a relatively low priority because priority goes to the problems in that country.'

On the other hand, the problem of international money laundering might be solvable, although it would take unprecedented international cooperation to produce a result.

'I think the major countries of the world can work together to eliminate the problem. If there is a political will this problem will be eliminated because ultimately it is the banks and the financial institutions of the major countries that are the big players in this offshore world. Without them, without the access to the international payment system that these people provide, and without access to markets, you can close this whole thing down in a minute.'

One way to deny laundrymen that access, he says, would

be for all the major industrial nations to pass laws which prohibit the right of anonymously owned corporations – that is, shell companies set up in tax havens where there is no clear indication of a beneficial owner – to open a bank account.

'You say to those entities, you may no longer do business here. Now, if you can't have a bank account, can't trade on the stock exchanges, can't conduct business in a country, then suddenly, the attractiveness of this kind of corporation goes way down. But the major developped countries have to agree and they have to work together on the problem. We cannot have one of the countries deciding that it will be the renegade that provides the doorway for people who want out.'

It has taken a long time but, at least where drugs are concerned, money laundering is being seen as both a crime and a symptom of other crimes. Accepting that the best way to combat drug trafficking must be to include methods which deprive criminals of their profits, one logical conclusion is: the day the drug problem is defeated, the money laundering problem will also be defeated.

Alongside comes the argument: if you really want to conquer drug trafficking, you have to eradicate the demand for drugs.

Yet, if the Ayatollah Khomeini couldn't keep drugs out of Iran, and if Fidel Castro can't keep drugs out of Cuba, and if Saddam Hussein can't keep drugs out of Iraq, how can anyone seriously expect elected leaders to keep drugs out of the west?

In reality, a drug-free democracy is a pipe dream.

One recent survey suggested that, even if law enforcement agencies throughout North America and Europe were able to increase their seizures by 40 per cent, the availability of drugs on the streets of New York, Boston, Philadelphia, Miami, Houston, Chicago, Detroit, Los

Angeles, San Francisco, Toronto, Vancouver, Montreal, London, Manchester, Edinburgh, Paris, Frankfurt and Rome would be virtually unchanged.

Confiscation is viewed by the traffickers as little more than a tax imposed on them for the right to do business. Either they write off the cargo entirely, or in some places, especially around the Caribbean, simply buy their cargo back for a handful of cash.

What's more, there are literally dozens of nations in this world where the government's revenue is less than the profits made by the drug cartels. Wherever this occurs, the danger is that those nations are ripe for picking. The traffickers move in and the country becomes a laundryman's playground. Imagine trying to enforce justice and protect citizens in a country where organized crime is wealthier and better armed than the government.

Speaking to *Time* magazine several years before his capture, Cali cartel boss Gilberto Rodriguez Orejuela wondered out loud, 'Why are countries such as Germany free to export materials used to refine cocaine? Why do countries like Switzerland, Panama and even the US protect money whose origin is dubious?'

The question clearly reflected his deep understanding of the narco-economy, that it could not possibly survive if otherwise honest men and otherwise legitimate businesses were not prepared to facilitate the laundrymen. He and others like him went on to prove that the devastation drug trafficking has wreaked throughout the world is monstrous. And the price is paid for nightly on the streets of North American cities.

How ironic that the very groups which could have the most immediate effect on the war against the laundrymen – bankers, lawyers, company formation agents, politicians and countries where financial secrecy is a growth industry – have the least incentive to take on the fight.

The game they play is one of plausible denial. As long as otherwise honest businessmen have half a thread on which to hang their belief that what they're doing is legitimate, they will continue doing it. They will ask, am I supposed to be a policeman? They may acknowledge that drugs equals money equals drugs but never in the context of their own money. They will insist, if I had to ask where my clients' money came from every time I got a new client, I wouldn't have any new clients.

As long as otherwise honest men can plausibly deny that they are as guilty of drug trafficking as the dealers they are serving, it will be business as usual.

And that business is usually death.

The North Vietnamese and the Viet Cong effectively used drugs as a weapon in the guerrilla war against the United States. The Mujaheddin rebels in Afghanistan took a leaf out of their book and made heroin easily available to the invading Soviets. They hooked the Red Army so badly that many soldiers were turning over their weapons in exchange for drugs. Mikhail Gorbachev pulled the soldiers out, not because the Afghans had rocket launchers but because his army had been soundly defeated by hypodermic needles and white powder.

Legalization of drugs, or at the very least decriminalization of some of them, are widely touted solutions. There is no disputing that both would help to keep some kids out of jail. But what it totally fails to do is keep drugs out of those kids.

In jurisdictions where they've tried to negate the obvious consequences of prohibition, the experiment has failed repeatedly. It has created massive health problems, spread drug consumption across wider sections of the population and fuelled other crimes. In the Netherlands, for instance, decriminalized drugs are the predominant ingredient feeding a growing and terribly violent white slave trade.

Legitimizing drugs also means legitimizing the traffickers and the money launderers. Turning the Treasury into a pusher so that it can tax drugs won't pay for the damage that drugs do, any more than it will put organized criminals out of business. So until someone can come up with a workable solution – and there are some people who have arrived at the tragic conclusion that the problem has now become unsolvable – the advantage remains clearly on the side of the laundrymen.

Anyway, modern technology is about to render the fight against them useless.

Rechargeable cashcards will allow criminals to bypass the banking system altogether and launder profits via the Internet. Computer chips weigh the same if they are carrying $10 or $10 million and unlike credit cards, there'll be no record of transactions. In its simplest form digital cash already exists. Phone cards carry a certain amount of credit. Deductions are made from the chip with each call. The next step will be cards carrying say $100 worth of credit which you'll use to buy gum, a ride on a subway, food in a restaurant or a new baseball mitt. Instead of handing the sales person a piece of plastic which sends the transaction to a central computer for billing later, or plastic which simultaneously debits your bank account and credits the seller's, you'll put your card into a machine and the proper sum will be moved off your computer chip and onto the seller's.

It will work the same way for drug deals.

Around the corner are smart cards embedded with enough memory to hold all sorts of data. Once encrypted software is developed to assure privacy, you'll download money from the cards onto your home computer – turning your hard disk into your virtual bank account – access the Internet with your modem and move assets from one jurisdiction to another instantaneously and invisibly.

Mastercard and Visa are both developing smart card systems, although theirs will deliberately generate an audit trail because that's the business they're in. Other companies however, including many banks, are developing smart cards that won't leave an audit trail because that's where the huge profits will be in digital currency technology.

There is no doubt that it will change the way we spend our money and therefore change the way we live. Eventually electronic money should replace cash. Consumer habits die hard and there is always great resistance to great change but once upon a time there were people who refused to believe that someday everyone would carry plastic.

Nor is there any doubt that cybercash risks undermining both the world's banking system and the administration of justice. The problem is compounded by lawmakers who, like generals, are always fighting yesterday's battles. By definition, cyberspace transcends governments and national boundaries. Unless governments get to grip with it in time, those people who stand to profit most from the future – and the most obvious two are banks and organized criminals – will have long ago worked out how to make the system government proof.

One solution to the drug war, which might be palatable to the electorate, is to officially recognize the difference between the professional, international drug trafficker and people who deal in small amounts simply to support their own drug taking.

When someone buys three grams of coke and sells two to make the money that one would have cost, technically that's dealing. And in some jurisdictions, a few ounces moved like that can put you away for a very long time. But when drug addiction is seen as an illness – much the way alcoholism is generally recognized as a disease – then this sort of 'amateur dealing' could rightfully be considered a symptom of that illness. The idea is not to decriminalize drug dealing at any level, but to treat 'amateur' dealing more humanely than many states currently do, while legislating that global trafficking must become a capital offence.

Establishing that difference could make a difference.

The thing that men like Escobar and the Orejuela brothers feared most was extradition to a legal system in which they could not buy justice. But simply indicting them and demanding that they be handed over – even with the possibility of the death penalty hanging over their heads – probably wouldn't put them out of business. However, by placing severe economic sanctions on any country giving them refuge; by sending special 'commandos' into the country to kidnap the traffickers and bring them back; and by putting a couple of million dollars on their heads, wanted dead or alive, it's a good bet that at least some of them would give up drug dealing in favour of full-time survival.

Hand in hand with that, anyone who has any professional dealings whatsoever with these indicted traffickers, would also be subject to charges of global trafficking and – like global traffickers – risk either capital punishment, in areas where that is legal, or life in solitary confinement without possibility of parole. It would be like charging laundrymen as accomplices to murder.

After all, in order to deal drugs the way they do, the global traffickers have set up huge corporate structures, taken several pages out of the best management books, and constructed their multinational organizations accordingly. They deliberately separate the marketing and financial sides of their business, keeping the two as far apart as possible, in order to create that all-important situation where the drug dealers never know about money laundering and the laundrymen – those white collar professionals whose business it is to handle money – never see drugs.

Now, by tossing street dealers, smugglers, marketing people, bankers, accountants, front-company people and lawyers into the same cauldron, the laundrymen would be forced to come face to face with the drugs and their 'plausible deniability' would fall on deaf ears. Their only way out would be a clause stating that citizens would have one chance to work a plea-bargain. In exchange for all of the global traffickers' assets, other accomplices and 'other invaluable information', they could trade the solitary confinement and 'without possibility of parole' clauses for something slightly less severe.

It is Draconian, to say the least.

And while the crime of global trafficking might not put an end to our drug problems, it would brutally focus the attention of the laundrymen.

Until something this drastic is done, the bad guys can bide their time, find helpful banks and buy crooked lawyers. They only need to find one country or one bank willing to do their laundry and it doesn't really matter if that country is half-way around the world or that bank is just across the border. The legitimate financial system will always be the neck of a bottle through which dirty money flows and as long as one country or one bank is willing to cheat on behalf of the laundrymen, there is nothing the others can do.

The good guys are hampered by a lack of human resources, limited by financial constraints and denied the tools they need by legislatures that must balance judicial concerns with the free flow of honest business.

The good guys were seriously outgunned five years ago when this book was first published. Today, it is even worse. Perhaps horrible problems really do require horrible solutions.

Bibliography

Books

Adams, J, *The Financing of Terror*, New English Library, London, 1986.

Adams, James Ring & Frantz, Douglas, *A Full Service Bank - How BCCI Stole Billions Around the World*, Pocket Books, New York, 1992.

Alexander, Shana, *The Pizza Connection*, Weidenfeld, New York, 1988.

Allsop, Kenneth, *The Bootleggers*, Hutchinson, London, 1961.

Anderson, Annelise Graebner, *The Business of Organized Crime*, Hoover Institution Press, Stanford, 1979.

Balsamo, William & Carpozi, George Jr, *Crime Incorporated*, W.H. Allen, London, 1988.

Beschloss, Michael, *Kennedy Versus Khrushchev - The Crisis Years 1960–1963*, HarperCollins, New York, 1991.

Black, David, *Triad Takeover*, Sidgwick & Jackson, London, 1991.

Booth, Martin, *The Triads*, Grafton Books, London, 1990.

Brashler, William, *The Don*, Harper & Row, New York, 1977.

Bresler, Fenton, *Trail of the Triads*, Weidenfeld, London, 1985.

Burdick, Thomas, *Blue Thunder*, Simon & Schuster, London, 1990.

Campbell, Duncan, *That was Business, This is Personal*, Secker & Warburg, London, 1990.

Charbonneau, Jean-Pierre, *The Canadian Connection*, Optimum, Ottawa, 1976.

Clark, T. and Tigue, J. J, *Dirty Money*, Millington Books, London, 1975.

Clifford, Clark, *Counsel to the President*, Random House, New York, 1991.

Clutterbuck, R, *Terrorism, Drugs and Crime in Europe after 1992*, Routledge & Kegan Paul, London, 1990.

Colodny, Len & Gettlin, Robert, *Silent Coup - The Removal of Richard Nixon*, Gollancz, London, 1991.

Cummings, John, & Volkman, Ernest, *Goombata*, Little Brown, Boston, 1990.

Dean, John, *Blind Ambition*, Simon & Schuster, New York, 1976.

De Grazia, Jessica, *DEA - The War Against Drugs*, BBC Books, London, 1991.

Di Fonzo, Luigi, *St. Peter's Banker - Michele Sindona*, Franklin Watts, New York, 1983.

Dinges, John, *Our Man in Panama*, Random House, New York, 1990.

Eddy, Paul, *The Cocaine Wars*, Century Hutchinson, London, 1988.

Ehrenfeld, Rachel, *Evil Money*, HarperCollins, New York, 1992.

Ehrenfeld, Rachel, *Narco Terrorism*, Basic Books, New York, 1990.

Eisenberg, Dennis with Dann, Uri & Landau, Eli, *Meyer Lansky*, Paddington, London, 1979.

Eppolito, Lou & Drury, Bob, *Mafia Cop*, Simon & Schuster, New York, 1992.

Faith, Nicholas, *Safety in Numbers - The Mysterious World of Swiss Banking*, Hamish Hamilton, London, 1984.

Frances, Diane, *Contrepreneurs*, Macmillan, Toronto, 1988.

Franklin, R, *Profits of Deceit*, Heinemann, London, 1990.

Franzese, Michael & Matera, Dary, *Quitting the Mob*, HarperCollins, New York, 1992.

Freemantle, Brian, *The Fix*, Michael Joseph, London, 1985.

Gardner, Paul, *The Drug Smugglers*, Robert Hale, London, 1989.

Garrison, Jim, *A Heritage of Stone*, Putnam's Sons, New York, 1970.

Garrison, Jim, *On the Trail of the Assassins*, Penguin, London, 1992.

Gugliotta, Guy & Leen, Jeff, *Kings of Cocaine*, Simon & Schuster, New York, 1989.

Gurwin, Larry, *The Calvi Affair*, Macmillan, London 1983.

Hess, Henner, *Mafia and Mafiosi*, Saxon Hall, New York, 1973.

Hogg, Andrew, McDougal, Jim & Morgan, Robin, *Bullion*, Penguin Books, London, 1988.

Ianni, Francis & Reuss-Ianni, Elizabeth, *The Crime Society*, New American Library, New York, 1976.

Intriago, Charles A, *International Money Laundering*, Eurostudy, London, 1991.

Jennings, Andrew, Lashmar, Paul & Simson, Vyv, *Scotland Yard's Cocaine Connection*, Cape, London, 1990.

Kaplan, David, *Yakuza*, Queen Anne, London 1987.

Karchmer, Cliff, *Illegal Money Laundering - A Strategy & Resource Guide for Law Enforcement Agencies*, Police Executive Resources, Washington DC, 1988.

Katcher, Leo, *The Big Bankroll*, Harper & Row, New York, 1959.

Kempe, Frederick, *Divorcing the Dictator - America's Bungled Affair with Noriega*, Putnam, New York, 1990.

Kobler, John, *Capone*, Michael Joseph, London, 1972.

Kochan, Nick with Whittington, Bob & Potts, Mark, *Dirty Money - The Inside Story of the World's Sleaziest Bank*, National Press Books, Washington DC, 1992.

Koster, R. M. and Borbon, G. S, *In the Time of the Tyrants*, Secker & Warburg, London, 1990.

Kwitney, Jonathan, *The Crimes of Patriots*, Touchstone, New York, 1987.

Kwitney, Jonathan, *The Fountain Pen Conspiracy*, Knopf, New York, 1973.

Lacy, Robert, *Little Man*, Little Brown, New York, 1991.

Lance, Burt, *The Truth of the Matter*, Summit, New York, 1991.

Lane, Mark, *Plausible Denial*, Plexus, London, 1992.

Lernoux, Penny, *In Banks We Trust*, Anchor Press, New York, 1984.

Loftus, John & McIntyre, Emily, *Valhallas Wake*, Atlantic Monthly Press, New York, 1989.

McAlary, Mark, *Crack War*, Robinson Publishing, London, 1990.

McCarl, Henry N, *Economic Impact of the Underground Economy - A Bibliography on Money Laundering and Other Aspects of Off-the-Record Economic Transactions*, Vance Bibliographies, Monticello, Illinois, 1989.

Marchetti, Victor & Marks, John D, *The CIA and the Cult of Intelligence*, Dell, New York, 1980.

Milgate, Brian, *The Cochin Connection*, Chatto & Windus, London, 1987.

Mills, James, *The Underground Empire*, Doubleday, Garden City, NY, 1986.

Mustain, Gene & Capeci, Jerry, *Mob Star - The Story of John Gotti*, Franklin Watts, New York, 1988.

Nash, Jay Robert, *Encyclopedia of World Crime*, Crime Books, New York, 1989.

Nash, Jay Robert, *Hustlers and Con Men*, Evans, New York, 1976.

Naylor, R. T, *Hot Money and the Politics of Debt*, Unwin Hyman, London, 1987.

Naylor, R. T, *Bankers, Bagmen and Bandits*, Black Rose, New York, 1990.

Nicholl, Charles, *The Fruit Palace*, Heinemann, London, 1985.

Nown, Graham, *The English Godfather*, Ward Lock, London, 1987.

O'Brien, Joseph, *Boss of Bosses*, Simon & Schuster, New York, 1991.

Perisco, Joseph, *Casey*, Penguin, New York, 1990.

Poppa, Terrence E, *Drug Lord*, Pharos Books, New York, 1990.

Posner, Gerald, *Warlords of Crime*, Queen Anne, London, 1989.

Possamai, Mario, *Money on the Run*, Penguin, Toronto, 1992.

Powers, Thomas, *The Man Who Kept the Secrets - Richard Helms and the CIA*, Pocket Books, New York, 1981.

Powis, Robert, *The Money Launderers*, Probus Publishing, Chicago, 1992.

Prados, John, *Keepers of the Keys - A History of the National Security Council from Truman to Bush*, Morrow, New York, 1991.

Prince, Carl & Keller, Mollie, *The US Customs Service - A Bicentennial History*, Department of the Treasury, Washington DC, 1989.

Reader's Digest, *The Greatest Cases of Interpol*, Reader's Digest Books, New York, 1982.

Roark, Garland, *The Coin of Contraband*, Doubleday, Garden City, NY, 1984.

Robinson, Jeffrey, *Minus Millionaires*, Grafton, London, 1988.

Scheim, David, *The Mafia Killed President Kennedy*, W.H. Allen, 1988.

Shannon, Elaine, *Desperadoes*, Viking, New York, 1988.

Short, Martin, *Crime Inc*, Thames Mandarin, London, 1991.

Short, Martin, *Lundy*, Grafton, London, 1992.

Sterling, Claire, *The Mafia*, Hamish Hamilton, London, 1990.

Stewart, James B, *Den of Thieves*, Simon & Schuster, London, 1992.

Tanzi, Vito, ed, *The Underground Economy in the United States and Abroad*, collected articles for the International Money Fund, Lexington Books, Lexington, Mass., 1982.

Truell, Peter & Gurwin, Larry, *BCCI*, Bloomsbury, London, 1992.

Tyler, Gus, *Organized Crime in America*, University of Michigan Press, Ann Arbor, Mich., 1962.

Villa, John K, *Banking Crimes: Fraud, Money Laundering and Embezzlement*, Clark Boardman, New York, 1987.

Walter, Ingo, *Secret Money - The Shadowy World of Tax Evasion, Capital Flight and Fraud*, Unwin Hyman, London, 1989.

Woodward, Bob, *Veil - The Secret Wars of the CIA*, Simon & Schuster, New York, 1987.

Woodward, Bob & Bernstein, Carl, *All the President's Men*, Secker & Warburg, London, 1974.

Woodward, Bob & Bernstein, Carl, *The Final Days*, Avon Books, New York, 1976.

Periodicals

ABA Banking Journal:
   July 1992: 'When money laundering law meets environmental risks.'
   January 1991: 'Spotting and handling suspicious transactions.'
   December 1990: 'Treasury takes next step on wire transfers.'
   March 1990: 'From the money laundering front.'
   March 1990: 'Stop the smurfs.'
   November 1989: 'Bank secrecy revisited.'
   July 1985: 'What you should know about money laundering law.'
American Spectator:
   June 1992: 'The great ruble scam.'
   September 1988: 'Losing the drug war.'
Atlantic:
   January 1986: 'Coping with cocaine.'
Baltimore Business Journal:
   25 June 1990: 'Ruling links 1st National with CIA: suit names CIA as a codefendant.'
Bank Management:
   April 1991: 'Wire transfer proposal: Treasury considers banker concerns.'
   March 1991: 'Money laundering experts team up - on and off the job.'
Banker:
   April 1990: 'What's in the suitcase?'
Banker's Magazine:
   March–April 1990: 'Money laundering.'
Banker's Monthly:
   June 1988: 'Panama's banks take it on the chin.'
Barron's:
   11 July 1983: 'Where hot money hides: havens spring up all over the globe.'
Boston Business Journal:
   15 July 1991: 'Brockton Financial Services.'
Boston College International and Comparative Law Review:
   Winter 1991: 'Bankers, guns and money.'
Boston Magazine:
   July 1990: 'Bad influence - the trial of Joe Balliro.'

Bottomline:
  March–April 1992: 'The bank secrecy law demands delicate decision making.'
Business:
  June 1988: 'Underworld hijacks underground banking.'
Business Horizons:
  September–October 1990: 'The continuing expansion of RICO in business litigation.'
Business Journal of New Jersey:
  November 1990: 'A crazy scheme?'
Business Journal Serving Charlotte and the Metropolitan Area:
  13 April 1992: 'Lawyer's conviction chills legal community.'
The Business Journal Serving Greater Sacramento:
  4 June 1990: 'Local money launderer prison bound.'
Business Journal Serving Phoenix & the Valley of the Sun:
  11 March 1991: 'Agreement reached on legislation aimed at money laundering.'
Business Week:
  1 March 1993: 'Cleaning up corruption is clobbering Italy Inc.'
  13 April 1992: 'How did so many get away with so much for so long?'
  6 April 1992: 'Germany's brash new import - dirt money.'
  16 December 1991: 'Zorro, Gorby and Howard the duck.'
  7 October 1991: 'Could China become a least favored nation?'
  23 September 1991: 'Psst, wanna buy a bank? How about a few dozen?'
  26 August 1991: 'Can Noriega drag the CIA into the dock with him?'
  22 July 1991: 'The long and winding road to BCCI's dead end.'
  20 May 1991: 'The days are numbered for secret accounts.'
  27 August 1990: 'Insider trading - The intricate case of Ellis AG'; 'Centrust, the Saudi and the Luxembourg bank.'
  4 June 1990: 'Grabbing dirty money.'
  19 February 1990: 'Gambling big to nail Noriega.'
  22 January 1990,: 'The Noriega "treasure chest".'
  2 October 1989: 'The drug war European style.'
  1 May 1989: 'He started at the top and worked his way down.'
  17 April 1989: 'Getting banks to just say "no".'
  24 October 1988: 'This bank may have been a laundry, too.'
  23 May 1988: 'The Oklahoma town that drug money bought.'
  18 April 1988: 'The Sicilian Mafia is still going strong.'
  16 September 1985: 'Big brother wants to see your bank book.'
  9 September 1985: 'The bank sting that's rocking Puerto Rico.'
  25 March 1985: 'Money laundering: the defense gets a star witness.'
  18 March 1985: 'Enlisting banks in the war on drugs'; 'The long and growing list of hot money havens'; 'In Colombia, dirty money passes through very clean hands', 'Money laundering; who's involved, how it works and where it's spreading.'
  11 March 1985: 'Two brokerages get tangled in the money laundering net.'
  4 March 1985: 'Bank of Boston.'

25 February 1985: 'An all out attack on banks that launder money.'

24 December 1984: 'How Deak & Co. got caught in its own tangled web.'

Columbia Journalism Review:

September/October 1991: 'Follow the drug money.'

Commuter-Regional Airline News:

25 May 1992: 'L'Express owner gets prison term for money laundering.'

Contemporary Crises:

March 1990: 'The Chinese laundry.'

Criminal Law Forum:

Spring 1991: 'Money laundering, an investigatory perspective'; 'Convention on laundering.'

Dallas Business Journal:

19 April 1991: 'Feds accused of misconduct in probe; defendants in money laundering case claim agents hired prostitute.'

28 September 1990: 'Reese deals probed as suits mount.'

7 May 1990: 'Law firms fight over allegations of misconduct.'

Economic Progress Report:

June 1990: 'Action on money laundering.'

Economist:

1 August 1992: 'The Escobar escape.'

9 May 1992: 'Cash at any price.'

25 April 1992: 'Cleaning up the rupees.'

4 April 1992: 'Calling earth, calling earth – the Noriega trial.'

22 February 1992: 'Cleaning up whose act?'

3 August 1991: 'The opening-up of BCCI; send for Richard Hannay; some of it will prove false but enough of the BCCI-spies story looks true to give the intelligence agencies some tough questions to answer.'

15 June 1991: 'Gilded cage – Pablo Escobar, head of Colombia's most important drug cartel, builds the prison where he will be held.'

16 March 1991: 'Oh, my brass plate in the sun.'

1 December 1990: 'Bombs and blackmail.'

27 October 1990: 'Closing down the launderette.'

7 July 1990: 'A clockwork future for Finanzplatz Schweiz?'

9 June 1990: 'Crime cracker.'

2 June 1990: 'A president with guts, and a bullet-proof waistcoat.'

5 May 1990: 'The muzziest of wars'; 'Flushing funny money into the open.'

27 January 1990: 'How BCCI grew and grew.'

9 December 1989: 'Stormy weather – Banking licences and politics of Montserrat.'

21 October 1989: 'Follow the money'; 'On the run.'

16 September 1989: 'Gun law – Colombia.'

9 September 1989: 'Real war – The Medellin cartel in Colombia.'

26 August 1989: 'Colombia's cocaine overdose.'

8 July 1989: 'Clive of Havana – General Arnaldo Ochoa Sanchez convicted of drug trafficking.'

24 June 1989: 'Limitless discretion - a survey of private banking; money talks, wealth whispers.'

11 March 1989: 'Dirty laundry.'
4 March 1989: 'Whitewash or crackdown?'
17 December 1988: 'BCCI stands accused'; 'Love, honour, obey and resign.'
12 November 1988: 'Check your case, sir?'
15 October 1988: 'Till drugs do us part.'
27 August 1988: 'Five tiny secrets of success.'
20 August 1988: 'Cleaning up dirty laundering.'
6 August 1988: 'Columbus's islands.'
28 February 1987: 'Taking crooks to the cleaners.'
Esquire:
  October 1983: 'Cocaine, how you can bank on it.'
EuroBusiness:
  June 1990: 'Cleaning up money launderers.'
Euromoney:
  July 1989: 'Can the UBS colonels win the overseas battle?'
  December 1988: 'Sailing into the grand harbour.'
  March 1987: 'Laundering law leaps across borders.'
Europe 2000:
  March 1990: 'Commission declares war on money laundering.'
European Journal of International Affairs:
  Winter 1989: 'Drug money, hot money and debt.'
Far Eastern Economic Review:
  15 March 1990: 'Japan - Dope dealers delight.'
Financial Post:
  6 July 1991: 'Bank shut in global crackdown.'
Financial Services Report:
  29 August 1990: 'Money laundering deterrence costs banks millions of dollars,
    survey shows.'
Financial World:
  15 May 1990: 'Dr. shoals.'
  21 March 1989: 'The IRS: the gang that can't shoot straight.'
  29 November 1988: 'The bank that knows too much.'
  18 March 1986: 'Secret money; the world of international financial secrecy.'
  18 September 1985: 'The flip side of the coin.'
Forbes:
  23 July 1990: 'Middle East'; 'The Americas.'
  13 November 1989: 'The paradox of antidrug enforcement.'
  30 October 1989: 'In the all out drug war, a low cost blow to the jugular.'
  29 May 1989: 'Scam capital of the world.'
  17 April 1989: 'The Bulgarian connection.'
  26 December 1988: 'Drug smuggler's startup.'
  14 November 1988: 'Too rich to ignore.'
  1 June 1987: 'The biggest drug bust.'
  6 April 1987: 'Stash accounting.'
  6 October 1986: 'See no evil.'
  5 May 1986: 'T-man videos.'
  7 April 1986: 'New hub for an old web.'

23 September 1985: 'America's Hottest Export - Funny Money Stocks.'
9 September 1985: 'How the smart crooks use plastic.'
28 January 1985: 'Guilt by association.'
5 December 1983: 'Everybody's favorite laundryman.'

Fortune:

5 November 1990: 'The S&L felons.'
20 June 1988: 'The drug trade.'
2 March 1987: 'Turmoil time in the casino business.'
1 April 1985: 'Money laundering – more shocks ahead'; 'Editor's Desk.'
4 April 1983: 'The feds eye the herd; Merrill Lynch swears off cash.'

George Washington Journal of International Law and Economics:

Issue #3 1989: 'Dollar diplomacy.'

Governing:

October 1990: 'To catch the drug kingpins, follow the money.'

Insight:

23 July 1990: 'Cleaning out money launderers.'
21 August 1989: 'Drug money soils cleanest hands.'

International Financial Law Review:

March 1990: 'Bank liability under the UN drug trafficking convention.'

International Management:

May 1991: 'Anxiety in the Alps.'

Jewelers Circular Keystone:

October 1991: 'Feds nab money launderers.'
May 1991: 'LU Kustom indicted in money-laundering case.'

Journal of Accountancy:

February 1992: 'IRS says more businesses are complying with anti-money-laundering rules.'
March 1990: 'The telltale signs of money laundering.'

Kansas City Business Journal:

2 August 1991: 'FBI eyes financing efforts for topless bar.'
25 September 1989: 'Ex-AMC exec indicted over embezzlement; money laundering, tax evasion also alleged.'

Kyodo:

29 July 1992: 'Bankers group compiles manual to tackle Money laundering.'

Law Enforcement Bulletin:

April 1990: 'Laundering drug money.'

Life:

March 1990: 'Our man in Panama: the creation of a thug.'

Los Angeles Business Journal:

3 June 1991: 'Cash pay going under the table erodes economy.'
13 July 1987: 'Barry Minkow's favorable treatment in press exposes reporters' own vulnerability to fraud.'

Maclean's:

5 August 1991: 'A scandal in waiting.'
23 October 1989, 'The laundering game: cleaning dirty money is crucial'; 'Canada's crackdown: a new law has led to more seizures'; 'Grabbing the drug bounty: the Miami tally is $150 million'; 'Hiding the drug money:

criminals are using Canada to launder billions of dollars in drug profits.'

11 September 1989: 'Terror in the drug world.'

4 September 1989: 'The cocaine war: Washington and Bogotá battle the drug lords.'

29 May 1989: 'Battling crime through the banks.'

31 October 1988: 'A dangerous trail; police pursue profits from drug sales.'

2 November 1987: 'Cashin in on ill-gotten gains.'

17 August 1987: 'The criminal element.'

25 March 1985: 'Trailing laundered cash.'

11 February 1985: 'Questions behind locked doors.'

4 April 1983: 'Offshore banking secrets.'

Management Today:

May 1990: 'The Mafia: the Long Reach of the International Sicilian Mafia.'

Multichannel News:

19 August 1991: 'Magness and Romrell tied to BCCI affiliate.'

Nation:

7 October 1991: 'The C.I.A. and the cocaine coup.'

4 February 1991: 'Tinker, tailor, banker, spy.'

19 November 1990: 'The looting decade: S&Ls, big banks and other triumphs of capitalism.'

9 July 1990: 'Minority Report - CIA involvement.'

26 March 1990: 'Drugs.'

13 November 1989: 'Get Noriega but don't touch the bankers.'

2 October 1989: 'Contradictions of cocaine capitalism.'

27 August 1988: 'Dealing with Noriega.'

20 February 1988: 'Our man in Panama.'

7 November 1987: 'The crimes of patriots: a true tale of dope, dirty money, and the CIA.'

5 September 1987: 'How the drug czar got away.'

29 August 1987: 'The Iran Contra connection: secret teams and covert operations in the Reagan era.'

21 February 1987: 'Crazy Charlie – Carlos Lehder Rivas.'

6 September 1986: 'The offshore money; Swiss banks still sell secrecy.'

23 February 1985: 'Stop blaming the system.'

18 February 1984: 'The Miami connection.'

Nation's Cities Weekly:

24 July 1989: 'Crime pays off for Torrance Calif.'

National Review:

30 March 1992: 'BCCI and Senator Kerry revisited.'

16 December 1991: 'Godfather Fidel.'

7 October 1991: 'The real scandal - BCCI.'

National Underwriter Property & Casualty-Risk & Benefits Management:

24 June 1991: 'La. regulator sent to prison; called "amoral".'

11 June 1990: 'Grand jury indicts La. commissioner in Champion case.'

New Internationalist:

October 1991: 'How to make dirty money squeeky clean.'

New Leader:

18 September 1989: 'A country under siege; fighting anarchy in Colombia.'

New Republic:

27 November 1989: 'The kingdom of cocaine: the shocking story of Colombia's habit.'

18 September 1989: 'A mess in the Andes: Columbia's government-by-cocaine.'

12 June 1989: 'Dear Manny.'

13 March 1989: 'Robbin' Hoods: how the big banks spell debt "relief".'

15 April 1985: 'Inside dope in El Salvador: where did d'Aubuisson's pal come up with $6 million in cash.'

New York:

26 August 1991: 'A Noriega laundry.'

22 January 1990: 'The Panama connection.'

31 October 1983: 'Money laundering: how crooks recycle $80 billion a year in dirty money.'

23 January 1978: 'Ladies of the night clean up their act.'

New York Times Magazine:

29 March 1992: 'Where the money washes up.'

New York University Journal of International Law and Politics:

Summer 1984: 'The use of offshore institutions to facilitate criminal activities in the United States.'

Newsweek:

16 November 1992: 'A CIA–BNL link?'

12 October 1992: 'The last martini.'

21 August 1991: 'The CIA and BCCI'; 'The bank that prays together.'

5 August 1991: 'What did they know - and when?'

18 March 1991: The pain of a power broker.'

10 April 1989: 'A drug crackdown in the Alps'; 'A bungled deal with Panama.'

27 March 1989: 'Scandal in Switzerland.'

22 February 1988: 'The dictator on the dock.'

23 September 1985: 'Hong Kong's funny money.'

20 May 1985: 'E.F. Hutton: it's not over yet.'

25 February 1985: 'Banking by paper bag.'

28 March 1983: 'Trying to shut down the money laundry'; 'The grandma Mafia on trial.'

Penthouse:

April 1984: 'Blood money.'

People:

6 August 1990: 'A conspiracy of crowns.'

19 June 1989: 'Masters of deception; a prominent Indiana family in exile is accused of running a drug ring.'

Philadelphia Magazine:

July 1985: 'The day they raided Shearson.'

Pittsburgh Business Times:

14 October 1991: 'Coastal Marketing owner pleads guilty to $2.2 million loan scam.'

18 March 1991: 'Local businessmen indicted in alleged drug-money deals.'
Playboy:
> May 1990: 'Just say nothing, Noriega; we created the monster we've now propped up on trial. Could be kind of awkward.'
> November 1989: 'Inside job; the looting of America's savings and loans.'
> November 1987: 'The crimes of patriots.'

Progressive:
> June 1992: 'The banker who said no to the CIA.'

Reader's Digest:
> September 1978: 'The Swiss connection.'

Regardie's Magazine:
> April–May 1991: 'What did Clark Clifford know, and when did he know it?'
> March 1990: 'R.I.P. DRG: the rise and fall of a real estate dynasty.'

San Antonio Business Journal:
> 21 June 1991: 'Feds crack down on exchange houses.'

San Diego Business Journal:
> 8 October 1990: 'Silberman is fined for money laundering role.'

Security Management:
> May 1990: 'When the walls come tumbling down.'

Social Studies Review:
> June 1991: 'Big crime - The international drug trade.'

SwissBusiness:
> May–June 1990: 'Keeping to the code; Switzerland's bankers have set up their own good-conduct guidelines.'
> January–February 1990: 'Tackling a tarnished image.'

Sunday Correspondent Magazine:
> July 1990: 'The Florida sting.'

Time:
> 12 October 1992: 'Follow the money.'
> 23 March 1992: 'Drug money fears halt state bond sale.'
> 16 December 1991: 'All that glitters.'
> 21 July 1991: 'The dirtiest bank of all.'
> 4 March 1991: 'A capital scandal.'
> 3 December 1990: 'The fling of the high roller: living in a ghetto, the coke trade from poverty to riches and into prison'; 'Meanwhile, in Latin America: with whole economies at stake, the drug war rages on.'
> 26 November 1990: 'Meanwhile, back in Panama: If the Noriega trial seems like a fiasco, consider the plight of his country one year after the U.S. invasion.'
> 25 June 1990: 'Grapevine - France may legalize brothels to combat AIDS, drug money laundering.'
> 19 February 1990: 'Too soft on the laundry.'
> 29 January 1990: 'Kink in the drug pipeline.'
> 15 January 1990: 'Noriega on ice.'
> 18 December 1989: 'A torrent of dirty dollars.'
> 16 October 1989: 'Putting an ear to the wires.'
> 21 August 1989: 'Wringing out a money laundry.'

24 April 1989: 'Crackdown on Swiss laundry.'
31 October 1988: 'Indicted, Patrick Swindall.'
24 October 1988: 'The cash cleaners.'
22 February 1988: 'Noriega's money machine; his former aides tell of corruption on a grand scale.'
8 February 1988: 'A briefcase for the general?'
18 January 1988: 'Afoot in a field of men.'
20 July 1987: 'ZZZZ Best may be ZZZZ worst.'
18 May 1987: 'Hooking some big fish.'
7 July 1986: 'Washday blues; scandal strikes Shearson.'
3 February 1986: 'Painful legacy; BankAmerica's bad days.'
2 December 1985: 'Fetal delusions; a shooting on Wall Street.'
28 October 1985: 'My, what a friendly customer.'
9 September 1985: 'Record fine for Crocker National Bank.'
1 July 1985: 'Cleaning up the cash laundry.'
25 March 1985: 'Crackdown on greenwashing; lawmakers warn banks to quit helping criminals launder money.'
11 March 1985: 'Boston's embattled bank.'
25 February 1985: 'Dirty cash and tarnished vaults; two large US banks struggle to recover from serious missteps'. 'Fighting the cocaine wars: drug traffic spreads, and the U.S. finds itself mired in a violent, losing battle.'
18 February 1985: 'Carry on cash connection.'
12 November 1984: 'Dirty money in the spotlight: a proposal to get tough on banks that launder cash.'

Travel Weekly:
4 June 1992: 'Helping the IRS.'
28 May 1992: 'Money-laundering regulations redefine cash.'
17 December 1990: 'Large cash sales must be reported.'
23 April 1987: 'Drug trafficking, money laundering and the travel industry.'
9 March 1987: 'Weak currencies and weak agencies recipe for riches in Nigerian scheme'; 'Airline crackdown shows results against money-laundering scam.'

United States Banker:
November 1989: 'Snaring the smurfs.'

US Department of State Bulletin:
September 1986: 'Narcotics trafficking in Southwest Asia.'

US Department of State Dispatch:
17 August 1992: 'Statement on Pablo Escobar Gaviria.'
11 May 1992: 'Narcotics activities in Panama: mutual legal assistance treaty needed' (address by R. Grant Smith).
2 March 1992: 'Progress in the international war against illicit drugs' (Melvyn Levitsky address); 'Fact sheet: combating drug money-laundering.'
10 September 1990: 'International narcotics control.'
3 September 1990: 'Narcotics: threat to global security.'

US Distribution Journal:

November 1989: 'Cash business targeted for laundering probe.'

US News & World Report:

19 October 1992: 'Cocaine kings and mafia dons – Crime in Italy and Colombia.'

23 December 1991: 'New target - the Cali cartel.'

26 August 1991: 'Washing the dirtiest money: why drug lords don't need BCCI to launder cash.'

19 August 1991: 'How BCCI banked on global secrecy.'

5 August 1991: 'Was there a BCCI coverup? In Washington and London, fallout from the rogue bank is spreading.'

28 January 1991: 'Jorge Luis Ochoa Vasquez.'

31 December 1990: 'Easing back in the war on drugs?'

30 April 1990: 'The drug warriors' blues.'

29 January 1990: 'The godfathers of cocaine cry uncle.'

15 January 1990: 'The case against Noriega.'

18 December 1989: 'To each according to his greed?'

21 August 1989: 'The drug money hunt.'

10 April 1989: 'Hot money: city of angels, indeed.'

24 October 1988: 'Caught in the money laundry wringer.'

4 July 1988: 'Psst -- Swiss accounts are no secret.'

30 May 1988: 'A king pin falls.'

11 April 1988: 'Inside America's biggest drug bust.'

15 February 1988: 'Tales of a pineapple pol.'

8 February 1988: 'How cocaine rules the law in Colombia.'

11 January 1988: 'The Honduras connection; drugs and money'; 'A narco traficante's worst nightmare.'

16 February 1987: 'Caught – cocaine's Mr. Big.'

8 December 1986: 'How White House built a "black ops" fund.'

2 June 1986: 'Why it's getting tougher to hide money.'

31 March 1986: 'Europe's immigration battles; slowdown of economies, ethnic discord set off backlash.'

3 February 1986: 'Busting the mob.'

11 March 1985: 'Banks caught in fed's squeeze on mobsters.'

5 November 1984: 'Asian gangs stake out turf in US.'

23 April 1984: 'Breaking up the pizza connection.'

1 August 1983: 'Computer cops: on the trail of runaway dollars'; 'Offshore tax havens lure Main Street money.'

Variety:

15 May 1985: 'Casino industry united in opposition to laundering regs.'

Vital Speeches:

15 July 1990: 'Money laundering; you make it, we'll take it' (Richard Thornburgh address).

15 April 1990: 'Dirty business - money laundering and the war on drugs' (Helen K. Sinclair address).

Washington Business Journal:

25 June 1990: 'Suit says Maryland bank masked CIA transactions.'

Washington Monthly:

June 1991: 'Cliffhanging; how the consummate counsel came to need a lawyer.'

October 1987: 'Hot money and the politics of debt.'

Washingtonian:

January 1992: 'Dirty money.'

Whole Earth Review:

Spring 1988: 'The Iran Contra Connection.'

Women's Wear Daily:

7 April 1992: 'Paris cops bust 100 laundering money in luxury shops.'

World of Banking:

September–October 1990: 'Money laundering - problems and solutions for the banking industry.'

World Press Review:

November 1985: 'Drugs and tax havens.'

Newspapers

Specific newspaper sources are too many to list individually. Suffice it to say that articles consulted appeared in, among other places:

North America – the *Atlanta Constitution*, the *Boston Globe*, the *Chicago Daily News*, the *Chicago Tribune*, the *Christian Science Monitor*, the *Dallas Morning News*, the *Detroit News*, the *Los Angeles Times*, the *Miami Herald*, the *Montreal Gazette*, the *New York Times*, the *Toronto Globe and Mail*, the *Wall Street Journal* and the *Washington Post*, also, the wires of the Associated Press.

UK – the *Financial Times*, the *Guardian*, the *Independent*, the *International Herald Tribune*, the *Mail*, the *Mail on Sunday*, the *Independent on Sunday*, *The Sunday Times*, the *Sunday Telegraph*, the *Telegraph*, *The Times*; also, the wires of Reuters and the Press Association.

Continental newspapers include leading dailies in France, Italy, Germany and Switzerland, in addition to the wire services of Agence France Press.

Miscellaneous Sources: Reports, Papers, Transcripts

Ashe, Michael, 'Money Laundering - Domestic Legal Issues', Paper delivered to the Conference on Money Laundering, Richards Butler, London, 1992.

Ashe, Michael, 'Reflections on Civil Liability', Paper delivered to the Conference on Money Laundering, Henry Stewart Conference Studies, London, 1991.

Bank of England, *Countering Money laundering*, London, 1992.

Bank of England, *Money Laundering - Guidance Notes for Banks and Building Societies*, London, 1990.

Bank for International Settlements, *Statistics on Payment Systems in Eleven Developed Countries*, Basle, 1992.

Basle Committee on Banking Regulations and Supervisory Practices, *Statement of Principles on Prevention of Criminal Use of the Banking System for the Purpose of Money laundering*, Basle, 1988.

Bosworth-Davies, Rowan, 'Money Laundering - Looking Towards the Future from a European Perspective', Private paper, London, 1992.

Bosworth-Davies, Rowan, 'What Money Is It?' Paper delivered to the Conference on Money Laundering, Henry Stewart Conference Studies, London, 1991.

Brightwell, Tony, 'The Laundering of Criminal Funds', Paper delivered to the Conference on Money Laundering, Richards Butler, London, 1992.

British Commonwealth, *International Efforts to Combat Money Laundering*, Cambridge International Document Series Vol. 4, Grotius Publishing, Cambridge, England, 1992.

British Commonwealth, *Scheme Relating to Mutual Assistance in Criminal Matters Within the Commonwealth, Including Explanatory Commentary*, London, 1990.

British Commonwealth, *Extracts from the Commonwealth Heads of Government Meeting*, Kuala Lumpur, 1989.

Brooks, Christopher, 'What the Police are Doing - When and How to Contact Them', Paper delivered to the Conference on Money Laundering, Henry Stewart Conference Studies, London, 1991.

Cassidy, William, 'Fei-Ch'ien - Flying Money - A Study of Chinese Underground Banking', annotated text of an address before the Asian Organized Crime Conference, Ft Lauderdale, 1990.

Clutterbuck, R, *Terrorism*, Wrexton Paper Series, Wrexton College, Wrexton Abbey, England, 1990.

Conway, Robert, 'The Techniques of Money laundering - Who Does What,' Paper delivered to the Conference on Money Laundering, Henry Stewart Conference Studies, London, 1991.

Council of Europe, *Recommendations of the Committee of Ministers on Measures Against the Transfer and Safekeeping of Funds of Criminal Origin*, Strasbourg, 1980.

European Economic Community, *The Convention on Laundering, Search, Seizure and Confiscation of the Proceeds from Crime*, Brussels, 1990.

European Economic Community, *Payment Systems in EC Member States*, Committee of Governors of the Central Banks of the Member States of the European Economic Community, Brussels, 1992.

European Economic Community, *Proposal for a Council Directive on Prevention and Use of the Financial System for the Purpose of Money Laundering*, Brussels, 1989.

Federal Bureau of Investigation, Criminal Investigation Division, *The Cosa Nostra in Canada*, Washington DC, 1985.

Federal Bureau of Investigation, Criminal Investigation Division, *Colombian Narcotics - Trafficking Organizations*, Washington DC, 1986.

Financial Action Task Force, *Notes from the Caribbean Drug Money Laundering Conference*, Aruba, 1990.

Financial Action Task Force *Report on Money Laundering*, Paris, 1990.

Financial Action Task Force, *Economic Declaration of the G-7*, Paris, 1990.

Gilmore, Dr William C, 'International Responses to Money Laundering - A General Overview', Paper given at the Money Laundering Conference of the European Committee on Crime Problems, Strasbourg, 1992.

Haines, Peter, 'How To Identify and Prevent Potential Money Laundering Schemes', Paper delivered to the Conference on Money Laundering, Henry Stewart Conference Studies, London, 1991.

House of Commons, Treasury Committee, *Report on Banking Supervision and BCCI - International and National Regulation*, London, 1991.

Hurley, Peter, 'Prevention and Staff Training', Paper delivered to the Conference on Money Laundering, Henry Stewart Conference Studies, London 1991.

Hyland, Michael, 'The British Bankers Approach', Paper delivered to the Conference on Money Laundering, Henry Stewart Conference Studies, London, 1991.

National Crime Authority of Australia, *Taken to the Cleaners – Money Laundering in Australia*, Canberra, 1992.

President's Commission on Organized Crime, *Cash Connection - The Interim Report on Organized Crime, Financial Institutions and Money Laundering*, Washington DC, 1984.

President's Commission on Organized Crime, *A Report to the President and the Attorney General of the United States: America's Habit - Drug Abuse, Drug Trafficking and Organized Crime*, Washington DC, 1986.

President's Commission on Organized Crime, *The Impact - Organized Crime Today*, Washington DC, 1986.

Rider, Dr Barry A. K, 'Fei Ch'ien Laundries - The Pursuit of Flying Money', *Journal of International Planning*, August, 1992.

Rider, Dr Barry A. K, 'Techniques of Money Laundering', Paper delivered to the Conference on Money Laundering, Richards Butler, London, 1992.

Saltmarsh, Graham, 'Understanding the UK Legislation', Paper delivered to the Conference on Money Laundering, Henry Stewart Conference Studies, London, 1991.

Solly, Mark W, *Offshore Havens - The Role and Responsibility of Financial Institutions to Assist in the Prevention of Money Laundering,'* Financial Supervision Commission, Isle of Man, 1989.

Stucki, Dr H. U., 'Swiss Banking Secrecy Revisited', private paper, Stucki & de Senarclens, Attorneys at Law, Zurich, 9 September 1992.

Tattersall, John, 'Providing Assurance That All Is Well - What Role for the Internal and External Auditor,' Paper delivered to the Conference on Money Laundering, Henry Stewart Conference Studies, London, 1991.

Tenth International Symposium on Economic Crime, *Hot, Dirty and Stolen Money - Identifying, Tracing and Restoring Flight Capital and the Proceeds of Crime*, Collected papers, delivered 12–18 July 1992, Jesus College, Cambridge.

Tupman, William, 'The Laundering of Terrorist Activities', Paper delivered to the Conference on Money Laundering, Richards Butler, London, 1992.

United Nations, *Political Declaration and Global Programme of Action of the General Assembly*, New York, 1990.

United Nations, *Convention Against the Illicit Traffic in Narcotic Drugs and Psychotropic Substances*, New York, 1988.

United Nations, *Comprehensive Multidisciplinary Outline of Future Activities in Drug Abuse Control*, New York, 1987.

United States Attorney for the US Southern Dictrict, Manhattan: 'Chronology of Events' (prepared for the jury considering the case known as 'The Pizza Connection'), New York, 1985.

United States Department of State, *Agreement with the Government of Venezuela Regarding Cooperation in the Prevention and Control of Money Laundering Arising from Illicit Trafficking in Narcotic Drugs and Psychotropic Substances*, Washington DC, 1990.

United States Department of State, Bureau of International Narcotics Matters, *International Narcotics Control Strategy Reports*, Washington DC, 1988, 1989, 1990, 1991.

United States Department of State, *Progress in the International War Against Illicit Drugs*. Transcript of an address by Melvyn Levitsky, Assistant Secretary of State for International Narcotics Matters, Washington DC, 2 March 1992.

United States Department of the Treasury, Financial Crimes Enforcement Network, *An Assessment of Narcotics Related Money Laundering*, Washington DC, 1992.

United States House of Representatives, Hearings before the Committee on Banking, Finance and Urban Affairs, *Bank of Credit and Commerce International (BCCI) Investigation*, Washington DC, 1991, 1992.

United States House of Representatives, Subcommittee on Financial Institutions, Supervision, Regulation and Insurance of the Committee on Banking, Finance and Urban Affairs, *Statement on Behalf of the American Bankers Association on Money Laundering Deterrence by Boris F. Melinkoff*, Washington DC, 8 March 1990.

United States Senate, Foreign Relations Committee, *Testimony of the Deputy Secretary of the Treasury, the Honorable John E. Robson, on the Work of the G-7 Financial Action Task Force on Money Laundering*, Washington DC, 27 April 1990.

United States Senate, Hearings before the Permanent Subcommittee on Investigations of the Committee on Governmental Affairs, *Drugs and Money Laundering in Panama*, Washington DC, 1988.

United States Senate, Hearings before the Subcommittee on Consumer and Regulatory Affairs of the Committee on Banking, Housing and Urban Affairs, *The Bank of Credit and Commerce International*, Washington DC, 1991.

United States Senate, Hearings before the Subcommittee on Terrorism, Narcotics and International Operations of the Committee on Foreign Relations, *The BCCI Affair*, Washington DC, 1991, 1992.

United States Senate, Hearings before the Subcommittee on Terrorism, Narcotics and International Operations of the Committee on Foreign Relations, *Panama*, Washington DC, 1988.

The United States Senate, Permanent Subcommittee on Investigations of the Committee on Government Operations, *Final Report of the McClellan Subcommittee - Organized Crime and Illicit Traffic in Narcotics*, Washington DC, 1965.

United States Senate, Report of the Subcommittee on Terrorism, Narcotics and

International Operations of the Committee on Foreign Relations, *The BCCI Affair*, Washington DC, 1992.

World Ministerial Summit, *Declaration to Reduce Demand for Drugs and to Combat the Cocaine Threat*, London, 1990.

Wren, Tim, 'Money Laundering Legislation', Paper delivered to the Conference on Money Laundering, Richards Butler, London, 1992.

Index